SHADOWS OF FREEDOM

(A POLITICAL THRILLER)

BY

YVONNE HART

To the memory of my late mother, Letitia Hart, who was always an inspiration to me.

ACKNOWLEDGEMENTS

I wish to acknowledge the help of the late Marian Marriot who proof-read the first draft and offered advice.

I also wish to thank Fiona Morgan for proof-reading the second and final drafts and for her useful comments.

CHAPTER ONE

Sun rays beat down relentlessly through the bars of the grimy, fly-specked window. On the floor of the prison cell, between the shadow pattern of the bars, a cockroach basked in the warmth. Listlessly Celia rose from her bunk and walked to the window. She stretched her face towards the sun, savouring its warmth, holding its light. Just one more full day to see the sun rise and wane. The day after that her execution.

Bouncer, the smaller and more aggressive of the two warders, shifted in her chair. A sallow-faced woman with close-cropped hair, Celia called her Bouncer because of her belligerent gait. Like black crows in their sombre uniforms, they watched her day and night. Watched her as if they thought she might find some way to cheat the hangman.

The other warder, whom she called Spider – a gaunt, awkward woman with sullen eyes – looked half asleep. But she was fully awake. Celia felt those half-closed eyes watching her every move. Spider was not the worst of them; although sharp-tongued and stern, she was never brutal. Bouncer was the one to watch; when roused to anger she would not hesitate to strike a prisoner in the face. They seldom spoke to her. Yet, forgetful of their prisoner's fluency in Spanish, they often spoke about 'la Inglesa' as though she were not there.

Lingering at the window, she turned her back slightly so as to seem indifferent to their scrutiny. They don't matter now, she thought. I'm already dead. She no longer felt terror save in her sleeping hours when she was prone to nightmares. Once she learnt the appeal had failed, she fixed her mind on the certainty of death. Now, numbed and without hope, the only feeling that penetrated her being was a profound sadness.

A tall tree stood outside the prison wall, its branches drooping over the high fortifications. A precious, solitary glimpse of nature. This, and the sound of birdsong, kept alive memories of a world she used to know.

But as she watched a bird rise from a branch and soar into the clear blue, Pacific sky, something stirred within her. Was she really so resigned? One month from now she should be twenty-four. A birthday she would never see.

With leaden steps she returned to her bunk and lay down. Images of London filled her mind. Walking through Kensington Gardens in the cool of evening. Watching ducks glide by on the Serpentine. Soon it would be autumn. The magnificence of the parks in autumn. Kicking those russet-brown leaves as she breathed the frost-nipped air. Never to see another autumn. Memories of people she knew flooded her mind. The children she taught in kindergarten school. Did they understand why she had not come back? The friends with whom she shared a flat in London. Her dead mother. The father she never knew.

As an aircraft flew over, her gaze turned towards the window again. Coming from the direction of Hong Kong it was heading towards the Philippines. The island republic of Costadora where she was imprisoned – a former Spanish colony – lay halfway between the two. Flying low, the aircraft's silver body gleamed in the sun. She shuddered as she saw the sign *Global Orient*. It was the company she had travelled with when she made her fateful journey to the Far East. Drugs had been found in her hand-luggage – a capital offence. How they had got there she could not explain. She had carried no drugs from London.

'I don't want to die. I'm innocent. Someone planted the drugs on me ....'

Spider interjected quickly to tell her to keep her voice down; she must not upset other prisoners in the adjacent cells. Only then did she realise that she had cried aloud her anguished plea of innocence. Bouncer made a move as though to rise from her chair. Quickly Celia raised her hand to protect her face, at the same time stammering out an apology: 'Perdón por la molestia.'

Then as Bouncer settled back into her chair, Celia turned her face to the wall fighting back the tears. Why did they still have that effect on her? Why should they matter any more?

She closed her eyes. What did it mean to be dead, to cease to be? The young priest had talked to her earnestly about having faith in God's mercy. He had promised to walk with her to the execution chamber. Despite her convent education, those old beliefs now seemed hollow. God had forsaken her. When the final hour came, would the priest's faith permeate her own being?

She must have fallen asleep. Or had she died? She could feel the rope around her neck. Darkness as the rope tightened. She was swaying, swaying, falling, falling.

Something hard struck her back. The floor vibrated. She was still alive. Still lying on the bunk of her prison cell. What was happening? A table had overturned and crashed to the floor. She looked towards the two warders. Neither looked at her. Panic on their faces as they stared at the widening crack in the concrete floor. Her bunk swung from the hinges which attached it to the wall. Bouncer gave a jerk and crashed to the floor. Spider was now propped against the wall, her head bleeding. Why was everything lopsided?

Something trickled down her cheek. She put her forefinger to it. Blood. Had Bouncer broken the skin this time? As the cell swayed like the sea, the bunk broke off its hinges and hit the floor. She could hear screams. The crack in the floor widened. It separated her from the warders. Earthquake! This was an earthquake zone.

Bouncer was bending over Spider. They weren't even looking at her. Stealthily Celia rose, her heart pounding with wild hope. She must move quickly. Silently. The crack in the floor might be wide enough to let through her slender body. She had no idea where it led, but like the bird facing an open cage door, dazed and half-aware, she edged towards it. A violent tremor threw her to the floor. Debris was falling. She stretched out her arm until her fingers reached the edge of the crack. Clutching the jagged edge, she eased her body forward. Now she was alongside the ever-widening fissure. A quick glance at Bouncer who was trying to rouse her stunned colleague. Bouncer had a gun which she would not hesitate to use. Act now. Act quickly. She had only one chance. Pushing her legs through the crevice, she jumped.

Landing first on her feet, she then fell backwards onto a bare, concrete floor. Unhurt, she rose stiffly. It was a store room. Shelves were stacked with cleaning powders, toilet rolls, soap bars – that rough prison soap – and disinfectants. And with the building still vibrating, some of these itmes were tumbling onto the floor. On a hook behind the door hung a pale blue overall, swinging madly with the vibrations. She held her breath, recognising it as the uniform of ancillary workers. Uniform which distinguished hired staff from convict labour. Quickly stripping off her prison navy-blue, she put it on. A square cloth hung out of a pocket. This she tied around her head in the style of the cleaning women so that it hid her gold-bronze hair.

A crack had appcarcd in thc floor of thc storc room. It was widening to a narrow crevice. Did it go all the way down the west wing, the women's block, to the ground floor? If so, it could be an escape route. Or was it a death trap? If the building collapsed, the chances of being buried in the rubble were greatest on the lower floors. It was a risk she would have to take.

At first the fissure did not seem wide enough to allow her to slip through. Desperately she began thumping at the area around the fissure with her bare hands. Aware that Bouncer would raise the alarm as soon as she saw the condemned prisoner had bolted, her thumping increased to a frenzied pace. A loud grating noise as the walls seemed to move, and then she saw that the fissure had widened a little.

She forced through her legs. Although the jagged edges tore her flesh, she felt no pain. Frantically she tried to ease through the rest of her body. Suddenly the area around the crack broke up and she fell with a thump onto the floor below.

Fresh blood poured from a gash on her left leg. For a moment she lay there shocked and disorientated. Then she dragged herself painfully to her feet and looked around. On one side toilets, on the other wash-basins. A staff wash-room, perhaps. Her gaze veered towards the door. A quickening of the pulse as she saw that it was a normal door. A door without locks. She hesitated. What was on the other side? Danger. Perhaps recapture. But she would surely be recaptured if she remained where she was. Heart pounding, she braced herself, pushed the door open and walked out.

The uniformed men and women walking past down that long corridor were pale and tight-lipped. Would they recognise her? As she hesitated, someone tapped her arm. 'Come on. Keep moving. You should know the evacuation drill by now. There must be no loitering.' The male warder who chided Celia gave her a shove.

She fell into step. Or tried to. But she was still doing something wrong. A woman warder snapped at her: 'Stop pushing. We *all* want to get out.'

She slowed her pace a little, trying to get into the same rhythm of movement as everyone else. She could feel her heart thumping – almost hear it. Her bolt for freedom had been a matter of instinct. Now, conscious that her chances of escape were slim, she was gripped by fear.

There was still a faint tremor by the time they reached the emergency staircase, but the worst was over. Not until she reached the ground floor did she see other prisoners. They were being herded at gunpoint to the left towards the prisoners' exercise yard. Turning to the right, Celia followed other women in pale blue overalls. The earthquake had now died down.

The guard at the exit raised his hand as though to stay her. He said something which at first she did not understand. It was the rough speech of the West Province, a corrupt form of Spanish that even native Costadoreans from other parts found difficult to comprehend. And then she grasped that he was not demanding identification; he was merely concerned about her injuries.

'Very bad, very bad,' he repeated as he shook his head and eyed her bloodied face. Her nose was now bleeding, the flow mingling with blood from the cut on her cheek. 'Hurt your leg too? Go have First Aid take a look at it.'

As she stared at him blankly, he continued encouragingly: 'You know where First Aid is? That building there beside the staff canteen.'

She nodded and walked out into the open air in the direction he pointed. A quick assessment of her position. The First Aid post was the nearest building to the main gates. Then she became aware of a voice blasting over a loudspeaking system directing the evacuation drill. Ancillary workers were to assemble in the staff canteen for a roll call. That she must avoid. The cleaning staff was not large, most domestic work being done by the prisoners themselves. Hired cleaners who worked in those areas out of bounds to prisoners would spot at once an imposter in their midst. Quickening her pace, she walked past the canteen building and into the First Aid unit.

* * * * *

'Nothing appears to be broken,' the nurse reassured her. They had cleaned the wounds, bandaged her left leg below the knee and applied a plaster to her cheek. Blood washed away, her skin had a striking whiteness, still pretty despite that strained look. Why was the nurse eyeing her in that curious way? Was she becoming suspicious?

'You look shocked. Feel any pain?'

'No. No. I'm all right,' Celia replied distractedly as she rose stiffly from the chair. 'Must go now.'

The bandage felt uncomfortably tight as she limped towards the exit. Now other casualties were arriving – people pulled out of the debris. No one paid her further attention as she went out into the prison forecourt.

A sudden feeling of weakness caused her to stumble. Then a fleeting sensation of blacking out. Was she dreaming? That recurring escape dream. She always woke at the moment when the prison gates flew open and rays of sun caressed her

10

face. A sharp pain in her leg reminded her that she was fully awake. Ahead she could see those great metal gates. Beyond lay a main road. And freedom.

A guard cocked his gun as she approached. Nerves taut, mouth dry, she continued walking towards him. He lowered his gun slightly, a look of curiosity on his face. Was he deciding whether or not to shoot? Her gaze was unflinching as she came ever nearer. Better the gun than the rope. At the gates he barred her way. 'We don't know yet what conditions are like in the city.'

'I've got to go – I'm worried about my family.' A look of irritation spread over his face. 'I'm worried about mine, too.' Another guard stepped forward and whispered something in his colleague's ear. Seeing the hesitation on the first guard's face, Celia pleaded: 'Can't you see I'm hurt – the doctor told me to get home as soon as possible.' His eyes went from her ashen face to bandaged leg. That she was injured was not in doubt.

'All right, then, go through. Wait one moment! I need to see your pass.' She stared at him helplessly.

'Your pass, señorita?' he repeated.

Was it all over? And with freedom just a few steps away. Desperately she pleaded: 'No, I don't have my pass – I don't have anything. My handbag and all my things are somewhere under that rubble.'

'Where were you when the earthquake started?'

'Back there in the West Wing.'

Instantly she regretted having mentioned the West Wing. Why hadn't she pretended not to have been anywhere near the death cell? The guard nodded. From where he stood, the West Wing looked to be the most damaged part of the prison. Yet he made no move to let her pass. His eyes held a hypnotic surliness as menacing as the gun he brandished.

Shots pierced the air. She swung round to see a man – he wore the navy-blue tunic of a prisoner – staggering helplessly. When gunned down he was only a few feet from where the prison walls had been partially demolished. Still too high to scale, it had been a desperate bid. He clutched at air, then fell, blood flowing from his mouth. The shrill voice of the

11

guard brought her back to the reality of her own predicament: 'Didn't you hear what I said, señorita? You must go now. This is no place for you. Either go back to the canteen or go home. You can't stay here.'

The guards stood aside and let her pass.

CHAPTER TWO

Avenida Monteverde snaked all the way downhill from Monteverde Prison to Plaza San Pedro. A suburb on the east side of the city, the area was well-known for its open air markets. On one side of the sloped roadway was a shanty town, on the other the back entrance to the Botanical Gardens. There in that leafy refuge a hapless multitude had gathered. Caught in the streets during the earthquake's first violent tremors, they had fled there for safety, away from the hazard of falling masonry.

Celia paused by the garden gates. Fragrance from flowers and shrubs wafted through the air. High in a tree which overhung the path, a bird trilled sweetly. The sounds, smells and colours of long ago. Dazed, as if in a dream, she ventured slowly down the garden path. But, as the clamour of human voices carried to her, she retreated to the roadway in panic.

Glumly and fatalistically the shanty town dwellers were gathering together their scattered belongings. The poorest of Costadora's citizens, they had the least to lose in any of those natural disasters – earthquakes, hurricanes or floods – which sometimes hit the island republic. Those rudimentary dwellings which fell apart with the first tremors were easily put together again.

A wide-eyed, bare-footed child, sitting amid the ruins of a damaged shack, gazed at Celia as she walked past. The first child she had seen in almost two years. Instinctively she smiled and waved to him. With a shy smile he returned her wave.

The glow of the late afternoon sun brushed the sky with a bronze tinge; its rays caressed her skin. That deadly tension within her began to evaporate. Am I really free? Free at last? She quickened her pace and, despite the stiffness of her injured leg, began to walk with an almost jaunty gait.

Nearing Plaza San Pedro, mayhem reached her ears – the screeching sirens of ambulances and police cars; shouts and screams; then a volley of gun shots. She stopped short. Should she retreat? But the knowledge that she was still close – too close – to the prison gave her the courage to go on.

At the bottom of the hill was a tall building. This was Keevers, the stylish, American-owned emporium, the only large department store on this side of the city. Its front entrance looked out onto Plaza San Pedro. Here at the side of the building – still on Avenida Monteverde – a damaged telephone kiosk had toppled over. As it lay across her path, she had to step off the pavement to get round it. Some debris lay beneath: plastic bags, newspapers and a bundle of something green which she couldn't identify. But she gave it only a passing glance; instead her attention was caught by the store's smashed windows. Looters had already been at work.

The Plaza was a scene of devastation. Buildings on the opposite side from Keevers, mostly small shops and restaurants, were almost completely demolished. It was here that the efforts of the rescue services were focused. Keevers itself, apart from broken windows, looked relatively intact. The famous statue of a mermaid, Keevers' logo, once standing over the entrance, had crashed to the ground. No other damage was apparent. Like most tall buildings erected since the 1978 earthquake, it had been built with articulated foundations, an earthquake-proof design copied from Tokyo.

But death had struck also on this side of the Plaza. On the pavement lay the body of a youth slumped over a television set, shot in the act of looting. Feverish efforts were in progress to board up the store's doors and windows so as to deter further theft.

'Move on. No loitering here!'

Swinging round, she looked straight into the mouth of a gun. The hard-bitten, scowling expression of the police officer who pointed the weapon at her warmed that he would not have the slightest hesitation in using it. She shivered. Then groping for excuses to explain her presence, she stammered: 'I – I only came to look for my sister – she works there – in the store.'

'Go look somewhere else. The staff of Keevers were evacuated.'

Turning, she walked away, half expecting a shot in the back. Once round the corner she tried to run, but the stiffness of her leg slowed her. Just ahead was the telephone kiosk, and once again she noted the debris trapped beneath. This time her gaze lingered. What was that green object?

A sudden gust of wind lifted into the air sheets of newspaper which had lain against the top end of the kiosk. Perplexed she stared at the fine alabaster-like features beneath. Was it a smaller statue of the mermaid which had fallen from the side entrance? Then, as her gaze lingered, she saw that it was a lifeless human face. A youngish woman. Face turned a little to the side, light brown hair falling to her shoulders. Her lips were parted as though about to speak. It was as if death had taken her before she had time to feel either pain or surprise.

Most of the body was trapped beneath the kiosk; only the head, shoulders and one arm were visible. A green silk scarf – that green object she had vaguely noticed in passing – lay draped across the dead woman's shoulders. She looked around hesitantly. Should she call the rescue services back in the Plaza? But if the woman were already dead, what was the point? To make sure she bent down and felt the pulse. There wasn't the faintest flicker. And then she noticed something else – a handbag partially hidden by the scarf. Gently easing it out from under the dead woman's arm, she looked inside.

Nothing unusual. Just what you would find in any woman's handbag: cosmetics, diary, some biro pens, a note-book and collection of papers. And then she noticed the leather wallet – a fat, well-padded wallet. Pulling it open, she stared in disbelief at the large wad of banknotes which, even before counting, she could see amounted to a considerable sum of money.

Steal from the dead? It was a shocking idea. But grim reality fought with her scruples. What price freedom, if it were only freedom to starve in the streets? And somehow she would have to get off this island. How this was to be done she still had no idea, but certainly not without money.

'Forgive me,' she murmured as she turned away, handbag clutched tightly to her chest.

CHAPTER THREE

Furtively she looked right and left. If it were not permitted to cross the Plaza, then she could only retreat. Where else to go but the Botanical Gardens.

Tyres screeched as army trucks swerved around the corner, speeding uphill. Instinctively she flattened herself against the wall, her body going rigid. Were they looking for her? And then relief as she saw the vehicles disappear in an arid dust cloud. A few steps uphill and then she stopped. That feeling of faintness again. Aware that each passing moment was vital, she tried to clear her mind. Where to hide? Oh, for some quiet place of refuge to plan and think! Glancing to the right she saw that behind Keevers was a narrow alleyway, the high wall on one side enclosing the lower end of the Botanical Gardens. Its shadowy gloom, its anonymity drew her like a magnet. Could this lead to a hiding place?

On entering the alleyway, a vaguely unpleasant odour wafted through the air. Ahead she could see the row of garbage bins. Here at the rear of the building all windows had iron bars. No danger of looting from this end. As the rumbling of the army vehicles died away, other noises reached her from Avenida Monteverde – voices, loud banging and hammering. From the snatches of conversation which carried to her, she figured they were now boarding up the side windows of the store.

A shout rose above the mayhem. 'Look over here. The telephone kiosk.'

'Is she dead?' someone asked.

'Don't know. Call an ambulance.'

Darting behind one of the garbage bins, Celia crouched down and continued to listen. The voices became louder – voices giving orders; voices urging caution. It seemed like twenty minutes before they managed to lift the telephone kiosk and remove the body. Then they went away and all was quiet.

Furtively she continued along the alleyway, at first scarcely noticing the door halfway down on the right. She had gone just a few paces past when some instinct of curiosity impelled her to stop and turn back. Gingerly she turned the door handle and pushed. To her surprise it opened. She was looking into a kitchen.

A trolley was laden with crockery, and on the table platters of daintily arranged sandwiches covered with cellophane. Alongside were dishes of apple pies – American-style apple pies were a Keevers speciality. Apart from a few pieces of broken crockery on the floor, the place seemed untouched by the fury of the earthquake.

A refuge at last! She stepped inside and closed the door. Overwhelmed by fatigue she sank into the nearest chair and momentarily closed her eyes. Sleep might have overtaken her but for the sounds of cataclysm and upheaval outside. A glance towards the daintily prepared food and coffee pot reminded her that she was hungry. Very hungry. Lunch had been over three hours ago. That revolting prison lunch – soggy rice and a tough piece of blackish meat which she had left untouched. Yet, hungry though she was, she hesitated. This was *other people's* food. She felt dirty, unworthy, someone who didn't belong. Her mind stunted by harsh prison discipline, she almost anticipated the rasping voice of a prison warder ordering her to move on.

Instead she turned to the sink and began washing her hands, rubbing them with fierce determination under the running water. Gripped by some burning imperative to get all the smell, dirt and feel of prison out of her skin, she continued washing for several minutes. Only then, with her hands tingling, did she feel able to touch the food.

Smoked ham on Keevers' home-made brown bread, a chicken sandwich flavoured with a spicy Costadorean sauce called kida, then a roll filled with soft cheese, added herbs, and shrimps. The best meal she had had for a long time. The coffee was cold, but it still tasted good. Now with food – good food – inside her, she felt more relaxed. It was inquisitiveness, not hunger, which caused her to look inside the fridge. Finding a carton of guava juice, she poured some into a glass. Pulling a chair up to the table, she turned her attention to the handbag.

First she counted the money. It added up to sixty thousand quederos: enough to live on very comfortably for a couple of weeks, or frugally for several weeks. Idly rummaging through the cosmetic bag, she pondered over the lipstick. Would this shade suit her? She squeezed a little moisturising cream from a tube, rubbing it on her face. It felt good – in prison her skin had become so dry. Then, removing the headscarf, she peered into the hand mirror to see if she had changed. Prison cells did not have mirrors. Her face had become thinner and paler. But her hair – that gold-bronze hair, tied up in a pony tail, was still a thing of beauty.

Looking through the jumble of papers, a slim red book in a plastic cover caught her eye. Pulling it out she found it was a European Community passport; the holder was a British citizen. Flicking the pages, she came to the photograph. The woman's laughing eyes stared back at her, her expression exuding vitality and self-assurance. At first glance there seemed little resemblance to the alabaster-like face of the person she had found beneath the telephone kiosk. But she had seen the dead woman only briefly. The passport was in the name of Helen Darcy (where had she heard that name before?) and she was aged thirty. Six years older than Celia.

Could this passport get her back to London? The excitement that this idea stirred in her almost instantly dissipated. Wistfully she scanned the woman's features. She doesn't even look like me. At least not *very* like me. The wrong hair colour, shorter nose, different shaped face. Replacing the passport she rummaged further, now eager to learn more about the woman's identity. The search revealed another photograph: that of an older-looking, more sophisticated Helen Darcy attached to a press card. No wonder the name was familiar. This was Helen Darcy, correspondent for the *Daily Courier*. But why was she in Costadora? Then,

19

as the chilling explanation flashed through her mind, she began to tremble: she was here to report the execution.

Suddenly the kitchen no longer seemed a place of refuge. Glancing upwards at the grid on the windows, she shuddered. She was still behind bars. In an erratic movement she swept money, press card and passport back into the handbag. Time to go. But even as she rose from the table she hesitated. Go where? Not outside. Too many police and soldiers out there. Best to slip away after dark. She had money now. Perhaps she could bribe a boatman to take her off the island.

Distant voices and shouts reached her from outside. Then voices not so distant. Were they coming this way? Rushing to the door, she quickly bolted it. Stay calm, she told herself. For the moment she was safe.

Her glance veered towards the other door at the far end of the kitchen. Cautiously she edged towards it and listened. It occurred to her that she might not be the only person in the building. Then, hearing nothing, she slowly turned the handle.

Through the almost impenetrable darkness she could just make out that it was a short corridor. Groping her way forward she came to another door. Again she hesitated. The darkness was disturbing – like prison walls once more reclaiming her. A bizarre notion came to her that if she opened this door she would come face to face with Bouncer and Spider.

She braced herself. Don't think of them now. Think only of survival. Cautiously she turned the handle, then stared ahead in surprise. She was looking into Keevers' famous coffee shop, mentioned in all tour guide books as a *must* for visitors. It was an extravaganza which overwhelmed her. Tables were arranged around a shimmering pool, in the middle of which was a mermaid perched on a rock. Despite the boarded windows, the place had an airy luminosity – the ill-fitted planks of wood did not reach the top of the tall windows, allowing chinks of light to flow in. Mirrored walls gave additional reflected light, as well as a feeling of immense space. A flight of marble steps led to a platform fringed with a riot of flowers and trailing ferns, like some ancient hanging garden. On the platform below chandeliers stood a grand piano. Beyond, trees in tubs flanked each side of an archway, leading from the coffee shop into the store. To the fugitive, fresh from a foul, grim cell, the place had an ethereal quality. Yet, instead of lifting her spirits, it left her disorientated. A sudden burst of birdsong caused her to look upwards. From a cage attached to the wall, a long-tailed parakeet looked down at her from its tiny prison.

Sinking into a chair, she continued to gaze around, wide-eyed and bewildered, her mind unable to cope with this unaccustomed spaciousness. Then a plastic bag on the floor caught her eye: doubtless something a panic-stricken shopper had dropped at the onset of the evacuation. Inside she found a pair of sandals in soft beige leather, and a smart pair of black shoes. Kicking off her own shabby shoes (the soles had begun to separate from the uppers) she slipped her feet into the sandals, then stood up and took a few steps. They felt so comfortable.

A movement of scarlet and gold drew her attention to the pool. At the edge she knelt down and peeped into the glimmering water. It was full of goldfish. Fascinated, she lingered, watching the fish swim with idle grace in and out of the green undergrowth. Another fish she could not identify darted past, a ray of light picking up the blue, green and gold of its swift-moving fluorescent form. And then she saw something else. Something menacing. A man's face, just a little to the left, was staring up at her.

CHAPTER FOUR

She froze to the spot. Then the face moved. An illusion? A rippling of the water as the fish swam past? She remained immobile, for the face seemed to have a hypnotic effect. Then the man's eyes – those big brown eyes – blinked. It was a reflection. Springing to her feet, she swung around.

He stood just a few steps from her. Instinctively she backed away. A sharp pain shot through her injured leg as she struck a chair. It toppled over with a crash. Swift as a feline creature he moved forward and grasped her in a firm grip. The scream which rose to her lips was stifled as his other hand covered her mouth.

'Be quiet!' he said softly. 'Don't scream. Don't make any noise. Understand?'

With a spontaneous pull she attempted to wrench herself free at the same time knowing that struggle was futile. As she ceased to resist, he relaxed his grip. 'The plaza outside is crawling with police.' The note of exigency in his voice demanded compliance. As her body went limp, he lifted his hand from her mouth.

They now stood face to face. A tall, broad-shouldered man with strong Hispanic features. The dark hair which fell on his fine brow looked dishevelled as if he had been running in the wind. He seemed to be in his mid-thirties. On catching sight of his tunic – that familiar navy-blue – her tension eased. 'Carcel de Monteverde' in white lettering was stamped across the chest. A fellow fugitive.

'You escaped - ?' The question died on her lips as he raised his hand motioning for silence. 'Anyone else here?' he whispered.

'I don't think so. Not on this floor.'

He cast his gaze around listening intently. The only sounds came from outside. Distant sounds. His expression relaxed, but he still spoke in a low voice.

'I scouted around upstairs as far as the top floor. No one there. That overall of yours had me worried. I didn't recognise you at first.'

'You were watching me?'

He nodded and pointed to a door marked *HOMBRES*. 'I was in there. I thought I heard a noise, so I came out to see what was going on.'

She looked at him warily. 'I never saw you in the exercise yard.' Instantly she regretted her words. For their own protection, kinky killers and rapists were segregated from other prisoners. He made a slight move forward. Instinctively her hand went to the butter knife on the table, at the same time knowing that this would be a feeble defence. With a celeritous movement he caught her wrist.

'I shouldn't bother. I'm pretty thick-skinned. Come on, let it drop.' Trembling violently she let the knife fall to the ground. 'Don't play those sort of games, chica.' His voice had a benign brusqueness. A hint of a smile appeared on his face. 'Your photograph doesn't flatter you.'

'My photograph?'

He lifted a newspaper from a nearby table and held it up. The photograph which stared back at her from the front page carried the caption: 'Appeal fails. Execution date set.'

She shuddered. Turning away, she sank into the nearest chair. He threw the newspaper aside and looked into a coffee pot. 'Want some? There are sandwiches here as well.' She shook her head. Sitting opposite he poured a cup. Pressing together a couple of sandwiches he began to chew them hungrily. His eyes scrutinised her with candid curiosity. Probing, analysing, evaluating.

'You speak Costadorean Spanish.'

'My mother was Costadorean.'

'And your father?'

'Norwegian.'

'Martinez! Norwegian?'

23

'It's a long story.'

'So – you seem to be afraid of me.'

'Oh, no – it's not that ....' She groped helplessly, trying to find some convincing words of denial. Picking up another sandwich, he gulped down the coffee. 'I was in D-Block.'

'The politicos?'

He spoke teasingly: 'Surely you know we don't have political prisoners in democratic Costadora. Or do your English newspapers tell you something different?'

Pouring out more coffee he continued, his voice edged with mockery: 'No, the Bianqui regime sent out its democratic special police with their democratic shields and democratic plastic bullets to beat up our undemocratic, peaceful demonstration against the Prevention of Sedition Act. Undemocratically we fought back. Most of the demonstrators got six months for assault. I was sentenced to ten years.'

'For taking part in a demonstration?'

'Attempted murder, they called it. The demonstration was peaceful until the police attacked *us*. I bashed a police special on the head with a banner pole. I'm Diaz. Roberto Diaz.' He spoke the name as though it explained everything.

Diaz! She had heard that name before. Something on BBC news. Wasn't he one of that group of intellectuals – they called them the Constitutionalists – who accused President Bianqui of subverting the constitution to remain in power.

'Roberto Diaz from San Miguel University?' She put the question tentatively. He looked at her approvingly. 'So you *do* know something about Costadorean politics. Yes, I'm *that* Roberto Diaz.' His voice changed as he rose abruptly. 'Come on. It's time we got ourselves out of here.'

'No, I can't. I'll be recognised. The photograph in the papers ....'

'You won't have this place to yourself much longer, chica.' He looked at her thoughtfully. 'Your hair was shorter at your trial.' He ran her pony tail through his fingers. 'If that's the way you had it in Monteverde, change it.'

'I have nowhere to go.'

'We'll work something out.' His voice was imperturbable, his eyes calm and alert. 'First you'll have to get some clothes from the Ladies Department upstairs. And pick up anything else you need from toiletries – toothbrush, soap or whatever. Grab a first aid kit as well. You might need to change that bandage. There's a washroom on the second floor if you want to freshen up. And don't forget a weekend bag for a change of clothes. Nothing too bulky. Something you can sling over your shoulder.

'Where – where are they?'

'Haven't you been in Keevers before? Oh, I forgot, you were arrested at the point of entry.' Sitting down again, he took a biro from his pocket, then with quick purposeful strokes began sketching a map of the store on the back of a menu. Without looking up, he said to her: 'That handbag. Did you get it here?'

'It belongs to a dead woman. Someone I found trapped under a telephone kiosk.'

'Anything useful in it?'

'Some money and a passport.'

'That *could* be useful.' He handed her his sketch of the store's layout. 'All right, go that way – through the archway. Take the stairs to the second floor. Don't risk the lift.'

She turned hesitantly in the direction he pointed. 'You must hurry, chica,' he urged. 'And don't leave that overall lying around here. We'll dump the prison clothes somewhere later.'

* * * * *

Returning twenty minutes later, she found him sitting at a table reading a newspaper. He did not hear her approach as she walked softly on the thick carpet. He now wore a bright red shirt – that Costadorean penchant for dynamic colour – with well-cut jeans and serge jacket. His silky dark hair, now well combed, had a slight wave as it fell forward on his forehead. At his feet lay a lightweight overnight bag. Exuding

25

an air of rugged good health, it was difficult to believe that this man had languished for almost a year in a grim penitentiary.

Dropping to the ground a weekend bag, she stood tentative and uncertain until he looked up.

'I didn't hear you –.' He paused in surprise. 'You *do* look different, chica.' His frank appraisal seemed to take in every detail. Very nice. Very nice indeed.'

It was a striking transformation. No longer in a pony tail, her gold-bronze hair, now glowing in a ray of sunlight, hung loosely on her shoulders. She wore a chic, dark blue ankle-length skirt, a style in vogue that summer in Costadora. Made from locally woven cloth, it had a delicate hand-painted floral motif. The plain blouse blended in well with the colour scheme of the skirt. On top she wore a light-weight jacket that had a designer look. She had removed the rough plaster from her cheek and replaced it with a smaller, transparent one. Her pale skin looked flawless.

His undisguised admiration brought a slight glow to her cheeks. It stirred within her a sensation of becoming alive. Then, as though suddenly mindful of the urgency of their situation, he got up. There was a distant chiming of church bells. The Angelus. A reminder that it was already six o'clock.

'I had a look at the back. The best way out is through the kitchen. We want to avoid the plaza. Come on, chica.' She followed him out into the bright summer air.

CHAPTER FIVE

The heat of the day had waned, but the sky was still brilliantly clear as they walked through the Botanical Gardens. A narrow roadway separated the gardens from the sports stadium.

'This way – through the sports ground.' Diaz pointed ahead. Dazed, unbelieving, Celia followed. Was she really free?

At the exit from the gardens they stopped to let the traffic pass. Horse-drawn carts trundled uphill in the shade of drooping trees. Peasant farmers returning from the market with their unsold produce – rice, nuts, corn, bananas, taro leaves and spices. Their weathered faces looked glum. The earthquake had disrupted the day's business.

'Tired?' asked Diaz as they entered the sports ground. She had begun to lag behind. 'Here, let me take your bag; I can manage both.' She handed him the weekend bag packed with new clothes. With her leg beginning to ache, it was a relief to be unburdened. The buzz of voices and cries of children floated through the air. Tents, distributed by the Costadorean Red Cross, had been erected in the stadium for those made homeless by the earthquake. People thronged around a truck for the distribution of food and blankets. Avoiding the crowd, they took a side path. She gave a backward glance at the scene of misery. 'I hope they get international aid.'

'Oh, they will,' he assured her blithely. 'And then it will go straight into Bianqui's Swiss bank account.'

The beach was now in view. She held her breath as she watched in the distance great white rollers thundering against the cliffs. Of late, images of the sea, and its restless freedom, had often penetrated her dreaming. It brought her back to the world of childhood holidays.

'My mother told me the beaches of Ciu Costa are the most beautiful in the world.'

He smiled at her careful articulation of *Ciu Costa*. With their penchant for abbreviation, Costadoreans always referred to their capital city, Ciudad Costadora, as Ciu Costa. Nowadays it was almost official, and was referred to as such in guide books.

'Once we get to the main gates, we're close enough to the city centre,' he told her. 'We can take a bus from there.' Searching in his pocket he pulled out some coins and began counting.

'I can pay the bus fares,' she offered. 'There's money in this handbag.'

'Keep it, chica. You may need it. I'm in my own city.'

'Are you sure buses will be running after the earthquake?'

'Hope so. The earthquake zone is usually the east side as far as Santa Monica. When we had the big one in 1978 the city centre wasn't hit.'

At the main gates they looked for a bus stop. A notice indicated that the service here was temporarily suspended; the nearest stop was outside the National Bank.

'This way.' Diaz's voice was purposeful, his demeanour confident. Nothing about him suggested that this was a man fleeing from the law.

They had reached the business area. Vast hordes of humanity swarming in all directions filled her with panic. After the tightly regulated discipline of prison, this uncontrolled movement seemed terrifying. As she hesitated, he caught her arm in a firm grip. 'Come on, we're not far from the bus stop.'

Abruptly she stopped. 'Roberto, that man!'

'What man?'

'There! Coming towards us. He's one of the prison warders. I used to see him in the exercise yard.'

'Just keep walking.' His grip on her arm tightened, forcing her to keep apace.

'Roberto, if he sees us ….'

'I said just keep walking.'

The warder was now almost alongside them. Wiry build, sleek black hair, his features were those of the Chinese Costadoreans. Now his cold, black eyes were scanning Celia's face. Paralysed by terror, only Diaz's firm grip kept her moving. For a moment the warder seemed to hesitate. And then he walked past without a word.

'Roberto, he recognised us!'

'I know. He won't do anything.'

'How can you know that?'

'I've some useful friends, chica.'

'He's a *friend?*'

'Just keep a look-out for the police. Don't worry about anyone else.'

Her heart was still pounding as he pointed casually to the building opposite. 'That's the National Art Gallery. Mario Carrillio's exhibition is still on.' She looked furtively around. Any minute now someone would arrest her. He laughed as they passed an old man lifting a violin out of its case. 'That's old Pepe. He's a hundred if he's a day. He used to play right here in the same place when I was a lad. He seemed old, even then.' She wasn't listening. There was a newspaper kiosk ahead. Would her photograph be staring out from a front page? Someone would surely recognise her. 'See that Bell Tower? It's one of the oldest buildings in Ciu Costa.' She turned her gaze towards the old tower, eyes lighting up. A famous landmark, she had seen it in picture postcards. He chattered on and on, pointing out this and that, gradually willing her, coaxing her, emboldening her to savour to the full the old city in all its vitality. She forgot that she was a fugitive.

Boarding a bus at the National Bank, they sat in a front seat in full view of the bustling streets. No trace here of the havoc of earthquake. Fascinated she stared ahead. Those attractive handpainted skirts. Wide-brimmed straw hats. People relaxing at pavement cafes. Earnest looking businessmen with briefcases. Ahead she could see rickshaws pulled by nimble men with bent shoulders ignoring the hooting of car horns as they threaded a path through thickening traffic. It brought to mind a song her mother sometimes sang: "The Streets of Ciu Costa". She started to hum a few bars, not conscious that she was doing so. He smiled. 'That's an old one. It goes back to the seventies.'

'It was one of my mother's favourites.'

'When did she leave Costadora ....?' The question died on his lips. He stared ahead. As the traffic ground to a halt, police were boarding buses. 'Come on, chica, we're getting off.' They quickly rose. He turned to the driver. 'Please, let us out here.'

'Not before the stop.' His tone was flat, like a man who knew the rule book inside out and would contemplate no deviations.

'Please, my wife is ill – she needs air.' A sideways glance at Celia's pale, strained face and he relented. 'All right. Be quick. Now! Before the lights change.' He opened the door and let them off. Avoiding the police check-point, they darted across the street and down a maze of side streets until they reached Paseo de Malecón, a fashionable promenade where wealthy Costadoreans had their beach homes. It overlooked Ciu Costa's main beach, Playa de Malecón. Longingly, wistfully she looked towards the sea. The billowy, restless waves seemed to draw her like a magnet. 'Roberto, can we walk along the beach?'

Cautiously he looked around. 'Why not? It's probably safer.' A narrow cliff path led them down to the sands.

'Let's rest a moment. Your leg hurting you?'

'Just a little.' She sat down. 'I think I'll take this bandage off. It feels like a tourniquet.'

Sitting beside her, he leaned back on one elbow. 'Is that wise? You could get infection.'

'Should be all right. I got plasters and antiseptic from Keevers.' As she peeled the bandage off, the pain instantly eased. Walking to a litter bin to dispose of the dressing, she found she no longer limped. The tight bandage, not the wound, had been the problem.

'That feels a *lot* better.' She looked towards him. 'Roberto, what do we do now?'

'I'm thinking about that, chica.'

Her gaze veered again towards the waves breaking on the pebbled shore. 'I'd love to paddle in the sea. Have we time?'

'Just a few minutes. We must move on soon.'

It was a quiet spot. Strong currents and submerged rocks made this end of the beach unsafe for boats and bathers. Further out in the sea were two starkly perpendicular rocks, the nearest one the shape of a man in silhouette. These were Los Centinelas – she recognised them from photographs – said to hold some sacred significance for the Terani, the indigenous people who were once the sole inhabitants of the island.

Perching on a flat rock at the water's edge, she watched the waves breaking over her feet. A thrilling sensation. The breeze blowing through her hair was warm and sensuous. On the horizon she could see the outline of an island shimmering and blurred in the early evening sun. Could this be King George Island, the British crown colony, she wondered? Halfway between Costadora and Hong Kong, it was sometimes referred to as Costadora's sister island. In reality they were very different. Costadora had been part of the Spanish empire during Spain's domination of the Philippines. Taking advantage of the upheaval which followed the dethroning of Isabella II of Spain in 1868, Costadoreans had declared themselves an independent republic. King George Island, lying nearer to Hong Kong, had been seized by the British at the start of the nineteenth century Opium Wars. Not included in the same treaty which governed Hong Kong, it remained under British administration after Hong Kong reverted to Chinese control.

'Want a drink?' Diaz called to her. She nodded and strolled back to where he was sitting. He took from his bag two cans of fruit juice, raided from Keevers' fridge.

'That's King George Island.' He pointed towards the sea. 'Here we just call it "George". 'I thought it might be.' She sat on the sand beside him. 'It's English-speaking, isn't it?' 'Officially. But there's also a small, Portuguese-

31

speaking community – migrants who came from Macau before it reverted back to China. And some rural people still speak Terani.' He smiled. 'You're looking at Britain's last bit of empire, chica.'

'Ever been there, Roberto?'

'A couple of times. Not much to see. It's a quiet place. Smaller than Costadora.'

As she continued gazing into the distant seascape she could see a boat on the horizon Was it heading for George? Or perhaps beyond to Hong Kong?

'It does liven up once a year,' he went on. 'The festival weekend.'

'I heard about that. Isn't it sometime in August?'

'Yes. The Feast of the Assumption. Boatloads go over from here. Must be this weekend.'

'I didn't know it was anything religious. I thought it was just a carnival.'

Diaz smiled. 'It's not religious in the sense that you folk in the west would understand. We do things our own way in this part of the world.'

Celia looked puzzled. 'But the Feast of the Assumption is just one of the traditional holy days.'

'Here it's a little different. The festival opens the nearest Saturday to Our Lady's Feast. It falls about the same time as an ancient Terani festival, so they are combined. The Portuguese open the festival by carrying a very old – some say miraculous – statue of the Virgin Mary through the streets. This is followed by the Terani celebration of the marriage of the Sky Goddess to the Lightning God.'

'It sounds fun.'

'It is. Three days of street theatre and dancing. Everyone joins in.' He looked at her pensively. 'If only you could reach that island, chica, your problems would be over.'

'I know, but how?'

'Let me see that passport.' She handed him Helen Darcy's passport. Looking carefully at the photograph, he then scrutinised Celia's face.

She shook her head. 'It's no use – I've thought about it. She doesn't even look like me.'

32

'Does anyone ever look like their passport photograph? Anyway this passport is nine years old. We all look different nine years on.'

'*That* different?'

Shrugging his shoulders, he handed the passport back to her. 'Photographs can be changed.' He sprang to his feet and cast his glance along the bay.

Changed? How? Did he know someone who dealt with passports, she wanted to ask. But she sensed the moment was not right; his mind was on other things. As she put the passport back in the bag, her hand brushed against something hard. Then she noticed for the first time that the bag had another compartment. Unzipping it, she found among some loose change a large key. Tentatively she fingered it. 'Roberto ....'

Still scanning the coastline, he did not hear her.

'Celia, can you walk that far? To the end of the bay?'

'Yes. My leg feels all right without the bandage.'

'Good. I don't want to risk any more buses.'

'Where are we going?'

'To see some friends.'

Rising to her feet, she looked at him bemused. 'Won't your friends be surprised to see you?'

He smiled enigmatically. 'I think they're half expecting me.'

CHAPTER SIX

The Orchid Bar of Hotel Metropole, favourite drinking den of foreign journalists, was crowded. Today the guests were mainly tourists. A few weeks back the place had swarmed with correspondents reporting on the visit of the US President Kirby, and shortly after a papal visit. With these dignitaries departed, only a few representatives of the foreign media had lingered on for the conclusion of the Celia Martinez case.

Tony Hepworth, correspondent for the British newspaper the *Daily Post*, leaned against the bar. A solid, greying man, fiftyish or thereabouts. Those who knew him well never remembered him looking young; yet with the passing years neither did he appear to get older. Colleagues attributed his apparent agelessness to the amount of whisky he consumed. Hepworth drank to cope with stress. It helped him through two failed marriages. Today he was coping with the stress that went with the job. The journalists had seen harrowing sights in the disaster area east of the city – crushed bodies; the anguish of the bereaved. Like Helen Darcy, Hepworth had been working in Hong Kong. But he covered assignments in Costadora and King George Island when the need arose.

Raising the glass to his lips, he cast his gaze around. Not a familiar face in sight. Although he assumed indifference, Hepworth was weighing up his fellow guests – men in well-tailored jackets and smart ties, languid women in chic dresses, all with the relaxed air of holiday-makers. Well-heeled holiday-makers, for the five star opulence of the Metropole was not for the budget traveller. Elegance permeated every nook and cranny. On the walls hung paintings by eighteenth century Costadorean artists. The plaster ceiling was bedecked with an intricate pattern of luxuriant flowers and birds. Once a summer residence of Spanish colonial governors, following independence it had been converted into a luxury hotel. Nowadays it was *the* place to stay in Ciu Costa.

Weird lot, thought Hepworth as he eyed his fellow guests with disdain. He disliked tourists. They booked out planes when he had to go somewhere in a hurry, slowed down service in bars and restaurants and generally got in his way. Not a sociable person, Hepworth mixed well only with members of his own profession.

Through clouds of cigar smoke and the whiff of perfume, snatches of conversation reached his ears. Grumbles about currency. Why did everyone prefer American dollars to the euro? The earthquake – did anyone know the death toll? And then he heard the name, Celia Martinez. Someone opined that even now, less than two days before the execution, Bianqui might yet pardon her.

Fat chance of that, thought Hepworth miserably. Hopes had been raised on the last day of the papal visit when His Holiness had made an impassioned plea for clemency. In a devoutly Catholic country like Costadora, Bianqui might be expected to listen. But the Costadorean president was rumoured nowadays to be lax in religious observance. The younger clergy were now amongst his fiercest critics. He had imprisoned for sedition a number of radical priests in the south who had supported the cause of landless labourers.

Then, once again, the name Celia Martinez carried to him. A phlegmatic-looking type, bow-tie and dinner jacket, was trying to interest his companion in a wager: how much would be bet on a last minute reprieve? Hepworth's expression firmed into an expression of disgust at this tasteless flippancy. While his professional detachment never outwardly deserted him, the Martinez verdict had touched him like nothing else in his professional career. Journalists who had covered the trial were stunned by its harrowing conclusion – that chilling moment when the ancient, black-robed judge solemnly pronounced the sentence of death.

35

That Martinez had been the victim of a shocking miscarriage of justice was an opinion shared by most foreign journalists. She had pleaded that the drugs found in her hand luggage had been planted on her. The British press inclined towards the view that the prosecution had not proved its case. There had been no proper witnesses. The custody of the drugs had not been satisfactorily documented. A rigorous security check at London Heathrow had not revealed any drugs in her luggage.

Hepworth believed that some of his press colleagues had not helped Martinez. Instead of concentrating on the flawed evidence, they persisted in seeing the judicial process as anti-British. That did nothing to create sympathy for the defendant. Martinez was not the first to be condemned under the current drug laws; a Terani tribesman had been executed a year or two past. But she was the first foreigner. Yet given the country's geographical location – the closeness of Hong Kong and Macau – it was perhaps inevitable that some sections of the Costadorean press saw links between the nineteenth century Opium Wars and the Martinez case. It was foreigners who had brought hard drugs into the area in the first place. They were still at it.

The appearance of Mike Delaney, correspondent for the *Irish Forum*, lifted Hepworth out of his despondency. Someone to talk to at last. Despite their professional rivalry, Hepworth got on well with his Irish colleague. Tall, affable, with an abundance of light brown hair, Delaney looked younger than his thirty years. Blue eyes bright with vitality, he had the fresh good looks of a country lad. On an assignment in Manila, he had been back and forward to Costadora throughout the year.

As the Irishman stood in the doorway looking around, Hepworth waved. 'Over here, Mike.' Delaney smiled in recognition as he edged towards the bar. He perched on a high stool next to Hepworth. 'So, how's it going, Tony?'

'Pretty hectic. Any news?'

'A London couple were killed in the earthquake.'

Hepworth grimaced. 'I meant any *good* news.'

'Sure. An Irishman came first at the Grenville,' replied Delaney, referring to the annual Fun Run on King George Island at which both tourists and locals took part.

Hepworth arched an eyebrow. 'My editor isn't interested in Paddies.'

'And mine isn't interested in Brits.'

The ethnic bantering was mere routine and offended neither. Delaney ordered drinks, then leaning towards Hepworth, spoke in a low voice. 'You know about Monteverdi prison? Damaged in the earthquake. They say Celia Martinez is one of the missing prisoners.'

'She's missing!' Hepworth's eyes widened. 'You're sure?'

'I'm sure. It was on TV.'

Hepworth shot a glance towards the bar television which was showing a football match. 'There was nothing about it here.'

'Well, you know the local news is censored. I picked it up on Channel Eight. Terrible reception. The government must be trying to block the international channels.'

The two men fell silent as they contemplated the significance of this. Then Delaney resumed in a sombre undertone. 'Let's hope she stays missing.'

Hepworth nodded thoughtfully. 'Could be dead, of course. They can't yet know the full death toll.' He pursed his lips. 'Might be the best solution. Better the quake killed her than what they were going to do to her.'

'Better still if she escaped. You know the Constitutionalists say they will abolish capital punishment.'

Hepworth smiled cynically. 'Don't count on it.'

'Their day will come,' Delaney spoke with conviction. 'Sooner than you might think.'

Hepworth's eyes twinkled as he sensed an argument. Delaney believed that the Constitutionalists, whose manifesto was based on Roberto Diaz's political tract *In Defence of the 1972 Constitution* would, sooner or later, seize power. Hepworth disagreed. Despite the now endemic unrest in the Eastern Province, a rigid police system kept Bianqui firmly in control.

37

'Mike, I wouldn't take too much notice of all that revolutionary blab you hear in the bars around here. After a few beers, they're all off to the mountains with their guns. Come the morning they go to work like good little citizens taking their hangovers with them.'

'The rebel army must be recruiting from somewhere. They now control large areas out east.'

Hepworth snorted. 'They don't control anything of strategic importance. Just a stretch of wilderness and hills.'

'That's not the point, Tony. They do have a power base. The working class hate Bianqui. So do most of the intellectuals. I can't help feeling that Bianqui must be on his way out.'

Hepworth spoke facetiously: 'So, how long would you give him?'

'A couple of months.' Delaney jerked forward with a grin. 'Want to bet on it?'

Hepworth gave Delaney a wily look. Was the proposed bet just a bit of sport, or did the Irishman know something the rest of them didn't know? Delaney, something of a linguist, had a sound knowledge of Spanish. He mixed well with local people, particularly in the bars and cares of nearby Fisherman's Cove. He also had contacts in Manila – Costadorean political exiles who were prominent Constitutionalists.

'You underestimate Bianqui,' opined Hepworth. 'He's got the army on his side. That's what counts.'

'The business community is turning against him.'

'You think so?'

'And the Americans. Did you read that piece in the *Washington Telegraph*?'

'Mike, the American *people* may be starting to question this uncritical support of Bianqui but President Kirby is standing firm ....'

Hepworth's voice trailed away. He began looking thoughtfully into space. Delaney cast a languorous gaze around the bar, as though suddenly captivated by a pretty hand-painted skirt and slender ankles. Both had spotted the lean, bald man who had edged close – too close – to Hepworth's elbow. They had seen him hovering around before. Egghead, they called him. Always alone, always with that listening expression on his skeletal face. A real creep. No one doubted that he was one of Bianqui's secret police. They were everywhere.

Egghead showed no sign of moving. 'Let's go onto the terrace,' Hepworth whispered. Delaney nodded, then called out impishly: 'Madam, do sit down. Here's a seat for you.'

'So kind,' said the little fat lady as she waddled towards him, followed by a bevy of voluptuous, ageing ladies. They seemed to swarm from all directions. A ladies' action group for the protection of the polanza, a supposedly endangered species of bird common to Costadora. These elderly campaigners had left leaflets all around the bar. Well-coiffeured, well-manicured, exuding good breeding, definitely Paso de Malecón types. Grabbing a few more stools, Delaney arranged them strategically around Egghead. He was now engulfed. The little fat lady oozed her thanks as she pinned a "Save the Polanza" sticker on Delaney's lapel. 'A cause dear to my heart,' he assured her, then grabbing his drink, bolted with Hepworth to the terrace.

'Phew!' gasped Delaney, as he sank into a sun chair. 'Let's hope they convert Egghead to the cause of the polanza.'

'Stupid cows!' grunted Hepworth. 'How many people were killed or made homeless in the earthquake today, and all that lot can think of is saving the polanza. How long are you going to wear that bloody sticker?'

Delaney pulled the sticker from his lapel. 'All right, Tony, you've made your point'

Hepworth cast his gaze beyond Delaney. 'Look who's here! Our cousin from across the Pond? I thought the Yanks had left.'

Turning around, Delaney saw Danny Jackson, correspondent for the *New York Globe* strolling towards them. A lean man with darkened, steel-rimmed glasses, his close-cropped, military-looking hairstyle added a touch of severity. Seeing his press colleagues, his face creased into a smile. 'Hi, you guys. Not many of us left.' Pulling up a chair, he sat down.

'Heard about Monteverde prison? Damaged in the quake. Celia Martinez is missing. So is Roberto Diaz.'

Delaney grinned in Hepworth's direction. 'How about that, Tony? Diaz on the loose. I told you things would get exciting around here.'

Hepworth looked sceptical. 'Could be dead or injured.' Escapes from Monteverde were rare.

Delaney shrugged. 'Well, you never know. Hope he got away. Any other news, Danny?'

'Something's going on in the Eastern Province. In Sonora.'

'Something's always going on in Sonora,' muttered Hepworth.

'Industrial trouble?' asked Delaney. There had been strikes in Sonora, Costadora's second city, all year. In recent weeks demonstrations often degenerated into violent clashes between police and workers. Rumour had it that the police were losing control and Bianqui was about to send in the army.

'Sounds more serious this time. Some strikers were shot.'

Delaney's eyes sharpened. 'Many killed?'

'Haven't heard the casualty figures. But, if you can believe Radio Libertad, it has triggered off some big trouble.'

'Good old Radio Libertad,' murmured Hepworth, his speech now slurred. If it weren't for the illegal, rebel radio station, they wouldn't know half of what was going on.

'Trouble is, I didn't understand everything,' Jackson continued.

Delaney downed his drink. 'I'll see if I can pick up Radio Libertad later on. I'll let you know what I make of it.'

Hepworth shifted in his chair. 'Were the strikers armed, Danny?'

'Not as far as I know. News is sketchy at the moment.'

Hepworth was now peering into his glass. 'Like my drink. That's getting real sketchy.'

'You mean you need a refill?' Delaney looked around for a waiter. He found one at his elbow.

'Pardon me, señor. I'm looking for Miss Darcy.'

'I don't think she's back yet.'

The waiter hesitated as though he still thought Delaney could help. 'It's a telephone call, señor. From London. The caller seems very anxious. He has phoned several times.'

'Anyone seen Helen?' Delaney asked. No one had. Delaney looked vaguely troubled. Where on earth was she? 'I'd better take a message, Tony. I'm seeing her this evening. We're eating in Fisherman's Cove.'

Hepworth nodded vaguely. 'It's probably from her editor.'

It was indeed her editor, Bob Smithey, and he sounded choleric.

'Delaney here. *Irish Forum*. Can I take a message for Helen?'

Where the hell was she? Smithey wanted to know. All the press agencies had the earthquake story but she hadn't bothered to ring or fax hers in. Delaney tried to calm him down. He assured Smithey that Helen had been in the San Pedro district, right in the thick of it. No, he hadn't seen her since, so she must still be out on the job. Phone lines were down on the east side, so it was likely she was not yet able to get through. 'I'll tell her to fax you from the hotel as soon as she gets back, Mr Smithey.'

Delaney in fact hadn't seen Helen since breakfast time. They had made an arrangement to meet for dinner that evening. She was dashing over to Keevers to do a bit of shopping, but would be back for the press briefing at Government House. She hadn't turned up. Caught unawares by the earthquake, he assumed she had stayed on the east side to report the disaster. That she hadn't yet contacted her editor *was* unusual. A sudden icy fear gripped him; a fear he tried to suppress.

Smithey appeared to have calmed down. 'You say you saw her in the earthquake area?'

'No, I didn't see her. But she told me this morning that she was going over to San Pedro – that's the district which was hardest hit. She must have been the first journalist on the scene.'

'Look, Delaney, do me a favour? Would you phone me if she *doesn't* get back. That is, if she's not back by tomorrow.'

There was a chilling silence. Delaney had no doubt as to what was in Smithey's mind. He tried to sound casual: 'Sure, I'll do that.'

'Was it from Smithey?' Hepworth asked as Delaney rejoined them.

'Yes, he's kicking up a stink because Helen hasn't contacted him.'

'We've been talking about Roberto Diaz,' continued Hepworth. 'Did you know he was born near here? Round the corner in Fisherman's Cove. They were a poor family. His father was a fisherman.'

Jackson began cleaning his spectacles with a tissue. 'If they were that poor, how come he ended up so smart?'

'I read something about him getting to college and university by scholarship,' replied Delaney. 'He's a very good historian.'

Jackson spoke disapprovingly. 'I should think the stuff he writes would be *very* leftish.'

Delaney smiled faintly at Jackson's penchant for affirming the obvious. 'With his background that's hardly surprising. His grandfather fled here from Spain when the Republicans were defeated in the Civil War. Quite a few Civil War veterans settled in the Cove.'

Delaney's explanation touched on a difference often noted between the Hispanic community of Fisherman's Cove and that of Paseo de Malecón: the former, of more recent European descent, had brought their revolutionary ideas with them. The latter, wealthy and conservative, liked to peddle the fantasy that they were descendants of First Families. Both hated each other.

Jackson continued to ramble on about Diaz's impact on political life. Hepworth, now sinking into an alcoholic lassitude, grunted amicably in the appropriate places. But Delaney was no longer listening. Looking out towards the sea, his attention was caught by small boats buffeted on the waves of an incoming tide. His eyes were troubled. 'I don't think anyone has seen Helen since this morning. Not since the earthquake.'

Hepworth's lassitude seemed to dissipate a little as he responded to Delaney's concern. 'Probably still out on the job. You know what she's like. A bit of a workaholic.'

Delaney was not convinced. 'Then why hasn't she contacted Smithey? We all got some sort of story through hours ago.' He fell silent for a moment. 'Should I phone the hospitals?'

Hepworth's eyes narrowed. 'Leave it for now. I'd say she's just held up. Transport's disrupted. Everthing's disrupted.'

In the distance church bells rang out. The Angelus. Delaney checked his watch. 'Look, I'm going to take a stroll on the beach. If Helen comes back, tell her to look for me there.'

* * * * *

As Delaney made his way down towards the sea, an invigorating breeze blew in his face. This was his favourite time of day. The stunning effect of a blazing red sky reflecting on the dark, mystic waters elated his spirit. Here in this idyllic spot, the idea of death and mayhem somewhere over there on the eastern fringes of the city seemed unreal. Make the most of it, he thought as he strolled along the beach. Soon it will be dark. He walked about half a mile, then retraced his steps. Reluctant to go indoors, he perched on a flat rock near the pathway leading up towards Hotel Metropole. There he watched the tide slowly edging further up the beach.

The sun was now setting. Bathers emerged from the water, and those who had been lazing on the beach had begun to drift away. A group of youths were playing football on the sands. Delaney could see in the distance a couple walking towards him along the water's edge. He was a tall, athletic-looking man; she was of slender build. Even from this distance she appeared to have a certain gracefulness. They were now alongside the young footballers. As the ball came flying towards the water the man dropped the bags he was carrying onto the sands and stopped the ball mid-air. He then kicked it back with some jocular remark which caused the boys to shriek with laughter.

The couple were now closer. As a large wave rose and fell onto the shore, the man tried, too late, to pull the young woman out of the way. She laughed as the water splashed on her skirt. The sheer delight on her face struck Delaney as extraordinary. She was like a child seeing the sea for the first time.

Then something else gripped him – a disturbing, incoherent memory. Where had he seen her before? The same features, but not that laughing face. No, she hadn't laughed – she groaned. That awful death-like groan. Two police officers steadied her as her legs gave way. They were propping her up as they led her from the courtroom. It wasn't easy to forget the moment when Celia Martinez was condemned to death.

But could this really be Celia Martinez? As he watched that woman on the beach he had an uncanny feeling he was seeing a living ghost – someone who walked between life and death.

The couple were now alongside him. Just a few yards away. He was now convinced that it couldn't be Celia Martinez. Yes, there *was* a certain likeness, but when she laughed you knew the resemblance was an illusion. The Celia Martinez imprinted on his mind was strained, ashen and with eyes full of hopelessness.

As they passed the woman looked fleetingly in Delaney's direction, then averting her gaze, slipped her arm through that of her companion. On reaching the path which connected the beach to the roadway, she stopped to empty sand out of her sandals. Her companion, now a little way ahead, stopped and waited for her to catch up. The man's voice carried to Delaney.

'Come on, chica. You can rest when we get to Habana Vieja.'

Delaney gazed after the couple as they disappeared onto the roadway. Habana Vieja! That was a well-known fish restaurant in Fisherman's Cove. The same restaurant where he intended eating that evening with Helen. Perhaps he would see them later.

CHAPTER SEVEN

They reached the roadway opposite Hotel Metropole. Gazing towards the fine edifice, Celia's steps faltered On the palm-shaded terrace guests sat chattering as they idly imbibed their drinks. Through great windows she could see people dining beneath chandeliers. The place exuded elegance. There was awe in her voice. 'So *that's* the Metropole. It looks even more splendid than in the photographs.'

Diaz's smile had a touch of cynicism. 'Not many Costadoreans get to see inside places like that. Rich tourists stay there. And foreign journalists.'

His words jolted her memory. 'Journalists! Now I know where I saw him before that man sitting on the beach.'

'What man?'

'Down there. We passed him when we came up the path. I'm sure he was in court at the trial. On the press benches.'

Diaz looked back sharply towards the beach. 'Do you think he recognised you?'

'I don't know – I think he wasn't sure.'

A look of unease momentarily clouded his dark eyes. Then he shrugged his shoulders. 'What of it? The foreign press were solidly on your side.'

Glancing back at the hotel, something else came to mind. The key in the handbag. She took it out. 'Roberto, I found this in Helen Darcy's bag.' She held it up so that he saw the inscription on the tag.

He stared in surprise. 'Hold onto that, chica. Could be useful. Very useful.'

It was cooler now. Plaintive strains of a Costadorean folksong – an old sea shanty – floated through the still evening air. Bars and restaurants along the seafront had begun to fill.

'Roberto, this restaurant you told me about. Is it really safe?'

'As safe as anywhere else. My friend Alfonso owns Habana Vieja. He'll give us something to eat.' He paused and looked at her thoughtfully. 'And then, chica, we've got to think of where you go from here.'

'Yes, of course.' She smiled bravely, but her tranquillity masked deep anxiety. Until a few hours ago she believed she had no future. In her despair there had been certitude. Now that she had briefly tasted freedom she had so much to lose.

They reached a bend in the road. A cliff head separated the Malecón beach from Fisherman's Cove. The smaller bay, Fisherman's Cove, was in full view. 'There it is! Habana Vieja ….' He stopped short, his expression becoming sombre. Looking in the direction he pointed, she shrank back in terror. Parked outside the restaurant was a police van. Her immediate instinct was flight. She had already started to back away, but he clasped her arm firmly.

'Don't even think of it. If you behave like a fugitive they'll give chase. Just keep walking.'

They advanced slowly. 'Come on, Celia, talk to me. Don't even look at them. Pretend we're lovers or something.'

Petrified, she didn't reply. An odd notion came to her that all passers-by could see her terror and knew the reason for it. Her bolt for freedom had been a mere deviation on the sure road to the gallows?

If Diaz felt anxiety he didn't show it. He squeezed her hand. 'This way, into the gardens.'

On the rocky projection separating the two bays was a patch of green called Marine Gardens. Among flowerbeds and trees, a pathway wound along from the roadway to the cliff head. On each side were benches. Finding an empty bench facing Fisherman's Cove, they sat down in full view of Habana Vieja. The stunning vista of both bays made this a popular spot for an evening stroll. Here people walked their dogs or sat on benches chattering. Voices and laughter reverberated in the still evening air. Her tension eased just a little. In this bustle of humanity there was anonymity. Warily her gaze veered towards the police van. 'Do you think they're watching us?'

'Don't make it obvious that you're watching *them*. Just talk to me. Come on, tell me something about yourself. What brought you out to Costadora, anyway?'

'As I said, my mother was born here. I always wanted to come.'

'You still have relatives here?'

'Not that I know of.' She sounded bitter. 'My mother's family abandoned her when I was born. I'm illegitimate.'

'Perhaps they were poor, and unable to offer support.'

'No, they were *rich*. They regarded it as a blot on the family's honour. When I was born they made it plain to my mother that they didn't want her to come back to Costadora.'

He put his hand on her arm, and then raised a finger to his lips to silence her. One of the policemen had jumped out of the van. Was he coming this way? He paused at the sea wall, then walked away, disappearing into the crowd.

'So your mother never came back to Costadora?'

'No, I think she would have liked to.'

'And your father. Where is he?'

'Dead. I never knew him. He met my mother when they were both students at an English language college in London. He went back to Norway before I was born ....' She stopped, again casting a fearful glance towards the police vehicle. His voice had a compelling calm. 'Don't look at them, chica. Come on, you're supposed to be telling me your life story. Didn't I read something about you working with children?'

'Yes, I'm a kindergarten teacher.'

'You enjoy that?'

'Oh yes!' Her eyes brightened. 'Small children can be such fun. Of course it's only an interim job.'

'You have other plans?'

'I go to college in the evenings for a degree course in Hispanic studies. When I qualify ....'

47

His hand touched her arm as though to alert her. 'What are the up to?' Two more policemen had alighted from the van.

She stiffened. 'Roberto, they're coming this way.'

He didn't answer, but continued watching intently as they turned into the gardens. With slow, aggressive gait they began walking up the path looking from right to left. He stood up.

'Right, chica,' he whispered. 'Go to the top end of the path – don't run, just walk. Take your bag with you. I'll try to hold their attention. There are steps down the cliff leading to a boat slip. Go there, and keep out of the way.'

'Roberto, they'll stop you.'

'If they do you must go to Habana Vieja and ask Alfonso for help. Say I sent you.'

'Come with me – please. We can both get away.'

'Do as I say. Quickly!'

She gripped his arm. 'Roberto, please don't get caught because of me.'

'Chica, go while you have the chance ....'

'We can both get away. Come .... Please.'

The two officers advanced with measured steps. No time to argue further. Diaz spoke tersely. 'All right, let's move.'

They walked slowly towards the cliff head, her arm slipped through his. Nerves taut, she could feel the pounding of her heart. At the top of the cliff path a white-winged bird soared. Free, languid and graceful. It hovered for a moment, then floated downwards towards the water. A sudden shout caused them to turn around. A man was running through flowerbeds and onto the road. In pursuit were the two nimble-footed policemen. Soon both pursuers and pursued were out of sight. She stared after them.

'Do you think they caught him?'

'More than likely, poor devil. As I said, if you behave like a fugitive, they give chase.' His gaze went towards Habana Vieja. 'Well, the police van is moving off. Shall we go to see Alfonso?'

* * * * *

'This way. The kitchen entrance.' Diaz waved his hand pointing the way ahead. She glanced briefly into the restaurant as they hurried past. Candle-lit tables, chattering diners, the aroma of fresh fish and herbs. Darting through the car park, they made their way to the rear of the building. At the kitchen doorway Diaz called to a pink-cheeked man with drooping moustache and white apron, busily stirring vegetables in a large pan: 'Amigo! Could you let Alfonso know I'm here.'

Dropping the spoon he came over smiling broadly and vigorously shook Diaz's hand. For a moment the man seemed speechless. Then in a hoarse whisper he told Diaz that Alfonso was waiting. They knew that if he got away he would come straight here. With a quizzical look, he offered his hand to Celia. He did not ask her name. She did not give it.

'This way, please.' He led them down a short passage and knocked on a door marked 'Private'. Someone shouted at them to come in. The door opened to a small, chaotic little office. A bearded man of medium height – he looked to be in his mid-thirties – came out from behind a desk. His eyes lit up as he embraced Diaz.

'You made it, amigo! You made it! We were so worried.'

'Alfonso, how good to see you!'

Alfonso gave a loud, jovial laugh. 'After all our planning, and in the end it was an earthquake that got you out.'

'Not just the earthquake.' Diaz stepped inside the room. 'I had unexpected help. I'll tell you about that later.'

A quickening of interest lit Celia's eyes. Help from where? She recalled that the warder they had seen in the street made no effort to have them apprehended.

Standing behind the two men was a pretty, petite woman, a hint of Chinese in her features. 'Dolores!' Diaz stepped forward and kissed her cheek. 'What's this I hear about a baby on the way?' Grinning, he slapped Alfonso on the back. 'This fellow has a lot to answer for.' Dolores laughed happily. 'They told me yesterday it's a boy.'

Celia remained awkwardly in the doorway. Forgotten, alone, out of place in this reunion of old friends. It was Dolores who noticed her, 'Roberto, your friend ....?'

Diaz swung around. 'Sorry. This is Celia. She needs our help, Alfonso.'

The two men looked at each other. A nod from Diaz and a finger to his lips seemed to answer some unspoken question in Alfonso's eyes.

'I'm so sorry. You weren't expecting me.' Her apologetic tone was born of habit. The prisoner did not get in the way; did not speak unless spoken to; was mindful at all times of being a non-person.

'You are most welcome.' Alfonso's tone was cordial as he shook her hand. 'You must stay to dinner. This is my wife, Dolores.'

Dolores extended her hand in greeting. 'Did you have far to come, Celia?' Very far, thought Celia. A death-time away. Diaz interjected. 'Celia has come over from the east side – San Pedro. It's a long story.'

Alfonso lowered his voice as he turned to Diaz. 'I've had orders from Wong to get you out of Ciu Costa tonight.'

'Wong! How did he know ....?'

'We knew nothing for certain. Only that if you got away you would come here.' Alfonso's voice gathered buoyancy. 'Anyway, we've time to eat first. You must be hungry.'

There was a discreet movement in the background. A young man emerged from a corner. Sallow-skinned, shrewd, humourless eyes, neat black jacket and well-polished shoes. Alfonso introduced him.

'Roberto, this is Pedro, your driver for tonight.'

'Good to see you, Dr Diaz. Will you be ready to leave in a couple of hours? About ten?'

'Whenever you are ready, Pedro.'

Where will I be in a couple of hours? Celia wondered. She fought back a feeling of panic. As Alfonso began issuing his instructions, it became clear that Pedro was a waiter in the restaurant. In Alfonso's absence he was to keep an overall eye on things.

Alfonso turned to his wife. 'Hang up Celia's jacket for her. She probably wants to freshen up. We'll join you in a few minutes.'

At the top of the stairs Dolores paused by an open door which looked into a pleasant room, the glass doors at the far end leading to a balcony. A heavy, carved mahogany table was set for a meal. 'We are eating in there. The bathroom is the last door on the right. Come back here when you're ready.'

The room was empty when Celia returned. Venturing in, she looked around. Photographs on the sideboard caught her attention. A younger-looking Alfonso and Dolores in Marine Gardens looked out from a silver frame. An old man leaning on a stick stood beside them. Fine crop of white hair, a glint of humour in his eyes, he was dressed like the local fishermen. Alfonso's father? There was strong resemblance. Then she spotted Diaz in a smaller photograph. A little thinner and about ten years younger. His arm was around the waist of an elegant woman. Dressed in white, dark hair pinned back in the Grecian coil, a style which enhanced her striking good looks and find bone structure. Head resting against Diaz's shoulder, her expression exuded happiness. Alfonso stood a little to the side.

Tentatively she lifted up the photograph and began scrutinising it. Who was this woman with Diaz? As voices from downstairs carried to her, she quickly put it down again as though ashamed of her curiosity. Then she walked through to the balcony.

The billowy sea which had so enthralled her was now subdued. A magnificent calm hung over the dark, glassy waters. All the bustle of the day had died. People drifted to and fro along the promenade, unhurried, savouring the nocturnal serenity. She gazed out fascinated, recalling the many stories she had heard about Fisherman's Cove. Folklore attributed to the area a turbulent past; a world of pirates, smugglers and shipwrecks. In her mother's childhood the area had been scarred by poverty – a stark contrast to the nearby stylish Paseo de Malecón. A tourist boom had changed all that. The seafood restaurants in Fisherman's Cove were now famous. Taking tourists on boat trips around the bay was a thriving business. Souvenir shops and small guest houses had sprung up everywhere.

She breathed deeply. The fresh, salty air and the gentle rhythm of lapping waves began to narcotise her senses. Reality was slipping from her. Monteverde Prison didn't exist; she had never been caged in that grim death cell counting the last days and hours of life ebbing away. It was a nightmare. She had woken in the fullness of life to a beautiful world.

'I'm sorry to have left you alone.' It was Dolores. She carried two bottles of wine which she placed on the table. 'We'll be eating soon.'

'You have such a wonderful view here,' Celia called from the balcony.

Dolores came through to the balcony and cast her gaze along the bay. 'Yes, isn't it beautiful? I don't think I could live anywhere else.'

'You were born here?'

'No, not here. Not in Ciu Costa. I was born in Sonora. Where the fighting is.'

'The fighting?'

Dolores looked at her curiously. 'Don't you know - ?' She hesitated. 'No. Perhaps you don't. You've been away from all this.'

'Then you know where I've been?'

'Yes, Roberto told me when I went downstairs for the wine.' She sounded unperturbed as though helping fugitives was mere routine.

'This fighting in Sonora, is it serious?' An avid reader of Costadorean history, Celia remembered the words of a guerrilla combatant of the first revolution: 'Whoever controls Sonora, controls the nation.' Sonora was the country's first capital. Although no longer so, as a major industrial centre it still dominated the nation's economy.

'It seems to be. We don't have all the details. It began with the strikes. The workers took over some factories. We've just heard on Radio Libertad that there is street fighting and some people were killed.' She paused. 'I mustn't forget – some table napkins.' The switch from revolutionary politics to domesticity was matter-of-fact, as though both were an aspect of daily life. Going inside she took napkins from a sideboard and placed them on the table. Celia followed her in and sat on the sofa.

'Is Roberto going to Sonora?'

'No. Not Sonora.' Dolores sat down beside her. 'He's needed somewhere else.' She seemed reluctant to elaborate. 'Did you meet Roberto in prison?'

'No, we never saw the politicos. We met when hiding in Keevers.'

'Oh yes, Roberto said you got some clothes in Keevers.'

Celia gave a rueful smile. 'I suppose that makes me a shoplifter. But I can't walk about Ciu Costa in prison clothes.'

'Of course you can't.' Dolores's commonsense voice implied that she viewed these things pragmatically. Lifting a corner of Celia's skirt, she studied the design. 'Very pretty. I'm glad you found something suitable. My clothes wouldn't fit you. You're taller than me.' Her glance fell again on the table. 'Serving spoons. I knew I had forgotten something.' She continued chatting as she fetched more cutlery from the sideboard. 'I feel sorry for Roberto. He would like to see his family again, but it wouldn't be safe just yet. A frank look as she scanned Celia's face. 'You know he's married?'

Celia smiled pleasantly. 'Well, I thought he might be. Costadorean men marry early.' She looked towards the sideboard. 'Is that his wife in the photograph?'

'Yes, that's Elena. The photo was taken about a year after they married.'

'Do they have children?'

'A nine year old daughter, Pilar. She's on a school exchange in George at the moment. At an English language college. Roberto left instructions that she should stay on George until the trouble is over.'

'Then you're expecting this fighting to spread?'

Dolores bit her lips as though she felt she had already said too much. Her reply had a studied vagueness. 'Well, anything can happen these days.'

Celia, so long starved for news of the outside world, wanted to probe further. 'I sometimes heard the prison warders arguing about politics. It sounded very serious, as though they expected a revolution, or something.'

Dolores sounded surprised. 'They talked politics in front of prisoners?'

'Why should they care? I was as good as dead ....' She stopped short as though aware she had said something that might embarrass. 'Or perhaps they just forgot that I understood Spanish.'

Dolores continued arranging the tableware. 'And did you get any impression as to which side they were on?'

'They didn't all seem to be on the same side. I found that strange. You would expect everyone working in the prison service to be government supporters.'

There was wisdom in Dolores's smile. 'Not necessarily. Politics tear workers apart, friends apart, families apart.' Her gaze veered again towards the photograph of Diaz and his wife. 'Elena's parents don't share Roberto's politics.' She gave a knowing shake of the head. 'Of course they *are* very rich.' Her tone implied that that explained everything.

Footsteps on the stairs and Alfonso's hearty laughter signalled that the men were about to join them. Dolores pulled out the chairs. 'You sit next to me, Celia. Roberto will sit opposite, and Alfonso at the top.'

Alfonso and Diaz entered, followed by a solemn-eyed, pale-faced youth carrying a tureen of soup which he placed on the table. Alfonso introduced him as his nephew Raul. His cheeks reddened as he shyly shook hands with Celia.

Alfonso looked approvingly at his nephew. 'Raul is a great help to me. He's a student, but he works in the restaurant during the summer vacation.' Glancing towards Diaz he added in a low voice: 'He keeps telling me, though, that he wants to go with you tonight. I can't get him to see sense.'

'Diaz placed an arm on Raul's shoulder. 'Raul, we need you here. Understand?'

While his arm rested on Raul's shoulder the lining of his jacket was visible. Celia noticed the revolver protruding from an inside pocket. Not something he picked up in Keevers.

'Go now and help Pedro in the restaurant,' Alfonso instructed his nephew. As Raul departed, he cast a backward glance at Celia. His look of admiration had a youthful intensity.

Platters of fish and vegetables followed the soup. Wine flowed freely. As Alfonso uncorked the second bottle and began filling glasses, Diaz raised his hand to indicate he had had enough.

'Come on, we're celebrating your freedom.' Alfonso sounded buoyant. 'And you don't have to drive.'

'No, but I might have to shoot.'

'So what. A drop of wine steadies the hand.'

'But not the eye. I want to shoot straight.'

Banter, slick repartee, easy laughter. It was difficult to believe that these people were serious, dedicated revolutionaries.

A quick glance at Celia, then Alfonso deftly changed the conversation to news of old friends. Had Diaz heard that Ernesto had married? Not a local girl – someone from the Western Province. Did he know that poor Antonio had lost his father a few weeks back? Very sudden. A stroke.

Does Alfonso distrust me? Celia wondered. Yet she knew that if she were recaptured and interrogated she could tell them nothing about Diaz that they didn't already know.

Then, without warning, the voices and laughter began to recede. A sense of disorientation engulfed her. Fatigue perhaps. She tried harder to concentrate. But the voices became ever more distant. Her mind was playing tricks again; she was somewhere else. The lights went out. Only that one light remained above her bunk which made sleep elusive. Those shadowy figures in the corner – warders who watched her day and night. That overpowering smell of pest control spray that did nothing to keep away mice or cockroaches. That deadly numbness and despair.

'I don't want to die.'

'Everything all right, chica?' Diaz's voice brought her mind back again.

Had she spoken aloud? Her voice assumed a brightness to hide her embarrassment. 'This is delicious. The sauce is so unusual.'

'Better than dinner at Monteverde?' Diaz's cheery tone implied that he had noticed nothing untoward.

'*Much* better.'

'Celia hopes to finish her degree course when she gets back to London. Hispanic Studies.' Diaz directed his remark to Dolores.

Dolores smiled at Celia. 'I had noticed you speak very good Spanish.'

They listened politely as she spoke of her plans for the future. She hoped one day to teach Spanish.

Good food, good wine, an ambiance of conviviality; the heady fusion began to lift her spirits. It was as though she had known these people all her life. As she sipped coffee she felt a warm glow inside. And then the jolt back to reality.

'The passport, chica.' Diaz's voice had a sudden urgency. 'Let Alfonso have a look at it.'

'The passport?'

'Yes. I told Alfonso that you found a European passport. He knows someone who could adapt it for your use.'

Alfonso leaned forward. 'He'll need a photograph, though. I'll take one of you before you go.'

Go where? She remembered that that was something she had not yet thought through.

'Alfonso, I could take the photograph,' Dolores offered. 'I want to try out my new camera. And I'm a better photographer than you. Come Celia, we'll do it in the bedroom. You might want to comb your hair first.'

As the two women disappeared, Alfonso went over to the sideboard and lifted up a radio. Sitting down again he began tinkering with the knobs until he picked up Radio Libertad. Both men listened intently to the rebel broadcast: a stand-off at two more factories in Sonora. Sporadic street fighting still going on, but police had regained control in the city centre. Barricades had gone up in nearby Puerto Bello. More army units going over to the rebel side.

Diaz's eyes conveyed anticipation, and just a hint of tension. 'It sounds as though I ought to be on my way.'

Alfonso agreed. 'I'll call Pedro. And then we must decide what to do with Celia. I don't think it's safe here.'

'The police raided you?'

'No. I'd feel happier if they had. It has to be our turn soon.'

They fell silent. Diaz leaned forward and clasped his hands. He seemed to be weighing up in his mind something that had no easy answer. 'I could take her with me. To the mountains.'

Alfonso poured himself another cup of coffee. 'You haven't time for that.' His face was impassive.

'She's in great danger here, Alfonso.'

'Would you be so anxious to save her if she weren't so pretty?'

Diaz raised his hands in a gesture of protest. About to speak, the words of denial died on his lips. With an easy smile he turned it to a joke. 'I'd save you, Alfonso, and you're not pretty.' Alfonso laughed and made a playful pretence of boxing Diaz's ears. Then his face resumed an expression of gravity.

'All the same, you must be sensible about this. Can you imagine the newspaper headlines? "Diaz in mountain hideout with blonde?" You would look frivolous.'

'Who cares what they think? You know what they were going to do to her. I couldn't just abandon her.'

'You've got to care. We need you.' Alfonso downed his coffee. 'You got her here safely. Leave the rest to us.'

'Then you will help ....?'

'I'll see what I can do.'

Diaz looked pensive. 'She has the key to Helen Darcy's hotel room.'

'Darcy! The English journalist? Darcy gave her a hotel key?'

'Darcy's dead. The earthquake killed her. Look at that passport.'

Flicking open the pages, Alfonso gasped in surprise.

'Celia found her body outside Keevers,' Diaz continued. 'The passport was in her handbag. We're probably the only people who know she's dead.'

'That's a real pity, Roberto. She was useful. Did you read her exposé on Bianqui? Published abroad. No, of course you can't have. It wouldn't have got past the prison censor.'

'We do need to get the foreign media on our side, Alfonso. What about the Yank?'

'Whatever he thinks, his paper supports Bianqui.'

'I was thinking of the woman. Katie Casper.'

'Casper? Television isn't she? I don't know where she stands.' Alfonso lightly tapped the table with his fingers, a gesture habitual to him when meditating the pros and cons of something. 'There's a fellow who comes in here sometimes. From some Irish paper. Delaney. I thought we might use him.'

'How well do you know him? Have you sounded him out? Remember the Ramos interview.'

Alfonso grimaced. Would he ever forget it? The ageing and respected poet, Ernesto Ramos, a one-time Prime Minister – he had won the Nobel prize for literature a few years back – was the man whom the Constitutionalists supported as a future President of Costadora. In exile Ramos had given an interview to a tabloid in which he was grossly misquoted. Alfonso stroked his chin ruminatively. 'Delaney does seem a good fellow, though. Says he met Luis in Manila.'

'If you're sure about him, then use him. We could do with ….' Diaz's voice trailed off as the two women reappeared.

'We were discussing where you could stop tonight, Celia,' Alfonso said. 'Let me see that hotel key.'

Taking the key from her, he scrutinised the tab. *Hotel Metropole Room 205* was embossed in gilt lettering. Turning towards Diaz he spoke in a tone which implied that that settled the matter. 'It's the last place they'd think of looking for her.'

* * * * *

58

The parting was painful. Habana Vieja had been a refuge. A warm and friendly place. Out there was a hostile world full of danger. She tried to look cheerful as she slipped on the jacket which Dolores handed to her. 'Remember to keep that key with you at all times,' Alfonso said. 'Go straight to your room. Don't go near Reception.'

'Don't ask for directions even if you're lost,' Diaz added. 'Look as though you know where you're going.'

Unzipping the weekend bag, Dolores slipped in a newspaper. 'Have a look at page four when you've time. There's an article there that will interest you.' She held up an envelope. 'I'm putting this in as well – a gift from Alfonso and me.'

Alfonso tapped his pipe against the chimney piece. 'I'll send someone with the passport later. Probably Pedro. It may be tonight. More likely tomorrow. Try to be out in the morning when the maid is making up the room. With a bit of luck you only need to hide for a few days.'

'A few days ....?' Celia looked puzzled. Alfonso's matter-of-fact tone seemed to convey that everything was in hand.

'I've got to contact some friends at the Ferryport. To find out when might be the safest time to take a boat.'

Diaz interjected. 'You don't have to do anything, Celia. Just wait for Alfonso to contact you.'

Alfonso was eyeing her appraisingly as she tucked her hair inside the jacket and turned up the collar. 'Shouldn't think anyone will recognise you. Do you want Pedro to carry over your bag?' Pedro had just entered with a tray.

'I'll be all right.' She lifted up the weekend bag. 'It isn't far.'

'I'll walk over there with her.' Diaz pushed back his chair and rose to his feet.

Alfonso raised his hand. 'She said she would be all right.'

Diaz stood slightly apart. She could feel his eyes – those great brown eyes, piercing her. Her mind groped for some appropriate words of farewell. Farewell and thanks. Thanks for bringing her so far. She would not be here, still safe, but for him – his chiding, his coaxing, his willingness to help when he could so easily have abandoned her. She turned towards him. No words came. He bent and kissed her cheek. 'Good luck, Celia.'

CHAPTER EIGHT

Delaney was hungry. It was now nine o'clock. No point in waiting any longer for Helen. Dinner plans, always tentative, depended on work. Something must have cropped up to delay her.

Leaving Hotel Metropole, he gave a backward glance towards the city before turning into Fisherman's Cove. Even from this distance you could see the old Bell Tower, floodlit, dominating the skyline. Beyond darkness. The east side was still without electricity. Probably also without transport. Was Helen still somewhere over there? He pushed a feeling of unease to the back of his mind.

The sea breeze blew his abundant, brown hair into his face as he skirted Marine Gardens with long, purposeful strides.

'Hullo there, Manuel?' he called to the old fiddler playing opposite Habana Vieja.

'How are you, Michael?' Manuel stopped playing as Delaney sat down on the wall. An amateur musician himself, Delaney's tin whistle travelled with him everywhere. He and Manuel had been trading Costadorean folksongs and Irish traditional music. Pleasantries exchanged, the old man took up his fiddle again.

'How about this one, Michael?' He smiled roguishly, then began playing a lively Irish jig. Delaney laughed, clapped the old man on the back, and told him what a big hit he would be at a ceili.

'And how's the revolution going?' Delaney put the question with a touch of flippancy that belied his serious concern. It wasn't that he thought the old man was someone with a finger on the political pulse, but he was a useful enough person to sound out for a man-in-the-street perception of things. Manuel looked around furtively. A police car had just sped past. Even at a distance the police had that effect. They froze people into silence. When the vehicle was out of sight the old man replied.

'You've heard Diaz is out?'

'I heard he's missing.'

'He's alive.' Manuel sounded confident. 'He must be. People are going off to the mountains.'

'What's happening in the mountains?'

The old man's white, bushy eyebrows came closer together, an expression he assumed when perplexed. 'I've heard people talk about a second front. I think it's something happening in the mountains.'

Delaney gave the old man a probing look. His information was sometimes confused, but never wholly inaccurate. Yet Diaz, if still alive, had been at large for just half a day. A second front had to be the result of long-term planning. Something didn't add up. Delaney tried another line. 'Manuel, it was on the news that Diaz is missing. There's no confirmation that he escaped. Are you certain he's out?'

'Well, Michael, people have been saying funny things. There's talk about fighting. My sons were listening to Radio Libertad. When the man on the radio said, "Diaz is out", my youngest boy said that means it's time to go to the mountains.'

Delaney weighed up the old man's words. How could Diaz's escape – if escaped he had - be a signal to go to the mountains? The earthquake which sprung him from prison could not have been predicted. "Diaz is out" must be a coded message – perhaps a signal for a rising – rather than anything to do with the whereabouts of Roberto Diaz.

Before taking leave of Manuel, Delaney glanced across at Habana Vieja, and then walked on. Another favourite eating place, La Roca, came to mind, a taverna at the other end of the Cove which was a popular meeting place for local musicians. There Delaney's impromptu performances on the tin whistle had won him friends.

Hands shoved in pockets, he pondered over the old man's words. A second front? It sounded feasible. The unrest in Sonora – the republic's industrial heartland – seemed to be escalating. Didn't half of Costadora's population live in Sonora? But the Eastern Province was some distance from the seat of Bianqui's government. The assault on Ciu Costa itself would have to come from somewhere else. Provably from the Sierra Guadeloupe, that great mountain range in the hinterlands of Ciu Costa which extended well into the Eastern Province.

Bianqui, old man, your days may be numbered, Delaney said to himself. Lost in thought, he didn't notice the police checkpoint until he was almost upon it. What was going on? People – mainly young men – were being apprehended. Others were allowed through. A ruffled tourist, red-faced and balding, was arguing with a policeman in a mixture of English and bad Spanish that he *had* to get past. His hotel was on the other side. No, he wasn't carrying identification. His passport was in his hotel room. Act cool, Delaney told himself. Pretend not to notice the hullabaloo. When a policeman blocked his way, Delaney oozed with courtesy. Nice evening. And hadn't it been a beautiful day? Would this do for identification? He produced his press card. No, that wasn't a gun in his inside pocket. It was a tin whistle.

Scowling, the policeman looked hard at the photograph on the press card, and then scrutinised Delaney's face. 'Where are you going, Mr Delaney?' Delaney pretended not to notice the two young men being bundled into the back of a police van. 'I'm going to eat,' he replied pleasantly.

'Where are you going to eat, Mr Delaney?'

'One of those fish places.' Delaney looked so relaxed that he might have been sleepwalking. The policeman handed him back his press card, but was still blocking his way.

'Well, must get moving,' smiled Delaney, shuffling sideways. He glanced at his watch. 'God, is that the time?'

A volley of stones showered the police van. It happened so suddenly that for a moment everyone stood, open-mouthed. The policeman turned from Delaney to rush to the assistance of a colleague who had been hit on the head.

Nonchalantly Delaney sauntered on. The tourist caught up with him.

'Did you see where the stones came from?' Delaney asked him.

'That side street beside the newspaper kiosk. Some youths. About a dozen of them. Dreadful business.' He sounded flustered. 'I thought this was supposed to be a civilised country.'

'They can be heavy-handed,' Delaney conceded. 'Best to keep calm. Don't show irritation. Are you all right?' The man nodded, cast a backward glance, then shook his head disapprovingly: 'I blame the parents.' Delaney shot a curious glance at the man as he grasped that their exchange had been at cross-purpose.

* * * * *

La Roca had an ambiance all of its own. Crude plastered walls, wooden beams, roughly-hewn tables, and that peculiarly pungent smell of Costadorean tobacco. Having eaten his fill, Delaney leaned back contentedly listening to the guitarist who played in the corner by an old-fashioned chimney picce. Snippets of conversation reached his ears. Comment on the stone-throwing youths. The latest news from Radio Libertad. Then someone opined that it wasn't too safe on the streets tonight.

What a cross-fertilisation of cultures we have here, thought Delaney as he absorbed the scene. In the music of the guitarist you could detect strains of something Terani, as well as Basque. The proprietor's grandfather was a republican Spanish Civil War veteran. These political exiles who had settled here in Fisherman's Cove had kept alive their music and folklore. La Roca was still a magnet for political radicals.

Between tables waiters moved nimbly carrying plates of food. Over calico trousers, they wore black high-necked tunics with colourful sashes, a design which owed something to the influence of Western Province lowland Terani.

'Michael! What are you doing here?' Turning around, Delaney stared in disbelief at the tall, bearded man – youngish despite his sprinkling of grey hair – who pulled out a chair and sat beside him.

'Luis! I thought you were in Manila. Did Bianqui pardon you or something?'

The bearded man laughed, then whispered as he leaned forward: 'Soon Bianqui will be seeking *my* pardon.'

'How soon?'

'Very soon. So what are you doing in Costadora, Michael?'

'Work. First Kirby's state visit, then the Pope's. I also covered the Martinez case. And now this war you're stirring up – it all keeps me busy. I didn't recognise you with that beard. Have all the exiles returned?'

'Maybe.' Luis sounded non-committal.

'On their way to the mountains?'

Luis didn't answer. Pulling out a packet of cigarettes he offered one to Delaney. 'So, how long are you staying, Michael?'

'Not sure. Would you advise me to hang around?'

Luis lowered his voice. 'Perhaps. Independence Day could be lively this year.'

Delaney gave his companion a searching look. Independence Day was an annual occasion of military parades in the Grande Plaza, with Bianqui himself, covered with medals commemorating God knows what, beaming down on the multitude from the balcony of the Presidential Palace.

'Something is happening on the big day, then? Things coming to a head?'

Luis didn't reply, but his thin smile conveyed a significance that was weightier than words. What was going on? Delaney's professional instinct told him that a tide in history had begun to turn. Luis – still on Bianqui's wanted list – had just strolled into La Roca like some casual holidaymaker. Had the revolution arrived?

'Staying over here for a while, Luis?'

'Hard to say.'

The dryness of tone suggested a reluctance to elaborate. Delaney ordered some drinks and their conversation took a trivial turn. That pretty girl in the corner. Her blouse left little to the imagination. Not that anyone was complaining, mind you. But Bianqui's police had taken to arresting girls whose blouses were too low, or skirts too high, under some vague Public Decency law. They teased each other over which of them she had her eye on when she cast that languorous look in their direction.

A passing waiter said something to Luis in a low voice. There was tension in his face as he replied, 'All right, amigo, I'll be ready.' Delaney pulled out a packet of cigarettes. Luis took one without a word. He now seemed deep in thought. Lighting one for himself, Delaney looked around. You didn't have to be a Sherlock Holmes to work out that the two men standing at the door, slick-eyed and alert, were on guard, ready to warn of danger. There seemed to be a number of emotional farewells. Young, earnest-looking men – and some not so young – embraced friends and then left. There was something about them that evoked Yeats' poem "1916". The opening lines were drumming through Delaney's brain:

> I have met them at the close of day
> Coming with vivid faces ....

The guitarist had stopped playing. He stood up and began talking to the proprietor in a low voice. As he put on his jacket, snatches of their conversation reached Delaney. Look after his guitar until he got back. Light a candle for them. Then he left with the others.

People now seemed subdued. 'Let's have a bit of music,' someone shouted. The proprietor tapped Delaney on the shoulder. 'How about it, Michael? Give us a tune.' Delaney nodded. Something to suit the mood of the moment, he thought as he put his whistle to his lips. He began to play an old Celtic folksong, the origins of which were lost in the mists of time. A theme of farewell and parting; love of country – of one's own glens and valleys; an unspeakable yearning. No one present would have known the words, yet eyes were misty as they looked towards him.

And as he played Luis rose, lifted his hand in a gesture of farewell and disappeared into the night.

* * * * *

There was an eerie silence on the streets. Delaney had almost reached Habana Vieja when he noticed the policeman sitting on a wall. Opposite a police van blocked the side street from where youths had been throwing stones. He had already pulled out his press card to show as identification, but as he approached he sensed the officer wasn't interested. Melancholy, ridiculously young-looking in his ill-fitting uniform, he seemed to be just staring into space. Delaney noticed some dried blood on his cheek. A stone had hit its target. You couldn't help feeling sorry for him.

'Nice evening. Are things quiet now?'

The young policeman looked at him in surprise. Passers-by didn't usually chat to officers of the law. Delaney held out his press card so as to allay suspicion. The little policeman seemed anxious to talk to someone.

'It's a bad business, that's for sure.'

Delaney nodded sympathetically and let him talk on. 'Can't they see it's not our fault? We've got a job to do. We're always in the front line. Not the bigwigs who sit at desks giving orders.'

'So you've had a tough day?'

He nodded miserably. 'And they say in the market that it's going to get worse. Wait until next week, everyone says. That's when the big trouble starts.'

Delaney decided on tactical ignorance. 'You can't believe everything you hear,' he said blandly.

'And what will happen when those rebels take over? I'll be put up against a wall and shot.'

'I don't think the Constitutionalists are into that sort of thing. Shooting ordinary people isn't their style. It's just the government they want to overthrow.'

The young policeman looked doubtful. Delaney elaborated. 'Well, if the Constitutionalists take over they'll also need police. Fellows like you with experience. Shouldn't think you'd be out of a job.' The policeman brightened up. He sounded almost cheerful as he bid Delaney goodbye.

As he rounded the bend, Hotel Metropole came into view. Delaney gave an upward glance, then held his breath. A lighted window on the second floor caught his attention. Helen's room. He had a fleeting glimpse of a female figure looking down, and then withdrawing. A smile of relief came to his lips. Fears that he hadn't dared articulate evaporated. Thank God she's back.

Hepworth was in the lobby. A cold sober Hepworth. No matter how much he had been drinking, Hepworth alwas came fully to his senses when he needed to get his mind into work mode. What Delaney called a well-adjusted, fully-operational drunk.

'Mike, this business is getting serious. The government may fall.'

Delaney nodded. 'I told you Bianqui is on his way out. What's the latest?'

'A unit of the army in the Eastern Province has mutinied. Gone over to the rebels.'

Delaney gave a low whistle. If true, then the net was closing in on Bianqui. 'When did you hear that?'

'They say it was on Radio Libertad.'

'Any reaction from Bianqui?'

'He's been on television just now. I wish you had been here. My Spanish wasn't up to it. I think he was claiming that everything is under control. Didn't look too happy, though.'

'Looks like we'll have a busy day tomorrow, Tony?'

'Care for a drink? A coffee or something?'

Delaney declined. 'I'm going up to see Helen.'

Taking the lift, he stepped out on the second floor, then glanced at his watch. A quarter to midnight. She wouldn't yet be asleep. Might as well find out if she's all right. At room 205 he knocked on the door. No response. He knocked again. He had just turned to go away when the door opened.

A girl stood there barefooted, wearing a flowing, white cotton nightdress. Her beautiful, gold-bronze hair framed a pale, bewildered face. He stared dumbfounded. Good God! Celia Martinez. *That* was what Helen had been up to.

'The passport ....?' She stopped short. Delaney was obviously not the person she expected to see. Quickly she tried to shut the door; he put out his hand and firmly held it open.

'Where's Helen?'

She eyed him warily but remained silent. He looked beyond her into the room. 'Helen, call off your kerbos.' No reply.

'Where is Helen?' he repeated. Now trembling, she seemed unable to reply. Seeing her fear, Delaney softened his tone.

'Look, love, I need to know where Helen is. Helen Darcy. She's a friend of mine.'

There was a look of recognition in her eyes. 'You're a journalist?'

He nodded. 'I'm Delaney. Mike Delaney.' He showed her his press card. 'May I come in? I'm sorry, I know it's late, but we can't talk here.'

She stood aside and let him pass.

CHAPTER NINE

Casting his gaze around the room, Delaney tried to quell a deep foreboding. Celia Martinez stood watching him, wary and wide-eyed, like a trapped animal at the mercy of the hunter.

'May I sit down?'

She nodded. He sank into an armchair. She remained standing, her arm resting on the back of the armchair opposite. He waited for her to speak. To tell him that Helen was safe and well. There was some logical explanation for all this. He pulled out a packet of cigarettes. 'You smoke?' She shook her head.

'Mind if I do?'

'No, I don't mind.'

He lit his cigarette and took a long pull. What was going on? Couldn't the girl say something? Had Helen helped Martinez escape? Crazy idea. But then Helen sometimes did crazy things. In any event it was clear that this was going to be a *Daily Courier* exclusive.

'Look, love, I'm confused. Would you mind telling me what's going on. Don't misunderstand me. I'm not trying to steal Helen's exclusive. I told you she's a friend of mine.'

'What do you want me to tell you, Mr Delaney?'

'I need to know where she is. Her editor is getting worried. He phoned from London. Does she know? Has she spoken to him?'

'She's a close friend of yours?'

'We've known each other for a long time.'

70

'Mr Delaney, I'm so sorry ....' As her voice faltered, he looked at her sharply. There was candour in her eyes as she returned his gaze.

'Is she injured? Ill?'

'I'm sorry, Mr Delaney. She's dead.'

What his ears heard, his mind failed to comprehend.

'Can I get you a drink, Mr Delaney?'

Numbed, he was unable to reply. He stared beyond her into space. 'Dead! No, she can't be,' he whispered hoarsely. Helen had survived a bombing in Jerusalem – one of the few to be pulled out of the rubble alive. Then that accident in Bosnia. A great little survivor, they called her. This had to be a mistake. His gaze veered again towards Celia, desperately seeking hope in that pale, anxious face. 'You're sure she's dead?'

She nodded. 'I found her body trapped under a telephone kiosk outside Keevers. There were things in her handbag to identify her – passport, letters.'

'You seem to have gone through it pretty thoroughly.' A sudden, unreasonable anger at this woman who was not Helen sharpened his voice. Startled, she took a step backwards. Then she met his gaze candidly. 'What can I say – I'm so sorry.'

Instantly regretting his anger, he made a vague gesture with his hand. 'Please, forgive me – this has been such a shock. I don't know what I'm saying.' Leaning back in his chair, his mind tried to grapple with what he had just heard. Dead! Helen is dead.

The girl's voice intruded his thoughts. 'You don't look well, Mr Delaney. Are you sure you won't have a drink?'

'Yes, I could do with a drink. Whisky.'

She took whisky from the mini-bar. 'Do you want anything with it, Mr Delaney? Soda?'

'Call me Mike. Yes, I'll have a little soda.'

'My name is Celia. But I think you know that.' Handing him the glass, she sank into the chair opposite him.

'It must be a great shock for you. Helen was your girlfriend ....?' She stopped short, her voice becoming

71

flustered. 'I'm sorry! What am I saying? I didn't mean to be so personal.'

He raised his hands as though to stem her apologies. No offence taken. It would have amused Helen to have been called his girlfriend. No, they were just old friend. He had known her since they were both junior reporters in London. Kept in touch after he went back to Dublin. They always looked forward to meeting up again on assignments abroad.

Delaney leaned forward. 'But what about you, Celia? You haven't told me how you got here.'

She sighed. 'Where do I begin?'

'Begin with the earthquake. It was the earthquake which got you out of prison. That much I know. You were reported as one of the missing prisoners.'

So she began with the earthquake which gave her the chance to escape. Meeting another escaped prisoner in Keevers. No, she couldn't remember his name. He introduced her to friends who gave her something to eat. She was using this room until they could fix up the passport for her. Helen Darcy's passport.

That she wasn't telling the whole truth was transparently clear. A vivid recollection came to him of Celia walking along the beach – yes he now knew that it *was* Celia. How she averted her head when he caught her eye. Slipped her arm through that of her companion, as though he somehow offered protection. Not the way you would behave with someone whose name you didn't know.

'Let me get this straight, Celia. Helen's room key was in that handbag? And these people you met have Helen's passport? They're putting *your* photograph on it?'

'Yes, someone's going to fix up the passport for me'

'Who?'

'I didn't meet him, but they told me he's the person who deals with passports.'

Delaney became silent for a moment; then he spoke as though to himself. 'This complicates things.'

She gave him an anxious look. 'You must hate me for it. But I've got to get off this island somehow. I don't like using her passport, but I have no choice.'

'No, you haven't, have you?' Delaney shook his head. 'All the same, it's a hell of a risk. Once Helen's body is identified, you won't be able to use that passport.'

Getting up, he went to the window and stared out. He seemed to have forgotten Celia's presence. Then he swung round. 'Well, we won't solve any of these problems tonight.'

'I'm very sorry, Mike.' She looked conscience-stricken, as though she thought she had somehow wronged his dead friend.

'It's not your fault, Celia. I'm not blaming you for anything. You just got caught up in this. We'll talk it over tomorrow.'

'You won't betray me?'

'Good God, no! Whatever gave you that idea?' He glanced at his watch. It was almost one o'clock. 'Look, I'll come to see you in the morning. Is nine o'clock all right?'

There was a smile on her lips, but her eyes had a haunted look. 'Nine o'clock is fine.' The tone of polite complaisance did not convince Delaney. You could sense her deep anxiety and mistrust.

CHAPTER TEN

'We're almost there,' Pedro told his passenger.

'Already!' Diaz looked out into the blackness of the night. The jerks and jolts told him that the road was now little more than a rough track, but it seemed too soon to have reached the mountains. At first he could see nothing. Then a great white moon emerged from behind dark clouds, illuminating the tree-lined route. Seeing a wooden cabin ahead, barely visible in the cluster of trees, he smiled. Polanza Lodge. Elena had given the place that name, for it was here that that beautiful bird was sometimes sighted. When a young graduate and almost penniless, he had bought the derelict shack cheaply. Rcnovating it himself, he transformed it into a charming cottage. Until recently, he and Elena had used it as a weekend retreat.

The car slowed to a halt. 'We're stopping here?' Diaz cast a surprised look towards his driver. Briefed only that he was required on a matter of some urgency, he assumed that he was on his way to join the insurgents.

Pedro nodded. 'There's a meeting of the High Command.'

'Everyone is here?'

'I was just asked to get you here as quickly as possible. Colonel Wong's orders.'

Diaz opened the car door. 'Well, let's go and see.'

As the walked up the rough pathway, the door opened. Francisco Wong's lithe frame emerged in the doorway. With a bound Diaz lightly scaled the wooden steps onto the verandah to embrace his old friend from their university days. Then a law student, Wong had joined the obligatory students' Reserve

74

Officers' Training Corps at the same time as Diaz. The military training given by the R.O.T.C. would stand the future revolutionaries in good stead.

Wong hadn't changed. The same wry smile. 'May we invite you into your own house? I hope you don't mind us using it as a temporary headquarters.'

'Glad you found it useful.' Remembering another university friend, he added: 'Is Jorge here?'

'You are the only politico.'

Diaz gave his old friend a searching look. What did they want from him? Son of a prosperous Chinese shop owner, Wong was a rising barrister when he successfully defended two of their members charged with sedition. He continued his association with the movement, advising on legal matters. Later he used his officer's training to acquaint rebel recruits with weapons. These were principally volunteers from the remote eastern hills – agricultural workers who had never handled a gun. He showed his mettle in a few skirmishes with government patrols. When the independent judiciary was dismissed on Bianqui's orders, Wong's military skills became more valuable than his legal expertise. The transition from advocate to soldier seemed to suit him.

'Why am I here, Francisco?' Diaz asked.

'The Irishman will tell you.' This was their name for Antonio Moreno McNulty, Chief of Staff of the rebel army, who attributed his shock of bright red hair to some Celtic ancestry.

A hurried farewell to Pedro, then they stepped into the bungalow. In the bright light Diaz saw that his friend had changed little since their student days. As always, a shade narcissistic. His khaki fatigues were finely tailored; his field-cap set at a jaunty angle, giving him a sort of insouciant elegance. His face was still young. The room was less recognisable.

Moreno sat at the head of a long, bamboo table. Once well-polished, usually bedecked with floral decorations – Elena's touch – now it was scarred with cigarette burns, despite the tin ashtrays. The Chief of Staff of the Costadorean Liberation Army rose and greeted Diaz warmly. 'The earthquake did our work for us. We planned to free you tomorrow.'

Diaz sensed the mood of urgency; the desire to get on with business. Obviously a military meeting. There was none of the witty polemics or passionate debate that typified political meetings. What does the High Command want of me, he thought? Why all the planning to get me out of prison?

With a brisk movement Wong seated himself at Moreno's right. Always half-barrister, half-soldier, Diaz wondered what he would be after the revolution. What will any of us be? Photographs surrounded by flowers on headstones?

Moreno looked towards the lean, white-haired man on his left, whose expressive eyes beamed at Diaz through rimless glasses. 'I think you know Julio Anzar.'

'By reputation.' Diaz smiled as he leaned across the table to shake hands with the elderly Cuban adviser, the legendary revolutionary who had fought alongside Che Guevara in the Santa Clara campaign. It was he who had trained the rebel army in the Sierra Guadaloupe and enlisted the support of the Western Province cooperatives. At his side was Emilo Paez, muscular and flat-nosed, a legacy from his days as an amateur boxer. Son of a Western Province factory worker; electrician by trade, gun runner by vocation. Across the table from him was a young Terani mountain tribesman whose features proclaimed the ethnic links between the indigenous people of Costadora and the Thai.

Diaz seated himself next to Paez and offered his hand. Paez took it but did not speak. The Terani met his eyes with a nod that acknowledged his presence. Handshaking was not a Terani custom. This must be Imi Timu, Diaz reflected. Imi Timu was son of the chief of the largest Terani tribe. It was Imi who had united the tribes in resistance to Blanqul's efforts to forcibly settle them in the lowlands, far from their ancestral lands. The same Imi who recognised the political expediency of linking the resistance of the tribal peoples to that of the Constitutionalists. Despite his youth, he was already a legend. His fearlessness was celebrated in the songs and sagas of his people. Like others around the table, he wore army fatigues, but an image of the Terani lightning god hung on a gold chain about his neck. Beautifully carved, it was unlike those crude imitations of Terani art sold in tourist shops in Ciu Costa. Diaz smiled warmly as Moreno introduced him.

'Your name is well known in Ciu Costa, Colonel Imi.'

The Terani's eyes remained impassive as he acknowledged Diaz's courtesy. 'As we shall know you, Dr Diaz.' His Spanish was grammatical, but careful.

What, Diaz wondered, did he mean by that? The mountain tribes rarely approached the cities. The more remote tribes were hunters who still used bows and arrows and spoke only their own tongue. Imi's semi-nomadic, pastoral tribe had guns his people had captured from the enemy in the first attempt to settle them one hundred years past. They soon became as adept in the usage of modern weaponry as any of their opponents.

Moreno called the meeting to order. Then a brisk nod towards Diaz. 'As you have been holidaying in Monteverde we had better bring you up to date' Rising, he picked up a pointer and went to a large map that covered most of the wall opposite. Diaz suddenly thought of that picture of a cat drawn by his daughter, Pilar, when she was five years old. Was it still handing there underneath the map? As Elena framed this early sample of Pilar's artwork, how they had laughed at the cat's ferocious scowl.

The map, which depicted Costadora, was pitted with pins. Green pins showed the rebel-held areas – the Eastern Province with the sole exception of the provincial capital, Sonora, and adjacent Puerto Bello, the mountains controlled by the Terani tribes where the rising began. Blue pins in the Western Province showed branches of the Union of Agricultural Cooperatives secretly affiliated to the movement, but presently controlled by General Varela's division of Bianqui's army. In the rich lands of the south, beneath the Sierra Guadaloupe range, a red pin pierced each large estate. These were the properties of landowners descended from conquistadors. They were staunchly loyal to Bianqui who had exempted them from his land reforms. In the south the Terani agricultural labourers toiled hard for subsistence wages on land once owned by their ancestors. They were now proving a steady stream of recruits for the rebel forces.

Moreno made a sweep of the Eastern Province with his pointer. 'We now control the whole of the Eastern Province – with the exception of Sonora and hinterland which is heavily garrisoned by government troops.'

Diaz carefully studied the map. It showed how rebel control had extended during his incarceration. Sonora was an industrial town. Bianqui kept the property of his foreign investors well guarded. Two regiments of elite troops had been deployed there. Not the conscripts who often slipped away to join the rebels. He looked towards Moreno. 'The strikers are organised?'

'As well as can be expected. But they are unarmed. Before we move on Ciu Costa we must take Sonora. We cannot leave a hostile city in our rear. How do we stand, Wong?'

Francisco Wong shuffled the typed papers before him. 'Our information is that Bianqui has reinforced the garrison with another division.' The wry smile. 'Conscripts.'

'More recruits for us,' Paez interjected.

Wong continued. 'In the past month 3,310 volunteers have joined us. We have arms for only 2,417 –'

'The bay is under surveillance,' Paez broke in. 'I cannot land arms there.'

'Upriver there is an inlet where the Rio Anguila runs into the sea.' Imi Timu knew the hill terrain of the Eastern Province as only a Terani could. 'You can land arms safely there.'

Wong nodded to him and continued. 'We lost two katushas in the bombing. Another damaged. Katushas and kalashnikovs are of little use against tanks and helis.'

'I can't supply tanks and helicopters like whisky from George,' snapped Paez.

'And I won't sacrifice my men in a failed attack,' Wong replied with asperity.

'*My* men will not fail.' Imi's black eyes burned with fierce pride. The mountain tribes had a courteous contempt for the lowland Terani who had adopted the tongue and lifestyle of the people who had conquered them.

We have spirit enough here, Diaz mused. But he also sensed a lack of unity. Courage alone did not win revolutions. Again he wondered why he was present. He recalled that Francisco had not answered his question.

Anzar raised his hands for calm, a smile on his lined face. 'Comrades, please! There have been developments in the past two days.' The Cuban looked at Moreno.

Obviously Anzar knew the details of these developments, but Diaz's political sense told him that this was something that must be put by a Costadorean.

Moreno was a direct man. 'General Varela psoposes that we join forces to take Ciu Costa.'

Varela! A defector? Diaz wondered if he had heard correctly.

Imi Timu tensed like a hunter who had heard the snap of a twig.

'Can we trust the bastard?' Paez barked.

Anzar pressed tobacco into his pipe. His eyes gleamed as he seemed to measure the opposition. 'If Varela generously presents us with the heavy artillery we require for the taking of Sonora, he will be so deeply committed he dare not turn back.'

'What does he want?' Wong asked.

'He was not pleased when Bianqui made his own nephew Paco generalissimo. Varela is a good soldier and the boy is an ass.'

Wong looked sceptical. 'So failing to be generalissimo he will agree to be colonel again?' Colonel was the highest rank in the rebel army.

'As long as no one outranks him.'

Paez's eyes blazed. 'You mean to make him Chief of Staff?'

'Not until this is over. We could do worse. He's not a man of politics. And he is loyal.'

'He's not loyal to Bianqui.' Wong looked reflective.

Diaz recognised the practised thoughtfulness. Wong would not show his hand until he had assessed the opposition. There was a glint in his eye like that of the seasoned gambler at the throw of a dice. The stakes were high: winning over Bianqui's most respected General could well be the turning point which led to victory. Anzar wanted Varela's adherence. Probably also Wong. It was Paez and Imi who had to be brought around.

'Loyalty goes two ways,' Moreno pointed out.

Varela had led the force Bianqui had sent to settle the Terani. That explained Imi's reservations. Diaz sensed a mounting tension. Moreno returned to the table and faced Imi. 'You will have autonomy within Costadora. You know that. Varela's authority will not extend to Terani lands.'

Imi's eyes met his and did not blink. 'So you say.'

Anzar cleared his pipe against the ashtray. It had the effect of a gavel, but he spoke to Imi as though in private conversation. 'I swear to you that Varela will not step foot on your lands.'

Imi's expression did not change. 'You swear by the Christian God who steals land.'

'I have no God.' The Cuban's voice was firm. 'Only a belief in something better here.'

'Every man should have his gods,' the Terani replied, then lapsed into silence.

Paez jerked forward with a scowl. 'We won the East without Varela.'

'We will win,' Moreno affirmed. 'Our strength equals Bianqui's. Exceeds it with the latest recruits.'

'My wives have more fighting spirit than such volunteers,' Imi scoffed.

'But we have no heavy artillery,' Moreno continued. 'It will be years. Not days.'

Diaz wondered if Imi's silence meant acquiescence. We know so little of them, he thought. The are part of our country. Most Costadoreans have some Terani blood, except a few southern landowners whose ancestors always took wives from Spain. Yet they are strangers. The sound of his name broke in on his thoughts.

'You will go up river to the Western Province tonight. Imi will go with you.' Moreno was addressing him. 'Acquaint Varela with our requirements.'

So that explained his presence. 'I'm not a military expert,' he reminded Moreno.

'Imi will see to that side of it.'

'What are my powers of negotiation?'

'You will have full powers to conclude an agreement.' Moreno paused. 'Gonzales, the Minister of Information, has also approached us.'

Paez's caustic quib masked his anger. 'Bianqui will want to join us next.'

'To be more precise,' Moreno continued, 'he wishes to meet with Dr Diaz.'

As Diaz's eyes met Moreno's, his expression gave no hint of the emotion that stirred within him. The first time Elena brought him to meet her family, Gilberto Gonzales had been a house guest. Diaz, then still a student, conveyed to Dr Betancourt his hopes of becoming engaged to his daughter. The tradition of suitors seeking parental consent was still observed among families of wealth and property. Dr Betancourt's courtesy to Diaz did not mask his disinclination to consider him as a future son-in-law. He advised against any formal betrothal until after graduation. Later Diaz discovered his father-in-law would have preferred Elena to marry Gonzales, then a promising politician with hopes of a ministerial post. Nonetheless a friendship of sorts grew between himself and Gonzales based on a mutual enthusiasm for tennis. Gonzales introduced him to the club where they played regularly. As Gonzales rose in government and Diaz became more immersed in radical activities, their tennis days became a political embarrassment to both. The friendship had not cooled, but they went their different ways.

'Gonzales is somewhat cautious.' The Cuban's eyes twinkled with cynical amusement.

Paez banged his fist on the table, causing the ashtrays to rattle. 'No! No! No! First Varela. Now Gonzales. It is too much.' He started to rise.

Wong evened the corners of his already neatly stacked papers as he might a legal brief. 'Perhaps we could discuss this another time.'

Moreno moved on to the next business.

* * * * *

The moon still shone brightly as they walked away from the bungalow in twos down the narrow path. The air was heavy with the scent of a myriad blossoms – camellia, azalea, the long flowered lily. A night alive with buzzing insects and chirping birds. It reminded Diaz of the first summer he had spent here with Elena. For a moment he forgot his companions.

Wong's voice broke in on his thoughts. 'When you have concluded negotiations with Varela, find out what Gonzales wants. What he wants and what he offers.'

A sudden irritation sharpened Diaz's voice. 'Have I no say in this? These damned army men.'

'You haven't changed. You never took orders well in the R.O.T.C.'

'Do you expect me to walk into the Ministry of Information and have myself announced?'

'You will meet Gonzales in a safe house. Alfonso will arrange that'

'I take it Paez and Imi Timu know nothing of this meeting.'

'They, too, do not take orders well. They will know in time. If Gonzales can deliver the broadcasting to us, it is worth six divisions.' Wong paused to light a cigarette. As the lighter flame illuminated his face, Diaz now saw that his friend had aged more than he previously thought. The weather-beaten features of the guerrilla fighter, not the smooth barrister. 'It would help to have it in our hands for Sonora, but ….' He shrugged. They fell into step again. 'I wish I were sailing upriver with you, Roberto.'

'Can my travelling companion be trusted with Varela?' Diaz looked ahead to the Terani walking with Anzar. 'He made his feelings clear on that matter.'

'That is why the Irishman ordered him to accompany you. As well as the fact that he is a born tactician. Trust him. A Terani's word is sacred. They will die before breaking it.'

He smiled slightly. 'Of course, if you betray them they kill you.'

'I hope Varela knows that.'

'We need air cover, Roberto. If Varela cannot give us air cover, then we must have ground to air missiles. I cannot take Sonora without something more up-to-date than katushas and kalashnikovs.'

'How is Varela to get them to you?'

'Leave that to Imi.'

'He seems to get on well enough with Anzar.'

Something Imi said had provoked a peal of laughter from the Cuban.

'Anzar is not Costadorean. The Terani tribes have little love of Costadora.'

Diaz shot his friend a bemused look. 'But they *are* Costadoreans, Francisco. Don't we call them the First Nation?'

'Well, that's the line nowadays, but they don't see it that way. The Spanish left the mountain Terani alone. Their lands are useless for cash crops. It was only after independence that efforts were made to settle them. What a fiasco that was. Bianqui was a fool to try it again.'

Diaz gave a short laugh. 'He wanted to show his American investors how he had westernised the country.'

'Well, perhaps he did us a favour. It was his move against the Eastern tribes that drove them into our ranks. I tell you, Roberto, those Terani make fine soldiers.'

'I do wonder, though, how they can eke out a living up there in those bleak mountains.'

'I used to wonder about that myself.' Wong put his hand on his friend's arm to stay him. 'After we took the Cabeza de Cabrio Pass, Imi decided I wasn't such a bad soldier so he invited me to his summer village. The mountains are full of game. They keep goats, grow vegetables and weave their own clothes. There is plenty of wild fruit.' He smiled. 'they showed me that you can have a good life, even if you work very little.' Wong ground out his cigarette and leaned against a tree trunk, his eyes animated. 'There is very little crime in their communities, Roberto. The tribes hold the land in common. No one is in want.'

'Sounds good to me. You're thinking of becoming a Terani?'

Wong grinned. 'The initiation ceremony is too painful. Besides I'm too much a man of the cities.'

'Imi's command of Spanish surprised me. Idiosyncratic perhaps, but sound. Unusual for a mountain man.'

'Imi and his brothers can speak and write basic Spanish. How they came to learn it is a strange story. Perhaps Imi will tell you about it when you go up-river with him tonight.'

'Army life seems to suit you, Francisco.'

'The law was my father's choice. Still, I would enjoy prosecuting Bianqui when we put him on trial.'

Diaz turned around as Moreno called out to them. It had been a long day, he thought, as he waited for the Chief of Staff to catch up. When, he wondered, would he get some sleep?

Moreno came alongside Wong. 'He knows what to do about Gonzales?' Wong nodded.

Anzar turned round and addressed Diaz. 'Impress upon Varela that speed is of the essence. Colonel Wong must take Sonora no later than a week from now if we are to move on Ciu Costa before Independence Day.'

'How am I to let you know when negotiations are concluded?'

'There are transmitters in some of the cooperatives. Our people will make themselves known to you.' He extended his hand. 'Good luck.'

They made light of farewells, Diaz knowing that he and Imi would be shot if recognised on the river. That without Varela's adherence, Francisco would probably not survive the battle. That until Sonora fell they could not take Ciu Costa. All of their lives hung on a spider's web of possibilities. And with the breaking of just one thread the whole could fall apart.

'See you in Ciu Costa, Francisco,' he called out.

'Don't forget you owe me a dinner.' It was an old bet, unpaid because Diaz had been arrested shortly afterwards.

'The best Alfonso has to offer.'

'To hell with Habana Vieja. You're taking me to the Metropole.'

Mention of the Metropole evoked an image of a pale-faced girl with gold-bronze hair. Would he ever see her again? Probably not. He must entrust her safety to Alfonso now. Lost in thought, he did not notice Imi Timu standing in the shadow of a tall tree, carefully assessing him.

CHAPTER ELEVEN

Dark clouds half hid the hazy moon. Its muted light reflected on the deep waters of Rio Verde as Imi and Diaz sailed upstream. The heat of the night – that humid heat which came with the north-west monsoon – filled Diaz with fatigue. It had been a long day.

Now and then movement in the undergrowth caused the fugitive to look uneasily towards the river bank. Was it man, beast or just the stirring or wind among ferns and long grasses? Both remained silent for Imi was trying to negotiate the most difficult stretch of water. The upper Rio Verde was where inexperienced boatmen sometimes came to grief. Leave it to Imi, Francisco had told him. Imi knew the river like the back of his hand. He recognised where there were contrary currents and where there were areas prone to sudden impetuous winds.

At a bend in the river, the moon suddenly emerged full-faced. Bathed in its light a long-legged heron stood poised at the water edge. Solitary, graceful, magnificent. It brought a smile of pleasure to Diaz's lips. And then a feeling of sadness. Why wasn't Elena here to share this moment with him?

Where the river divided – the confluence with Rio San Tome and Rio Cauca – the vegetation became thicker. Their route was up the Cauca, which flowed through the terrain of lowland Terani. Further on were the great forests of the midlands; after that the farming cooperatives.

Exhausted, Diaz stretched out at the bottom of the boat, intending only to relax for a while. But he was quickly overtaken by sleep. He woke to a clear sky touched here and there with a fluff of white cloud. Imi in a wide straw hat sat in the bow of the boat, legs crossed, his hand resting on the AK at his side as though the weapon were a companion, an old friend.

Diaz sat upright and stretched. 'Sorry. I fell asleep. It must have been last night.'

'Every man must sleep.' The Terani replied with neither warmth nor animosity. Then he motioned to the broad-brimmed straw hat which, with their baggy peasant clothes, completed the disguise. 'Sometimes there are eyes on the shore.'

Diaz placed the hat on his head. 'Want something to eat?' he asked as he pulled open a bag with provisions. The Terani shook his head. As Diaz ate some cold rice, washed down by tepid tea from a flask, he wondered if the Terani had eaten or slept at all. 'What sort of man is Varela?'

'A good enemy,' Imi replied. 'His troops are better than the others.' Diaz nodded as he recalled what he had heard about low army morale. The troops stationed in Ciu Costa and in the Eastern Province were badly paid, badly fed young men who resented conscription. But those who served under Varela in the Western Province fared better. Varela, who had a formidable military reputation, treated and trained his conscripts as though they were a professional army.

'Do you think we can trust him?'

'If he betrays us he will die.' Imi spoke as though that finished the matter.

Much good Varela's death would do us, Diaz thought. He wondered if the Terani would use the meeting with Varela to settle old scores, then recalled Francisco telling him that Terani never lied. He hoped his old friend was right, and if he were, that Varela's word was as good as a Terani's. The capture of Colonel Imi Timu would be a powerful propaganda coup for Bianqui, as well as his own return to Monteverde. He kept his reflections to himself. Imi did not appear to feel the need of conversation. His black eyes seemed concentrated upon some inner point of thought.

The gentle river current strengthened. Imi rose to paddle the boat back on course.

'Let me do that,' Diaz offered. Imi did not answer; his eyes were fixed on the horizon where a cloud darkened. Two or three drops of rain fell on the bottom of the boat. 'The Sky Goddess weeps. A bad omen.'

Diaz wondered at the Terani's superstition, at the same time inwardly cursing the shudder within himself. 'Imi, it cannot be a bad omen. The farmers need rain for their crops.'

'When the rain pours down, that is a blessing,' the Terani explained. 'A few drops only tell us that the Goddess weeps.'

Imi returned to the bow and seated himself again, his right hand unconsciously seeking the AK. 'If Varela has F-22s he must give them to us.' The Americans had given Bianqui thirty F-22s. 'Do not let him deceive you.'

'I wouldn't know one plane from another.'

'I will know.' The Terani sounded confident. 'There are only old Tornados in Sonora now. If he gives us stealth fighters, they are nothing.'

A bamboo fishing pole lay in the bottom of the boat. Diaz picked it up and rolled it in his hands, enjoying the familiar feel. He searched through his kit to find a bright red slice of pepper in the food packet. Halving it, he baited the hook. Imi was watching him quizzically. 'You know how to do that?'

'My father took me out in his boat when I was a boy. When I was too young to help with the nets, he taught me to fish with a pole.'

'My father did not give me a gun until I could bring down game with my bow.' The Terani's sombre features softened to a smile as though remembering happy times. Diaz returned the smile as he dropped the line over the side. Perhaps their boyhood had not been so different. The sea had formed him just as surely as Imi had been a child of the great mountains.

'You teach your sons to fish?'

'I have no sons, Imi.' He laughed. 'Not yet. Just a beautiful little daughter.'

A sudden tug on the line diverted his attention. A fine, fleshy silver fish emerged gleaming in the sun. He tossed it to the bottom of the boat, baited the hook again and threw it over the side. 'You speak Spanish well, Imi.'

'I learnt it in your capital.'

'You know Ciu Costa?'

'As well as I need.'

Imi continued as though to himself. 'Two men of our tribe went into Sonora to buy blue dye for the clothes we wear on the Festival of the Sky Goddess. One of the men came back and said that Oma, the other man, had been taken by the police and locked in a prison. My father took me, and the two brothers born before me, into Sonora to bring him back. At the Sonora prison there was only one man who spoke our tongue. He told us that Oma had committed a bad crime and had been taken to the great prison in the capital.'

Diaz smiled cynically. 'My own recent lodgings.'

'We then walked to this place.'

'You walked from Sonora! How long did that take?'

Imi's smile was enigmatic. 'Until we reached it No man in the great prison spoke our tongue. One wrote down the address of the Office of Terani Affairs.' He gave a sardonic smile. 'What have Terani affairs to do with Costadora? There was no Terani in that office, but a man who spoke our tongue better than the other one. He told us that Oma must die.'

Diaz's expression sharpened. Could this be the same Oma who was the first to die under Bianqui's tough new drug laws? Tribesmen understood little of Costadorean laws, and there had been a campaign against the death sentence at the university.

Imi continued. 'We told him this is not a Terani punishment. If Oma had done great wrong, my father would punish him by sending him from Terani lands forever. He said Terani law meant nothing here. He gave us a pass to visit Oma in the prison.'

As Diaz hooked another fish, he listened intently.

'When we saw him he was in a room with many men in dark blue clothes. Oma, too, wore these clothes. He told us he had done nothing wrong. After he had bought the dye he went into a tea house to wait for his friend and smoked gunja to pass the time.'

Diaz remembered that as a student Francisco had smoked gunja. Its use was not then widespread; it was mainly the richer students who indulged. 'You know, Imi, it was to please his western friends that Bianqui tightened the drug laws. Yet it was the west who first brought hard drugs to this part of the world.'

The Terani acknowledged Diaz's intervention with a nod. 'A man came to sit at the table next to Oma and asked him for gunja. Oma gave it to him. This man was a police agent.'

Diaz landed another fish. 'Did he take money for it?'

'Take money! For a gift?' The Terani spoke in wonderment.

'How did you find out he was a police agent?'

'He spoke to the police like a friend when they came to take Oma away. Oma told us that only Minister Zamora could ….' Imi's Spanish faltered.

'Commute the sentence?' Diaz suggested helpfully.

'Commute the sentence,' Imi repeated carefully. 'We went to Minister Zamora. He knew the name of my father. We explained to the Minister that no Terani could refuse when asked for a gift, even if it were the clothes he wore. Minister Zamora promised us we could return to our lands in peace. Oma would not die. We did not return. We waited to take Oma back with us. The sun had risen and set no more than five times when we saw Oma's picture in a newspaper wrapped around lemon grass. My father asked the vegetable seller what it said beneath. He said it meant the man in the picture was dead. Muerto. It was the first Spanish word I learnt. Muerto. Then the vegetable man made the sign of hanging. Minister Zamora lied to us. He had to die. We stayed in Ciu Costa.'

'How did you live?'

'We lived where the streets are dirty and it smells bad. No one offered us food. Costadoreans do not give food to strangers. Our stomachs felt empty. We could not steal or beg as Costadoreans do. We are Terani.'

Diaz felt another tug on the line. 'Not all Costadoreans steal and beg, Imi.'

'In our lands one man's hunger is the hunger of all. One man's shame is the shame of all. My brother wanted to sell his gun, but I told him that selling his gun would be selling his warrior spirit. We took what work we could find. Washed plates. Swept floors. Carried boxes. Working with Costadoreans we learnt Spanish. And we watched Minister Zamora. When two of us worked the other would watch him. We watched him from his office to his house. To his speech-making and his dinners. We watched him and learnt his ways. Always there were men with guns about him.

'Each morning when he came out of his house he stopped to look at the buds on a flowering bush. Then he walked to his long car where the men with guns waited. I learnt that when the señora went to church, when the children were at school, there were no men with guns about, and the servants grew careless. So at this time one day I climbed a tree near his house. From there I could see into his garden. Then next morning Minister Zamora came out and stood longer at the bush, as I knew he would, because the buds had opened. When he put out his hand to a flower, I shot him.'

Diaz recalled the assassination of the Justice Minister. Bianqui's speech at the state funeral had described Zamora's death as the work of left-wing terrorists. It gave the government the pretext to crack down further on political dissent.

'I don't think any of us guessed that Zamora died at the hands of a Terani.'

Imi smiled proudly. 'I went to my brothers and told them I had given Oma back his honour. I was now older than my brothers, although they were born before me.'

'Where are your brothers now?'

'One commands a platoon. The other will command the Terani regiment when Francisco attacks Sonora, if Varela kills me and you. What are you going to do with those fish?'

The question was put in the same tone as the narrative, and the matter-of-fact statement of their possible fate. Diaz glanced at the four fat, succulent fish in the bottom of the hull. 'We could eat them if there were somewhere to cook'

Imi cast his gaze towards a clearing on the shore. 'We can cook here.' Lifting the paddles he began steering the boat towards the river bank. They came ashore at a rocky inlet where Imi tied the boat to a tree which overhung the waters.

Diaz seasoned the fish with soya sauce and the chilli paste they had brought to flavour their cold rice, while Imi made a fire. 'If my friend Alfonso were here he would make a delicacy of this. If I had some lime I could do better.'

Imi cast his gaze about, then leapt up and ran a few metres into the thick foliage, taking the AK with him. Swift and sure-footed, he climbed a lime tree. He returned with limes tied in his loose shirt. As he untied the knot, one rolled away down the incline into the river. Watching it sink he began to recite:

> *Cortó limones redondos,*
> *Y los fue tirando al agua*
> *Hasta que la puso de oro.*
>
> *(He cut round lemons*
> *and tossed them into the water*
> *making it golden.)*

To Diaz's surprise he went on to recite the rest of Frederico Garcia Lorca's poem from *Romancero Gitano* in his strange, soulful intonation.

'You know Lorca?'

'My friend Francisco said this poem once. I liked it and asked him to say it again so I could put it in my head. He told me the Spanish police killed the man who made it.' His expression darkened. 'It is a bad thing to kill a poet.'

Diaz squeezed lime juice on the fish, wrapped them in seawood, and smiled over his shoulder at Imi. 'Some would say it is a bad thing to kill a Justice Miniser.'

Imi appeared to consider this for a moment, then began to laugh. Diaz's laughter joined his. Together they covered the fish with plantain leaves and laid them on the hot stones.

As Diaz savoured the freshness of the fish, he thought of the dull, meagre diet in Monteverde. It was good to be free. As they ate, Imi recited tales of the fish-eating lowland tribes in the time when there were only Terani, before the Spanish came. He spoke of the ghost tiger that ravaged the villages. A bad omen foretelling the coming of the pale-faced strangers who took their lands. He recited the love poems of his people and tales of ancient battles.

Diaz listened contentedly, the urgency of their mission briefly forgotten. The dark, mystic forest and the great river made a perfect theatre for this recital of Terani folklore.

'Francisco tells me there are many stories about you, Imi.'

Imi nodded. 'His name, too, is in our songs.'

Diaz felt pleased that not all Costadoreans lived in Terani folklore as enemies. They fell silent. The gentle sound of lapping waters soothed the fugitive's spirits like a narcotic. Leaning back idly, he looked around. Through drooping foliage he could see a radiant splash of colour. Wild orchids. The ferns which bent towards the river swayed gently in the breeze. In this primeval world the revolution no longer seemed real.

A brisk stirring of tree branches disturbed the tranquillity. Abruptly. Not like a mere gust of wind in the foliage, but rather the intrusion of some unseen presence. Diaz's hand immediately went to his revolver. Imi grabbed his AK. Then Diaz saw it. A parting of the leaves revealed the polanza. Blue and white, its graceful neck a paler blue. The long, yellow tail fanned out, diaphanous and shimmering in a stream of sunlight. Diaz held his breath. Never before had he been so close to this beautiful creature. Then he saw Imi's hand tighten on the AK. 'Don't. Imi, please. Don't shoot it.'

Imi stared at him in disbelief. 'Kill the sacred bird of the Sky Goddess! Never would I commit such an impiety.'

They watched as the polanza opened wide its wings and soared into the air.

'That,' said Imi, 'is a good omen.'

* * * * *

Diaz failed to persuade Imi to part with his kalashnikov when they arrived at the army base. Would the sight of two shabby peasants, one heavily armed, be sufficient to cause a nervous sentry to shoot before they had time to show Varela's safe conduct?

93

The sentry appeared to be forewarned of their arrival. He demanded papers, examined the seal of the safe conduct, then let them pass.

The barracks looked freshly painted, unlike the usual tumbledown quarters that housed Bianqui's conscript army. No rats rummaged through litter on the ground. The few troops he saw wore complete uniforms and appeared well fed.

A corporal caught up with them. He asked for their papers, lips moving as he read, retained it and accompanied them to HQ where they were shown into Varela's study.

It was an austere room. One wall was lined with books; on the other hung a large framed portrait of a military man, in the uniform of the last century. Across from it in an antique gilded frame, a man and woman in the dress of seventeenth century Spain. The general sat behind a fine, mahogany desk. Diaz recognised it as eighteenth century Spanish. Elena's father had a similar one.

General Alejandro Varela was a spare, white-haired man. As he fixed his piercing blue eyes on his visitors, Diaz calmly returned his gaze. Each man measured the other. Dismissing his aide, the general rose and came around the desk. He was not a short man, but Diaz had expected him to be taller.

'You have arrived in good time.' Varela exuded no warmth, but there was grace in his greeting. 'We shall dine shortly, but first a drink.'

Imi declined. Diaz knew the Terani had not yet decided to trust Varela, reserving his right to kill the general if he lied. This could be difficult. His eye went to a silver-framed photograph on the desk. It was a family group: the general's late wife, his daughter Concha taken about five years ago when she was nineteen – the year she was chosen Miss Costadora – her two brothers: Captain Juan Varela, and the younger brother, fair-haired as his father once was, a look of suppressed laughter in his eyes as he posed for the formal photograph.

Diaz recognised at once those eyes bright with intelligence and idealism. 'I didn't know that Raphael Varela was your son.'

'But I knew him to be your student.' The general's dry smile seemed to give the words some hidden meaning 'Campari or vermouth? Or something else, perhaps? Please be seated, Dr Diaz. And you, Colonel Imi.'

The General continued. 'I forbade him to take part in your demonstrations. He called me a reactionary. An exploiter of the people. I told him I would beat him until he had no skin on his back if he attended another.' He extended a cigarette box to his guests. When both declined, he lit one for himself. 'So when he came back with a black eye and an arm broken by a police baton, I told the police he had fallen downstairs. I am still a reactionary and an exploiter. You are his idol. And I pay a fortune in bribes to keep him out of jail.'

Diaz sank back into the large leather chair. Imi remained standing.

'I cannot believe that you wish to help us in order to gain your son's esteem, General.' Diaz sipped his vermouth slowly, glad the fish had been a substantial lunch.

'I haven't the slightest wish to help you, sir. Your political games with Bianqui are of no interest to me.'

'You approached us.'

'When politics affect the army, the army must defend itself.' He turned to Imi. 'You have seen my troops.'

'When they invaded our lands.'

'I obey my orders, as you do yours.' His eyes met the Terani's. 'Or you would not be in this room.' He walked to the window and looked out. 'You will have observed that my men do not loot. And you, Dr Diaz, will have had no complaints of extortion of civilians.' He turned about and faced them. 'You may, of course, confirm that in the Cooperatives when you use that secret transmitter hidden in the grain stores. My men, you see, are paid regularly although their annual pay is less than the cost of one of Paco Bianqui's uniforms.'

'My men have no pay,' Imi said. 'They do not loot or harm civilians. They are warriors.'

'My men are not warriors. They are conscripts. But they have three good meals a day, and there are severe penalties for breaches of discipline. They are good soldiers.'

'Your troops have always had a good reputation.' Francisco Wong had told Diaz that. 'Why approach us now?'

'Bianqui has made a commitment to the Americans. I do not know the details, but he received his first payment in the shape of thirty F-22s.'

'You have them here?' Imi interjected.

'Alas, no. Bianqui considers them more useful in Ciu Costa to impress foreign visitors.' He smiled 'Did the flyover impress King Leon, or the O.D.U. delegation, Dr Diaz?' The General made no attempt to conceal his contempt of Bianqui. 'Those F-22s will not be our last gift from America. Bianqui is determined to crush your rebellion. It is becoming more than an embarrassment.'

'The people are with us.'

'The people are nothing against his new hardware. But you too have friends. The Chinese will support you.'

'We seek no outside intervention.'

'But, if it comes to the crunch, you will accept it. The survival instinct is a strong incentive. You are too young to remember the Vietnam war.' The General's face became sombre. 'I do not wish Costadora to become another Vietnam.'

'That is your sole reason for approaching us?'

'Of course not. A man motivated by only one reason is a fool or a fanatic.'

'Your other reasons, General?'

'I want Costadora to have a good professional army. End conscription. Pay our troops properly. Quarter them in barracks fit for human beings. Send our best officers to St Cyr or Sandhurst'

'That is a Ministry of Defence matter.'

'Politicians are incapable of understanding our needs. Such decisions should be left to the commander-in-chief.' Varela's tone was casual. His eyes were not.

'So you wish to be Commander-in-chief.' Irony entered Diaz's tone. 'Is that …. *all*?'

'One or two personal matters. His face softened slightly as he glanced at the photograph on his desk. 'My daughter Concha lives in Madrid, but she frequently visits Ciu

Costa. She has a good enough income to maintain her lifestyle. I have seen to that.'

'With foreign investments taken from Costadora's wealth?' What, Diaz wondered, did a fashion icon like Concha Varela have to do with all this?

The General frowned. 'With some family lands I sold opportunely before Bianqui's pay-offs beggared me. His land reforms have made that peasant's grandson a very rich man. Concha is protected financially even if you people win and confiscate the rest of my lands, but I wish her to be able to continue visiting Costadora, as and when she wills.'

'You put personal matters in the plural. What are you asking for yourself?'

'I am a man of simple tastes. I can live on my pay as a soldier. But my son Juan will have divided loyalties. Many of his friends and fellow officers will choose exile.'

'I am certain you have provided for him also.'

'He is a good officer. Not meant for exile from his country. A posting as military attaché to one of our embassies for a year or two would reconcile his loyalties. Western Europe. He likes his pleasure. He is much as I was at his age, although he looks like his mother. I know he will become of more serious mind when he marries.' The general paused and sighed. 'As for Raphael, he already belongs to you and your movement and wants nothing from me. But come, gentlemen, we can discuss this further over dinner.'

Diaz knew that Varela's terms would alter little during the course of a dinner, or a year. Their need for him was immediate and crucial. His ambitions for the Costadorean army were not unreasonable. Wong and Moreno both considered a conscript army inefficient. The General had no love for the Constitutionalists, only contempt for Bianqui and his corrupt government. He was a man of integrity according to his lights, but Diaz could not easily forget that, until now, he had loyally served Bianqui.

He had once met the late Doña Cristina Varela at one of his father-in-law's dinner parties. A charming woman with dark hair and large, dark Andalusian eyes. How he hated those dinner parties! And he had seen photographs of the frivolous

Concha in newspapers and magazines. Looking towards the photograph on the General's desk, he noted how Concha resembled her elder brother. Cold eyes, handsome and proud, Captain Juan exuded all the self-confidence of his class. Did these people really deserve to have their privileges protected? He thought of all those ordinary people now struggling to make Costadora a better place. No privileges for them. When the revolution was over they would return to their daily grind in farms and factories. He thought of comrades still in prison for daring to speak out against injustice and corruption.

But the General was not a venal man. His world was the army and his family. He was not political and could be a good enough commander-in-chief. If his terms were not accepted, Diaz knew he would use his troops against the Costadorean Liberation Army. His men were the only disciplined units in the Costadorean army, apart from Bianqui's two brutal elite regiments.

Should he accept the General's terms? He wished the decision did not lie with him.

CHAPTER TWELVE

Celia woke with a start. Bewildered she looked around. The light of morning flowed through a window draped with fine brocade curtains – a window without bars. No warders watching her. The pillows felt soft. The cool, clean sheets had a faint lavender scent. On the wall hung a delicate watercolour. Was she dreaming? Then as her gaze fell on Helen Darcy's handbag, events of yesterday came flooding back. She was free.

Rising, she went to the window and looked down. The tide was out. On a hazy horizon she could see the blurred outline of fishing boats. Marine Gardens was deserted now, save for one man walking his dog. In the brightness of morning it did not look like the same secluded spot where she had sat with Roberto the evening before. Would she ever see him again? Probably not. He belonged now to his revolution.

What should she wear? Opening the weekend bag, she looked through the clothes hastily snatched from Keevers. The envelope put there by Dolores the evening before – she had forgotten about it – caught her eye. Tearing it open, she found some crisp banknotes. They were enclosed in a sheet of paper with the scribbled message: "Just a little cash to help you over the next few days."

For a moment she stared, uncomprehending. Then, gripped by some abstruse emotion, she brushed away a tear. In that grim world from which she had escaped, kindness was something that had receded from her memory. She counted the notes. There was enough – probably more than enough – to buy a ferry ticket to King George Island. No need to use Helen Darcy's money. That somehow made her feel more at ease at the thought of seeing Mike Delaney. Then she noticed the newspaper. Hadn't Dolores said something about page four? Lifting it out of the bag – it was the *King George Island Observer* – she thumbed through the pages. Catching sight of her own photograph, she winced. A first instinct was to cast it aside, but the caption held her attention: "Governor General appeals for stay of execution". She read on: "Sir John Blacklad argued that the drugs trial in Manila had implications for the Martinez case. It is now known that Peter Surrey, the Global Orient air steward accused of planting drugs in a passenger's hand luggage on a flight to the Philippines, was also on the same flight to Costadora as Celia Martinez. Speaking at the Residency to a press conference, the Governor said: 'It would be unthinkable for President Bianqui to permit the execution to proceed until this new evidence is investigated.'"

As the words sank in, an involuntary cry escaped her lips. A cry of hope. Eagerly she read on. Then interest changed to puzzlement. She bit her lips. Another cry – this time of despair – as she read the final paragraph. "Costadora's Justice Minister, Mr Lopez, told our reporter that he saw no reason to reopen the case. Martinez, he insisted, had had a fair trial."

Throwing herself face downwards on the pillow, she wept. She lay there listless and despondent until the telephone aroused her. Who could it be? A message about the passport? Or perhaps a call for Helen Darcy. The ringing was penetrating, threatening, persistent – it demanded to be answered. Apprehensive and hesitant, she lifted the receiver. 'Yes?'

'Señorita?' It was a man's voice. A soft tone as though the caller didn't want to be overheard.

'Who is it?'

'I have a gift for you. I was asked to deliver it personally.'

'Could you bring it up, please.'

Grabbing Helen Darcy's dressing gown from a chair, she hastily put it on and waited.

The tapping on the door was light and surreptitioius. So light that at first she thought she had imagined it. Then a more robust knock. She opened the door cautiously. A young man stood there, a small package in his hand. Dapper moustache, and well-groomed sleek hair, he wore a white waiter's jacket with *Hotel Metropole* embroidered on the pocket.

'May I come in?' He gave a nervous backward glance before stepping inside and shutting the door.

'The passport, señorita.' His voice was low and furtive. 'I've been told to tell you that the best day to go is Saturday morning. One of our people is on passport control then. Someone will be in touch with you beforehand about getting to the boat.'

Taking the packet, she murmured her thanks.

'We will tell you which sailing time, but be ready early. The boats will be crowded – people going over for the festival. Bring your room key with you.'

She shot him a surprised look. 'The room key! Why?'

'Because if you fail to get away you might still need it.' He opened the door and was gone.

* * * * *

The bombing of the army barracks, San Remo district of Ciu Costa, hit the early morning headlines. Early risers learnt of it when a newsflash interrupted the 6.30 television Keep Fit programme. One window of the building was badly damaged. As yet no details about casualties. Viewers would be kept informed.

Delaney heard the news on Radio Libertad. Heard it and thought of Luis. Then he put the thought out of his mind. Radio Libertad referred to it only briefly. No details or analysis. No claim of responsibility. Could it be the work of a rebel splinter group? Tinkering with the knobs he found himself tuned into an English language broadcast from King George Island. No reported casualties; motive not established, the announcer said. Next he picked up the official announcement from Costadora National Radio. CND described it as a bomb left on military premises by "left-wing terrorists". This was contradicted by a pirate radio station which interrupted their pop music programme to announce the news, describing it as a rocket attack launched from the Sierra Guadaloupe.

It's escalating, thought Delaney, as he jotted down some notes on a pad. The first incident of its kind in the capital. He smiled absently as he anticipated the argument and political analysis with press colleagues over breakfast – Jackson dogmatic as usual, Hepworth dry and caustic, Helen disagreeing with everyone else. Helen! The smile froze instantly on his lips as he remembered. This morning there would be no Helen.

To work, he told himself grimly. First he must draft the contract. Could he persuade Celia to sign it? It was to her advantage. She would surely see that. His newspaper would pay a large sum of money for her exclusive story.

It was now seven o'clock. Three p.m. in London. Remembering his promise to Helen's editor, he grimaced. No, he wouldn't phone. Helen's death must remain secret until Celia got away safely. He would send a fax. Regular faxed reports from Helen should pre-empt any more frenetic phone calls from London. A few finishing touches to his own copy, and he was ready for breakfast.

In the restaurant he found Hepworth seated with press colleagues, already demolishing a platter of bacon and eggs. All over the world Hepworth insisted on an English breakfast. Years of working abroad had not diminished his suspicion of "dodgy foreign food".

They were discussing the bombing. Hepworth thought it curious that there had been no reported casualties. Jackson was unconvinced by the rocket theory. Yves Renoir, the sleek, moody-looking correspondent for the French left-wing daily L'Univers, had his own theory. A Middle-East connection. The rebels had been importing arms for some time.

'Come on!' Jackson sounded dismissive. 'How could they finance that sort of thing?'

Renoir shrugged his shoulders. 'How do *any* insurgents fund that sort of thing? Who funded the IRA?'

Hepworth gave Delaney a rakish look. 'Ask the expert.'

Delaney, in no mood for polemics on the "Irish Question" retreated into flippancy. 'The national lottery .... Oh, and I did the odd sponsored walk.'

A distant explosion froze everyone into silence. Then a buzz of questions. What was it? Where was it? Who caused it? At the next table a buxom woman in a flowery sun-dress called anxiously to the waiter. Were they in any danger, she wanted to know?

'Demolition work,' the waiter replied blandly. A little too bland to be convincing. 'They're pulling down buildings damaged by the earthquake.'

'He's lying through his teeth,' growled Hepworth. 'I'm going over to the San Remo barracks to see what's happening. Anyone want to share my taxi?'

Jackson accepted the offer. Delaney, remembering Celia, declined.

'Go without me, Tony. I've a few phone calls to make. I'll see you over there later.'

'Where's Helen?' Hepworth cast his gaze casually around the restaurant.

'Left.' On the spur of the moment Delaney couldn't think of anything else to say.

'La Belle Helene has left already?' With a pose of Gallic charm, Renior managed to look suitably devastated. Delaney nodded. The easiest thing was just to agree.

Hepworth gave him an odd look. 'I thought you said last night that Helen was back.'

'Gone off again to the Western Province.' Delaney spoke with studied vagueness. 'Early start.' Why did he get the impression that Hepworth didn't altogether believe him?

* * * * *

At a quarter to nine Delaney phoned Celia. Was it too early to come up? 'No, it's not too early.' That polite – over-polite – voice. Did she still mistrust him?

At Room 205 he knocked lightly on the door. 'Mike here,' he called out. As she opened it cautiously, it struck him that she looked different. Her simple navy, wrap-around skirt, shorter than the one he had seen her wear yesterday on the beach, had the primness of a uniform. It also revealed a very shapely pair of legs. The sleeveless cotton blouse, a delicate floral patters, had a crisp, summery look. Hair shining, a touch of colour in her cheeks, she had the freshness and fragrance of someone who had just stepped out of the shower.

'May I come in?' Noting that nervous flicker in her eyes, he tried not to sound forceful. Had she slept well, he asked as she stood aside to let him pass?

'Very well.' Her tone had a forced brightness. 'It's more comfortable here than my previous lodgings.'

He cast his gaze around. The place seemed charged with Helen's presence. Her laptop computer, biros and notebooks on the table. That faint, discreet smell of perfume. A muted smile came to his lips as he noted the bowl of fruit on top of the mini-bar, testimony to Helen's good intentions to give up smoking. She had argued somewhat implausibly that it was easier to stay off the smokes if you had something to chew. He half-expected her to walk out of the bathroom and explain everything.

Celia's voice intruded into his thoughts. 'I've tried not to disturb any of Helen's things.'

'Oh, that's all right.' A feeling of guilt shot through him as he remembered last night speaking to her sharply for having Helen's handbag. 'Look, there are some things I need to talk over with you, but it's getting late. I've got to get over to the San Remo district pretty soon. Can I see you sometime this afternoon?'

She acquiesced with a disarming politeness, but it was difficult to fathom the real feeling behind those watchful, blue eyes. Did she have breakfast, he wanted to know? She pointed to the hospitality tray. 'I made some coffee.'

His eye fell on Helen's sunglasses lying on the dressing table. He lifted them up. 'Here, Celia, put these on.'

'Why?'

'Just to see what you look like.'

Puzzled, she lifted the glasses hesitantly, put them on, then glanced in the mirror. He stood behind her. 'There you are, that looks all right, doesn't it?'

'All right for what?' She stiffened. 'No, I can't go out, if that's what you mean. I can't do it. I cannot leave this room.'

'Celia, I don't know how long you plan staying here. But if the maids can never get in to make up the room, they're going to become very suspicious. Anyway it will do you good to get out for a breath of fresh air. Let me take you out for breakfast.'

'I might be recognised'

The newspaper with her photograph lay on the dressing table. He held it up. 'Take a good look at this. Does this really look like how you are now?' Not just clothes. But hair – everything. He smiled. 'You're much prettier than your photograph.'

She swung around. '*You* recognised me.'

'I sat in court throughout the trial. If I had only seen this photograph, I wouldn't have recognised you. Believe me, the sunglasses really do make a difference.'

As she looked towards the window he noted her wistful expression. 'You'd like to go out, wouldn't you?' She nodded. He took her by the hand. 'Come on, then, let's go.'

* * * * *

At the little self-service café a couple of blocks behind Hotel Metropole, Delaney found a corner table. He left Celia sitting there while he fetched the food. Full Costadorean breakfast for Celia; an orange juice for himself.

Off the tourist track, it was a place used by locals. Straw mats on the floor, bamboo furniture of the style peasants fashioned themselves, the place had a rustic touch. At a window table bronze-faced fishermen, still smelling of the sea, talked of the morning's catch while eagerly ingesting copious breakfasts. At a nearby table country people – they wore the wide straw hats of the farming folk – were complaining about the price of goods in the market place. The laughter of a group of youths at a centre table caused everyone to look towards them. One had just made a bawdy joke about Bianqui's mistress. Delaney, then paying for breakfast, noticed at once the fear in the proprietor's eyes. Excusing himself, he left Delaney and approached the youth who had made the joke. It was obvious that he had whispered some warning for the young men immediately fell silent.

As he placed the tray in front of Celia, it struck Delaney that she was looking more animated. She smiled. 'I'm glad you brought me here, Mike. I always thought Ciu Costa would have little cafes like this tucked away in side-streets.'

'I'm sorry I can't spend much time with you here. We'll catch up with things this afternoon.'

She looked at him quizzically. 'What things? What do you want from me, Mike?'

'Let's leave it until this afternoon, shall we? I must be off in about twenty minutes.' He pulled some money out of his pocket. 'Look, take this, just in case you need anything when I'm not here.'

She shrank back. 'Mike, I do have some money of my own.'

'Take it,' he urged indifferently.

She took it hesitantly. 'I'll repay you when I get back to London.'

'Forget it.' He lowered his voice. 'Celia, you know you must take sensible precautions. I think you should stay out of your room until about midday. Don't be around when the maid is making up the room.'

'But I can't stay here until midday.'

'No, you can't stay here. Nor would I advise you to go wandering around the streets. I've thought of a hiding place. The flat roof of the hotel. You'll like it there. The view is superb – the full stretch of Malecón beach, and from the back the foothills of the Sierra Guadaloupe. I'll leave you with some papers and magazines to read.'

She looked doubtful. 'Do other people go up there?'

'Sometimes.' He sounded unperturbed. 'If they do, take no notice. Just read your newspapers. Whatever you do, don't take off those glasses.' He downed his orange juice. 'This passport. When did your friends say they would drop it in?'

'They've already done so. About an hour ago.'

'An overnight job! That's very impressive. So, when do you intend to leave?'

'Saturday, I think ….' Then she hesitated. 'I think it will be Saturday.'

Her hesitation disturbed Delaney. 'Have you thought this thing through, Celia? Is anyone helping you? Or is it just a case of making a run for it and trusting to luck?'

There was a nervous flicker in her eyes. 'I think it will be Saturday,' she repeated. Her apprehension was transparent. It struck Delaney that she wasn't taking her escape for granted.

On the way back to the hotel they stopped at a newspaper kiosk. A photograph of Bianqui, dour eyes and wispy moustache, stared at them from one tabloid. "Situation under control", the caption said.

'That was from his speech last night,' Delaney explained as he handed papers and magazines to Celia. 'Even Bianqui wouldn't argue that everything is under control this morning.'

'Mike, what is happening?' She lowered her voice. 'I heard an explosion earlier on.'

The man hovering behind Delaney spoke in English. 'It's enough to give you the jitters.' Uttered with the distinct twang of London's East End, the voice sounded familiar. Swinging around, Delaney saw the balding British tourist, head now buried in a newspaper, whom he had seen at the police check-point the evening before.

Delaney greeted him cheerily. 'Hullo again! Things do seem to be hotting up.' The man lifted his head out of the overseas edition, business section, of London's *Times*. He nodded glumly. 'You're right. The economy *is* over-heating.' Shaking his head gravely, he added: 'The Chancellor will have to put up interest rates.'

'Who is that man?' Celia whispered as they walked away.

'Don't know his name. Some Innocent Abroad.'

CHAPTER THIRTEEN

Ten o'clock. The morning was now half gone. Delaney's voice took on a driven urgency as he spoke down the phone to Carlos, the young freelance photographer he sometimes hired.

'Can you meet me in half an hour, Carlos? Usual place. The old Bell Tower. Sorry about the short notice.' Carlos agreed to be there.

As Delaney spotted his photographer's thin, rakish form slumped against a wall puffing clouds of smoke, it occurred to him that it was truly miraculous that he hadn't been arrested long ago for something or other. The hated "Stop and Search" laws were supposedly used only if the police had reasonable grounds for suspicion – at least that's the line the Information Department gave to the foreign press. The reality was somewhat different. Enthusiastic officers of the law often stopped youths who looked inebriated, dissolute or were allegedly giving, or about to give, public offence.

Carlos certainly looked dissolute. Dark brown hair, erratically curly and uncombed. Crumpled shirt. Shrewd eyes that always looked half-closed. Judging by appearance, the epitome of decadence. But Carlos didn't give a damn. He didn't have to. He was a superb photographer and he knew it.

Unusually for Delaney, who spoke to local people in Spanish, he communicated with his photographer in English. He knew that Carlos liked to practise his quirky English, a variety strongly influenced by American gangster films he had watched when doing student vacation work on George. His employer ran a cine-club and Carlos had made the most of this opportunity to view vintage Hollywood films and cultivate what he regarded as a sassy way of talking.

Carlos greeted him with a grin. 'OK, gimme the lowdown.'

'First some photos at the San Remo Barracks ....' Delaney hesitated. 'That's if they let you. After that perhaps the sports stadium for a few shots of the earthquake relief work.'

They got into a taxi. 'Anything else of interest going on around the east side?' Delaney asked.

Carlos munched nonchalantly on his chewing gum as he considered this. 'Shouldn't be surprised if we had a spot of street fighting.'

Delaney scanned his photographer's languid face. 'Who do you think was responsible for the San Remo job?'

'The soldiers.'

'The soldiers blew up their own barracks?'

'Yup.' Carlos continued chewing as he glanced idly out of the taxi window.

'You mean Bianqui's soldiers. Not the fellows in the mountains?'

'Yup, yup,' replied Carlos, looking as though he might fall asleep. Yup was an expression of affirmation that had become trendy among young Costadoreans. A sort of code word denoting you were anti-establishment, not necessarily in any political sense. Delaney knew from experience it was one Carlos used when he didn't intend to be communicative. Attempting to tease more information out of him by jest and small talk, he finally gave up. Carlos, if he had anything to say, would say it in his own time.

The taxi took a diversionary route, avoiding areas where earthquake rescue work was still going on. The city centre – a mosaic of colonial buildings with baroque facades alongside modern, high-rise business premises – began to recede. The eastern fringes of the city was an older, Asian world. Delaney's gaze scanned the narrow side-streets where people moved to and fro like ants. One-storey buildings, itinerant vendors in wide straw hats crying out their wares; the only vehicles to be seen in those cramped lanes were rickshaws pulled by men who moved at a measured trot.

Another turning to the right, and then the taxi climbed steeply up a winding, bumpy road which separated the Botanical Gardens from the Sports Stadium. To the left, across the gardens, Delaney could see the stark, grey walls of Monteverde prison. Remembering Celia's rendezvous with the hangman – just eighteen hours away – he shivered. Then in his idiosyncratic fashion he prayed to that unfathomable something he often believed in and could never wholly forget: 'Please God, don't let them find her.'

At the top of the craggy hill, open countryside came into view. Infertile terrain useless for agricultural purposes, it was now used for army training. A turn to the right, and then the taxi stopped within sight of the barracks. Sensing the driver's nervousness, Delaney told him not to wait

The barracks, now almost half demolished, was cordoned off, surrounded by a hostile crowd. The raw, young soldiers guarding the building looked nervous and unequal to the job. At the cordon, some thirty yards from the main gates, twitchy-looking policemen were trying to prevent the crowd getting too close. Now and then they pointed guns menacingly at those who pushed forward.

What struck Delaney was the sullen boldness of the crowd as they edged closer. For once they seemed uncowed by the forces of the law. A risen people who had lost their fear? He cast a quizzing look at Carlos. But his photographer simply shrugged as though he, too, were perplexed.

Delaney spoke in a whisper. 'Carlos, isn't it here that the National Service men are billeted?' Delaney had heard that many young men resented the call-up.

Carlos raised his camera ready for action. 'Yup, National Service guys come here.' His face creased into a canny grin. 'Didn't do any myself. Excused on health grounds.' By way of demonstration he gave a theatrical cough from the depth of his nicotine-sodden lungs. 'This old chest problem served its purpose.'

They were now on the fringes of the crowd. 'Careful now,' Delaney cautioned. 'Don't let them see what you're doing.' He remembered how tetchy the security forces could be about photographers. Carlos's laugh had a ring of derision. 'Just look at them. You'd think they were guardians of some great superpower, instead of Bianqui's little holiday island.'

They moved in closer. Carlos surreptitiously poised the camera, then took two shots: one of the damaged building, another of a woman angrily remonstrating with one of the policemen. Her son had been seized during the night in a police raid and she was demanding to know where he was. The officer was arguing that it had nothing to do with him. The night raids were done by the plain-clothed men, not the ordinary police. From the wrathful murmurings of the crowd, it seemed that a number of local lads had been seized.

Just how and why the mood of sullen anger changed so dramatically to something volatile and terrifying was to remain an enigma in the memory of those who were there. First stones began to fly in the direction of the police. As one hit an officer on the head, causing him to raise his hands to shield his face, another policeman cocked his gun. 'Careful, Carlos! That's close enough,' hissed Delaney as Carlos edged ever closer with his camera. Then remembering other conflicts, he put a restraining hand on Carlos's shoulder. 'For God's sake, man, watch those guns. Plastic bullets aren't harmless. They have blinded people.'

Carlos, with cool detachment, shrugged off Delaney and pushed himself to the fore. The first shots rang out. Live rounds, not plastic bullets. A woman fell to the ground, blood flowing from her mouth. Nearby a youth slumped to his knees, then toppled over lifelessly. Carlos caught both on camera. The risks could no longer be justified; Delaney reached out to pull his photographer back, prepared if necessary to overpower him. His hand had almost touched Carlos's shoulder when someone pushed between them. Two policemen fell lifelessly to the ground in quick succession. Somewhere in that angry crowd snipers lurked and they were in the firing line. Time to bolt for safety. Screams of pain and terror now pierced the air. People pushed against each other in frenzied panic, trying to get away. Hell had broken loose. Somehow he managed to grab Carlos.

'Come on. Out of here fast.' Carlos didn't resist this time. Having caught the police casualties on camera, the job was complete. He grinned with satisfaction. 'I've got you the first pictures of the revolution.'

'Carlos, run like hell or we'll be with the first corpses.'

In the general stampede they made for the main road. Delaney, the fitter of the two, easily outstripped Carlos. Pausing every now and then for him to catch up, he could see people attempting to drag or carry away injured friends to safety.

As he turned a corner, someone yelled, 'Mike! Over here. Quick!'

It was Hepworth hanging out of a taxi window, Jackson's anxious face peering behind him. As Delaney reached the car, they moved over to make room for him.

'Hold it just a second, Tony. I've got my photographer with me.'

As Carlos caught up, Delaney bundled him into the car, then jumped in beside him. The taxi sped off towards the city centre. Hepworth cast a backward glance. 'What the hell was going on there?'

Still panting, Delaney gasped out: 'Didn't you see? There was a shoot-out.'

'Tony and I had just left to look for a taxi,' Jackson explained. 'Then we heard shots and screams.'

Delaney shook his head grimly, as though he still couldn't believe it. 'There were people killed. Two of them policemen.'

'Christ!' said Hepworth. 'Bianqui will declare a state of emergency.'

'He already did eight years ago. That was never lifted,' Delaney reminded him. 'Isn't that how he managed to abolish elections and rule by presidential decree? He'll have to call today's little ructions something else.'

Carlos chuckled hoarsely. 'A state of ructions! Yup. Yup. I like that. Very Costadorean.'

Hepworth peered crookedly at carols, then turned his gaze to Delaney with arched eyebrows, his expression seeming to say: where the hell did you pick him up?

* * * * *

Delaney and Carlos got out at the old Bell Tower. They dropped into a small café in the business area. Carlos had once more become uncommunicative, probably because he would have preferred a liquid lunch. Delaney suspected that Carlos lived on too many liquid lunches. It occurred to him that if he didn't buy his photographer something substantial to eat, he might break down or fade away.

'We'll forget about the Sports Stadium,' said Delaney as the waiter placed in front of them platters of chicken kida and rice. 'The earthquake is yesterday's story – oh, what are you having to drink?' he added, noting Carlos looking around as though something were missing.

'Beer – white polanza.'

Delaney ordered two of the local beers, then continued his briefing. 'I've got to get back to the hotel. Someone I have to interview. If anything happens – street disturbances, barricades going up – anything like that – get me some pictures. But for God's sake take care. It isn't necessary to put yourself in the firing line. You might be a terrific photographer but you're no bloody use to me dead.'

Carlos grinned. Was he coming to life again?

* * * * *

Police cordons prevented Delaney from crossing the road to reach a taxi rank. Before he had time to ask what was going on, the motor cavalcade sped past. First escort cars, and then the sleek, black Presidential car. Bianqui himself.

'Bastard!' a woman screamed from the pavement. Scuffles broke out as police made moves to arrest her. People shambled this way and that as the police pushed into the crowd. From where Delaney stood it was difficult to see whether she managed to get away. You got the impression the crowd were trying to impede the officers of the law. Such boldness was unusual.

The puffy-faced President in military attire seemed not to notice the rumpus. With a slight incline of the head, he raised his hand to acknowledge the wave of a well-wisher. Delaney caught only the briefest glimpse of Costadora's first citizen before the car sped past.

He changed his mind about the taxi. Seized by a sudden yearning for space and solitude, he decided to walk back to the hotel – a long walk along Malecón beach. As he skirted the water edge, the rhythm of waves gently rising and falling onto the shore lulled his spirits. Enviously he looked towards the swimmers in the cool waters. Would he have time for a swim later on? By now the bloodshed and mayhem that he had seen at the San Remo barracks seemed unreal and distant.

The sight of a police patrol descending onto the beach brought him back to brutal reality. Intently and malevolently they stared around, giving the impression of being on the lookout for someone. I wouldn't fancy being on their wanted list, Delaney thought. Up on the promenade he could see more police. Then, remembering how only yesterday Celia and her companion had walked along this way, he chilled. Today they wouldn't have stood a chance.

The sea breeze was blowing in his face – that refreshing breeze that made the afternoon sun bearable. Just ahead, a young woman kicked off her sandals and walked towards the water. She reminded him of Helen. With a devastating feeling of loss, he realised that Helen was slipping from him. Helen was yesterday's death. His feelings were confused. As well as pain there was acceptance – the certainty that he would never see her again. Then a sense of guilt. Was it not a sort of betrayal to be able to accept her loss? Death was for the old. Death was not for people like Helen.

He reached the roadway by the cliff path, just opposite Hotel Metropole. The little policeman – the same one he had chatted to the evening before – was leaning against the wall, still looking aimless and distracted. Delaney tentatively held out his press card, half expecting not to be recognised. The policeman flinched at first, as though he thought Delaney had pulled a gun; then a faint smile of recognition.

'Hullo again! Things getting busy,' Delaney said breezily.

The little policeman looked round furtively, then whispered. 'They're shooting policemen now. There was big trouble up at the San Remo barracks.'

'It might blow over,' replied Delaney, not very convincingly. It was obvious that the young officer's nerve had completely failed; he had no stomach for the impending strife.

'I don't think so.' He gave another stealthy glance around. 'I'm worried about my wife. She's expecting a baby. Who will look after her if I'm killed?'

It struck Delaney he was a simple sort of fellow. Policing was probably just a job, the source of steady income. It implied no conscious loyalty to Bianqui.

'I don't think it will come to that.' Delaney's cheery words were glib; he knew he was in no way qualified to give this reassurance.

The little policeman's woebegone eyes widened as he scanned Delaney's face. 'You know Bianqui was on television this morning?'

'He was?' Delaney recalled that he had seen the First Citizen just an hour ago in the city centre. 'What did the President have to say?'

'Says the terrorists will be hunted down. There'll be a lot of new regulations.'

'What sort of regulations?'

'A ten-thirty curfew.'

'That should go down well in Fisherman's Cove!' Delaney retorted dryly. He remembered that bars and restaurants there were at their busiest between ten and midnight.

The little policeman gave a worried shake of the head. 'They won't like it in the Cove,' he conceded.

'What else did Bianqui have to say?'

'The national reserve has been called up. There will be more police and army patrols on the streets. People must carry identification at all times.'

Delaney nodded. 'I'll remember that.'

115

The young policeman seemed to suddenly remember that he represented the forces of law and order. He stood upright and braced his shoulders as befitted his office. 'Well, I wouldn't take too many risks if I were you.' His briskness was forced. 'Stay indoors if you can. Keep away from the east side.' Then his voice faltered. 'All the same, I wish this were all over.'

'It probably won't last long,' said Delaney as he turned to go. 'I hope things go well for your wife.'

The oncoming traffic caused him to pause before darting across the road. Costadorean drivers must be the worst in the world, he thought as one car, which jumped the lights, brushed past him. Manoeuvring his way to the other side, he did not notice Celia's terrified face staring down at him from a second-floor window.

CHAPTER FOURTEEN

Celia stood motionless at the window. Uncomprehending, stupefied, rejecting what she saw. Then, her inner numbness gave way to terror. Aghast, she backed away. Delaney in conversation with a policeman!

No! No! He couldn't betray her. Or could he? Perhaps he thought it his duty to turn her in. Then a more chilling explanation flashed through her mind. There was a reward in it for him. That was it. Blood money. He was doing it for money. She had begun to trust him – even to like him. And now this!

Frantically she began stuffing her clothes into the weekend bag. Best to bolt for it. To get to the docks in time for the next sailing. What else did she need? Handbag with passport and money. She looked towards the dressing table. No time to separate her things from Helen Darcy's. With a frenzied sweep of the hand she brushed into the handbag an assortment of items: cosmetics, biros, room key. Slipping on her jacket, she slung handbag and weekend bag over her shoulder and fled down the corridor towards the lifts.

One of the two lifts was marked "Out of Order". The other was on the ground floor. Feverishly, frantically, she pressed the button. She kept on pressing. As a maid with a trolley of linen approached, the lift moved to the first floor, Was it stuck there? Why the delay? In an eternity of waiting she could feel her heart pounding.

Then she remembered Delaney's promise to see her as soon as he returned. Could he be on his way up? Perhaps he was already in the lift. And the policeman as well. Looking around wildly, her eye caught the sign at the far end of the corridor "Emergency Exit". She dashed towards it.

'Señorita, the lift is here,' the maid called after her. Ignoring the call she darted down the fire staircase, almost losing balance. Breathless she arrived at the rear of the lobby. Only then did she remember she had forgotten to put on the sunglasses. It was too late to go back.

But wasn't it Delaney who had suggested that she wear those glasses in the first place? So that she wouldn't be recognised. That surely meant he wanted to protect her. Conflicting images of Delaney caused her to hesitate. That affable, good-natured Delaney who had taken her out to breakfast. That sly Delaney who was passing on information about her to the police. Yes, she *had* seen him talking to the policeman. No mistake about that. For a moment her mind was in a turmoil of indecision. Then that icy fear again. There was treachery behind his charm. He wanted her to wear those sunglasses so that *nobody else* would recognise her. She was *his* blood money.

The lobby was full of people checking in and checking out. As she pushed her way forward, a man in the uniform of hotel staff enquired politely if she needed a porter. No, she didn't. A friend was picking up her luggage. No, her bag wasn't heavy. 'A taxi, señorita?' the doorman asked as she reached the main exit. Breathlessly she nodded. As he stopped a taxi she fumbled in the handbag for a tip. He opened the taxi door to let her in.

A firm hand gripped her arm. 'We won't need the taxi, thank you,' Delaney said. Tightening his grip until it hurt, he smiled at the taxi driver. 'Sorry we stopped you. We have a lift.' He turned to Celia. 'It's all right. The car has arrived.'

Firmly and silently he propelled her back into the hotel. Helplessly, with leaden steps, she kept apace. At the entrance she stumbled. He lifted the weekend bag from her shoulder. 'I'll carry that.' His voice was terse. Leading her back through the lobby with determined steps, he continued clutching her tightly. Then someone called out.

'Got back all right, Mike. How about a drink?'

Delaney turned his head in the direction of the voice. 'Not now, Tony. See you in the bar later. I've an interview to do.' Looking around, Celia saw a middle-aged man, vaguely familiar. Hadn't she seen him before on the press benches in the courtroom? A first instinct was to scream out for help. But would he help? Would anyone help? The man edged closed to Delaney.

'Before dinner, then. In the Orchid Bar ….' His voice trailed away. He was staring her straight in the face. Eye to eye. A candid stare. A look of recognition. Now right beside Delaney, the man whispered hoarsely: 'Christ, Mike, what is this? Are you crazy?'

'I must be. See you later, Tony.'

He remained staring after them as they entered the lift.

'Hold it there.' A youth rushed forward just as Delaney raised his finger to the button. Then turning round, he called out to a matronly woman weighed down with shopping bags. 'Hurry up, mum, the lift is waiting.'

Was this her chance? Celia made one desperate effort to wrench herself free. But Delaney was on his guard. His grip remained unyielding.

Mum was the talkative type. 'Blouses are just sixty queredos in Pablos.' The remark was addressed to Celia. 'Have you been to Pablos, dear? Everything is half price just now.'

Delaney gave her no opportunity to reply. Shaking his head at mum, he jested, 'Oh, no, not shops. If we do any more shopping I'll have to remortgage my house.' Mum shrieked with laughter. Getting out at the first floor, she turned and wagged her finger at Celia.

'You mustn't let these men have it all their own way, dear. I find shopping *so* therapeutic. Do have a look at the blouses.'

They continued to the third floor. 'Out here.' Delaney gave a determined tug.

'Where are you taking me?'

'My room.' His tone of voice made it clear that he was brooking no arguments. 'Come on. We're almost there.' Even as he pushed the key into the lock his grip on her arm did not relax. Opening the door, he pushed her inside with enough force to cause her to stagger. Losing her balance, she stumbled, falling onto the bed. Then banging the door behind, he leaned against it as though to impede any escape bid.

CHAPTER FIFTEEN

Delaney slumped back against the door in an attitude of exasperation. 'Are you out of your mind? Just where did you think you were going?' She rose from the bed, trembling, face ashen, tears filling her eyes. In a distracted sort of gesture he pushed his hair back from his forehead. Bombs, bullets and earthquakes he could take in his stride. Such were the hazards of the job. But a woman's tears unnerved him.

'Celia – please! Just calm down.' He lowered his voice in an effort to strike a note of reason. 'I *had* to stop you. Don't you know there are now police check-points all along the promenade? How far do you think you would have got in that taxi?' He paused to gauge her reaction. There was none; just a blank stare.

'Celia, Bianqui has been on television just now talking real tough about stepping up security. He means business. Not the best time for someone on the run to be taking taxi rides.'

She was now backing away from him. He looked at her puzzled. Her eyes had a wild, vacant look – as though nothing he said was getting through. She was somewhere else. Furtively she edged towards the window. Then, in a frantic movement pushed it open. Was she ill? Needed air?

'Oh, my God, no! Celia don't! Please!' He darted forward as she raised herself onto the ledge. Looking down she seemed poised to jump. He reached her just in time. With a powerful grip he caught her around the waist and dragged her inside. Her body went limp; there was no fight left in her. Quickly he slammed shut the window and swung around to face her. She stood paralysed and transfixed like a small animal watching a predator. Seeming to sway, she grabbed the back of the armchair to steady herself. Then she sank into the chair and buried her face in her hands.

Shaken to the core, for a moment he could only stare at her, stupefied. Then as what had happened – or almost happened – sank in, he pulled himself together. She was his responsibility now. Or was she? Getting involved with a fugitive from justice was surely playing with fire. But he knew he was already involved – involved from the moment he found her hiding in Helen's room.

Sitting in the armchair opposite he took a deep breath to steady his nerves. 'Celia, why did you try to jump from that window?'

She seemed to stifle a sob. He spread out his hands in a gesture of bewilderment. 'I mean, why now …. When things were going so well? You got yourself out of prison. I tell you not many people escape from Monteverde. And you were planning to get away on Saturday …' Pausing, he shot her a searching look. 'Or has something gone wrong with your plans for Saturday?'

She still didn't answer. Her silence was beginning to irk him. 'Celia, I can do without this. Would you mind telling me what's going on?'

She raised her head suddenly. There was a sharpness in her eyes that he hadn't seen before. Now the cornered animal was prepared to fight. 'Mike, why did you betray me?'

For a moment he was stunned. 'Celia, what the hell are you talking about?'

'Why do this to me, Mike? I've never done you any harm.'

Getting up, he walked towards the window, perplexed and troubled. Then he swung round. 'Look, Celia, I know I snapped at you last night for having Helen's handbag. I know I should have shown more restraint. God knows you've been through hell enough without me yelling at you. If I haven't behaved like a perfect gentleman, I'm sorry. But try to understand I've got feelings too. Losing Helen hurts. Can't you just accept my apology and forget all this nonsense about betraying you?'

As she looked at him blankly, he realised he was on the wrong track. 'So it had nothing to do with anything I said last night? What is it, then?'

'I saw you just now. From the window.' She paused as though to measure the impact of her words. 'I saw you talking to that policeman.'

He shrugged his shoulders dismissively. 'So? I was talking to a policeman.'

'You were telling him about me, Mike.'

He stared at her. Then as the implication of what she was suggesting sank in, he gave a dry laugh. 'Oh, I see. That's what bothered you. You thought I was giving him the tip-off about you hiding here? Don't you trust me? No, you obviously don't.'

The vigour of his protest seemed to leave her confused. She spoke as though to herself. 'But Roberto told me to avoid police.'

It hadn't escaped Delaney's attention that she had dropped a name. A fellow fugitive? The name of the man who had walked along the beach with her yesterday?

'Well, of course you avoid policemen if you've just broken out of jail. And sure Costadoreans aren't too fond of their police. But I'm a journalist. I talk to everyone. How the hell do you think I sound out opinion? I'd talk to Bianqui himself if the bastard would give me an interview.'

She started to speak, then hesitated as though about to cry again.

'Look, Celia, hadn't you better start trusting me? Can't you credit me with some human decency? If there's any way I can help you ....'

'Why should you want to help me?'

'Let's get something straight. I didn't ask to get mixed up in this. I found you hiding in Helen's room. Remember?'

His rebuke seemed to sting. She murmured softly: 'It's not my fault she's dead.'

Instantly he regretted his sharpness. 'I know I was a little rough with you just now. But how do you think I would feel if the police had found you in that taxi and I had done nothing to stop you?'

123

She remained silent, seeming to waver between doubt and trust.

'Anyway, what motive would I have for going to the police? What would I get out of it?'

'Money?'

He laughed loudly. 'Money! Reward money? Are you serious?'

She bristled. 'Have I said something funny?'

Her indignation heartened Delaney. This was easier to deal with than tears. 'Celia, get real! You think I'd be tempted by a reward in *queredos*? My editor will pay me far more in *real* money to turn all this into an exclusive story. I'm not interested in mickey mouse money.'

Chagrined and distracted, she pushed back her hair from her eyes. He sensed she now doubted her accusation.

'Anyway, why do you think they would offer a reward for you? Whether you live or did, life goes on as usual in Costadora.'

'Glad you think I'm dispensable.' She spoke acidly.

Delaney had an impression that in that flash of anger the colour of her eyes changed. The blue became mauve. They were very fine eyes. 'Look, love, in case you haven't noticed, this country is falling apart. Yes, your escape *is* an embarrassment to the government. But it's no threat to them. They're a lot more anxious to get the insurgents behind bars. Revolutionaries like Roberto Diaz.'

There was a note of entreaty in her voice. 'Mike, do you really think they've stopped looking for me?'

'Oh, they'll go on looking for you. So you can't afford to do daft things like taking taxi rides along the promenade. Not when the place is crawling with police. But with a revolution on their hands you won't be their priority just now.'

As she leaned back in the armchair she appeared drained and confused. 'What do you want from me, Mike?'

'We could be of use to each other.' Now, Delaney decided, was the moment to broach the subject. He smiled as though half jesting. 'Forget what I said about human decency. Let's talk business.'

'What business?'

124

He lifted the contract he had prepared earlier from the table. She gave him a puzzled look.

'Go on, read it,' he urged. 'It's a proposition I'm putting to you. I want your story. My paper will pay you a lot of money for it.' She began to read. At first listlessly, then with growing interest. A gasp of surprise escaped her lips.

'Mike, this fee – it's more than I could earn in a couple of years. Do I really get this just for giving you an interview?'

'Well, there are conditions. Have you looked at clause three? It must be an *exclusive* interview. You can't talk to any other newspaper.'

She hesitated. 'I didn't want any publicity …. But I suppose I can't avoid that.'

'No, you can't. So why not make some money out of it? Take your time to think it over. You don't have to sign now.'

'What is there to think over?' She sounded weary. 'When I get back to London I have nowhere to live. I don't know if I can get my job back. This money would help me until I get my life sorted out.'

'So you need the money and I need your story?' Drawing his chair close to hers, he sat down. Grinning, he gave her a nudge. 'I think that makes us a team.'

CHAPTER SIXTEEN

It was six thirty. Hepworth, who had just showered and changed for dinner, adjusted his tie in front of the mirror. Nagging disquiet returned to plague him. Delaney was up to something. Something murky. Something best left alone.

Or was he being paranoid? As he combed back his greying hair, he reminded himself that foreign correspondents were always "up to something". Delaney was probably just onto a good story.

But parading Celia Martinez through the lobby was an uncharacteristic act of bravado. Something wasn't right. Delaney was no fool. He surely knew to keep her out of sight.

He had known Delaney a long time. Since their reporting days in London. Despite all their baiting and teasing, their wrangling over politics, their professional rivalry, they remained good friends. Neither would fail to help the other in any sort of trouble. On an impulse he picked up the phone.

'Mike, Tony here. Ready for that drink?'

'A drink? Is it that time?' Delaney sounded as though he had forgotten.

'Would you mind dropping in here first? There's something I want to ask you. Can't talk privately in the bar.'

'Sure. I'll be down soon.'

Delaney tapped on the door some twenty minutes later. As Hepworth let him in, it struck him that he looked unusually strained.

'Anything wrong, Tony?' Delaney asked as he sank back in an armchair.

Hepworth settled into the armchair opposite. 'I want to ask you the same question.' His eyes narrowed as he scanned the face of his younger colleague. 'You seem remarkably careless about your safety. Taking a few risks, aren't you?'

Pulling out a packet of cigarettes from his pocket, Delaney offered one to Hepworth. 'My last before kicking the habit,' he said brightly. Hepworth got the impression that he was trying to avoid the question. He repeated it doggedly. 'I'm talking about your safety, Mike. Aren't you pushing your luck?'

'Well, you know what it's like.' He affected a casual tone. 'Danger can flare up at any time. I tell you I didn't hang around up there at San Remo any longer than necessary. Once the bullets started flying, you couldn't see me for dust ....'

Raising his hands, Hepworth cut in impatiently. 'Mike! Cut the crap, will you. You know very well I'm not talking about that San Remo business.'

'What, then?'

'What do you think?' Hepworth's voice took on a tough note that warned he intended to get to the bottom of the matter. 'If *I* saw you strolling through the lobby with Celia Martinez, God knows who else saw you.'

Delaney made no attempt at denial. 'Well, it's unlikely she was recognised. You saw her umpteen times in the courtroom. Most people only know her from a photograph. She looks different when she's not wearing prison clothes. I did tell her, though, not to go out without sunglasses.'

'You did, did you?' The bland explanation seemed to irritate Hepworth. He jerked forward with a scowl. 'Mike, this is Costadora. Not the place where I would choose to be on the wrong side of the law.'

'Nor I, Tony.'

Hepworth gave him a trenchant look. 'How did you come to be mixed up with Celia Martinez?'

Delaney took a long pull at his cigarette. Hepworth guessed from his ponderous expression that he was vacillating. He hadn't yet made up his mind whether or not to take him into his confidence. He continued to probe.

'Where is Celia Martinez now?'

'In Helen's room. Sleeping, I think. She's rather over-wrought at the moment.'

'So Helen is in on this as well?'

Delaney's composure deserted him. He seemed near to tears.

'Tony, there's something you ought to know – I would have told you sooner but ….' He faltered, unable to continue.

'What is it?'

'Helen is dead!'

'Dead! Helen is *dead?*' Hepworth looked stunned. 'But how? When did it happen?'

'Yesterday. In the earthquake.'

'Yesterday! You've known since yesterday? Well I thought something was wrong. It didn't seem right Helen rushing off to the Western Province this morning when the action is here. Why the secrecy?'

'It was Celia Martinez who found the body – she's got Helen's handbag and passport. The room key was in the bag. When I went up to Helen's room last night she was there. It was she who told me that Helen is dead.'

'Are you sure she's telling the truth?'

'Why would she want to lie?'

'To cover the fact that she had just stolen Helen's handbag.'

'Tony, my finding her last night was a complete surprise. She had no time to invent stories.'

Hepworth spoke dryly. 'Well, maybe.'

'Tony, I'm sure she told it to me the way it happened.'

Hepworth got up and stared out of the window looking troubled and uncertain, then he sat down again. 'And how did it happen?'

'I don't know everything. She seems to be protecting someone who helped her. Probably another jail breaker. As you know, it began with the earthquake ….'

* * * * *

Having finished the story, Delaney was emotionally drained. The secret of Helen's death had weighed heavily on him. Hepworth's face settled in an expression of gravity. 'I'm sorry about Helen. Really sorry.' He stubbed out his cigarette.

128

'What are you going to do about Martinez? I assume you have signed her up for an exclusive.'

Delaney nodded.

'You know this is a risky business, Mike?'

'I can't just turn my back on her.'

'Oh, I haven't forgotten they were going to string her up sometime.'

'Tomorrow morning.' Delaney's voice was grim.

'Tomorrow! Yes, I had forgotten it was tomorrow.' Hepworth shook his head sombrely. You must make her understand that she can't go wandering about the place. How do you intend to get her off this bloody island?'

'Not me – other people are helping her. As I said, she's using Helen's passport.'

'Helen's body may soon be identified – if it hasn't been already. That would blow Martinez's cover.'

'Celia has all her identification.'

'She'll be recognised eventually. You know you haven't got much time. When does she intend to leave?'

'She said something about Saturday. I don't know the details. Tony, we can't say anything about Helen's death until Celia is on her way.'

Hepworth sprang to his feet. 'You look as though you need a drink.' Taking a bottle of Jamiesons from the minibar, he held it up. Delaney nodded.

'To Helen!' Hepworth raised his glass.

'To Helen!' Delaney's voice quivered with emotion. Helen should have been here drinking with them.

Hepworth studied the golden liquid in his glass. 'You know I never really got on with her.' He shrugged his shoulders as though trying to make sense of something. 'I don't know why – I didn't dislike her, but we seemed to be always arguing.'

'She didn't dislike you either, Tony. But I think she found your style of argument ....' He faltered, trying to find the right word.

'Belligerent?' suggested Hepworth dryly.

'Challenging,' replied Delaney. 'She enjoyed all that creative tension.'

'Creative tension?' Hepworth arched an eyebrow. 'I suppose that's one way of putting it.'

They fell silent for a moment. A strange expression spread over Hepworth's face – an expression of sadness. Delaney looked on in wonderment; he had never before seen his old friend looking sad. Then Hepworth broke the silence: 'Anyway, she was a damned fine journalist. One of the best.'

CHAPTER SEVENTEEN

The Orchid Bar was crowded. Ripples of laughter mingled with buzzing voices as guests sipped their aperitifs. As always, Egghead hovered in the background. Despite his vacant expression, he still managed to look conspicuous.

'Bloody tourists,' muttered Hepworth as he peered around the door. 'You'd think it was Disneyland the way they take over the place.'

Delaney smiled at his friend's crankiness. Hepworth clearly never considered that others might see him as part of the crowding.

Hepworth continued grumbling. 'No room anywhere.'

'There's plenty of room. Look, there's Guy and Danny over there.' A most incongruous pair, Delaney thought as he saw his press colleagues. Jackson and Renoir were forever arguing about Costadorean politics, Jackson defending Bianqui's right to maintain law and order, Renior taking a "power to the people" perspective. But for once they didn't seem to be arguing, Renoir leaning languidly against the bar, dark smooth hair well-groomed; Jackson fussily brushing a piece of fluff from his jacket as he talked in a flat, monotonous voice.

'Busy day?' Delaney asked.

The Frenchman shrugged. 'Comme ci, comme ca.'

Removing his spectacles, Jackson cleaned them with a tissue. 'One of the escaped prisoners has been recaptured. Caught at the ferryport trying to board a boat.'

'When did you hear that?' Hepworth asked.

'About half an hour ago. On television.'

Delaney chilled. Only a few hours back he had stopped Celia fleeing to the ferryport. 'Anyone important, Danny?'

'Someone called Cheng Kuo. Don't think he's political.'

Renior toyed with his wine glass. 'All the same, the police can't be feeling too happy. Five prisoners still missing, including Martinez.'

Jackson cleared his throat as though he had something important to say. 'I overheard something very strange. Someone claiming to have seen Celia Martinez yesterday afternoon walking along the beach.'

'Balderdash!' Hepworth spoke with unexpected vehemence. 'The poor woman is just one day dead and they're already dreaming up apparitions.'

'You don't know that she's dead.'

'Died in the earthquake, didn't she?'

'There's been no confirmation ....'

Hepworth snorted. 'Use your commonsense, Danny. If you had just broken out of Monteverde Prison, would you stroll along the beach looking like you were on holiday?'

Renoir gave a short laugh. The idea of Jackson as a jailbreaker evidently amused him. He looked towards Delaney as though wishing to share the joke. Delaney, with an eye on Egghead, thought only of turning the conversation away from Celia's escape. 'Anyone know what conditions are like out there now?'

'Some street fighting,' Renoir replied.

Hepworth sounded surprised. 'I thought the San Remo business was now under control.'

'Something else flared up on the east side. Near Plaza San Pedro.'

Delaney's expression sharpened. 'When did you hear this, Guy?'

Renoir looked vague. No, he hadn't heard it on Radio Libertad, nor had it been on television. Puffing a cloud of smoke into the air, he referred enigmatically to his "contacts". Renoir was like that; he enjoyed an aura of mystery. Delaney thought he would probably change direction mid-career and become a writer of political thrillers.

'Well, I'm meeting my photographer in about an hour in the city,' Delaney said. 'I suppose I could scout around the east side as well. Anyone want to share my taxi?'

Hepworth wasn't interested. 'The revolution can wait. I'm having dinner. Anyone going to the Grill Room?'

Renoir was of the same mind. One barricade was very much like another. Blood was the same colour anywhere in the world. God knows they had been running about enough all day. Sometimes you just had to switch off. If necessary they could do what was expected of newspaper hacks. Concoct the news.

Jackson too had had a busy day, so he declined. 'Don't get caught out in the curfew,' he cautioned.

'Damn the curfew,' replied Delaney irritably.

* * * * *

Much of the area east and north of Plaza San Pedro was cordoned off. 'It's still unsafe,' a policeman told Delaney. Then he shook his head. 'Bricks and mortar falling everywhere.' He didn't hear – or pretended not to hear – the gunshots which rang out close by. The police seemed reluctant to acknowledge that there was a simmering revolution. Street unrest was attributed to "looters and gangsters taking advantage of the earthquake situation".

Delaney retreated from the plaza and found himself in a street leading to the harbour. Apart from one seedy café, "The Sailors' Tavern", business premises were boarded up. Here and there a girl in a doorway called out to him. Prostitution was not illegal in Costadora, but soliciting in the streets was. However, with the deteriorating political situation, the police had other things on their mind. For the moment the girls were free to ply their trade.

A loud volley of shots followed by screams startled him. It sounded dangerously close. Time to move on.

Returning back towards the plaza, he noticed a barricade a short distance down a side street. Two men with rifles guarded the narrow opening between an upturned vehicle and the wall of a derelict house. Hesitating for a moment, he braced his shoulders and walked towards them. The younger man – he looked about eighteen – wore a black leather jacket; the middle-aged one a shabby, coarse hemp tunic. Both had red scarves tied around their sleeves. Sharp-eyed and suspicious, they tensed and raised their guns as he approached. Delaney smiled as he walked towards them. The younger man stuck out his jaw defiantly like someone ready for a fight. Delaney held out his press card, then immediately realised the futility of this. Even if they could read English, it was too dark to see. He called out: 'Buenos noches. Soy periodista. Quiero hablar con ustedes, por favor.' They did not answer but continued staring at him fixedly. 'Expecting trouble?' he asked as he came alongside them. Almost unconsciously he had adapted his Spanish to the rough dialect of the east side.

'Yes, big trouble.' It was the older man who replied. He scowled as he scanned the press card.

'Care to give me a statement. For the *Irish Forum*.' Noting his obdurate, distrustful expression, Delaney added: 'I won't use your name, if you don't want me to'. The two gunmen looked at each other, then the older one nodded.

'What do you want to know?' the younger man asked.

'Why are you prepared to fight?'

The younger man answered. The other just looked on, cigarette dangling from his mouth. He never lowered his rifle.

Their motivation was simple enough. The right to work. Here in the San Pedro district one person in four was unemployed. The right to have their independent trade unions restored. Few workers even bothered to join the government-sponsored Urban Workers Association. Too much government corruption. Too big a gap between rich and poor. Too much hunger in the mean streets here on the east side.

Delaney, jotting it all down in his notebook, continued firing questions.

'Why has it all come to a boiling point at this particular time?'

The young insurgent was vague about the timing of the thing. People higher up in the movement decided these things. No, he didn't think it was altogether planned. At least not by the workers. Solidarity action in support of the Sonora strikers had been going on for some time. But the earthquake brought things to a head. Their factory had been destroyed. They knew from Radio Libertad that those Constitutionalist fellows were now squaring up to Bianqui. It seemed a good time to decide which side you were on.

What did they think of Robert Diaz and his proposals for reform? The two insurgents looked at each other, then the younger one shrugged. 'Diaz? The University chap? Don't know much about him. Seems all right.'

Shoving his notebook in an inside pocket, Delaney smiled. 'Well, thank you for talking to me. I'm most obliged.' As he was about to leave, the older man took his cigarette out of his mouth and gave Delaney a shrewd look. 'I say, amigo, could you possibly make a contribution to our Emergency Reserve Fund?'

'Sure,' replied Delaney pulling a banknote out of his wallet. He didn't bother to ask what was the purpose of the fund. Food or guns, what did it matter? In a state of siege they would need both.

Moving on, he met Carlos in a taverna near the city centre. With the ten thirty curfew in mind, it had to be brief. Carlos had some photographs for him. They stuck to small talk as they downed their drinks. You never knew who was listening. Outside in the street they stopped in a shop doorway. Carlos told Delaney that there were heavy military reinforcements all around the Presidential Palace, Government House and the Defence Ministry. 'They don't allow you to take photographs of the military on duty,' said Carlos as he blew cigarette smoke into the air. The he flashed a sardonic smile. 'But I got you a few shots just the same.'

Delaney picked up a taxi on Avenida de la Independencia. Cruising through the business district, it took a right turn into Calle Marina. There they ran into a police checkpoint.

'Just half an hour to curfew,' the police officer warned as he checked their identification.

The driver could scarcely hide his irritation. 'We're only going as far as the Metropole.'

135

'Don't get caught out,' the police officer continued, then waved them on. They had now reached Paseo Malecón. No sign of revolution here, thought Delaney as he eyed the opulent beach homes. He cast his mind back to the two men at the barricades and their very different lifestyle. Their objectives seemed modest enough – a charter for social justice. Apart from the demand for free trade unions, they were all bread-and-butter issues. No mention of human rights; no reference to freedom of speech and press; nothing about constitutional matters. If only he could interview a leader of the Constitutionalist movement he might get a different perspective. The Constitutionalists had their programme of social reform, but you didn't eliminate poverty overnight. It suddenly struck him that Costadora about a couple of years *after* the revolution might be a fascinating place to visit. Would the workers get their social justice? Would the Constitutionalists remain pure and uncorrupt? Had purity of vision any place in *realpolitik*?

'On holidays?' the taxi driver called back to him.

'No. Work. I'm a journalist.'

'You'll be writing about all this, then?'

Delaney decided to be evasive. He didn't know who the hell the man was. Bianqui's agents came in all shapes and guises – taxi drivers, barmen, porters or even that friendly stranger who just happened to be at your elbow when you wanted a light for your cigarette. 'I've finished the job here,' he replied vaguely. 'Got to get back home.'

'So soon? Aren't you waiting for the weekend?'

'Why? What's happening at the weekend?'

The taxi driver sounded surprised. 'Don't you know about the festival? On George. There are extra sailings.'

Delaney relaxed his defences just a little. 'I'm told it could be just as exciting here.'

'Here? In Ciu Costa? Don't know about that. This curfew. It kills everything – restaurants, bars, all the night life. No late business. Bianqui's a bloody fool. What the devil is he trying to do? Empty the place of tourists? We live off t he tourists, for God's sake.'

In the car mirror he could see the irritation on the driver's heavy-jowled face. Then he glanced towards the beach. The reflection of the moon on a satin-black sea was awesome. I'll always remember this place, he thought. The beach was deserted now, save for a solitary couple walking along the water edge. The scene evoked a memory of Celia yesterday evening walking along the sands, hair blowing in the breeze. But who was her companion? That was the question that had been teasing his brain all afternoon. Hadn't she said to him that *Roberto* had told her to avoid policemen? Could this be Roberto Diaz? Was it possible that Celia could lead him to this man whose political writings has aroused international interest? But Roberto was a common enough name in Costadora. He would first have to check the Christian names of the other escaped prisoners.

The driver's voice broke in on his thoughts: 'I wonder, amigo, if you could sell me some American dollars?'

'Dollars!' Delaney feigned surprise.

'Even a small amount,' the driver continued. 'I'll give you a better rate than the banks.'

'Sorry,' Delaney replied. 'I've nothing but queredos.' Delaney was well aware that the penalties in Costadora for currency irregularities were severe. He had seen it all before in East Europe and elsewhere. As repressive regimes collapsed, an underworld came to surface.

'He's not wasting any time,' thought Delaney as he hopped out of the taxi and paid his fare.

Delaney dropped into the Orchid Bar to let his press colleagues know the situation on the east side. No he hadn't seen any street fighting but had heard enough shooting to know that it was going on, at least sporadically. Army reinforcements around the presidential palace and elsewhere seemed to suggest that the trouble was expected to get worse.

Jackson frowned ponderously. 'You think Ciu Costa is about to fall?'

Delaney grinned. 'What do you mean by *fall*, Danny? That's the wrong political line. You're supposed to say *liberated*.'

Jackson replied testily: 'If this island is on the verge of a Communist take-over, then it's going to *fall*.'

'Come on, Danny. There aren't just Communists in this. The Liberals, Social Democrats and all sorts of dissident groups want to see the back of Bianqui.'

Renoir, perched on a stool next to Jackson, rolled his dark eyes and shrugged, a gesture which young women found sexy. 'Does it matter whether or not it goes communist, Danny? It's *their* country, isn't it? Nothing to do with the West.'

Jackson adopted a didactic tone. 'Aren't you forgetting Cuba?'

'No, mon ami, I'm *remembering* Cuba. A good example of how *not* to treat a smaller neighbour who happens to choose a system of government you don't like. How can you justify this trade embargo?'

When Renoir and Jackson got onto that subject, it could go on all night. Delaney turned to go. Hepworth, his speech slurred – it always was at that time of evening – asked him if he wanted a drink. Delaney didn't reply; his attention was distracted by Egghead edging closer to the pressmen. As Delaney reached the door, Hepworth called after him: 'Mike, where the hell are you going? You're like a bloody whirlwind. Stop and have a drink.'

'Not now, Tony.'

Hepworth smirked. 'Going to see the pretty little lady?' Delaney stiffened. Hepworth was clearly the worse for drink. Would he in some unguarded moment say something to betray Celia? Seeming to read his thoughts, Hepworth put his finger to his lips and uttered, 'Sshhhhh!' Face flushed, hair falling in his eyes, he looked thoroughly rakish. Giving Delaney a knowing wink, he then turned his attention to the serious business of drinking.

Jackson was looking on bemused. 'Helen is back, then?'

Hepworth gave a non-committal nod. 'Think so.'

Delaney eased up. Hepworth was sufficiently in control. Alcohol might be playing havoc with Hepworth's liver, but it didn't seem to affect his mind.

* * * * *

Celia looked pleased to see him. She brushed aside his apologies about being late. 'I guessed you must be busy.'

'I've ordered dinner for us. In my room,' Delaney told her. 'They're bringing it up in about twenty minutes.' He glanced at his watch. 'Celia, you must be ravenous. I've just remembered you've had nothing to eat since breakfast time.'

'I did have something to eat. A late lunch. About four o'clock.'

'Where? You didn't go out?'

'No, the waiter brought it. The one who gave me the passport this morning. I was surprised – I hadn't ordered anything.'

Delaney held his breath. Then he feigned an offhand tone. 'I expect Alfonso told him to look after you.'

'You know Alfonso?' She looked surprised.

'Sure, I eat sometimes in Habana Vieja. Often chat to Alfonso. And the waiter. What's his name? Pedro?'

That wary look again. 'But how did you find out that *I* knew Alfonso?'

'I saw you on the beach yesterday. You passed me and walked up the pathway. When you sat down and emptied sand out of your sandles, I heard what your friend said to you.'

She hesitated. 'Did we speak? I don't remember .... Yes, I do remember. He told me to hurry. I could rest when we got to Habana Vieja.'

Delaney nodded. 'Yes, that's how I knew you were eating in Alfonso's place.'

'All the same, Mike, you only knew I ate there. How did you figure out that I knew Alfonso?'

'It wasn't difficult.' Delaney was now bluffing. 'Roberto Diaz is a friend of Alfonso. So after breaking out of jail he went to his friend for help.' He smiled knowingly. 'It was a real piece of luck you meeting Roberto Diaz like that.'

139

She tensed, but said nothing. Observing her closely, Delaney continued. 'I didn't realise Diaz was so tall. Tall for a Costadorean. But he looks like his photograph. Prison doesn't seem to have altered him.'

'You recognised Roberto from a photograph?'

'Straight away,' Delaney lied glibly. 'No mistake.' He guessed that Celia would never willingly betray Diaz's identity; nonetheless she had done so unwittingly.

* * * * *

Dinner eaten, Celia leaned back in the armchair. 'Mike, that was delicious.'

He refilled her wine glass. The turmoil of the day behind him, he felt wonderfully relaxed. 'You like hot spicy food?'

'You bet I do. Remember, I'm half Costadorean.'

She seems more at ease with me now, he thought. That augured well for the interview. He eyed her appraisingly. Still the same prim-looking navy skirt that she had worn during the day, but a different blouse. Instead of the floral cotton, she now wore a silky mauve top. The colour suited her.

He put the suggestion tentatively. 'Maybe we could have a Costadorean meal together sometime in London. Do you know any Costadorean restaurants there?'

'As far as I know there isn't one. But if ever I get a place of my own I'll cook you a Costadorean meal.'

'Where will you go when you return to London?'

Her expression clouded. 'That's something which worries me. We had a shared flat in Kensington – three of us.'

'Your flatmates don't want you back?'

'I don't know.'

'You've had no contact with them?'

'My friend Judith wrote to me when the trial was going on. After the death sentence was passed, I heard from her only once. A very stiff letter, as though she didn't know what to say. She told me someone else was using my room. A temporary arrangement as they needed the rent.' A note of bitterness crept into her voice. 'She asked if I had any

140

instructions about the disposal of my belongings. I thought she could at least have waited until after the appeal.'

'Look, Celia, I've an idea. Just a short-term arrangement, mind you. My newspaper has a flat in London. In Hampstead. A place we use when hotels are booked up. You could go there.'

'They would let me use it?'

'For a month or two. While you're looking around for something more permanent. Would you like me to arrange it?'

'Please – if it's not too much trouble.' Then she added softly as though to herself: 'If I ever do get back'.

'Oh, come on! Of course you'll get back. The folk will put on a great homecoming. Champagne corks popping and all that.'

'What folk? Mike, are you forgetting I have no family?'

'Sorry. I had forgotten.'

'You know when in prison, in a funny sort of way that made everything more bearable. When I thought I was going to die, it seemed better that there was no one to grieve for me.'

As Delaney leaned back in his chair, he tried to remember all the biographical details published at the time of her trial. 'I know your mother died some time ago. And I remember something about you being ....'

As he faltered, she promptly supplied the word. 'Illegitimate. You don't have to be shy about it. It seems to be common knowledge.'

'He raised his hands in a minimising gesture. 'Celia, no one cares about things like that these days.'

'They do in Costadora. At least they did in my mother's time. That's why she couldn't return here.'

'Your father? You've had no contact with him?'

'He's also dead. I never knew him. He met my mother when they were students in London. He went back to Norway before I was born. My mother got a job as a housekeeper. I was sent to a convent boarding school. An expensive place. I always thought my mother's employers paid the fees, as I knew she couldn't. My mother died when I was still at school. Two years later, when I was in fifth form, Sister Teresa, the

141

headmistress, broke the news to me that my father had also died. That was when I knew he had been paying my school fees. I wasn't angry with him after that. He must have cared for me to have paid for my education.'

'You were able to finish your schooling?'

'Yes, the sisters were very kind. They said that as I had been a good pupil I had earned a scholarship. They let me stay until I took my A level exams. Sister Teresa also explained that my father already had a family – a wife and child – at the time of my birth. That's why he couldn't marry my mother.'

'You must have felt very alone.'

She suddenly stiffened. 'Mike, this isn't the interview, is it?' She blurted out the question as though in a panic. 'You mustn't write anything about what I've just told you.'

Her change of mood surprised him. 'Celia, if it were an interview I'd have told you. I won't write anything you don't want me to.'

'What are you going to write?'

He shrugged. 'Something about your thoughts in the death cell. Your sensational escape. Enough material there without probing into an unhappy childhood.'

She responded with alacrity. 'I didn't say it was unhappy.'

'Celia, do you have to be so defensive? I said I wouldn't write anything you didn't want me to.'

'Sorry. I'm all tensed up. A stay in Monteverde doesn't improve your temper.'

She's pretty when she's riled, he mused. All bright-eyed and intense. He was beginning to sense that the interview might not be easy. 'Shall I make some coffee?'

'Coffee!' She looked towards the clock. 'No, it would keep me awake. I'll go now.' She stood up. 'I'm very tired. Mike, thank you for a wonderful dinner.'

He sprang to his feet. 'I'll see you tomorrow, then. We must make a start on this interview.'

'Tomorrow!' She looked startled. 'Wouldn't it be safer to wait until I get away from this place?'

'Best do it tomorrow while I've time. Don't worry, it will be embargoed.'

142

'Embargoed?'

'That just means it won't be published straight away. We'll delay it until you get back to London.'

'What time will I see you tomorrow?'

'The morning. About nine. I need to see Alfonso in the afternoon.'

'You won't mention that I spoke to you about Roberto? – Alfonso might think I've blabbed – that I'm not to be trusted ….'

He cut in briefly. 'Celia, I recognised Diaz from his photograph. I don't remember you telling me anything about him.' Now he was turning over in his mind the possibility that Alfonso could lead him to an interview with Diaz. His gaze veered towards the clock. 'Nine o'clock is all right, then?'

She was looking at him strangely as though she hadn't heard the question. 'I hate tomorrow. I don't want to think about it.'

He didn't at first understand. 'The interview is nothing to worry about, Celia. Just an informal chat, like we've been having all evening.' He beamed a persuasive smile. 'The only difference is that I'll be making some notes.'

'I wasn't worried about the interview, Mike'

'What, then?'

'Have you forgotten, Mike? Tomorrow might have been the last morning of my life?'

'Don't dwell on it, Celia.' As his hand touched her arm, his thoughts turned to Helen. 'Just be glad you are still alive.'

* * * * *

It was after midnight when Delaney and Renoir went up to the hotel roof. Not easy to gauge the state of things while a curfew was going on, but from this vantage point they hoped to gain a general impression.

All seemed quiet. Only the occasional distant sound of gunshots disturbed the serenity of a star-lit night. So distant that neither man could be sure of what he heard.

'Nothing much happening here,' murmured Delaney. The police check-point he had seen earlier on the promenade had gone.

'Must be that Bianqui is concentrating his security on the east side. Where all the trouble is.'

Delaney nodded thoughtfully. In that part of the city where poverty was greatest, resentment of Bianqui was strongest. Following any act of sabotage, it was usually east-siders who were rounded up for interrogation.

Raising binoculars to his eyes, Renoir looked towards the city centre. 'Some army trucks near the Cathedral.' He slowly veered around in the opposite direction until he was looking towards Fisherman's Cove. 'Ah, ha!' His exclamation suggested he had spotted something significant.'

'What's going on, Guy?'

'Some soldiers.'

'What are they doing?'

'Nothing much. Just talking to people.'

'What people? Isn't there supposed to be a curfew?'

'Theoretically.' The Frenchman extended the binoculars to Delaney. 'Want to have a look?'

Delaney focused the binoculars in the direction of the Cove. 'What the hell is going on? Those people aren't taking a blind bit of notice of the curfew.'

'Nor the soldiers of curfew breakers.'

It was difficult to make sense of it. Parked near Marine Gardens was an army truck, around which a small group of people had gathered. The rapport between soldiers and civilians seemed convivial and relaxed. Beyond a few people strolled about as though unconcerned by the military presence. It seemed some amicable arrangement existed between soldiers and local people.

'I wonder if this means that Bianqui has already lost control ....' Delaney stopped sharply. 'Guy, look at this!' He handed the binoculars to the Frenchman. 'Look at their sleeves.'

Bemused, Renoir took the binoculars and looked again towards Fisherman's Cove. 'Yes, yes, I see The soldiers are wearing red armbands. Don't rebels wear red armbands?'

144

'Defectors, maybe. On their way to the mountains.'

'Careful, Guy, don't let them see you looking at them.' It was Hepworth who had approached silently. He appeared to have completely sobered up. 'I'd stand well back if I were you.'

Renoir lowered the binoculars. 'We aren't breaking the curfew, Tony. This is hotel premises. We haven't gone outside.'

Hepworth's face creased into a cynical grin. 'I doubt if those guys are bothered by such technicalities. If they care to raise their guns in this direction, you're sufficiently outside to stop a bullet.'

CHAPTER EIGHTEEN

At Varela's headquarters, near the village of Arganda, a military helicopter took off in a whirl of dust. Unusually it carried a civilian passenger. Having spent the night on the nearby farming cooperative, Diaz accepted Varela's offer of an airlift back to Ciu Costa. From the cooperative he had transmitted a message to Moreno: Terms accepted. Agreement concluded.

Peasant clothes discarded, he now wore jeans and an open-neck shirt. As the aircraft soared into a cloudless sky, he leaned back and relaxed. The meeting with the General had gone better than he expected. The main objective – Varela's agreement to provide the necessary back-up for the Sonora campaign – had been fulfilled. A joint assault on Ciu Costa would follow. He had done his bit. Or almost. There was still Gonzales to deal with.

Below he could see deep ravines, then beyond heavy forests which flanked the winding river. Here was terrain inhospitable to man. How little of this country we managed to tame, he mused as he scanned the savage earth below. Still no sign of life, animal or human. Then suddenly in a clearing he espied a steep donkey track winding down a rocky hill, from which descended a solitary mounted figure. Beyond, as the forest thinned, a hamlet with small thatched houses. Ciu Costa could not be far off.

But what of Gonzales? Would his meeting with the Minister for Information go so smoothly? He could not suppress a feeling of disquiet. Gonzales had fitted so snugly into the social milieu of his in-laws that the notion of him as a defector seemed incongruous.

But perhaps it was not so strange. The man was a blatant opportunist; hedonistic, someone whose cynicism exuded a debonair touch. Diaz remembered well the first time he had poured forth his views on the erosion of democracy under Bianqui. He had hoped to provoke a political debate. Instead the imperturbable Gonzales had flashed him a sardonic smile. 'You're quite right, Roberto,' he said, 'but the President is running a country, not trying to get himself canonised.'

That Gonzales had chosen this moment to defect was perhaps a reason for optimism. A man who put pragmatism before principle would have weighed up Bianqui's chances of holding onto power. He obviously didn't think much of them.

All the same, thought Diaz, he still needs watching.

He continued scanning the landscape. Lines of fatigue marked his handsome face. On the horizon he could see the sea, now calm and hazy. It was a deceptive calm. Storms were forecast for tomorrow. He recalled the magnificent storms which had so overawed him as a child. Turbulent winds bearing down on Fisherman's Cove with great waves rising up twenty feet or more before breaking over the promenade. But it was the fury of the sea that had taken his father's life. The sea had given him everything, and taken everything from him. He loved it; he hated it; but it was forever part of him.

The officer's voice broke in on his thoughts. 'We're almost there, Dr Diaz.'

* * * * *

The telephone rang as Celia, still in a nightdress, was brushing her hair. It was Delaney, his voice sounding easy and pleasant. He hoped he hadn't woken her. Was she ready for the interview, or was it too early? Glancing at the travel clock on the dressing table, she chilled. Two hours beyond the time of her tryst with the executioner. Two hours of stolen time. With an effort she banished from her mind the image of a dangling rope.

'No, it's not too early, Mike. Just give me a few minutes to get dressed.' She tried to sound calm; to suppress her feeling of panic. More than anything else at that moment she craved for the nearness of another human being.

'Shall I come down? Or will you come up here?' he asked.

Looking around it occurred to her that being in his room, still surrounded by Helen's belongings, might be painful for him.

'I'll come up.'

'Fine. I'll have coffee ready. Then we'll get started on the interview …. Oh, and wear something pretty. I'm going to take a photograph.'

'Well, I don't have much choice,' she thought as she put down the phone. She rummaged in the travel bag, examining the random selection of clothes taken from Keevers. A couple of skirts, some blouses and a cool-looking cotton dress. Perhaps the hand-painted skirt was the prettiest. Then her gaze fell on a chic, crimson blouse – expensive-looking – in the half-opened wardrobe. Helen Darcy's blouse.

No, don't even think of it. It would make Mike angry. The blue blouse I have will do. Or the white.

Yet her eyes still lingered on Helen's blouse. She tried to imagine the person who once wore it. Self-assured, yet with a sense of fun. Someone difficult to forget. Lifting the blouse out of the wardrobe, she held it up against her and glanced in the mirror. How close had Helen been to Mike, she wondered? The idea had been drumming through her mind that perhaps they had been lovers. Oh, yes, he had dismissed the idea that Helen had been his *girlfriend*. Just old friends, he had said. But why would he tell her the truth? You didn't bare your soul to someone you had just met. It was something, she guessed, she would never know. Wistfully she put the blouse back in the wardrobe.

* * * * *

Mid-afternoon a car drew up at the side of Habana Vieja. Diaz stepped briskly out. As he turned to murmur his thanks to the driver, he was struck by the sultriness of the air.

148

Oppressive and humid, this was no ordinary heat. Rather the sort of heaviness that always preceded a storm.

Alfonso rushed to the car to meet him. A brief greeting, then he ushered his friend quickly through the kitchen and into his small office.

'Things went well?' asked Alfonso as Diaz settled back in the settee.

'Fine. I've got Varela's agreement to provide ground-to-air missiles.'

As Alfonso sat down beside him, his heavy eyebrows shot up. 'Varela! You met Varela? He's helping *us*?'

'I went downriver to Arganda to discuss terms with him.'

Alfonso gave a low whistle. 'They told me they wanted you for something important. But I didn't guess *that* important.'

Diaz's shrug and easy smile seemed to minimise the compliment. 'I thought I was going to see some action. Instead they made me the messenger boy.'

Alfonso's elbow shot out to give his friend a playful shove. 'Some messenger boy! Fancy winning over Varela.'

'There's someone else I have to see, Alfonso. Have they told you?'

'You mean Gonzales. Yes, I know about that. I'm to fix up a safe house. Trouble is, what he thinks is safe may not be safe for you.'

'I hope he's not in a hurry. I could do with a breathing space.'

Alfonso scanned his friend's weary face. 'Who needs Gonzales? Tomorrow should be soon enough. Let him sweat a little longer.'

'Alfonso, we don't need him, but we could *use* him.'

'For what? He's Bianqui's puppet, for God sake.'

Diaz shook his head. 'No, he's very much his own man. No loyalty to anyone.'

Alfonso shrugged. 'Perhaps. All the same, I don't trust these government ministers.'

A glint of humour crept into Diaz's eyes. 'that's a pity. We were thinking of making you one'

'No thank you. My own restaurant was all I ever wanted.'

Diaz was now smiling broadly. 'I know that, Alfonso. Your business flair showed early. I remember you as a youngster out there on the beach, cooking fish over a barbecue and selling them to tourists.'

'And it soon proved to be a nice little earner Talking about fish, are you hungry?'

'I had lunch in Arganda.'

'Feel like going upstairs for a siesta? We'll wake you for dinner.'

'I *am* tired.'

'Well, go then. Have a sleep. You'll get little rest in the next few days. The comrades have arranged a meeting for tomorrow ....'

'They have, have they?' A sudden irritation sharpened Diaz's voice. 'Has it occurred to no one that I would like to see my wife? Does Elena even know that I'm alive?'

'She knows. She also knows our rules. The escaped prisoner does not go near his family.'

'She may be in danger, Alfonso.'

'Shouldn't be. So don't put her in any. She's playing her part very well at the moment.'

Diaz tensed. 'What part?'

'The anxious wife. Enquiring at hospitals about casualties. Going along with the official line.'

'They're saying I'm dead?'

'They're saying you went missing in the earthquake. According to Bianqui, political prisoners don't escape.'

'Well, don't let that fool you. They'll go on looking for me.'

'I know. And they'll be watching Elena like a hawk. You mustn't go near her. Not yet.'

Diaz stood up. 'What was that trouble at the San Remo barracks yesterday?'

'The bombing. You heard about that?'

'Yes. I told Varela it had nothing to do with us .... Or has it?'

'Not that I know of. Our people have been told to hold their fire. Not to rise prematurely.' Alfonso's tone took on an impatient edge. 'I wish they'd take down those bloody barricades over on the east side. It's too early'

'Things will move fast enough from now on.' Diaz spoke with a quiet intensity. 'Perhaps we shouldn't delay this meeting with Gonzales. It *is* important. I'll see him tonight, if that's what he wants.'

'I'll try to arrange it before ....'

His voice trailed off as Raul put his head around the door. 'Uncle Alfonso, I'm sorry to interrupt you, but someone wants to see you.'

'Who is it, Raul?'

'Delaney. A foreigner.'

'*Michael* Delaney?'

'I think his name is Michael. The one who chats to you sometimes. Speaks good Spanish.'

'All right, Raul, tell him I'll see him in a minute.' Turning to Diaz, he pointed his thumb towards the door. 'Go now and get some sleep. Same room you used last time. I'll talk to Delaney in here.'

'Delaney? You mentioned that name before.'

'Yes. Writes for some Irish newspaper. I wonder what he wants.'

Diaz spoke with vigour. 'Sound him out. See if we could use him. God knows we could do with some decent publicity.'

'We'll have to go carefully on this one. Remember Ramos?'

'Oh yes, that damned newspaper article.' Pausing at the door, he put the question tentatively. 'By the way, how is Celia?'

'All right, I hear. Filipe brought the passport over to her yesterday. We should get her away by Saturday.'

* * * * *

'Can I get you something to drink, Michael?' Alfonso asked as Delaney leaned back in a chair.

151

'Mineral water, please. This heat! It has you drinking like a fish.'

As Alfonso poured the water into a glass, they exchanged banter about the threatened storm. Would it come tonight or tomorrow? Had Delaney ever seen a *real* Costadorean storm?

Handing the drink to his visitor, he lit his pipe before sitting down. Delaney was well aware that his easy-going manner was a façade; the Costadorean was on his guard. He knows I'm not here to chatter about the weather, he thought.

'This curfew must be killing business.'

Alfonso shrugged. 'It doesn't help.'

Delaney assumed an off-hand tone. 'It didn't seem to be so strict in the Cove. I was up on the hotel roof last night. Could see quite a few people milling around.'

Alfonso nodded. 'Well, you know that the folk in the Cove are like. Don't care much for rules and regulations.'

'But I hear the city centre was like a ghost town.'

Alfonso smiled non-committally.

'So the Cove is pretty solid rebel territory. A no-go area?'

Alfonso took a deep pull of his pipe. 'So they say.'

Delaney was warming up. 'Then the story I want – the rebel viewpoint – is right here. Under my nose.'

'Could be,' Alfonso replied vaguely.

Delaney continued to probe, shading his comment to make it appear he knew more than he did. 'It would help me if I could speak to someone high up in the movement.'

'Movement. What movement?' Alfonso took his pipe out of his mouth. Delaney noticed that he didn't move a muscle in his face; teasing information out of him wasn't going to be easy. He resorted to bluff. 'Come on, Alfonso. We all listen to Radio Libertad. Real rousing stuff, that is. We know things are hotting up in Sonora. And the rebel army is advancing.'

There was a flicker of humour in Alfonso's eyes. 'Yes, I heard those wild fellows out east are stirring up trouble. Hope it doesn't spread.'

Delaney's laugh had a sardonic edge. 'But it *has* spread, hasn't it? It's here in Ciu Costa. I was up at the San Remo barracks yesterday. Bianqui isn't in control any more, is he?'

'Isn't he? I thought he was still in the Presidential Palace.'

'But for how long?'

Alfonso shifted in his chair. 'Michael, tell me something. Your newspaper – what's it called?'

'The *Irish Forum*. I'll send you over a few back copies if you like.'

Alfonso repeated the name slowly, as though wishing to imprint it on his memory. 'And what sort of paper is it?'

'You've never read it?'

Alfonso shook his head. 'I don't read English. My wife does. She sometimes looks at the foreign papers to see how they report Costadorean affairs.'

'And how do they?'

'It's as though we didn't exist.'

'Then you need to get your side across.'

'What do you mean, *my* side?'

Delaney gave a short laugh. 'I think you know what I mean. Look, Alfonso. I'm a journalist, not the secret police. I don't expect you to incriminate yourself. But if you could arrange a meeting for me with Roberto Diaz, I could get Costadora into the headlines.' He paused, scanning Alfonso's face for a reaction. 'We know Diaz's writings in Europe. I need a well-known personality to give the story a focus.'

Alfonso stiffened. In the moment of silence Delaney held his breath. Slowly and deliberately Alfonso tapped his pipe on the ashtray. It seemed at first that he was not going to answer. Then he looked Delaney straight in the face. 'Diaz might be dead. Haven't you heard? He went missing in the earthquake?'

'He was very much alive when I last saw him.'

'You saw him? When?'

'Tuesday. Day of the earthquake. He was walking along the beach with Celia Martinez.'

Alfonso's face remained impassive. 'Interesting. Where do you think they are now?'

'Well, I know where Celia Martinez is. I think you do as well.' He raised his hand. 'All right, I don't expect you to confirm that.' Flashing a convivial smile, he rose to his feet. 'You know where to contact me. The Metropole. Think about it, Alfonso.'

CHAPTER NINETEEN

Leaving Habana Vieja, Delaney made his way through the rear of the car park to the back entrance. This opened onto a narrow street which skirted both Habana Vieja and the back of the Metropole. Winding his way down more narrow streets, he found himself in the Chinese Quarter. A closed world; a closed community; an Asian oasis on the European western side. Tourists who ventured down this labyrinth of small streets and alleyways often seemed bewildered and lost.

Aimlessly he continued to amble right into the heart of China Town. It was a fascinating place. Heady smells drifted through the air – sweetly-scented flowers, fried food from open air take-aways, incense, tobacco. He tarried at a stall where a tiny woman with a grandmotherly face was peddling ingredients for traditional Chinese medicines – dried sea horses, sharks' fins and a variety of herbs. As Delaney lifted up a handful of fragrant green leaves to take a smell, the vendor was quick to press a sale.

'Improves the memory. Very good for blood pressure.'

About to argue that there was nothing wrong with his memory or blood pressure, as the old woman fixed her genial gaze on him, he sensed there was already a contract between them. It was too hot to resist. As the pleasant aroma held the promise of a good herbal tea, he bought some.

While he continued to stroll further into the oriental maze, the buzz of conversation reached him from steamy tea houses – pleasant voices of people not driven by any sense of urgency. Only the voice of Radio Libertad floating down from an upstairs window reminded him that this bit of old China was in fact a world within a world.

Something in the illegal news broadcast caused him to look up sharply. Had he heard right? Arms had reached the strikers in Sonora? He would have to check that out. He had asked Celia to listen in to Radio Libertad for him; a distraction, he thought, from her own mental turmoil. She seemed pleased that he thought she could be of use. The interview that morning had gone better than he dared hope: with very little prompting form him, she had opened her heart, describing in harrowing detail those last anguished days in Monteverde prison awaiting death. Delaney was touched by her candour and trust; he felt closer to her.

The distant chiming of church bells caused him to pause and check his watch. Six o'clock. Too early for dinner. Just ahead was an old-world tea house with an upstairs wooder verandah. Somewhere to rest for half an hour.

'An outside table, please.'

'Yes, sir.' The smooth-faced waiter gave a deferential nod of the head, then led him to a seat at the corner of the verandah. Ordering jasmine tea and a slice of spicy nutcake that was a speciality of the Costadorean Chinese, he leaned back and watched the bustling street life below.

It's like a different country altogether, he reflected. Sipping idly from the delicate porcelain cup, he watched below an elderly woman taking slow, careful steps as she leaned on the arm of a female companion. Dressed like the people of the market place – high-necked tunics and trousers – they belonged to that generation which resisted western fashions and western lifestyles. Ciu Costa, Delaney reminded himself, was reputed to have the most traditional China Town in the world.

Or was that changing? The young people at the next table clearly represented a different kind of Costadorean Chinese. Probably college educated, their conversation switched with a striking effortless between Chinese and Spanish, as though bilingualism was second nature to them. One of the girls wore the cheongsam, the other an ankle-length cotton, hand-painted skirt, the height of fashion that summer. The two boys looked entirely westernised with T-shirts and shorts. Delaney's gaze lingered on the cheongsam which so elegantly accentuated the woman's shapely form. He recalled an article Helen had written on the youth of Costadora. She had noted the tendency of some well-educated young people in the Chinese community to revert to traditional styles once common in the fashionable milieu of an older China. Helen saw it as some sort of political statement, or cultural assertiveness. Where do their loyalties lie come the revolution, he mused?

It was a question he had discussed with Carlos. The Chinese were a minority often resented for their prosperit. In the last revolution, believing they owed loyalty to neither side, they had remained neutral. Carlos, however, thought that the younger Chinese thought differently. Most of his Chinese friends at college claimed to be admirers of Roberto Diaz. Diaz's first published book "The Awakening" was a history of the last revolution. He had argued that that revolution represented so many lost opportunities – he opportunity to offer ethnic minorities reserved seats in Parliament; the opportunity to offer bilingual education to the Chinese; the moment to reflect that whatever its origins, modern Costadora was a pluralistic society. A revolution worthy of its name cherished all its children equally; a true revolution should seek to create a united country proud of its diversity.

The drone of aircraft caused Delaney to look upwards. Were they military aircraft, someone asked in Spanish? The four young people at the next table stopped chattering and looked towards the sky, their anxious faces suggesting they were fully aware that their country stood on the brink. While there was nothing unusual in seeing a military aircraft now and then, Delaney had never before seen so many flying in formation. They were going eastwards.

What is going on in this damned country, he thought? Glancing at his watch, he rose to his feet. This interminable waiting for something to happen – God know what – had begun to fill him with restlessness.

As he strolled back towards the hotel, the swarm of humanity from all directions impeded his progress. In no great hurry he moved with its rhythm, savouring all the nuances – incense wafting through the air, street vendors crying their wares, the clamour of a myriad oriental voices exuding a vitality and exuberance. Approaching the Temple of Heavenly Peace, the main Buddhist Temple, he hopped off the pavement to avoid a group of young men squatting in a circle as they played some gambling game. The Temple was a landmark which told him that the exit from China Town was just two streets ahead. At the next corner was a small church. Taoism, Buddhism and Christianity were the religions of the Costadorean Chinese, in that order of importance. He had once attended Mass in the Chinese Catholic church and noted that the statue of Christ resembled more some ancient oriental scholar – Confucius perhaps - than the traditional image of the preacher of Galilee.

At market stalls in a small cul de sac he cast his eye idly over the wares: embroidered blouses, miniature statues of Buddha, silk scarbes, hand-made jewellery, paint brushes and ink sticks. A tall, auburn-haired woman lifted a scarf and tied it round her head, gypsy-style. 'How do I look?' she called to her companion in an accent of American's mid-west.

'Hold it there,' he replied, lifting his camera. She flashed a smile as he pressed the button.

The stallholder's ancient face was adorned with a long, wispy beard. Smiling graciously at the American woman, he spoke in stilted English. 'Just eighteen queredos. Three for the price of two.'

'Go on, dear, get three. I'll pay,' said her companion. As the woman selected two more scarves, Delaney looked on in fascination. It never ceased to amaze him how women could so dramatically alter their appearance by some simple touch – a scarf tied in a certain way, or the strange things the did with a dab of cosmetics. Helen was the one for scarves; the last time he saw her she had a green one draped over her shoulders.

Whilst the woman continued browsing through the knickknacks on the stall, an image of Celia came to his mind. Tentatively he fingered a scarf – dark blue bordered with a floral motif.

'That one *is* pretty,' opined the American woman.

'You think so?' Delaney replied awkwardly. 'Would it suit someone with fairish sort of hair?'

She smiled approvingly. 'On, I should think so. The design is *so* delicate.' The stallholder was quick to push business: 'Three for the price of two.' Delaney chose another two at random. Then, in the time-honoured fashion of oriental bazaars, he began to haggle over the price.

'Well done,' murmured the American woman when he managed to get a few more queredos knocked off the final price.

* * * * *

'Like this?' Standing in front of a mirror, Celia placed the scarf on her head, then tied it behind at the nape of her neck, gypsy style. Delancy nodded as he looked on appraisingly. Apart from a lock on her forehead, and a wisp at the back, it covered most of her hair. A touch of mascara both darkened and lengthened her eyelashes. A few deft touches with an eye pencil to give her eyes a slanted look. Then a dab of blusher to transform her face, so that she now seemed to have high-cheeked bones. She has become someone else, Delaney noted with a tinge of regret. He preferred the pale, wide-eyed girl she used to be.

'Well, I hope that's all right,' she said doubtfully as she replaced the makeup in Helen Darcy's cosmetic bag. 'I don't usually wear all that stuff on my face.'

'Yes. Fine. It makes you look different. That's all that matters.'

'But not all *that* different. Hardly a disguise.'

'Forget about a disguise. The last thing you need is any theatrical stuff.'

'What do you mean by theatrical?'

'Anything that makes you look conspicuous – hair some outlandish colour, dark glasses ....'

Celia looked surprised. 'You don't want me to wear the sunglasses?'

'Not now – not when the sun has gone down. Who on earth would walk through China Town after dark wearing sunglasses?'

A glint of excitement came into her eyes. 'We're going to China Town?'

'I thought we'd have dinner there'

In that sudden swing of mood that he was becoming accustomed to, she now looked apprehensive. 'Is that safe?'

'Safer than anywhere else. You won't see police patrols there.' It was well-known that the police regarded China Town, with its labyrinth of crowded, narrow lanes and jam-packed bazaars, as a security nightmare. Once a policeman had been shot there.

'China Town.' Celia repeated the name slowly as though it evoked some distant memory. 'My mother told me a lot about Ciu Costa's China Town. One of the most traditional Chinese communities in the world, she said. Is it true that they do their own policing?'

'Yes. As far as I know. Unofficially. You hear rumours of them meting out their own justice to offenders. They like to keep the police out of their area. And, from what I hear, the police are happy to stay out. The say that triad gangs from Hong Kong settled here after the colony was ceded back to mainland China.'

'Here? In Ciu Costa? What are they up to?'

'Well – if you can believe all the yarns you hear in the bars – there's a lucrative trade going on in illegal immigration from Vietnam and Cambodia. The place of course has always been awash with unlicensed gambling dens.'

She walked towards the window and cast her gaze along the moonlit beach. For a moment she seemed to retreat into a world of her own. Then she swung round. 'Mike, I don't know if I should risk it.'

He shrugged. 'It's up to you. But I'd say you're safer in China Town than anywhere else. Have you seen this morning's papers?'

'I didn't want to read about it, Mike.'

'Well, if you had, you'd see you aren't the government's priority right now. They're a lot more keen to catch all the political boyos on the run.'

Cheated of an execution, the morning's newspapers concentrated on the political news. Celia was referred to only briefly as "still missing". One newspaper opined that she was probably dead. A headline in the government newspaper *La Nation* struck Delaney as ironical: "Was Martinez an earthquake victim?"

As she looked towards him, Delaney saw that nervous flicker in her eyes. She was vacillating. His voice took on a cajoling note. 'Come on, Martinez! Stop your moping and come with me for a bite to eat?'

* * * * *

Descending in the goods lift, they left the hotel by the rear exit. Delaney took her arm as they crossed the road. Every now and then she seemed to hold back, her haunted eyes glancing nervously at passers-by. Each time she hesitated, his arm slipped round her waist to guide her on. 'Come on. Don't be afraid. Remember, you're just a tourist.'

That distinctive fusion of smells – fried food, incense and tobacco – signalled that they were on the threshold of China Town. Rounding a corner they could see just ahead Chinese street signs in neon lights. 'You'll love it here, Celia,' he enthused. Her eyes brightened; she now seemed less tense.

From a murky doorway, lit on either side by lanterns, a man emerged. Thin, bent shoulders, care-worn oriental features, he swayed slightly as he looked around, inebriated by God knows what. Here, if you knew the right dens, illegal brews came cheaper than licensed drinks. The man staggered down the street ahead of them, swaying from side to side. He reminded Delaney of Hepworth who was probably at that moment knocking back spirits in the Orchid Bar. Hepworth's words of caution sprang to his mind: 'Tell Celia Martinez she can't go wandering about the place.' Tony would have a fit if he knew I was right now walking with her through China Town, he thought. But then, Tony need never know.

They dropped in at Eddie Chang's place. Although many foreign visitors believed otherwise, Eddie Chang did not really exist. Moreover, no one outside the Chinese community ever remembered either the restaurant's real name, or the name of its owner. But it once provided the setting for a Hollywood

161

movie thriller, "The Secret Lives of Eddie Chang". And so the name "Eddie Chang's place" stuck.

They were led to a table at the rear of the restaurant. Delaney smiled teasingly at Celia after the waiter had taken their order. 'I think that must be Eddie Chang himself,' he said, indicating with his thumb the keen-eyed man with dark jacket and bow tie who paced the floor. 'You should get his autograph.'

Celia laughed, then cast her gaze around at the colourful wall murals depicting vistas of an ancient, imperial China.

How lovely she looks when she laughs, he thought. For a few moments, utterly absorbed in her surroundings, she did not speak. The place was full, mainly with Chinese people. At the far end of the restaurant he thought he recognised – but in the subdued light could not be sure – the American couple he had seen earlier at the market stall. On a raised platform a young Chinese woman was playing the piano.

'And that's Lily Wong,' he said with an impish grin. Lily Wong was the name of Eddie Chang's erstwhile girlfriend. Her suspected infidelity had driven Eddie to contemplate a more gruesome retribution. Lily might have suffered a terrible fate if she hadn't been rescued by an American sailor, a great hulk of a man called Bob.

'It's just like the film, isn't it?' said Celia, her eyes aglow with animation. To Delaney there was something touching in her child-like wonderment. But then, he reflected, for Celia Martinez life itself was a bonus. With so many anguished yesterdays, and no guarantee of a tomorrow, all she had was the passing moment.

'I hope you can handle chopsticks,' he said when the waiter placed platters of steaming food in front of them.

She smiled cheerily. 'You just watch me.'

* * * * *

Afterwards Delaney never remembered what exactly they talked about. Small talk, certainly. But they seemed to laugh a great deal. They laughed spontaneously, both their minds interacting with all the nuances of their surroundings. They laughed when a sailor entered the restaurant, his muscular frame filling the doorway. 'Bob the sailor!' they said in unison, pretending to believe he had come to rescue Lily Wong. They laughed when the waiter who skidded on the floor deftly regained his balance and walked on with cool nonchalance without spilling anything from his loaded tray. They laughed at everything and they laughed at nothing. Just for a brief space of time the dangerous world outside had ceased to exist.

And then at ten minutes to ten Delaney looked at his watch and announced regretfully: 'Just forty minutes to curfew time. I think we should move. Best not leave it until the last minute.'

CHAPTER TWENTY

Minister Gonzales smiled evenly as he faced Diaz across the table. 'I'm sorry I had to insist on meeting tonight. I believe you would have preferred tomorrow.'

Diaz gave a dismissive wave of the hand as he leaned back in his chair. 'No problem.' He had the air of one not greatly inconvenienced. That was how he intended to play it. Let Gonzales lay his cards on the table. And make it clear to him that if the terms were not right, they could do without him.

Gonzales had expressed some reluctance to meet at this cottage in Fisherman's Cove. Ostensibly a holiday home with an absentee landlord, it was in fact on Alfonso's list of safe houses. The Minister had pressed for the meeting to take place in an apartment near the Grand Plaza. Diaz hoped his firm refusal had sent the right message: be prepared for tough bargaining; expect no favours on the grounds of past friendship.

Pulling out a gold cigarette case from an inner pocket, Gonzales flicked it open and stretched across the table.

'Cigarette?' He smiled affably. As Diaz declined, he added: 'I forgot you don't smoke. Still no bad habits, Roberto?'

A hint of a smile lit Diaz's dark eyes. 'I wouldn't say that. I still keep bad company.' He couldn't resist a teasing quip. 'I hear, Gilberto, that you too might like to join the bad guys.'

'Perhaps.' The Minister lit his cigarette. Although his sensual lips were still smiling, his eyes had a shrewd look as he fixed them on Diaz. 'We still hold Sonora.'

Diaz's reply was swift. 'As long as we let you.'

164

Gonzales's eyebrows arched slightly. 'Come on, Roberto! Bianqui's army is first-class.'

There was a shade of mockery in Diaz's smile. 'I know, Gilberto. That's where most of our fellows got their training.'

The irony of this was not lost on Gonzales. He laughed dryly. 'Yes, I see what you mean. Our government does seem to have trained both sides. And to think I opposed the abolition of conscription.'

'We don't just rely on conscripts, Gilberto.'

'Quite, quite,' murmured the Minister with a studied indifference. While Gonzales could not yet know of Valera's defection, Diaz suspected he was well aware that there had been a steady stream of defections from the rank-and-file of Bianqui's army. Gonzales was silent now, toying ponderously with his cigarette, but his keen, grey eyes never left Diaz's face. Then he continued in an easy, detached voice.

'But it's still not a level playing field, is it Roberto? Where are your tanks? Your aircraft ….?'

Diaz cut him short. 'Gilberto, military matters are not my brief.'

'Quite.' Gonzales got up, walked to the window and looked out. Nonchalantly, as though he had all the time in the world. He's aged, thought Diaz in surprise. Lines now marked the corners of his eyes and mouth; his cheeks seemed to sag. Although a mere six or seven years older than Diaz himself, he now seemed to belong to another generation. But it remained an impressive face – the face of a man sure of himself. And he still had a fine head of wavy, brown hair.

'Still play tennis, Roberto?' the Minister asked without turning round.

'Monteverde didn't have a tennis court.'

'Quite. Quite. I'm out of practice myself.'

Continuing to gaze towards the sea, for the moment he seemed to have forgotten Diaz's presence. Diaz decided to do nothing, or say nothing, to remind him of it. Then he turned and walked back slowly, a smile on his face as he settled into the chair. Thoughtfully, he watched the ash from his cigarette drop into an ashtray. Then looking immensely sociable, his eyes turned again towards Diaz. 'How is Elena?'

Diaz picked his words guardedly. 'Elena is very well.'

'Glad to have you out, no doubt?' Gonzales spoke casually, but a strange flicker in his eyes suggested a keen interest.

'We'll both be glad when this is all over. So that we can get on with our lives.' Diaz hadn't forgotten that time when both he and Gonzales loved the same woman. A poor man then, Diaz might well have been the loser. But it was he, not Gonzales, that Elena had chosen to marry.

'Quite. Quite. These are unsettling times.' The Minister paused again, as though deliberating something. When he spoke again there was an unexpected edge in his voice. 'You know, Roberto, this movement you're in is very well infiltrated.'

Diaz eyed him coolly. 'So we have observed.' He flashed the Minister a sardonic smile. 'Those spies of yours are real clumsy fellows. But we don't stand for anything illegal.'

'Bianqui *banned* the Constitutional Alliance.'

'He did. And he was acting illegally.'

'Perhaps. But I'm not just talking about the Alliance. Your military wing is certainly not legal. Their activities are treasonable.'

There was a cynical detachment in Diaz's smile. 'I see we differ on the definition of treason.'

'Roberto, there must be a better way than this.'

'Than what?'

'Than fighting. Think of the last revolution. Brother against brother. Neighbour against neighbour.'

'If there is a better way, you tell me about it, Gilberto.'

Gonzales stubbed his cigarette into the ashtray, as always half-finished. He leaned back, stroking his chin, the expression in his eyes suggesting that he had momentarily switched off from the problems of the moment. His buoyancy of tone when he spoke again seemed forced – as though trying to convince Diaz of something that he didn't altogether believe himself. 'You know Bianqui has some positive qualities.'

'Has he, Gilberto? And what are they?'

'He gave Costadora thirty years of peace.'

Diaz's eyes blazed. 'Peace? What sort of peace? Well, I suppose if dissidents are all in the graveyard, the prisons or in exile, that makes life quiet enough for men like Bianqui. But silence isn't peace.'

'Quite. Quite. Bianqui does tend to extremes.' The look in Gonzales's eyes as he lit another cigarette suggested that he was still weighing up something in his mind.

'You smoke too much, Gilberto.' Diaz spoke lightly – an attempt to ease the tension.

He smiled. That old, easy smile. 'So my doctor tells me. But then, if you remember, I always did everything too much.'

'And how is Marcela?' It was a polite question. Diaz had not seen Gonzales's wife for years.

'Well, I believe. In Santa Cruz at the moment. Don't see much of her these days.' His sigh was just a trifle histrionic as he added, 'Politics play havoc with a man's personal life.'

Remembering Gonzales's reputation as a womaniser, Diaz made no attempt to conceal his amusement. 'They never got in the way of yours, Gilberto.'

By now he was beginning to suspect that Gonzales's composure was a façade. This was a seriously worried man. Worried, but still in control. Diaz would have to strike a fine balance between reassurance and ultimatum. A few more pleasantries about the old days, and then Diaz came to the point.

'Well, Gilberto, time is running out. Have you decided what you are going to do?'

'That depends on you.'

Diaz held his breath. 'We don't really have to offer you anything?'

The Minister gave him a sharp look, and then shot an uneasy glance towards the door. Did he fear he had walked into a trap? Diaz continued evenly: 'But I won't deny that we could be of use to each other. You control national broadcasting.'

'Are you serious?'

'Deadly serious.'

'I just hand it over to you! To you? I would be in jail before morning.'

'When the time comes you will know.'

'Hypothetically, of course. How would I know?'

'Someone will tell you. But you will already know. You aren't a fool.'

Gonzales fell silent again; Diaz leaned back and waited. Outside they could hear the sea lashing against rocks. Was the storm breaking? Then the long mournful cry of a seabird. Gonzales got up again and looked out of the window. Then he swung around.

'I'm not a poor man. I could live quite well in Madrid or Barcelona.'

'You are a politician, not a playboy, Gilberto. What will it be? Minister of Tourism or playing dominos in some café in Madrid?'

Gonzales sat down. His eyes stiffened as the hard bargaining began. 'I quite like the Information ministry.'

Diaz eyed him coolly. 'You know better.'

'The Foreign Ministry?'

'You can't speak Chinese, and we have someone else for that.'

'Ah, Francisco.' Gonzales scrutinised Diaz's face, hoping for some confirmation that he had guessed correctly. Then he thought of an objection. 'You know Francisco will sell out to Beijing.'

Diaz spoke with unexpected sharpness. 'Francisco is not for sale.'

Gonzales shrugged. 'Transport?'

Diaz shook his head. 'Tourism.'

'Commerce? Actually I could be quite useful. I know most of the corporate heads.'

Diaz paused to deliberate. This was no easy decision. Wong and Paez would want to nationalise everything immediately, whereas Diaz believed that for the foreseeable future a mixed economy best suited Costadorean conditions. Gonzales, not driven by ideological belief, would be pragmatic.

His very flexibility might make him best suited for this important portfolio during the transition period.

Gonzales was now looking at him intently in a way that told him the Minister had come to his bottom line. Smiling, Diaz rose from the table to indicate the interview was over. 'I'll let you know our decision in a couple of days.'

* * * * *

Now alone, Diaz sank into a chair and leaned forward on the table. In his mind's eye he could still see Gonzales sitting there in the empty chair. Suave smile, shrewd eyes. The pungent smell of his Cuestra Negra cigarette still lingered.

Minister for Commerce! The deal was not without merit. An incipient government would benefit from Gonzales's considerable executive experience. But some comrades would not easily forget that this man once served Bianqui. Could he persuade them to look beyond the armed struggle to the building of peace?

'Are you ready, Dr Diaz?' Looking towards the door he saw a fresh-faced man in navy anorak.

'Ready? Where am I going, Pablo?'

'Victor's place. It's safer there.'

Diaz gave a cynical grin. 'Are they afraid Gonzales will send someone back here to arrest me?'

The man shrugged. 'I've got my orders. A car is waiting.' He looked at his watch. 'We must hurry. I'm told there's someone else to see you.'

CHAPTER TWENTY-ONE

They crept up the back staircase.

'Some tea, Celia? The green stuff? In my room?'

Exhilarated, bright-eyed, slightly intoxicated, Celia nodded happily. Green tea, she agreed, was just what she needed.

At the top of the staircase Delaney looked down the corridor. No one there. He grabbed her hand. 'Come on.' Then he added with a grin, 'We're behaving like a couple of burglars'.

She giggled. 'We might have a flair for it, Mike.'

While the kettle boiled, Delaney sprawled out in an armchair. Sitting opposite, she pulled off her headscarf. As Delaney eyed the bronze tresses falling on her shoulders, he thought of making love to her. Thought of it, then put it out of his mind.

'It was fun tonight, wasn't it, Celia?'

'It was wonderful. I can tell my friends in London that I ate in Eddie Chang's place.'

'Only one more day.'

She nodded. 'It's hard to believe that by Saturday I'm on my way.' She tensed just a little. 'Well, I hope so.'

Delaney's eyes narrowed. 'It's all arranged, isn't it?'

'Yes, so I'm told. It's just that I don't know *what* exactly has been arranged.'

'They haven't told you yet?'

'I had a message from Alfonso that I would be contacted Saturday morning. I don't have to do anything. Just wait.'

170

Delaney got up to make the tea. As he handed her a cup of the steaming brew he saw that she was looking at him strangely.

'You do trust Alfonso, don't you?'

Lifting his own tea from the tray, Delaney sat down. He hesitated before answering. 'Celia, I have no reason whatever to distrust Alfonso.' He became silent as he looked into his cup, his attention momentarily caught by the play of light reflecting in the green liquid.

When he looked up again she seemed to be trying to read something in his face. 'Are you thinking it could go wrong on Saturday?' she asked.

His assurance was cheerful but facile. 'Why should anything go wrong?'

'But something is worrying you, Mike.'

'Not really. It's just that I would have liked to take you to the boat on Saturday. To see you off safely.'

She spoke eagerly. 'I'd like you to come ….'

'But I may not be able to.' Her smile faded as he continued. 'You know I'm not here on holiday. It's my job to go wherever there's trouble. And there's plenty of that in Sonora just now. The rebel army is advancing. There was something in the news about an explosion in the centre of Sonora. Don't know the details ….' Pausing, he looked up at the electric light which had just wavered erratically. Something atmospheric, he thought, remembering the expected storm. When he looked at her again he caught, just for a second, an intensity of expression in her face, as though she were probing the very depth of his soul. As their eyes met, her face relaxed into a smile. How little I know of her, he thought. 'So if I'm not around on Saturday, will you be all right?'

'Don't worry about me, Mike.'

'Taking you out to Eddie Chang's place this evening was a sort of farewell celebration, I guess.'

'It was a wonderful farewell.' Her voice became wistful. 'Something good to remember about Costadora.'

'But it's only farewell to Ciu Costa. We're having dinner together next time I'm in London?'

'It's a deal. Don't forget.'

When Celia left Delaney turned on the radio hoping to pick up the rebel station. Radio Libertad was jammed. The government did all it could to stop the rebel broadcasts. CNR, the government-controlled station, was blaring out its usual strident and unconvincing propaganda – workers denouncing their union leaders for having misled them; rebel army recruits deserting in their multitudes; the Christian Mothers' Union calling for peace; and just about everyone declaring their undying love for Bianqui. One news item convinced Delaney that the government must now be in a real funk – little Pilar Diaz's alleged plea to her father. Delaney gave a sardonic laugh as the newscaster's voice took on a sickly-sweet piety. 'Please, Daddy, don't let there be a war. If you are still alive give yourself up.'

Leaning back in the chair he absently lit a cigarette. Then remembering his declared intention to give up smoking – something he and Helen tried to do on and off – he immediately stubbed it out and flung the packet into the wastepaper basket. He had begun to pace the room restlessly when the telephone rang. The caller, a male voice speaking softly in Spanish, conveyed a secrecy and urgency.

'Mr Delaney. Could you come down to the lobby. Straight away?'

CHAPTER TWENTY-TWO

The car slowed to a halt. 'We're here, Mr Delaney.' The driver, who had been taciturn during the journey, smiled. Well almost a smile. 'I'm sorry about the bumpy ride. This is not a main road.'

What godforsaken place is this, thought Delaney? Alighting from the car, he followed the man up an uneven path towards a cottage. It appeared to be desolate countryside, yet they could not be far from the city since the journey had taken not more than twenty minutes. A moment of doubt. Had he been wise to get into a car with this stranger on the pretext that Diaz had agreed to an interview? He recalled how journalists and aid workers had been taken hostage in places like Beirut, Indonesia and Pakistan. But there was now no turning back.

The man knocked three times on a heavily curtained window, then called out something which Delaney took to be some sort of password. The door swung open and Roberto Diaz's athletic frame filled the doorway. Blue jeans, rough hemp tunic of the fishing folk, the fugitive looked very much part of the local milieu. He smiled as he proffered his hand in greeting.

'You must be Mr Delaney. Sorry I couldn't see you earlier. I've had a very full day.' He turned towards the driver. 'No need to wait. I can get Lucio to take Mr Delaney back.'

'Thank you for agreeing to this interview, Dr Diaz.'

'My pleasure.' There was a formal courtesy in Diaz's voice as he ushered his guest inside. Delaney's quick eye took in the details of his surroundings. Low ceiling with timber beams. In the corner a roughly-hewn table and chairs which had a peasant do-it-yourself look. In the centre a couple of faded, well-used armchairs. Straw mats on the floor. A strictly utility place. On the wall just one picture to relieve the bareness – a print depicting the Sierra Guadaloupe. No knickknacks, no books, no family photographs. Nothing to denote that Diaz actually lived here. Delaney guessed that he probably didn't. More likely he moved from one safe house to another, his movements known only to his closest associates.

Diaz waved towards an armchair. 'Please sit down, Mr Delaney.' He placed himself in the chair opposite. 'I believe we have some friends in common.'

'Yes indeed.' Delaney wondered if he meant Alfonso, or his Costadorean contacts in Manila Or was he thinking of Celia? A quick assessment of his host. Diffident, perhaps, but there was a touch of warmth in his dark, pensive eyes. Delaney sensed a vitality behind his reserve. Diaz, no doubt, was also sizing up his visitor.

'A drink? I'm afraid we've only beer. The local brew. White polanza.'

Delaney, anxious not to delay the interview, declined. He drew a notebook from his pocket. 'Enjoying the sweet taste of freedom?'

'It takes a little getting used to.'

'In what way?'

'In so many ways. Like forgetting that you can open a door and walk out. You don't have to wait for someone else to unlock it.' He laughed. 'And I was away only ten months.'

Delaney nodded. He remembered that Celia had been locked up for almost two years. 'Long enough, I guess, when you're anxious to get on with your revolution.'

'You wanted to talk to me about the revolution.' Diaz's tone became guarded. 'You do know I'm not a military man?'

'Yes, I know that. I don't need military men – at least not yet.'

Diaz leaned forward. He fixed a penetrating look on his visitor, like a tutor about to tease information out of his student. 'I'm puzzled to know why you should be so keen to interview me, Mr Delaney. I'm not the only dissident they locked up. Nor am I the first one to escape. Juarez managed it a year ago without the assistance of an earthquake.'

Delaney nodded. 'Juarez is a brave man. There are plenty of brave men out there. But you are the only one they call the Conscience of the Revolution.'

Diaz gave a short laugh. 'I've no idea why they call me that. The real liberators are those who have taken up arms and are prepared to fight. You know I've never fired a shot in anger. Oh, yes, I do carry a gun – but only for my own protection. I'm a writer, a historian; I have certain ideas on the way forward. But ideas don't win wars. They only help people understand why they are fighting.'

Delaney's eyes had a glow of expectancy; he sensed that Diaz was beginning to open up. 'Ideas play their part in the grand scheme of things – at least according to our poet Yeats.'

'Yeats?' An abstracted expression as he appeared to be digging up some half-forgotten memory. 'I remember as a student reading his poem on the Irish uprising of 1916 and discussing it with Elena ….' He smiled. '….the girl who became my wife. If I remember correctly, in that poem Yeats referred to a patriotic play he had written. He agonised as to whether that had been the influence which brought men into the armed struggle, eventually leading to their deaths.'

Delaney nodded. 'You remember these lines:

Did that play of mine send out
Certain men the English shot?'

'Yes, yes indeed.' There was a bemused expression on Diaz's face as though he wondered where this was leading. Delaney shifted in his chair. 'Neither did Yeats ever fire a shot, yet T. S. Eliot once said that Yeats was one of those few writers whose history is the history of our own times; who are part of the consciousness of their age, which cannot be understood without them. It is in that sense that people see you as the Conscience of the Revolution.'

Diaz gave a quizzical smile. 'So I'm to blame for all that upheaval out there. Perhaps I should be more careful about what I write.'

'You certainly helped me understand what it was all about.'

'I may have helped *some* people understand. But not all that many. Remember Bianqui banned all of my political works.'

'Still obtainable if you know the right people.' Delaney drew from an inner pocket a copy of Diaz's last political work, "The Betrayal".

'Well, yes that ....' There was a touch of ironic humour in Diaz's voice as he slipped into English. 'That ruffled a few feathers.'

'Would you care to autograph it?' Delaney handed him a pen.

'Of course.' He started to write, and then looked up. 'Your name is Michael – a variation of Miguel, I suppose – spelt M I C ....' Delaney confirmed the spelling of his name. 'May I call you Michael?'

'Please do.'

'You must call me Roberto.' He handed back the book. Delaney saw he had written: "To Michael. I hope my book gives you some understanding of what Costadora is and what she is striving to be. Fraternal greetings, Roberto Diaz."

As he replaced the book in his inner pocket, he felt Diaz's eyes still assessing him. 'Perhaps, Dr .... Roberto, you could clarify something you wrote in "The Betrayal". I was impressed by what you said in the second chapter: "There can be no liberation without education." Would you care to elaborate?'

'Certainly.' Diaz leaned forward and clasped his hands as though deliberating how best to approach his subject. 'You've seen much of our country ....?'

'Only Ciu Costa and Sonora. I've never been south.'

'Ah, the south. Now that's a prime example of what I had in mind. Another world altogether. Home of the big land barons. A kind of aristocracy with their roots in the old world.' He raised his hand in a minimising gesture. 'Don't misunderstand me. I've no ideological objections to gracious living – as long as it's not built on the misery of others.'

Delaney, notebook on lap and pen poised, nodded silently as Diaz warmed to his subject.

'You've no doubt heard it said that I oppose private property. That is to misrepresent my views. What I oppose is latifundia – large land holdings belonging to often absentee owners, where great estates are worked by hired labour for near starvation wages.'

By now Diaz, who had retreated into his own world of ideas, seemed to have forgotten his visitor. And Delaney, lured by the prophet's voice, at times found himself carried into the same visionary world. Only with difficulty he resumed the role of objective observer. Not hard to see why Bianqui locked him up. That charismatic voice holding forth on social justice must have seemed like dynamite to young students, already eager to right the world's wrongs. A dynamite that would one day blow apart the world of the rich and powerful. Not difficult to see why the announcement: 'Diaz will speak' brought thousands of students and workers flocking to participate in an illegal demonstration.

A smile at Delaney as though he suddenly remembered his visitor's presence. 'But you are probably thinking, Michael, that there's nothing new in this. Just the basic tenets of socialism adapted to Costadorean conditions.'

'I think you put a greater emphasis on education than other writers.' He leaned forward. 'Could we stay on this theme for the moment. I presume you mean that education would open the minds of the poor to abstract ideas such as democracy …. Could stir them into wanting to fight for things like civil rights ….?'

'More than that. Make them aware of rights they *already have* under the 1972 constitution. You probably know that the constitution allows for free primary and secondary education, with university scholarships reserved for gifted young people from poorer families.'

'Yes, indeed. With a system like that you should be the best-educated country in south-east Asia. Why isn't it working?'

'Because the whole social structure of Costadora is in need of reform. In rural areas you find children as young as eight no longer at school, labouring long hours for a pittance on the landed estates.'

'There is still child labour!'

An enigmatic smile from Diaz. 'Don't just blame Bianqui for that. Blame it on the penchant of the poor to feel eternally grateful. The man of no property faced with starvation is grateful to whoever gives him a job. If there are too many mouths to feed he is even more grateful to whoever gives his child a job. The poor are encouraged to think of themselves as mere units of labour – not creative beings with a potential for better things.'

Delaney assumed an affable expression so as to rob the question of its sting. 'How would you answer those of your critics who say that what you call education is simply indoctrination?' He remembered that Jackson had once dubbed the Constitutionalists "a bunch of communists". Diaz was simply a more interesting "commie" than the others.

Diaz gave a dismissive laugh. 'Are these critics arguing for the status quo? Remember we have something like eighty percent illiteracy in the south. No, it is not our intention to replace Bianqui with some other repressive system which silences dissent, bans books or prevents workers from organising.'

'Since the constitution makes provision for universal education, how do you explain the south's eighty percent illiteracy rate?'

Diaz shrugged. 'Even before ruling by decree, Bianqui was adept at exploiting loopholes in the constitution. He held it to be the responsibility of local authorities, not the state, to provide schools. That's fine in Ciu Costa and Sonora. It works well in the western farming cooperatives where they provide good, community-funded schools. But in the south the only local authorities *are* the land barons. Universal education conflicts with their labour needs. Elsewhere most village councils are too poor to provide for anything more than primary education.'

A mournful cry like that of a sea bird caused both men to look towards the window. 'The storm. It must be on its way,' said Diaz thoughtfully.

Delaney nodded. He remembered his childhood in the west of Ireland where the migration of seagulls inland always preceded bad weather.

'It would appear then, Roberto, that your vision of a new Costadora must include land reform. If you abolish child labour and diversify the economy in the south, you will have to find some other system for working the land.'

'Yes indeed. I haven't spelt that out in any detail in "The Betrayal". What sort of land reforms we set up is for a democratic government to decide. But I personally would favour the cooperative system.'

'Like they have in the Western Province? Near Arganda?'

'That's exactly what I had in mind. The western cooperatives are a find example of local democracy – good schools, good standards of living – they even have their own hospitals.'

'I'd like to visit there sometime.'

'That could be arranged. When …. when the country is more settled.'

Delaney leaned back. 'So, in effect, you believe that without education all other reforms are meaningless.'

'That about sums it up. Would it surprise you to know that my friend Francisco – that is Francisco Wong – has met landless labourers in the south who didn't yet know that they had the right to vote. That even their fathers had had that right?'

'Well, I can see who profits from that.' Delaney's eyes sharpened at the mention of Wong's name. Could this be the same Francisco Wong, a defence lawyer, who had made a reputation for himself as defender of political dissidents. He gave up legal practice when Bianqui abolished the independent judiciary and was now said to hold high rank in the rebel army? Delaney framed his question carefully knowing Diaz was unlikely to confirm Wong's rebel activities. 'Wasn't he the defence lawyer in the Juarez and Gomes sedition trial a few years back?'

'The same. He no longer practises law.'

'You say he's a friend of yours?'

179

'Since our schooldays. We both attended Sancti Spiritus College.' He smiled. 'I was a scholarship boy. We were also at university together.'

Diaz recognised an opportunity to get Diaz talking about his boyhood. 'Yes, I heard it said you were the first lad from the Cove to make it to university. Your family still lives in that area?'

Sadness clouded Diaz's eyes. 'My father died in a drowning accident when I was a student. Mother died just months later.'

'You have brothers and sisters?'

'There were three of us. One died in childhood. My sister now lives in the United States. San Francisco. She married a Mexican.'

'Your father was a fisherman – a precarious occupation. Did that influence you politically?'

Diaz paused as though weighing up this proposition. 'We did know some hungry times. But I wouldn't change anything. There's no better place to grow up than Fisherman's Cove.'

'Any special memories?'

A note of nostalgia crept into Diaz's voice as he reminisced about that innocent world of long ago. Going out in the boat with his father in the freshness of morning, face to the wind. Playing football on the beach. A few anecdotes about boyish escapades and pranks – the same normal boyhood that matched Delaney's own. He touched only lightly on the hard times; stormy weather when it was too dangerous for the boats to go out and therefore they had no income. That seemed to have impressed him less in terms of hardship than as a memory or the courage and dignity of his parents in all their difficulties.

'So, how come you ended up an academic?'

Diaz smiled as though he, too, found this a little odd. 'Well, like most lads in the Cove, I grew up thinking that I would be a fisherman. Winning a scholarship to a prestigious school, Sancti Spiritus, changed all that. I remember how proud my father had been when the letter arrived offering me a scholarship place. Mother, however, was a little anxious. She worried about how a poor boy from the Cove would fit into a smart place like Sancti Spiritus.'

'And how did you fit in?'

'At first I felt lonely. Lonely and bewildered. I think it was my passion for football which broke down barriers. I got on the school team. One of the first friends I made was Francisco Wong.'

Delaney's tone remained casual, but his eyes showed keenness. How much information about Wong could he tease out of Diaz? 'This school you won a scholarship to. It must have been a real hotbed of radicalism.'

'Why do you assume that?'

'You and Wong there at the same time. Two of Bianqui's most wanted men.'

'I don't recall that we were very political at Sancti Spiritus. All our combative energy went into things like sport. We discussed political theory certainly, but it was all very bookish. I don't think any of my contemporaries thought then that we would one day have to fight a revolution. At university it became more serious. Francisco and I were both active in the Federation of Costadorean Students.'

A smile from Delaney as though the question were mere rhetoric. 'Wong is an odd sort of socialist, is he not?' Delaney recalled rumours he had heard of Wong's reputation for womanising; his predilection for expensive couture and fast cars – if indeed the rumours were true. A slight arching of Diaz's eyebrows sent a message that he was prepared to defend his friend. Delaney retreated glibly into generalities. 'From what I hear he comes from a very privileged background.'

'Yes indeed. His father owns several shops in China Town. Very rich. Francisco was always a bit of a rebel.'

'Weren't you also a founding member of the Constitutional Alliance? Set up at university?'

'Yes, but not in my student days. That happened later, after I became a lecturer at San Miguel University.'

'So, how did you change from a football-loving college boy into a political activist?'

'Gradually. There was no defining moment when I decided I was a revolutionary. You could perhaps say that for my generation the deteriorating political situation coincided with our growing to maturity. It fell to our generation to find the solutions.'

Diaz was now talking easily as though to an old friend. Without any further prompting from Delaney he went on to describe the gradual drift into a revolutionary situation: curbs on the press, the abolition of an independent judiciary and eventually the widespread arrest of dissidents on so-called grounds of sedition. 'Believe me, we did try all the peaceful options. Now there is nothing left but to fight for our freedom.'

It was a suitable quote to round off the interview. Delaney glanced at his watch. 'Almost midnight.' He rose. 'Roberto, thank you for giving me so much of your time.'

A courteous smile from Diaz as he sprang to his feet. 'Glad I could be of help. I'll call Lucio to drive you back.'

As Delaney shoved his notebook back into an inner pocket, his expression exuded quiet satisfaction. It had been a good interview.

* * * * *

Delaney kicked off his shoes and flopped onto the bed. It was good to be back. Lucio had proved to be a reckless driver. He would probably be a menace even on a well-lit city highway, but careering down a desolate, bumpy roadway in the darkness of night was an exercise that seemed to have overtones of suicide. Curfew or not, it was a relief to see the city lights. Foreign journalists were sometimes exempt from curfews, if they sought permission. Delaney had no prior permission and his driver no exemption. Nor had he forgotten the penchant of the police to shoot first and ask questions later. Near to the back entrance of Habana Vieja he had seen groups of men loitering in the street. One, who seemed to recognise Lucio, raised his arm to wave him on; he wore a red armband. Clearly Bianqui's writ did not hold in all parts of the city.

Now it was well after midnight. Would Radio Libertad still be broadcasting? As he reached out to switch the radio on, the telephone rang. It was Hepworth asking if he could come down to the bar.

'Anything wrong, Tony?'

'No, nothing wrong. Fielding has arrived from Sonora. If you want a word with him, come down now. He's staying overnight in Ciu Costa.'

'Just one night?' Delaney sounded surprised. He had got to know Eric Fielding, the British television journalist, when in Bosnia. Fielding didn't normally cover this part of the world. 'Why is he in Costadora?'

'Says he came because Thompson couldn't make it. He's in the Middle East.'

Delaney's pulse quickened. If they sent a camera crew to Sonora, things must be coming to a head. 'Right, Tony, I'll be down straight away.' Before leaving he phoned the switchboard to book an alarm call. An early rise was advisable as he needed to warn Carlos as soon as possible to be ready to go to Sonora.

* * * * *

Celia was wakened by a high wind howling, wailing, ululating. The storm had broken. Rising from bed, she went to the window and looked out. A primeval fury had gripped the world. Seized by a bizarre impression that the swollen seas were advancing towards her, she instinctively stepped backwards. Over in Marine Gardens, through sheets of rain, she thought she could make out the dark, straggling outline of an uprooted tree. Then something without shape whirled past the window; some debris driven by the wind. For a moment she felt herself to be part of the turmoil. An oddly liberating feeling. Enthralled, she continued to gaze. And then a feeling of sadness. Had the storm come too soon? When Mike had talked to her last night about going to Sonora – a possibility, nothing definite – she found herself hoping, almost believing, that the impending storm would delay him in Ciu Costa. That he would be stormbound at least until Saturday.

As she continued gazing into the tempestuous world outside, she was seized by a strong compulsion to throw a

183

jacket over her shoulders and walk out into the night. To walk alone. Free. No one out there but herself. No need to avert her head or worry that she might be recognised. She tried to remember what freedom felt like – the way she used to feel a long time ago.

A caprice she dare not indulge. She remembered stories she had heard of people caught out in Costadorean storms being swept out to sea. I'm still a prisoner, she thought as she got back into bed.

For a while she lay wakeful and alert, listening to the winds and seas Something miraculous was going on out there – frightening, but still wonderful. Nature at its most terrible had always some element of renewal. Something destroyed; something rekindled. She owed her life to an earthquake. Was there something benign even in the fury of this storm? She began to visualise the damage – roads blocked by landslides and fallen trees. Broken rail communications. Perhaps it wouldn't be possible to get to Sonora just yet. Would the storm leave Mike with her for just one more day?

* * * * *

The storm also woke Roberto Diaz. Unable to sleep again, he rose and sat at a table by the window. These few hours of solitude were his opportunity – the first since his escape – of writing a letter to his wife.

For a moment he sat staring at the notepad trying to collect his thoughts. The turmoil outside was distracting him. Storms brought in their wake swollen rivers and blocked roads, not ideal conditions for transporting Varela's missiles over to the East Province. Was it beginning to abate? The wind was now blowing fitfully, convulsively, like someone crying. There was no way of knowing before morning the extent of the storm damage. Resolutely he cleared his mind and began to write:

My darling Elena,
By now you will know that I am no longer in Monteverde. While it is wonderful to be out of that vile place,

184

it pains me that I cannot yet be with you and Pilar. As I did not leave Monteverde with Bianqui's blessing, it would not be safe for me to come to you yet.

Pausing, he looked again towards the window. Dawn was beginning to break but the sky was still black with storm clouds. A shrill wind rose to a crescendo. Like the fury of war. Soon, very soon, another storm would break. The furore unleashed by the revolution might be even greater than anything nature could send. His hand stole to a gold crucifix around his neck – Elena's gift. Let the conflict be short, he prayed. And let it be decisive, so that Costadorean lives might be spared.

If the revolution fails, I might never see Elena again. He shuddered, at the same time cursing his weakness in even contemplating such a thought. No, that was unthinkable. They would not fail. With Varela's adherence, a rising now had more chance of succeeding than at any previous time. Yet in his heart he knew that even if the revolution succeeded, at least some of his comrades would fall. His own survival was not guaranteed. Bracing himself, he dismissed his doubts and continued writing.

At this moment there are many things in my mind. Things that must be left unsaid. I'm sure you always understood that sacrifices would be demanded of all of us. But I am hopeful, dearest, that the conflict will be a short one and that we will soon be together again.

I have one lovely memory which sustained me during those dark days in Monteverde. It sustains me still. You and I, still students, walking along the beach. The last day of the vacation. You were wearing a white dress and the shell bracelet I had bought from that old pedlar down at the boat slip. I remember well pushing back a wisp of hair that the wind had blown on your forehead. You then clasped my hand in yours and pressed it to your lips. It was that day we decided, despite your father's disapproval, that we were already secretly betrothed.

I send a thousand kisses and hugs to our little Pilar.

185

As Diaz was penning his signature there came a light knocking on the door. A thin-faced man with stubby moustache looked in. 'I've made some breakfast.'

'Any news, Lucio?'

'Things seem quiet.'

'What about Sonora?'

'Haven't heard anything.'

Diaz's face firmed in an expression of concern. Did that mean the weapons had not yet got through?

* * * * *

Just after day-break Bianqui stood at the window, looking out on a troubled world. Still stormy, but less so than when he first woke. He stood upright, feet apart and hands behind his back. Despite the military stance, he cut a squat figure in his white linen suit. Somewhat different from the photographs of that leaner, younger Bianqui which hung in public buildings. Bianqui was waiting for breakfast to be served. A working breakfast, during which Brigadier Miranda would brief him on the military situation. As he continued to gaze out onto the Grande Plaza, the sallow-faced President twiddled with his sleek, black moustache. It was a recently acquired adornment which some said, unkindly, gave him "that Hitler look".

Why did Miranda want to see him so urgently? Some problem about the Western Province, he gathered. His brow furrowed as he thought irritably: Haven't I enough problems already in the East? And anyway what had the Western Province to do with Brigadier Miranda? Varela had not reported anything amiss. Miranda was normally an unassuming man. Efficient, loyal but unpretentious. His bold insistence on speaking to the President alone was uncharacteristic – and, to tell the truth, a little worrying. Was something going on out in the west that he didn't know about?

The sight of young guards crossing the Plaza, wet, bedraggled and despondent, evoked images and feelings from long ago. As a young soldier from the Western Province, a

186

gauche country lad then, he himself had done guard duty at the Palace. Memories flooded back of another famous storm which had caused widespread devastation – they called it the night of the Great Turbulence. Shivering and hungry, he had stood guard there while bitter winds bore down with uncontrolled fury from the Sierra Guadaloupe, lashing his face and almost sweeping him from his feet. That had been the longest guard duty in memory. Hitherto proud to be a palace guard, that night the first feelings of disloyalty had stirred within him. How he had resented the nation's first citizen sheltered within those splendid walls, warmly attired, deferentially waited upon and dining beneath the chandeliers.

An uncomfortable thought crossed the President's mind that although his government had invested heavily in propaganda, the loyalty of no one, not even his own soldiers, could ever be taken for granted.

CHAPTER TWENTY-THREE

Saturday morning. Nerves taut, Celia waited for the tap on the door. The waiter who had brought the passport – he called himself Felipe – was to signal the time for departure. The instructions were precise. Be ready by seven thirty. She would be fetched not later than eight. She was to leave by the back entrance. A car would be waiting. She mustn't speak to the driver, who already knew were to take her.

To get her through formalities as quickly as possible she was given a boat ticket in advance. Two passport control gates would be operating. She was shown a photograph of a passport official – tall with moustache. 'Remember what he looks like,' she was told. Go through the control gate where he is on duty. No other. When she disembarked at George she would have to work things out for herself. As government administrative offices would be shut over the festival period, she should go straight to the Residency.

She glanced around the room. Initially a place of refuge, it now had an uncomfortable emptiness. The room of a dead woman. Nothing to relieve the monotony of waiting. No Mike with whom to chat and joke – to make her forget for a while that she was a fugitive. Mike seemed in a hurry when he came to say goodbye yesterday morning; the escalating unrest in Sonora meant he could not delay his departure. He reminded her that they would meet again in London. Kissing her goodbye, he seemed full of breezy optimism – as though he were brooking no possibility of the escape bid failing. When he had gone, a feeling of loneliness overwhelmed her.

Felipe arrived just before eight. He lifted her weekend bag and told her to follow him. Avoiding the lifts – usually busy at this hour – they descended by the back staircase. Normally taciturn, Felipe chatted to her as she followed him downstairs. Tense, absorbed in her own fears, she was only vaguely aware of what he was saying. Something about the currency; she could change her queredos into George pounds on the boat. Something else about favourable weather conditions; she should make the crossing in a couple of hours.

The car was waiting by the back entrance. As though seized by a sense of urgency, Felipe ceased to be talkative. Briskly opening the car door, he waited until she was seated, then handed in her bag. As she uttered some words of thanks, he turned on his heel and was gone.

The car pulled off quickly. Out by the rear exit of the car park and down a long street which ran parallel to the promenade. The driver, thin-faced and stony-eyed, uttered not a word. Just once Celia caught his eye in the car mirror. Tensing, she noted a flicker of interest. He knows who I am, she thought.

They stopped at traffic lights. From the open window of a nearby car, a radio broadcast blared out: parts of Sonora ablaze last night, the rebels had been repulsed. In the car mirror she could see grim foreboding on the driver's face. A foreboding that touched her own being as she remembered that Mike was somewhere out there in the middle of it. And what would happen to Roberto if the rebellion failed? Would he forever be a fugitive? Or worse still, hunted down and recaptured? Would Alfonso and Dolores suffer for having backed a losing side? No, the rebels *mustn't* lose. It was unthinkable. She surprised herself by the vehemence of that inner protest. Costadora's revolution had taken on a personal significance.

Thickening traffic, taller buildings and multitudinous humanity indicated that they were nearing the city centre. Then a police check-point. 'Have your passport ready, señorita,' the driver called to her. But even as her trembling hand pulled the passport from the handbag, the policeman waved them on. They were doing only random checks. The sign for a traffic diversion caused the driver to take a sharp turn to the left. Just ahead she could see the sea. A calm expanse of silvery blue; it was as though the storm had never been.

Now at the far end of Paseo de Malecón, she could see a cliff pathway. The same pathway that she and Roberto had used on the day of their escape. And there was the rock on which she had sat looking out towards King George Island. All that now seemed a lifetime away. Another ten minutes along Calle de Puerto, then the docks came into view.

The car slowed to a halt. Hopping out briskly, the driver opened the door. He case a furtive gaze around as he lifted out her weekend bag. 'That queue over there, señorita. The shorter one. That's for passengers who already have boat tickets.'

She looked in the direction he pointed. 'When does the boat sail?'

'In forty minutes. But they will let you on board in about a quarter of an hour. Good luck, señorita.' He hopped back into the car and drove off.

For a moment Celia stood still, staring around. Now utterly alone, she felt afraid. Then, pulling herself together, she walked slowly towards the queue, head erect, breathing evenly. Only a quarter of an hour to wait – nothing could happen in that short time. Everything fine so far. Help me, God – please!

An assortment of people waited to board. Young people talking in loud voices, hyped up in anticipation of the festival, some carrying musical instruments. Tourists chattering in a variety of languages, cameras slung over their shoulders, many sporting colourful T-shirts. Just ahead of her in the queue was a tubby man of about fifty wearing a baseball hat back-to-front, shorts, a bomber jacket and bright red socks stretching halfway up his hairy legs. Celia's tense expression softened to a smile. What weird fancy dress some people wore when on holiday, she thought.

Not all were on a pleasure trip. There were those with sad, anxious faces – whole families by the look of them – sitting on enormous piles of luggage. Were these Costadoreans attempting to flee the country before the fighting began? At least they take attention away from me, she thought, as she saw a policeman eyeing them suspiciously while pacing up and down. Catching his eye she managed a smile which, curiously, he returned.

Glancing around, she noted a dreary shabbiness. The grim docklands contrasted starkly with chic Paseo de Malecón, or picturesque Fisherman's Cove. It is as though I had already left the country, she thought as she eyed the dingy, one-storeyed restaurant with faded curtains, wedged between two stark, grey warehouses. Grinding winches were lifting cargo onto a number of ships. The port was a hub of commercial activity.

The interminable waiting. Why had the queue not started to move? Surely she had been here more than fifteen minutes. Then a shuffling forward. Glancing ahead she could see that the people at the top of the queue were now going through the ticket barrier. Quickly, in an orderly fashion, no hold-ups. The policeman who stood at the side regarded them indifferently. She was on her way. Or almost. There was still passport control. Carefully she memorised the details of the passport official whom she should approach – moustache, tall, about thirtyish.

There were now a mere dozen people ahead. She felt her heart pounding. Soon she would stand on the ship's deck and see the coastline of Ciu Costa receding. Then freedom.

A hand touched her arm. 'Miss Martinez?' Terror transfixed her. As her name was called a second time, she swung around. Staring at her with sombre expression was a man dressed in blue denims, sun-bronzed face, with receding hairline.

'No, no. You're mistaken. My name is Darcy.'

Speaking in a low voice, the man tightly gripped her arm. 'You must come with me, Miss Martinez. Quickly, please.'

Trembling violently she attempted to free herself from his grip. 'No, no. I tell you, you've made a mistake. My name is not Martinez.'

The man's sharp eyes pierced her. His voice became insistent. 'Please, Miss Martinez, don't make a scene. It won't do any good. Just come with me. Quietly.'

A bizarre sensation that something was tightening around her chest – it impeded her breathing – enfeebled her attempts to pull away. Her legs began to weaken. Was she going to fall? The man's grip tightened. Even as she continued trying to wrench free she knew that resistance was futile. Or was it? If she put up a fight they might shoot her to prevent escape. Better that than the gallows.

'Get a move on,' someone shouted from behind. An impatient traveller who didn't understand why the queue had stopped.

The man holding Celia gave a powerful wrench, pulling her out of the queue. 'Go ahead, the lady isn't travelling.' Another sleek-faced man stepped forward unobtrusively and picked up her weekend bag. 'This way, Miss Martinez, we've got a car waiting.'

Tears blinded Celia's eyes as she was led away, stumbling, almost fainting.

CHAPTER TWENTY-FOUR

'Nice car,' Carlos remarked as he tried to edge their hired vehicle past the horse-driven cart in front. 'Pity about the traffic.'

Delaney looked out uneasily from the front passenger seat. So far progress had been slow. Although a primary route connecting Costadora's two main cities, the roadway coped ill with modern traffic. Two hours along the road and ahead was a jumble of horse-driven carts intermingling with a few motor vehicles and bicycles. To add to their frustration, the farmer just ahead in a wide straw hat was herding sheep along the road at leisurely pace, obstructing the traffic flow.

Coming in the opposite direction was a thirty-year old, brightly painted bus, filled to capacity. Cheap luggage and boxes were piled on the roof, excess passengers sitting astride their luggage. These were the "earth-diggers", a nickname Costadoreans gave to the wide-eyed, guileless peasants from remote rural areas who poured into Ciu Costa looking for work.

Delaney jerked forward as Carlos swerved suddenly to avoid a jay-walking sheep. 'Where do we hang out in Sonora?'

Carlos was a good photographer, heedless of his own safety. He got shots that agency photographers would die for, but his driving left a lot to be desired.

Delaney leaned back in his seat. 'The Imperial Hotel.' Then he grinned as he remembered that Carlos affected not to like what he called "those swanky joints". 'Hope you brought a tie and change of shirt.'

'You booked? When the Pope was here the television guys took it over and we had to sleep in the lounge. Remember?'

I remember. I booked this time.' An image of Helen, bright-eyed and laughing, came into his mind. Why did he think of her now?

'What the hell ....' Delaney jerked forward once more. Carlos had almost collided with a water buffalo meandering across the road. Carlos gave a cheeky grin. 'Sorry. But it's not the Pan-American highway.'

Another jerk and they came to a complete halt.

'Why have we stopped? An accident?'

Carlos munched on his chewing gum. 'Check-point.'

The sun was radiating down on the car top. It was hot and stuffy. A cyclist edged his way ahead, trying to avoid the sheep which got in his way. Delaney stretched forward to try to ascertain how far away they were from the guards. A gasp of dismay escaped his lips as he saw a BBC van being turned away. The guards were not media-friendly.

Carlos saw it too. With an alacrity that scarcely seemed possible given the limited scope for manoeuvre, he managed to turn around, bumping into the car behind. A volley of abuse from the driver rang in their ears as he turned the car up a side road. Not quite a road. More a twisting, country lane, intended for donkeys, not motor vehicles.

'Carlos, where the hell are we going?'

'There's more than one way to Sonora.'

Delaney eyed the desolage, craggy hillside 'Is this the scenic route?' He reached for the road map.

'You won't find it on the map.'

Delaney slumped back in a gesture of resignation. He would just have to trust Carlos. Stones pounded the bottom of the car like a hail of bullets. Would they hit the petrol tank?

A couple of hours along the godforsaken mountain route seeing neither man nor beast, then they descended to rejoin the main highway. Distant high-rise buildings towered against a smoky skyline. They were about three kilometres from Sonora. Thickening traffic, which forced them to slow down, and a wider roadway suggested that they were approaching a busier metropolis than the elegant capital they had left behind. They did not notice the next security check-point until they were almost alongside it.

Eyeing the khaki uniforms, Delaney tensed. This time there was no convenient side road to offer escape. Carlos cursed in Spanish as he always did when his English gave out.

A gawky, pasty-faced young soldier came alongside the car. Delaney proffered his press credentials. The soldier eyed it up and down with the scrutiny of an illiterate. Spotting that the words were not in the right place, a crafty look came into his eyes. 'Where is your permit?'

'Didn't think I needed one,' Delaney lied glibly. The Ministry of Information often refused permission for foreign journalists to move to an area of conflict.

Carlos held up a card which showed him to be a member of the National Association of Costadorean Photographers. 'He's with me,' he said blandly, as though that somehow legitimised Delaney's presence.

There was a note of finality in the guard's voice as he glared at Delaney. 'You can't go into Sonora without a permit.'

Delaney was in no mood to give in. 'I'm an accredited journalist.'

'You must have a permit,' the soldier repeated like a broken record.

Carlos beamed a brash smile. 'Couldn't we come to some arrangement?' Leaning forward he waved a US dollar note under the guard's nose, its denomination roughly equivalent to what a private would earn in a month.

The guard's eyes glittered but his tight lips had a sullen doggedness. Carlos produced two more banknotes. 'Are these the right papers?'

The guard smiled sheepishly. He reached out, his fingers almost touching the banknotes. A crisp voice from behind caused him to swiftly draw back. 'What's the hold-up here? Are you having some trouble?' Carlos quickly pocketed the banknotes as an officer came alongside them.

'No trouble, sir,' the soldier stammered out. Raising his voice he frowned ferociously at Delaney. 'Go now. You cannot enter Sonora.'

Holding up his press card, Delaney replied blandly: 'I'm an accredited correspondent.'

The officer's expression was obdurate, his tone snappish. 'No one enters Sonora without a permit. You apply for one to the Ministry of Information. Go now!' He scarcely glanced at the card Carlos held up showing his membership of the photographers' association.

Delaney knew it would take days for an application to be processed. 'May I know the reason why?'

'Terrorist criminals attacked the city. They have been repulsed but a state of emergency exists until order has been restored.'

* * * * *

'Not so fast,' Delaney cautioned as Carlos sped back down the main roadway. 'I've got to think.'

'Don't you want to get to Ciu Costa before curfew?'

'I'm here to report a war. We've got to stay in the East Province.'

Carlos munched languidly on his chewing gum as Delaney deliberated. The last news broadcast some hours ago reported that, after fierce clashes with government troops, the rebels had retreated. If an army can't go forward, presumably it goes back to its previous position. He knew that the rebels had controlled Las Pampas, that vast expanse of flat terrain south of the city.

'Carlos, can you get to Las Pampas?'

Carlos's normally languorous eyes widened in surprise. 'Could do. It will be a roundabout way. We can't go through the city.'

'Want to give it a try?'

'Yup.' He moved into another lane to prepare for an exit from the highway.

After what seemed like an interminable twisting and turning through inconsequential byways and mean little streets, they reached the fringes of an industrial suburb. Graffiti on factory walls – slogans such as "Death to Bianqui" and "Free Roberto Diaz" – suggested that this was a district sympathetic to the rebel cause. It had an eerie emptiness. Only the sporadic sound of gunfire indicated that somewhere out in those shadowy streets where was a human presence.

Delaney pressed his face against the window. 'I wish I knew what the hell is going on,' he muttered in a tone of frustration. It was a most elusive war. After the rebel retreat, there had been a news blackout. Music was played from the national radio station. Nothing at all from Radio Libertad.

Buildings thinned out. Open fields came into view. No sign of any other traffic. Just a desolate landscape.

Carlos was looking vaguely troubled. 'This is the beginning of Las Pampas. Where do we go from here?'

'Stop the car, Carlos. I want to look around.'

As the car screeched to a halt, Delaney jumped out and scanned the flat expanse of countryside which stretched monotonously to a distant mountain. He raised his hand to his eyes to shield them from the glare of the setting sun. The land looked bare and arid. Rain storms which had raged out in the west and central provinces had not reached this far east to nourish the thirsty earth. There were few trees; only a farmhouse here and there to relieve the dreary flatness. No human life stirred. Lifting binoculars from the car, he raised them to his eyes. His expression sharpened. 'Carlos, look over there.' Taking the binoculars, Carlos focused them in the direction Delaney had pointed. He gasped. On the mountainside were a number of look-out posts, and at its foot what was clearly an encampment.

Delaney jumped nimbly back into the car. 'Right, Carlos, we head in that direction.'

Carlos stared at him in disbelief. 'That's the rebel army. We'll be shot.'

'We could get shot anywhere. Rebels might be more media-friendly than Bianqui's lot.'

'We don't know that, do we?'

Delaney eyed his photographer quizzically. 'Carlos, I told you I wanted pictures of the conflict. What did you expect?'

'Street fighting and stuff.'

'Well, I'm sorry. The commanders didn't let me in on their plans.'

Carlos was looking unusually edgy. 'Let's go home. It's all over, isn't it? The rebels have been pushed back.'

Delaney waved a hand towards the rebel camp. 'Does it look all over? An encampment that size! They're just regrouping.' This was the last thing Delaney had expected. Carlos afraid! It was not only his exceptional photographic flair but also an impetuous disregard for danger that had made Carlos seem peculiarly suited to covering conflict situations. 'I've never known you to lose your nerve before, Carlos. When the shooting started at the San Remo barracks, I had to drag you away.'

Carlos grimaced. 'That was different. You knew what was going on.'

Delaney slumped back in his seat. So that was it. The danger you knew, even if it were death staring you in the face, got the adrenalin flowing and stirred you to action. But the unknown was too terrifying to contemplate. He was learning something new about his photographer every day.

'All right, Carlos. Stay here, then. I'll go on without you.'

'And leave me to walk back,' Carlos protested.

'*I'll* walk. You keep the car.' He jumped out and removed a jacket and haversack from the boot of the car. Coming round to the front he held up his own camera. Carlos's mouth had firmed into an expression of resignation but his eyes betrayed his nervousness. 'Well go, dammit.'

Delaney turned into a rough sidetrack which, as far as he could see, seemed to be heading in the direction of the encampment. The car engine started up. Now the rumble of the engine sounded nearer. Probably Carlos using the opening of the sidetrack to manoeuvre the car around in the opposite direction. Delaney wanted to turn round and wave just to show there was no ill-feeling, but somehow he could not bring himself to do so.

'Christ! Are you trying to kill me?' Delaney leaped to the side as the car stopped just at his heels. Carlos leaned out of the window. 'Get in, Mike.'

'You're coming after all?'

Carlos spoke airily as though he were now in charge. 'Can't go wandering around on your own at a time like this.' He rolled his chewing gum around his mouth with an exaggerated lethargy. 'Hell, man, you'd get lost without me.'

CHAPTER TWENTY-FIVE

They reached the fringes of the camp. Delaney pointed towards an army vehicle standing beneath a tree. 'We'll park there.' Carlos manoeuvred the car around, pulling up beside the army vehicle. As Delaney got out, his photographer lingered a moment at the wheel, eyeing dubiously the sea of tents. He appeared unable to grasp that getting into the rebel camp could be that easy.

A splash of water caused Delaney to turn around. A duck had flipped across the surface of a nearby river before settling on the smooth, black waters. I'll have a bathe in that river later, he promised himself, conscious that he was sweat-soaked and sticky. He could see fireflies hovering in the night air above the water. Glad to stretch his legs, he ambled a pace or two towards the river. Sweet-smelling and mystical, it was one of those warm, languid nights which belied the reality of war.

'Want some tea?' Carlos was pouring the green brew from a flask into plastic cups.

'Why not?' Delaney's tone suggested he had only half heard. He was still looking towards the river.

'What do we do now?' Carlos asked as they sat on the grass sipping their drink from plastic cups.

Delaney ignored the question. He waved his hand towards the bank of the moonlit river. 'Carlos, look back there. Isn't that another camp at the bend of the river?'

Carlos looked in the direction Delaney was pointing. 'Yup. Looks like the Terani.'

'How do you know?'

'The oula poles outside some of the tents. Something to do with ancestor worship. Or maybe dead warriors.'

Delaney's keen, blue eyes sharpened. It was known that some Terani tribes had thrown in their lot with the rebels; they were reputed to be fierce fighters. But hard facts were difficult to come by. Many of the astounding escapades attributed to a supposedly fearless Terani colonel called Imi Timu were probably myth. Some of his colleagues – they included Hepworth – doubted if Imi Timu even existed.

'What do we do now?' Carlos posed the question again in a tone which suggested that he had not altogether shed his anxiety.

'I don't know, Carlos,' Delaney admitted. 'We ought to make ourselves known to some senior officers.' As he ran his fingers through his hair, his tone became apologetic. 'Trouble is, I don't know where to find one.' His other concern he kept to himself; he had learnt from his experience of war zones that commanders of defeated armies were never anxious to talk to the press.

The signs of defeat were clear enough. A despondency, palpable and oppressive, hung over the camp. Young men stood around dejectedly, some staring into space, seeing perhaps in the mind's eye comrades fallen in the day's battle. Others sat in huddled groups on the grass, faces downcast, talking in low voices. There was an absence of all the usual activity that occupies off-duty soldiers: no card-playing, no football, no laughter. Just a blanket of gloom.

But he did owe Carlos some explanation. 'Carlos, I'll try to sort something out this evening, but I'll have to choose my moment ....' He stopped as he saw that Carlos was now stretched out on the grass, eyes closed, and appeared to have fallen asleep. Not surprising. It had been a long day. He turned his gaze back towards the velvet-black waters, where some river creature – he could not make out what – had just plunged below the cool waters. Soon the heavy air began to narcotise his senses. Lying down, he too closed his eyes. A thousand noises harmonised together – the cry of water birds, buzzing insects, lapping water and men's voices – becoming a nocturnal symphony. It might have lulled him into a deeper sleep, but something in the conversation which drifted through the air snapped him back to wakefulness – talk about the day's battle. A gruff, throaty voice, like that of a heavy smoker, complained loudly. 'It was the tanks, the bloody tanks ….'

Another voice, like that of a youth whose voice had just broken, chipped in. 'I thought I had that plane. I was sure.'

The third voice sounded like an older man, 'Not your fault, chico, it was those damned katushas. Inaccurate. In the old army we had the latest weapons.'

'You were in the old army too, Pablo?' The question was put by the gruff-voiced soldier.'

'Yes. Artillery. I came over to the Liberation Army after the attack on the Montenegro barracks. And you, Ernesto? When did you come over?'

'It was six months ….' The gruff voice faltered 'Or maybe seven …. before Montenegro.'

Delaney was now listening intently. So the rumour is true, he thought. Bianqui's troops are going over to the rebels. The gruff voice continued, 'They took me prisoner. Me and six others. Scared stiff, I was. Gave us something to eat. I thought they were going to shoot us.'

A dry laugh, and then a voice which hadn't spoken before. 'Why the hell would we feed you if we were going to shoot you?'

The gruff voice continued. 'The Colonel came out and asked where we were from. Told us to go back to our villages. We would be safe. Government didn't rule in those parts any more, he said. He talked to us about how Costadora would be when they won the war. It sounded so good I wanted to sign on right then. The others laughed at me, but we all signed on next day.'

'Good man, the Colonel,' the older man opined. 'I was with him when we took the Cabeza de Cabio Pass. He went in with the advance. He doesn't lead from behind a desk like the brass in the old army.'

No longer interested in sleep, Delaney sat bolt upright. Who was this Colonel who had led the rebel army in that notable victory? Taking the Cabeza de Cabio Pass had given the rebels their first foothold in the Eastern Province. Delaney sensed a good story. The four soldiers, sitting just a few yards away, had now lapsed into silence. Delaney noticed only two were in full rebel uniform. The other two wore khaki jackets over jeans. If defections from the government army were as substantial as rumoured, it was likely the supply of rebel uniforms could not meet the demand.

The older soldier, heavy-jowled and sharp-eyed, broke the silence. 'Where are the Terani? There is no movement. No lights.' He waved his hand towards the encampment further up on the river bank.

The gruff-voiced soldier turned his weather-beaten face towards the Terani camp. 'Strange bastards. Can't understand a word they say. But by God they've got guts.'

The boy soldier who seemed to be in his early teens also looked back towards the other camp. 'They say that the Terani colonel has some sort of magic that makes bullets bounce off him. He can't be killed.'

The older soldier gave a humourless laugh. 'Don't believe it, chico. I saw him bleed at the Cabeza de Cabrio Pass when the Colonel saved his life. Any man can die.'

A glum silence fell on the group, sobered perhaps by the older man's reminder that they were all mortal. And then amid a general hum of voices, the words floated through the air. 'Yes, yes, thank you, Colonel Paez.' Pulse quickening, Delaney looked around into the shadow night. Paez! He had heard that name before. Surely one of the High Command. Who were the leaders known as the Big Five? Paez, Moreno, Wong, a Cuban by the name of Anzar, and the legendary Imi Timu.

A man in officer's uniform was walking through the groups of men. Medium height, fortyish, his solid-looking features had a morose look. As he came closer Delaney could see a number of pips on his shoulder signifying high rank.

Paez – if it were him – had his jacket open, a touch of informality that made his rank seem less intimidating. Giving a curt but reassuring nod to the soldiers he had engaged in conversation, he moved on to another group. As a soldier attempted to spring to his feet, he put out his hand to stay him.

'No, don't get up, comrade. I know you've all had a tiring day.' As he moved closer, Delaney could hear his words of encouragement: tomorrow would be a better day. Try to get some rest. Despite his unsmiling face, Delaney could see that the men respected him and he cared for them.

He was now with the group to whose conversation Delaney had been listening. The boy soldier spoke first. 'Sir, we haven't seen the Terani since the retreat. They say Colonel Wong is missing as well. Is there any news of them?'

The older soldier's elbow shot out, giving the boy a nudge as though warning him that you shouldn't speak so freely to a commanding officer. Paez paused before answering; he seemed to measure his words. 'Colonel Wong has survived tighter spots than this. Remember the Cabeza de Cabio Pass? It's too early to write off anyone as missing.'

Delaney's pulse quickened. This was his first hard news of the day's battle. The crack Terani regiment unaccounted for, as well as Colonel Wong, a member of the High Command. He sprang to his feet and on impulse called out, 'Colonel Paez. May I have a word with you, sir?'

Paez swung round sharply. From the look on his face Delaney realised he had acted unwisely. His hard eyes appraised Delaney's clothes.

'Are you a civilian?' Paez spat out the words.

'Michael Delaney. I'm ….'

Paez interrupted sharply, giving him no time to explain anything. 'What the hell are you doing here?'

'I'm an accredited correspondent.' Delaney proffered his press credentials, stamped by the Ministry of Information.

Paez gave the press card no more than a cursory glance. 'Gonzalez's writ doesn't run here.'

Delaney felt his temper rising. 'I'm well aware of that.' Affecting not to hear, Paez gave a mocking laugh as he turned towards the soldiers. 'Did you hear that, lads? He thinks Gilberto Gonzales says who comes and goes here.'

Some of the soldiers laughed heartily; others looked on apprehensively. Paez turned again to Delaney.

'How did you get in here? Who told you where to find us?'

It was too much for Delaney. Tired, hungry, sweat-soaked, an interrogation was the last thing he wanted. 'No one told me. I'm here to report a war.'

Paez wouldn't let up. 'I asked you how you got in here.'

Delaney knew better than to show his mounting anger. He muttered in English: 'It was easy. I lied about my age.' A titter in the background told him that his joke had gone down well with someone. Not with Paez. Although the colonel did not understand English, his face had the fury of thunder; he sensed Delaney's defiance. As Delaney braced himself for the backlash, he did not notice another officer edging towards them. The tall, red-headed colonel, of similar age to Paez, with pale, handsome face put an arm around Paez's shoulder. He spoke in a low voice. 'Emilio, what is this? What's going on?'

'A stranger in the camp. Says he's the press. I'm trying to find out how the hell he got here.'

'It's all right, Emilio. I'll see to it.'

Paez's bullish face creased into a frown. 'Do we need this? The press! At a time like this?'

'We'll talk it over later, Emilio. Look, the meeting is about to start. Go now. I'll catch up with you in a moment.'

Paez gave a shrug, muttering something inaudible as he turned and walked away. The red-headed colonel turned to Delaney. There was a pleasant cordiality in his voice. 'It has been a bad day. People are tensed up.'

Delaney took his proffered hand and shook it warmly. 'I understand, sir. I guess we've all had a bad day. Finding you wasn't easy.'

'You came here alone?'

Delaney shook his head and pointed to Carlos's prostrate figure. 'That's my photographer, Carlos Garcia.'

Moreno smiled as he looked down at Carlos, now snoring loudly. 'And your own name?'

'Delaney. Michael Delaney. Correspondent for the *Irish Forum*.'

The colonel's eyes widened with interest. 'Ah, Ireland! My ancestral home. Never been there, mind you. But one of my ancestors had to flee from Ireland after the failed rebellion of 1798.

So revolutionary fire is in the genes, thought Delaney. A smile gathered on his lips as he sensed a good story. 'Should I know your name?'

'Moreno. Antonio Moreno McNulty. They call me the Irishman.' Realising this was the Chief of Staff of the rebel army, Delaney held his breath. A string of questions was forming in his mind – anything to detain him. Moreno turned to go, his expression now anxious. 'You must excuse me. We have a meeting just now. Urgent business. Don't leave the camp. We will have a talk later.'

'I'll make sure we do,' Delaney thought as he looked after him. In that brief encounter with two of the Big Five, he had warmed to Moreno just as surely as he loathed Paez.

* * * * *

The faces around the table were grim. 'We should never have trusted Varela,' Paez bellowed. Anzar raised his hands for calm. 'It's too early to know if he has betrayed us.'

Paez spat out his words. 'How did Bianqui know to send more planes? Why no missiles from Varela? Would we have moved on Sonora today if we knew we'd only have katushas? I tell you Varela tricked us. He engineered our defeat.'

Anzar remained unruffled. 'Emilio! Emilio! We aren't defeated yet. The fight goes on.'

Moreno's voice was heavy. 'All the same I think we moved prematurely.'

Paez banged the table. 'I warned you not to trust Varela.'

Moreno placed his hand on Paez's arm. 'Let us reserve our judgement until we know the facts. I suspect the weather held up supplies.'

As Paez gave a hard laugh, Moreno raised his voice. 'Come on, Emilio, be reasonable. You cannot blame Varela for the storm.'

Paez was in no mood to be reasonable. 'If Varela has double-crossed us, I'll string him up myself.'

The Cuban's wise, old eyes twinkled through his rimless spectacles. 'Have you forgotten our pledge to abolish capital punishment?'

Paez frowned implacably. 'Varela's treachery has cost us Wong and Imi.'

Moreno's intervention was brisk. 'Missing in action. Not casualties.'

'And an entire Terani regiment. No survivors. Is it also missing? Spare us your fine definitions.'

Once again the Cuban raised his hands, that characteristic gesture which seemed to inject reason into the most passionate argument. 'Emilio, it's too early to assume the worst. They may yet return.' He paused to let his words sink in. 'On the other hand, they may have been taken prisoner. But they are soldiers; we are soldiers. The revolution goes on.'

Paez lapsed into sullen silence. Anzar looked across the table at Moreno. 'What now?'

Moreno hesitated. 'I'm reluctant to risk men's lives in another failed attack. I think we should clarify the position with Varela.'

'No, we mustn't wait.' Anzar sounded adamant. 'Tomorrow we must move again on Sonora. We must not lose the momentum.'

Moreno stared in disbelief. 'Are you serious?'

'Absolutely. If Varela's missiles have not arrived by tomorrow, then we use katushas.'

'We had katushas today. You are happy with the result?'

Anzar leaned back in his chair. 'There's more to winning a battle than hardware. We must change our strategy. The government forces will expect another attack from the south. What if we came at them from two fronts – say a separate attack from the south-west?'

'Imi's idea,' Moreno murmured softly as though speaking to himself.

The Cuban nodded. 'He was right all along. We should have listened to him.'

Paez shifted in his chair. 'It's a hell of a risk.'

The Cuban shrugged. 'More risky the alternative. To wait too long is to lose control. Today we lost a battle – our first major setback – but we haven't lost the war. The revolution goes on.' There was a glint in the eye of the veteran revolutionary which showed his intensity of conviction. 'The men are demoralised. They need a victory – even a small one – to lift their spirits and restore their pride. Well, what's it to be? Do we fight on?'

Moreno and Paez eyed each other. A curt nod from Paez and Moreno broke the silence. 'Time is short, comrades. Let us now discuss the strategy for tomorrow's battle.'

* * * * *

Near to midnight the meeting broke up. Leaving the commanders' tent they walked out into the warm, star-lit night.

'What can that be?' Moreno pointed to a blazing sky in the distance.

'It's in Sonora, surely,' said Anzar. 'Or near it'

Paez turned to the soldier guarding the commanders' tent.

'How long has that fire been burning, comrade?'

'At least an hour, sir. No one knows what it is.'

A shuffling in the shadows and a tall man emerged. It was Delaney, now spruced up with clean shirt, hair still wet from his dip in the river. As he put his question he avoided Paez's surly gaze. 'I would be obliged if someone could tell me the reason for that fire.'

Moreno smiled. 'We've been asking the same question.' He turned to Anzar. 'Let me introduce Michael Delaney. A journalist from Ireland. And this is Colonel Anzar.'

There was a charming courtesy in Anzar's voice as he shook hands. 'Ireland! You've come a long way.'

'I haven't come directly from Ireland. I've been on an assignment in Manila.' As their gaze met, there was a swift assessment in the old revolutionary's shrewd eyes.

A commotion caused them to look round sharply. The screeching of brakes and then a loud cheering. 'What's going on?' Moreno asked, peering into the shadowy night. Even as he spoke, Imi and Wong emerged from the darkness. Both dishevelled and grimy-faced, Wong's tunic blood-stained. As the rebel leaders embraced their missing comrades, Delaney watched from the sidelines.

'Send the medics to our men.' Wong spoke without expression. 'We have a few wounded.'

'Otherwise the Terani regiments are intact?' Moreno asked.

'Three casualties.' Imi spoke proudly. 'They will be reborn warriors.'

'Over fifty men of the fourth Costadorean are missing,' Moreno told him. 'We believe they were taken prisoner.' He turned to Anzar. 'It would hearten the troops if we could rescue them tomorrow.'

Wong gave a brisk shake of the head. 'Bianqui has a new policy. No prisoners taken.'

'You saw this?' Moreno asked. Paez spat and muttered something through his teeth

Wong nodded. 'As soon as they laid down their arms they were shot.'

Paez's voice gathered anguish. 'Couldn't you have stopped this, Francisco?'

'Not without sacrificing twice as many. From the resistance we encountered I judged that the government had thrown its entire Sonora strength against us.' He lit a cigarette, the lighter flame illuminating his taut features. 'That left the Sonora airbase deserted except for a skeleton guard. So we fell back on the base and seized it.'

'Terani are good with mortars.' Imi's grin held no mirth.

The Cuban's eyes glowed with expectancy. 'You destroyed the base?'

'We mortared as many planes as were on the ground,' Wong explained. 'I should say they were the ones Bianqui sent up here on Thursday. A good third of their force.'

Anzar looked at the distant fire. 'And still burning.'

'A fine funeral pyre for the dead prisoners.' Imi touched the amulet at his neck in a gesture of reverence.

We torched the H.Q. as well.' Wong passed his hand wearily across his brow. 'But I daresay they managed to save most of it.'

'Francisco .... Imi ....' Paez broke in. 'We've been discussing our strategy for tomorrow. We need to update you ....'

Wong shook his head. 'Sleep is what I need. Wake me early. You can brief us then. I doubt if I could take it in now.'

Delaney stepped forward holding up his press card. 'Colonel Wong, I would be obliged if you could answer a few questions.' Moreno intervened to introduce Delaney. Wong displayed neither surprise nor hostility at the journalist's presence. 'Tonight we evened the playing field a little.' He turned away indicating that that brief comment concluded his press statement. Delaney saw him exchange a smile with Imi that had in it a quiet optimism. The wearied warriors were well pleased with their night's work. Then Wong walked slowly towards his tent. Imi set off in the direction of the Terani bivouac. Painfully, as though his limbs were aching. But he held his head high.

CHAPTER TWENTY-SIX

Delaney woke to see the light of dawn casting a hazy glow over the countryside. Carlos was asleep inside the car. Finding the car too cramped, Delaney had smothered himself in insect repellent cream, then stretched out in a sleeping bag on the grass. To his surprise he slept soundly.

A flurry of activity caused him to sit bolt upright. Voices shouting orders, soldiers hastily folding tents, a general clearing up. There was a vibrancy in the air which contrasted strongly with the sombre mood of the day before.

'We're moving,' a passing officer said in reply to the question Delaney fired at him. 'In about half an hour.'

Delaney hastily woke Carlos. 'Get ready to move.'

Hair dishevelled, Carlos sat up grinning sheepishly.

'Where's the loo?'

'Where do you think? Behind the nearest tree. And there's the river if you want a wash.'

When Carlos returned, Delaney handed him a mug of green tea and a warm chunk of flat bread which the soldiers had been making over camp fires. A simple breakfast, available from a nearby supplies tent.

'This will have to do. No time to brew our own coffee.'

'Where are we going?'

'How should I know? Sonora perhaps.'

'When do we get to Sonora?'

'Will you ask me something I can answer.' Delaney jumped into the car. Carlos placed himself in the driver's seat.

Looking towards his photographer Delaney thought he sensed an eagerness and expectancy. He knew the retreat had been a disappointment to Carlos but it was difficult to know if this had to do with missed photographic opportunities, or whether the revolution meant something to him. His dislike of Bianqui was no secret, but Carlos never expressed his likes or dislikes in ideological terms – just part of his general antipathy for "fat cats and big bums". It occurred to Delaney that he didn't know anything about his photographer's politics – if indeed he had any.

An army truck pulled over in front of the car. The driver leaned on the wheel, looking around expectantly as though he thought an order to move was imminent. Just ahead was another truck. Delaney spotted the sturdy shape of Paez chatting to the driver.

'Carlos. The press sticker! Where the hell is the press sticker?'

Carlos munched into the bread. 'Dunno. Did we bring one?'

'Oh, there it is!' Delaney was patently relieved to find the sticker between the pages of the road guide. Quickly he slapped it on the front window. As he leaned back again in his seat, he gave Carlos a wry smile. 'The last thing I want is another brush with Paez over our credentials.'

'Paez!' Carlos's eyes widened. 'Is he here?'

'Yes, over there.' Delaney waved his hand in the direction of the truck in front. 'Why? Do you know him?'

'Yup. Sort of.'

'What do you mean, *sort* of?'

'Everyone knows him. Used to be a smuggler.'

Delaney's eyes sharpened. 'What did he smuggle?'

'Whisky from George. Things like that.'

'Anything else? Guns? Ammunition?'

'Dunno. Any more tea?'

As Delaney watched Paez stroll away and disappear among the troops, he ruminated over the information Carlos had so casually let slip. Paez a whisky smuggler! Trivia such as that added a human dimension to the grim tale of war.'

A wild whoop from Carlos intruded on his reflections. 'Look at that woman soldier. Doesn't she look sexy the way she waggles her hips?'

Delaney grinned. 'I wouldn't upset her if I were you. She looks like she knows how to use that gun.' This was the first woman he had seen in the camp. Fascinated, Carlos continued eyeing her. 'She looks just like a girl I used to know.'

'She's too old for you. More my age.'

'She *does* look like the girl I met last year on George,' Carlos insisted. 'The weekend I went over for the festival.'

Mention of King George Island reminded Delaney that this was Saturday, the opening day of this year's festival. Also the day that Celia would flee to the British dependency. He wished he could have stayed to see her safely away. She was so frightened. So alone. A momentary feeling of guilt. Had he let her down?

Then he realised that Carlos was talking to him again. Pointing to another woman soldier, he asked Delaney's opinion. Wasn't she pretty? No, she didn't have the same swing of the hips as the other one, but there was something about her smile that he liked. 'Now, *she's* more my age than yours, Mike,' he said buoyantly.

They were still discussing the charms of the woman soldier when a young officer stepped up to them. No more than nineteen or twenty. A lieutenant or a captain. Insignia was somewhat vague in the rebel army.

'Colonel Wong extends his apologies for your night's discomfort.' He seemed proud of his duty in conveying the Colonel's message. Erect bearing, his manner polite but brisk. Delaney wondered what he had been a year or two past. A student? A farm boy? 'We regret you were not given proper sleeping quarters. This was very bad, but much happened last night and we were very busy.'

Delaney's head swerved as he heard a familiar click. Carlos stood camera to his eyes. Another click. The officer scowled. Then his brow soothed, his face became impassive and he held out his hand. 'Your camera,' he demanded briskly. Delaney gritted his teeth. Carlos had gone too far this time.

'You don't want that.' Carlos smiled. Almost miraculously a £20 sterling note appeared between thumb and forefinger. More than many Costadoreans earned in a month at

213

black market exchange rates. And rebel soldiers were unpaid volunteers.'

The officer's eyes blazed, but his voice remained constrained. 'This is a military zone. Photographs are forbidden.'

Carlos rubbed the banknote in time-honoured Costadorean bribe gesture. 'Amigo ....' he began.

'Do not insult me.' The young officer drew his revolver but did not release the catch. 'Your camera,' he demanded again. 'Now!'

This time Carlos complied. The officer returned the revolver to its holster. 'You shame Costadora. Do not judge Costadoreans by this man's behaviour, Mr Delaney. Now your car keys, please.'

'My car keys?'

'I am sorry, but we cannot permit you to leave at this time. Colonel Wong's orders.'

Delaney smothered the upsurge of anger. 'I should like to speak to Colonel Moreno.'

'He is no longer here.'

'Then Colonel Anzar.'

'He, too, has gone.'

Indignation sharpened Delaney's tone. 'Wong has no right to hold us prisoner. I'm a neutral citizen; we are representatives of the press.'

'I'm sorry but those are my orders.'

'What the hell does Wong think ....?' Delaney broke off as he saw Wong approaching.

The Colonel was close-shaven, his uniform neatly pressed, dark shadows under his eyes the only remnant of the weary, bloodied warrior of the previous night. He turned first to the young officer. 'I'll see to this, Raphael.' Relieving the officer of the camera, he dismissed him, then took a silver cigarette case from his pocket and extended it to Delaney. 'Spanish or Chinese. We do not smoke Costadorean. It is a government monopoly. I regret I cannot offer you one of Anzar's Havanas. I'm not a cigar smoker.'

'I don't smoke.' Delaney spoke coldly. 'I must protest ....'

'A matter of security. Either you remain here, or you come with us.' Beneath Wong's urbane manner Delaney discerned something of the soldier's contempt for the soft civilian.'

'We'll accompany you,' Delaney replied without hesitation.

'Mr Delaney, you are no fool. You can see for yourself that we aren't going to Sonora just to parade in the Plaza.'

Delaney's gaze went about six metres beyond to a field where troops had loaded ground to air missiles onto a lorry. American manufacture. Bianqui had paraded them in a display of Costadora's defence capacity a few months ago. Missiles and launchers so unlike the old katushas he had viewed the previous night. The troops had changed, too. None of the lassitude of yesterday. They looked determined. Ready for action.

'I didn't see those missiles last night.'

'Weather conditions temporarily held up our supplies.' A frown gathered on Wong's brow. 'Mr Delaney, you ought to reconsider. We can take no responsibility for your safety, or that of your photographer.'

Delaney spoke decisively. 'We'll take our chances.'

'As you will.' Wong affected indifference but there was a touch of new respect in his eyes. He dropped the cigarette and stubbed it out. Then he opened the camera, removed the film and handed the camera back to Carlos.

'Do not attempt to bribe any of our men. For your own safety. They may not be as forbearing as Lieutenant Varela.'

Varela! Delaney looked sharply at the departing figure of the young officer, the name triggering a myriad of questions. That well-articulated accent denoting a certain class; that fair complexion suggesting the lineage of an elite which intermarried only with its own race. It was a long shot, but Delaney was adept at long shots: 'Lieutenant Varela looks like his father,' he said casually. Very casually.

From Wong's startled expression he sensed that he had guessed correctly. But he wanted to make sure. 'I met General Varela once,' he lied glibly.

215

Wong nodded curtly. 'Revolutions do sometimes split families.' He waved towards a convoy of departing vehicles. 'It's time to move, Mr Delaney.'

CHAPTER TWENTY-SEVEN

Monday evening Delaney and Carlos, dishevelled and strained, appeared in the Rainbow Bar of Sonora's Imperial Hotel. The raw patch on Carlos's cheek had been caused by a bullet that had whizzed past his face, lifting a piece of skin. Death had been a cat's whisker away. Delaney was limping slightly. When a bomb sent the fabric of a building high into the air, he had been hurt by flying bricks and mortar.

Looking around, Delaney at first felt disoriented by the glare of colourful wall lamps. It was a glitzy place. Plush, gaudy carpet, prints on the walls depicting Sonora street scenes, and curious, irregular-shaped tables which were the latest creation of a local designer. He recoiled slightly. The exuberance of big, ultra-modern, international hotels was less to his taste than the old-world charm of the Metropole.

Then he spotted the familiar shape of Hepworth, draped over the bar, looking as dissipated as ever. Flushed and bleary-eyed, hair rumpled, his stance suggested he was far gone with drink. A flick of a lighter, then Delaney saw that the man next to Hepworth lifting the flame to his cigarette was Renoir. Wearing a loose Terani cotton tunic, his dark hair appeared well-coiffeured. Renoir always managed to look debonair, even in the middle of a war.

'Guy! Tony!' Delaney pushed his way towards his press colleagues, followed by Carlos.

Renoir smiled as he saw Delaney. 'Mike! Where have you been?'

Hepworth turned his head, looking slightly perplexed as he focused his eyes on Delaney. 'Something I have to tell you,

Mike.' He shook his head woefully. 'But I bloody well can't remember what it is.'

A deafening explosion blotted out the rejoinder that was on Delaney's lips. Lights went out, the bar vibrated. Some people ducked, others fell face downwards on the floor. Then the lights flickered on again. It had not been a direct hit. Sighs of relief that no one was hurt. Hepworth was helped to his feet complaining loudly that it was supposed to be the "happy hour". Couldn't both sides have the decency to call a ceasefire when a man was trying to enjoy his drink?

'Just like Beirut.' Recognising that distinctive English public school accent, Delaney swung round to face the British television journalist, Eric Fielding. About Hepworth's age, he had a shrewd, creased face and slightly bent shoulders. Fielding greeted Delaney warmly. They had last met in the Metropole bar on Thursday when Fielding had updated them on the deteriorating situation in Sonora. That was a lifetime away. A whole bloody war away. What was Delaney's latest news?

'Long story,' murmured Delaney. 'Who needs a drink?' There was another explosion as he ordered a round. Not so close this time. 'Carlos and I tried to reach Sonora on Friday. Were turned back ....'

Somebody called for quiet. Television news had just come on. Everyone looked expectantly towards the screen. The smooth-faced newscaster, speaking from Ciu Costa, affected a stiff smile that was mere habit as he delivered the "good news". Government had the situation in Sonora under control. This provoked peals of laughter and derisory comments. Control? With whole streets ablaze. And fighting going on all around them. A call for silence again as the newscaster announced 'Our beloved President'. And then Bianqui himself, military uniform bedecked with medals, beaming a fatherly smile. The enemy, he announced, had been thwarted. Even as he thanked the army for putting down the coup attempt, a loud volley of gunfire almost drowned his voice. Then his countenance became stern as he continued: 'My government was legitimately elected Any further attempt to take power by force will be severely punished.'

218

'Bloody crap!' It was the voice of an Australian journalist sitting at a corner table. 'That isn't live – it's an excerpt from his speech last week.'

'True,' murmured Carlos in his detached voice. 'Our beloved President is probably playing golf.'

As the stock images of the army on parade came onto the screen, people turned away uninterested. Renoir grimaced. 'We certainly miss Radio Libertad. I wonder if the government found out where it is and smashed it.'

'They broadcast this afternoon,' Fielding reminded him. 'Didn't you hear?'

'Didn't hear anything this afternoon. I was trying to get Danny to hospital.' Jackson had had a bullet lodged in his arm.

'Is he all right?' Delaney and Fielding spoke in unison. Renoir nodded. 'He'll survive.'

Delaney pushed back his hair from his eyes. 'No, Guy, they won't find Radio Libertad. It's mobile. In a van. God knows where it is now.'

'How did you find that out?' Fielding asked. Hepworth's eyebrows shot up. He had that look on his face that said he was about to sober up – something he appeared to be able to do at will.

'I've been with the rebels.'

'How the hell did you manage that?' Hepworth asked.

Delaney gave an enigmatic smile. 'Luck and genius.'

'You met any of the Big Five?' Renoir's moody eyes sharpened.

'The full pack.'

His impression of the rebel leaders, Fielding wanted to know.

Before he had time to reply, a woman's voice calling his name caused Delaney to turn around. 'Helen!' He didn't seem to realise he had spoken her name aloud. Renoir was looking at him strangely. Hepworth put a hand on his arm. 'I remember now what I wanted to talk to you about.' Delaney saw standing beside him Katie Caspar, a telejournalist for the American channel Cosmos Vision. A tall, bony woman, about thirty, with an unkempt mop of brown curly hair, her faded anorak looked as though it had seen several wars. She had a deep-throated voice which gave an impression of toughness. Hepworth had unkindly dubbed her "a Chicago gangster in drag".

Quickly hiding his sadness that it was not Helen, he managed to look pleasantly surprised. 'Katie, I haven't seen you for some time.'

'Not since Bosnia. I owe you a drink.'

'I won't argue with that.'

Arching one eyebrow, she motioned surreptitiously to an empty table behind. 'A word?' Delaney couldn't suppress a smile. Katie had a way of injecting a hint of conspiracy into the most innocuous utterance.

Placing the drinks on the table, she seated herself opposite him. 'Did I overhear correctly? You've been behind the rebel lines?'

'Yes, trouble is I don't know what's happening on the government side. What's your news?'

I interviewed the General today.'

'Varela?'

'No, Crespo. There's a rumour that Varela has defected.'

Delaney whistled softly.

'Just a rumour; nothing confirmed.' Her voice was downbeat. 'I wouldn't give odds on it.'

'What did you think of Crespo?' A comparative newcomer, the journalists knew little of Bianqui's youngest general.

'Very dedicated. Nerves of steel. Not much time to talk, though. Rebels attacked the army H.Q. during the interview. We got good film of the attack. If it falls to the rebels in the next hour, it will make the next news in New York – London – Tokyo.'

'You think it will fall?'

'Looks like it.' She smiled shrewdly at Delaney. 'Where did the rebels get their interesting new hardware?'

'It appeared miraculously overnight.'

'And if you don't believe in miracles?'

He gave a teasing smile. 'Oh, believe in them, Katie. In our job how else could we explain the impossible.'

220

'Then you don't really know?'

He shook his head. 'I haven't a clue. Rebel leaders aren't very forthcoming.'

'You met all of them?'

'Yes. Moreno was the only one I talked to at any length.'

'What are they like?'

'Off the record?'

'A usually reliable source.'

He started to give a brief description of the Big Five, then stopped as he saw Hepworth gesturing towards him, as though wanting to impart something urgent. Delaney called over. 'See you in a minute, Tony.' He gave Katie a probing look. 'How are you getting that tape out?'

'Brian is flying it to George.'

'You have flight permission?'

'Sure. Permanent. Cosmos covers the world.' She smiled brightly. 'Someone was paid for thinking that up.'

'Katie. Do me a favour. Would you send something out with it. To be faxed to the *Irish Forum*?'

She looked at her watch. 'Have your copy ready in an hour. No later. The leaders, Mike.'

'Moreno's a decent fellow. Trade Union background. Self-educated Knows his history. I interviewed him on Sunday. Wong is a cool bastard. Smooth, but brave. Paez is a cantankerous fellow; doesn't like journalists; I kept out of his way. I saw the Terani colonel only briefly ....'

'Imi Timu! He's for real?'

'As large as life,' Delaney assured her. 'And the Cuban. Anzar. A sprightly old fellow – difficult to believe he was a contemporary of Che Guevara.'

'The top man?'

'Moreno? But Wong commands the Sonora campaign ....' A booming voice from behind interrupted. 'Mike! Didn't know you were here. How are you?' It was Barney Mackenzie, formerly of the *Scots Telegraph*, now working for a new independent TV channel, Scotland Two. A powerfully built man, his roughly-hewn features were embellished with a spectacular bushy beard. Ferociously cheerful, he reminded

Delaney of the sturdy fellow who once appeared in an advertisement for Scots Porridge Oats. Only the kilt was missing.

Delaney sprang to his feet and shook the Scotsman's proffered hand. 'Barney! I haven't seen you since ….' He faltered, trying to remember.

'Hong Kong. The handover of power,' Mackenzie reminded him. Then his genial features became sombre. 'Mike, I'm sorry – really sorry – about Helen.'

Delaney stared at him stupefied.

'Christ, Mike, don't tell me you didn't know.'

Delaney's voice was hollow. 'Know what, Barney?'

'That she's dead. I'm sorry to be the one to break it to you. You two were such pals. She died in the earthquake.'

'How do you know?'

'Fielding identified her body. On Friday, I believe.'

Delaney felt a chill run through his being as Celia's pale, frightened face loomed into his consciousness. A note of panic crept into his voice. 'What time was she identified?' Celia had planned an early morning departure on Saturday.

'It's true, Mike.' Mackenzie saw the desperation on Delaney's face, but misunderstood the reason for it. 'Sorry to break it this way.'

The passport! Had Celia managed to use the passport before the news broke about Helen? Delaney struggled to hide his anguish. 'Could there have been a mistake …. were there any personal belongings to show that it was Helen ….?'

He felt an arm on his shoulder. It was Fielding who had joined them in time to hear the latter part of their conversation. 'Sorry, old chap, but there's no mistake. It was Helen all right.'

'How did you find out?'

'Almost by accident. I had to go to the Familia Sagrada Hospital on Friday afternoon to identify some people. An English couple I knew who were reported missing. When I was there I was asked if I would look at another body. The thought from some labels on her clothes that she might be English. There was a letter in her pocket that gave a few clues.' He shook his head grimly. 'It seemed like a bit of a long shot, but I said I'd do it. It was Helen.'

The world seemed to recede from Delaney. Somewhere a long way off he could see people leaning on the bar, hear the hum of voices and the clink of glasses. But he himself was somewhere else. Questions whizzed through his mind. Before he had time to utter one of them, there was a loud shattering of glass; lights flickered, then went out plunging the bar into utter darkness. Like the extinction of a life.

CHAPTER TWENTY-EIGHT

Grim foreboding darkened Delaney's expression as he skirted the side of Habana Vieja. Having found the front entrance boarded up, he feared the worst: the occupants had been arrested. And if Alfonso had been taken away, who wlse was there to tell him what happened to Celia?

Rounding the corner, he looked towards the kitchen entrance. An immense relief welled up within him as he saw Alfonso's sturdy frame filing the doorway. 'Alfonso, there's something I need to know.' A touch of uncertainty entered his voice. 'I suppose it's an inconvenient time to call ....' As if to underline his words, a thundering explosion shattered the evening stillness. There could be no convenient moment in the middle of this life and death struggle.

Neither the explosion nor Delaney's unexpected appearance seemed to affect Alfonso's habitual impassivity. 'It's all right, Angel. This is a friend.' A backward glance told Delaney that Alfonso had aimed his remark at two men with rifles who were closing in on him. They backed off.

'Come in, Michael. This way.' Alfonso waved his hand to indicate the way ahead. 'We can talk more freely in my office.'

As Delaney sank back into a chair, he could hear sporadic gunfire. It had been like that all day. This time it sounded near. Very near. Alfonso, seating himself opposite, lighted his pipe. 'So, Michael, you've been in the thick of battle in Sonora. Even spoken to Colonel Moreno.'

'How did you know that?'

Alfonso lifted a copy of the *Irish Forum* from a table and extended it to his visitor. His article was front page of the international section.

Delaney's short laugh conveyed surprise. 'How did you get that?'

'Some of our people returning from Manila brought foreign newspapers with them. Good article, Michael. Dolores translated it for me.'

Alfonso's praise engendered a warm glow of professional pride. He responded modestly. 'The government doesn't share your enthusiasm. I've been ordered to leave the country.'

Alfonso puffed pipe smoke into the air. 'Ignore it.'

'I intend to.'

'If needs be I can arrange a hiding place for you.'

'Thanks. I'll let you know if I need it.' There was a shrewd assessment in Delaney's eyes as he scanned Alfonso's face. 'The last time we met I asked you to fix up for me an interview with Roberto Diaz. Now I wonder if I could ask another favour?'

Alfonso fixed a quizzing gaze on Delaney. 'How do you think I can help you, Michael?' The dryness of his tone suggested that help should not be counted upon. Delaney was not put off; he had become accustomed to Alfonso's ways. 'I'd like to interview Ramos – if that could be arranged.'

Drawing the pipe from his mouth, Alfonso shot his visitor a startled glance. 'Ramos? Ernesto Ramos?'

'Yes, *that* Ramos.'

'But, amigo, he isn't even in the country.'

'Not all that far away. He arrived in Manila yesterday. All the foreign papers have the story. There's speculation that his next stop might be Ciu Cota.' Delaney was carefully scanning Alfonso's face trying to read confirmation of things he was only guessing. Ramos, the elderly statesman and one-time Prime Minister, had resigned office when Bianqui abolished the independent judiciary. He had spent the last eight years with his daughter's family in Canada. To dissidents and political exiles he was President of the Provisional Government.

Alfonso shook his head, a gesture of wonderment rather than refusal. 'Michael, you don't know what you're asking. Getting hold of Diaz is one thing – but Ramos!'

Delaney's smile was disarming. 'It could only help your cause.'

Alfonso fell silent for a moment. Delaney became aware of movement among tree branches outside as wind stirred the leaves, and then the cry of a seabird. Nature had its own way of reminding you that even in the midst of war there was a timeless something that man could not destroy. And then a loud explosion. Alfonso raised his eyebrows only slightly as though he hardly noticed. 'I would have to ask ….,' he paused as though carefully considering his response …. 'ask the appropriate people. You understand that something like this is not in my power to agree to.'

Delaney nodded. 'I understand.' Was Alfonso's response a tacit admission that Ramos was expected to return? 'Alfonso, I came about something else ….'

He stopped short to greet Dolores who had just appeared in the doorway. Wearing a loose overall, her pregnancy was beginning to show. She apologised for the intrusion. First aid things were kept in here, she explained as she opened a cupboard. Her manner suggested a haste and urgency. 'We'll need to re-stock soon on bandages and antiseptic.' She spoke as though to herself. What was going on in Habana Vieja, Delaney wondered? He could hear voices from other rooms. Subdued voices.

Alfonso looked towards his visitor. 'You said you wanted to ask me something else?'

Delaney pushed back his hair in an abstracted manner. His need to know the truth was no less a torment than his dread of the answer. 'What I really came here to ask you …. Did Celia get away safely last week?'

There was an eternity in the silence that followed. Delaney could hear a clock ticking monotonously as he fixed his tortured gaze on Alfonso. Sombre-eyed, Alfonso shook his head. 'Helen Darcy's body was identified ….'

'I know that. What happened to Celia?'

Dolores intervened. 'Michael, we helped Celia to the best of our ability.' Getting up, Alfonso whispered something in his wife's ear. She nodded her agreement and left. He sat down and looked thoughtfully at Delaney. 'Michael, if I could have got Celia away on Saturday, I would have done so. I promised Diaz I would help her. But once we found out about Miss Darcy it was too late. The passport ....'

'Alfonso, please tell me! Is she dead?'

Alfonso raised his hands as though to protest something. He was about to speak when the door swung open. 'Alfonso, you wanted to see me ....' She stood there looking at first bewildered, then a smile of recognition.

'Mike!'

'Celia!' Delaney stared for a moment as though hardly believing what he saw, then sprang to his feet and kissed her cheek. 'Celia, thank God! I was so worried about you.'

'And I about you. The pictures we saw of Sonora. It looked like an inferno.'

'It was no picnic.' He stood back a pace and eyed her appraisingly. 'You look different.'

'You caught me in my working clothes.' She glanced down at her white overall. Sleeves rolled up, hair held back in a neat, black hairband, she had the air of someone thoroughly immersed in household routine. The touch of colour in her cheeks suggested that a working life suited her. She laughed at his bemused gaze. 'Well, it's time I did an honest day's work instead of living rent-free at the Metropole.'

Alfonso waved to a chair. 'Sit down, Celia. You and Michael must have things to talk about.'

'Have I time?'

'We can spare fifteen minutes or so.' He rose. 'I'll see about getting us some coffee.'

Delaney looked from one to the other. 'But I don't understand. What *did* happen on Saturday?'

Alfonso paused in the doorway. 'Celia had already left for the boat when I heard the news about Miss Darcy. I sent two of our men after her. Told them to bring her back here.'

They were now alone. He felt curiously awkward. She didn't look the same, fragile Celia he had said goodbye to just over a week ago. Sure of herself now. Still pretty, but in a robust sort of way. Her serious cast of face seemed to have a new determination and purpose. She smiled – a warm smile that made him feel at east again. 'I'll never forget that Saturday morning. I thought those men who stopped me getting on the boat were plain-clothed police.'

'And you've been here ever since?'

She nodded. 'Alfonso pointed out the risks but left me to decide. He reminded me that if the rebels lose, they were all in danger. But if I wanted to take that risk, I was welcome to stay here.' There was serenity in her eyes as she added: 'I haven't regretted throwing in my lot with them. I'm half Costadorean. I'm beginning to feel it's my revolution too.'

'What do you do here?'

'A bit of everything – first aid, preparing food. They bring casualties here. When news came through of the fall of Sonora, some of the trade union boys took to the streets. Government troops fired on them. The restaurant is closed for the moment, but we still provide food for the men on active service.'

'You're not afraid?'

'I'm too busy to be afraid.'

* * * * *

Leaving by the back entrance, Delaney crossed the car park towards the narrow street behind. It was cooler now. The dying sun had brushed the sky with gold. Soon, with the suddenness with which night descended in this part of the world, the gold would turn to black. A black sky that would be lit by the fireworks of war. He turned round to wave goodbye to Celia, still standing in the doorway.

Would he ever see her again? The thought had no sooner crossed his mind than he wondered the reason for it. Why shouldn't he see her? He would be back again to Habana Vieja. And hadn't they agreed to meet up again in London?

The screeching of brakes startled him; a van swerved suddenly from the back road into the car park. The driver jumped out. Delaney recognised the trim, neat figure of Pedro,

Alfonso's senior waiter. From the other side a taller man with torn tunic descended, his manner exuding vitality and a sense of urgency. Celia ran to meet him.

'How many?'

'Four – one serious. Get help, chica.'

But even as she turned to go, help was at hand. Alfonso and his nephew, Raul, had appeared, ready to assist in unloading the wounded. As Pedro opened the back of the van, the other man looked towards Celia. It was then that he saw it was Roberto Diaz. What he said was inaudible but Delaney was just close enough to see that brief smile which passed between them. It evoked a memory – an enduring image that had become imprinted on his mind. That first time he had seen her with Diaz. Both walking along the beach in the brightness of a late summer day. How his laughter mingled with hers as he pulled her back to avoid the wave which had risen suddenly, splashing her skirt. At that moment they had seemed as wild and free as the sea itself.

And once again that question flashed through his mind: what did Diaz mean to her?

* * * * *

'Are you staying on, sir?' Although the receptionist's tone was politely deferential, Delaney detected a hint of curiosity in his eyes as he handed him the room key.

'Yes for the moment. Perhaps for another week.' Or month, year – for as long as it takes, he thought. Revolutions didn't follow any pre-arranged timetable.

'Very good, sir.' He smiled. 'Most of our guests left today.'

Delaney sounded upbeat as he returned the smile. 'All good things come to an end. Even holidays.' Like the receptionist, he was keeping up the pretence of normality. Does he know I've been ordered to leave the country, he wondered uneasily? There was only one way to buy his silence. He pulled a banknote from his wallet. The man showed no sign of surprise as he took the bribe. 'Thank you, sir. Let me know if there is anything you need. If your room isn't satisfactory I can move you into one with a better view.'

Delaney nodded. He know the man wasn't referring to any of those frills that guests sometimes demanded, such as a sea view or vista over the Sierra Guadaloupe, but where best to see the action.

As he made his way to the lift he was struck by an unusual emptiness; a lack of bustle and vitality. Just a small group of guests sitting in a corner surrounded by luggage. They talked in low, tense voices as they waited for their transport to the airport.

That the Metropole had almost emptied of guests was not surprising. After government forces had been routed in Sonora, foreign embassies had advised their nationals to leave the country. This morning came a terse warning from the US Secretary of State to American citizens who had lingered on: don't defer evacuation until too late. If Ciu Costa comes under attack, the airport may shut down. Delaney wondered if the flights leaving tonight for Europe and the USA would be the last this side of the revolution. It occurred to him that if he wanted to obey the expulsion order, there was still time to do so. Just a passing thought.

* * * * *

Half an hour later Delaney returned to the lobby. Crisp clean shirt, hair still damp from the shower, his demeanour had a touch of restlessness. He paused by one of the great terrace windows which overlooked the seafront. The soft glow of a hazy moon lit the dark waters. It was normally the time of evening when bars and tavernas came to life; the time he loved to wander down those narrow, twisting alleyways behind the Cove where In strange, sequestered hovels called Troubadour Houses, musicians gathered and storytellers told their tales – music and stories which owed as much to the Terani culture as the Hispanic. This was Delaney's world; at heart he was a creature of the night. But where was that world now? Even the musicians had gone aground. Out there the promenade was deserted, save for a group of men by the entrance to Marine

Gardens, their dark, menacing silhouettes striking a pose of vigilance. Resistance men, or Bianqui's plain-clothed police? Who could tell? And then he spotted Manuel the fiddler. Poor old Manuel, white hair blowing in the breeze as he stoically played under a street lamp; the same spot where he played every evening. One of the men detached himself from the group to toss him a coin. This he acknowledged with a smile which had more a shade of sadness than gratitude. No one else to pay him for his performance. The tourists were gone; the restaurants boarded up.

And then he saw someone else. Someone he thought he recognised. Wasn't that man crossing the road just opposite the gardens the British tourist whom he had dubbed "The Innocent Abroad". In the shadowy dusk he couldn't be sure. Almost immediately he dismissed the idea. With the rebel army nearing the city no one, not even the Innocent, could be unaware of the impending danger.

A familiar French accent broke in on his thoughts. Renoir, breathless and wind-blown, like a man in a hurry, had just entered and was exchanging a greeting with the doorman. Then he spotted his press colleague.

'Mike! When did you get back?'

'Today. And you?'

'Last night.' Renoir lowered his voice. 'Didn't expect to see you still here.'

Delaney shrugged. 'I'm not the first foreign correspondent to ignore an expulsion order.'

Renoir regarded his colleague soberly. 'You must take care, Mike.'

'I'll keep my head down for the moment. I've a feeling it won't last long. Should be safe to surface soon.'

'That, mon ami, depends on which side wins.'

CHAPTER TWENTY-NINE

Delaney rose at five. It had been a fitful sleep, interrupted at times by gunfire and once by an eerie cry in the night. Animal or human, he could not tell, but it penetrated his dreaming, jolting him to full consciousness. It was t hat kind of tense, unearthly cry which evoked the Celtic legends of his childhood – stories of the Banshee's piercing wail that was said to be a foreboding of death. He no longer believed in the Banshee, but who could doubt that death lurked out there in the streets of Ciu Costa?

Further sleep was impossible, yet it was too early for breakfast. Filling the kettle to make coffee, he then turned on the radio. Although he moved the button around the position where he normally picked up Radio Libertad, he found nothing. Nothing save intermittent whistling noises. But then perhaps nothing meant everything. He reminded himself that in those very hours which preceded the rebel attack on Sonora, nothing could be heard from Radio Libertad. He tried George 3, a commercial radio station which transmitted all night from King George Island – a phone-in programme for insomniacs, sentimental music for romantics and brief news bulletins. Just in time to catch a news update. 'Situation in Costadora deteriorating,' said the newscaster.

'We know *that*,' uttered Delaney impatiently. About to try another station, his attention was arrested by a dramatic announcement: 'Unconfirmed reports say that late last night Monteverde Prison was besieged by an armed mob. Freed inmates included both political prisoners and common criminals.' Delaney's expression sharpened. News from George 3 was usually accurate, though meagre in detail. If the report were true, it would surely be confirmed by Costadora National Radio. CNR, however, was broadcasting only music – but then that's what it did on the day of the assault on Sonora.

* * * * *

As Delaney stepped out of the lift into the lobby, he spotted a familiar figure leaning back in an untidy heap on a sofa, straw hat dipped forward as far as his nose. The cigarette which dangled from his lips sent a lazy stream of smoke curling upwards.

'Carlos, what are you doing here?' Delaney looked at his watch. Just eight o'clock and he hadn't yet had breakfast. Moreover he didn't recall sending for his photographer.

Carlos immediately sat up and pushed his hat backwards.

'Don't you need me any more?' There was an unmistakable reproach in his voice. Delaney looked around cautiously, before sitting beside him. 'It's not that .... I certainly could use you ....'

'But you didn't phone me since we got back from Sonora. Didn't you like the Sonora photographs?'

'Of course I liked them. They were first class. Carlos, we've only been back a couple of days.'

'Yeah! And what a couple of days! More tanks around the Palace. Guys throwing petrol bombs. Shootings and stuff like that. But who's taking the photographs? Have you found someone else?'

'No, of course I haven't found someone else ....'

Pausing, he gave another cautious look around, then lowered his voice. 'The problem is, Carlos, I'm not supposed to be here. I've been ordered to leave the country.'

Carlos somehow managed a broad grin without the cigarette dropping from his mouth. 'What did you do? Shoot someone?'

'Yes, myself. In the foot.'

'You did? Does it hurt?' Carlos looked down curiously at Delaney's feet. Delaney gave a laconic laugh. His photographer often misunderstood the most commonplace of English idioms.

'I didn't *really* shoot myself. I don't carry a gun. I'm a journalist, not James Bond. I just managed to ruffle the feelings of someone at the Ministry of Information.'

'What did you do, then?'

'I wrote something the government didn't like.'

'Is that all?' He sounded disappointed.

'Well, it's enough, isn't it? I have to be careful of where I go. Avoid police checks and all that. That's why I didn't send for you. I could be putting you in danger.'

'Hell, man, everyone's running away from the police. They can't catch all of us.'

'Are you telling me you're on the run as well?' Delaney's question was facetious. As far as he knew, Carlos was apolitical.

Carlos nodded. 'Yup. Think so. I was out yesterday scouting around where the fighting is. When I got back Dad gave me some money and told me to go hide somewhere.'

'Hide! Why?'

'Because the police have been rounding up the young guys. Some were taken from our street. They asked about me, but Dad said I had gone to George for the Festival and hadn't come back.'

'So where are you staying now?'

'With guys I knew at college. In Calle Bolivar.' He waved his thumb. 'Just back there. You know it?'

Delaney nodded. Calle Bolivar was a small street skirting part of the east side of China Town. 'Quite near here, isn't it?'

'Yup. Kind of convenient. I can call in whenever you need me.' Carlos spoke as though the matter were now settled. Smiling triumphantly he added: 'I already have some good shots of the Palace. Tanks all around it. Taken from the window of a fourth floor flat.'

* * * * *

234

Bianqui stood at the window overlooking the Grande Plaza. The heavy blue velvet curtains, tied back with gold cord, framed his well-rounded figure. Tanks in the Plaza gleamed in the bright light of a fresh, sunny morning. Everything looked clean, efficient and orderly. It was as though the defeat in Sonora had never been. Sonora, he told himself, was only a temporary setback.

The shootings and rioting of the night before had sounded distant. With all streets leading to the Palace sealed off, he felt secure within his citadel. Things were quieter since his order that curfew-breakers should be shot on sight.

Not that he was complacent. He couldn't afford to be. That damned Monteverde business last night had probably released more political undesirables onto the streets. He had spoken directly to the Prison Governor on the phone an hour ago. The Governor assured him that everything was now under control. When asked about the number of escaped prisoners, the Governor had vacillated. A headcount of inmates was in progress; the situation was 'still unclear'. A sudden anger flared up within him as he recalled the Governor's words. Too many things these days were unclear.

'Brigadier, what is the current position?'

He addressed the question to Brigadier Miranda, a tall, spare man with greying hair who stood a few feet away. Miranda was invited to a working breakfast whenever the President needed a quick update on the military situation. Miranda, looking ill at ease, evaded the question. 'Excellency, it might be wiser not to be seen at the window at a time like this.'

Swinging around, Bianqui snapped the question. 'Why, Brigadier? Is someone planning to assassinate me? You know something that I don't know?'

Miranda's patience was infinite. 'I have no knowledge of any plot, Your Excellency. But it is reasonable to suppose that while the Emergency lasts we are all in danger.' A thin smile as he continued. 'My own car has acquired some fresh bullet dents.'

Bianqui walked slowly away from the window. The spring had gone from his step. He seemed intensely preoccupied. Pulling out the chair at the head of the table, he sat down. With a wave of the hand he indicated that Miranda should sit next to him. 'Brigadier, I want you to be frank with me ….'

A knock on the door signalled the arrival of the breakfast trolley. The President and Miranda lapsed into silence as the food was served. The President gave a nod of dismissal to the waiter and maid, then turned to Miranda with that hard stare that warned he was in no mood for bad news. 'Brigadier, how far have the rebels advanced?'

'The position is uncertain, sir.'

The President snorted impatiently. Uncertain! Unclear! Unknown! Why could no one give him unequivocal information? 'Brigadier, can we contain the situation in Ciu Costa? Or do I need help from Varela?'

The Brigadier looked pale and intent as he cleared his throat. 'Excellency, I have just received some intelligence, the details of which are still somewhat vague. It would appear that General Varela is already preparing to mobilise.'

CHAPTER THIRTY

An air of expectancy hung over Varela's military base. Leave cancelled; army on alert; but no one knew why. Senior officers, looking stern and secretive, seemed to have something momentous on their minds. But what they new they were keeping to themselves.

The soldiers had a few theories of their own which they discussed over the midday meal. A youth from Ciu Costa provoked derision when he opined that it might have something to do with the Chinese. An invasion of Taiwan from mainland China, followed by the conquest of Costadora. A less fanciful theory put forward by someone else was that there had been another Terani rising in the Sierra Plata. If true, it would be the second in a decade. But then why the secrecy? No, it had to be something else. In this military outpost there were few sources of information for the ordinary soldiers. Everyone knew about Radio Libertad – well, most people did – but the soldiers were forbidden to listen to rebel broadcasts.

As he pushed a fork into his pork and rice, a raw young recruit from Santa Fe in the deep south wondered aloud if it had anything to do with elections. There had been elections only once in his lifetime – it seemed a long time ago. But he remembered there had been a lot of shooting and people were afraid to go outdoors. His father said it was better not to vote. The landlord wouldn't like it.

A short taunting laugh made everyone sit up. It was that fellow from Arganda – his name was Jorge. A real know-all. Like all the Arganda fellows he could read and write and thought he was a cut above the country lads. 'You don't get it, do you? With half of Monteverde's prisoners on the loose, and martial law in Ciu Costa, isn't it obvious why we're put on alert?'

The lad from Santa Fe, wide-eyed and foolish, looked towards Jorge. 'Ciu Costa is so far away. I've never been there.'

'Prepare for the trip, chico. I'll wager you that we'll be heading there before the end of the week.'

* * * * *

'Thank you, gentlemen, that will be all. You each know what you have to do.' As General Varela indicated that the meeting had concluded, the senior officers rose to their feet.

'Just one other matter, gentlemen. In case I do not have another opportunity to tell you, I want you to know that I am deeply grateful for your continued loyalty and support.'

As the last officer filed out of the Council Room, the General's habitual calm changed to an expression of gravity. Events of the last twenty-four hours were forcing his hand. He cursed those indisciplined civilians for wrecking his plans by rising before the rebel army reached the capital. It had been agreed that in Ciu Costa the Resistance would hold fire until the arrival of the military. Moreno was advancing from the east. As the rebel army neared the capital, his own army was to advance from the west under air cover. Latest intelligence, however, indicated that the revolution was taking its own momentum. Rioting in the capital had intensified leading to the imposition of martial law; barricades had sprung up all over the city; the army was shooting indiscriminately at civilians. With Bianqui deploying his strength to defend Ciu Costa, the effectiveness of their agreed strategy had diminished. If he moved now the element of surprise was lost; not to do so could mean the slaughter of the rebel army as soon as it reached the city. There was now only one option. Immediate mobilisation.

Grimly he rose from the table and crossed the corridor to his private office. Pausing by the window, he looked down. A sense of pride surged within him as he saw the soldiers drilling. Fresh-faced, enthusiastic, exuding professionalism. The best-trained army in Costadora, he told himself.

Sitting down, his steel-blue eyes pierced the pile of letters and briefings on his desk. Pierced them without seeing them. Having made one of the hardest decisions of his life, he needed a quiet moment to reflect. He had made that decision without hesitation once he became convinced it was the right thing to do. Nonetheless, he pondered over its implications. He once believed you left politics to the politicians, and military matters to the generals. Was there a way out? With a distinguished army career behind him, he could have brought forward his retirement date and bowed out with honour.

A glance towards the window. The soldiers were still drilling. Could loyalty to a corrupt President be balanced against responsibility to these men? As the answer flashed through his mind, he at once recognised the bizarre paradox: for the true patriot the only option might well be treason. History would vindicate him. But what of those he loved most? He glanced at the wall clock, then reached for his pen. His first letter was to his elder son, Captain Juan Varela.

My dear Juan,

I do not ask you to judge me lightly, but to understand, if you can, the action I now take.

For years I have tried, and found it increasingly difficult, to do my duty to the men I command and to carry out the responsibilities entrusted to me. I need not tell you what our army has become: ill-trained, ill-fed, quartered in tumbling barracks, a disgrace to Costadora.

When I held my eastern command I gained some respect for the rebel forces. Haphazardly formed as they are, they have some good officers, the men are well disciplined and morale high. They will not lose this war, Juan, although they may not win.

I am in a position to know that Bianqui expects more sophisticated hardware from America by the end of the month. This leaves no option for the rebels but to take whatever China offers. If the war continues on such a scale, nothing will be left but the broken and bleeding carcass of our country whoever wins. You are too young to recall the Vietnam war. I do.

After my last futile meeting with Bianqui, I came to a decision, believe me not easily made, and contacted the rebel High Command. They sent two of their leaders, a Terani colonel and a politician, Raphael's idol, the one your mother always called poor Elena's folly. He impressed me more than I had expected, although he is not an army man. In matters concerning the army I have never trusted politicians of any ilk.

In brief, their Provisional Government agrees not only to my proposals for improvements in the armed forces, but to give me the authority to carry them out. I believe they will keep their word. Their years of fighting have taught them the value of a first-rate army.

By the time you read this you will know that I have thrown in my lot with the rebels. So, my son, we face one another as enemies. I pray that that remains a metaphor. Yet should we meet in battle, do your duty. It is the least I should expect of you.

Your loving father.

Another anxious glance at the clock. Was there time for a letter to his daughter Concha, his favourite child? Scarcely had his pen touched the paper when he was distracted. His aide, looking harassed and intent, came in bearing a message from the rebel command. Liberation army now thirty kilometres east of Ciu Costa. Are mortaring the military airport. 'Send Colonel Llerena to me at once,' he instructed the aide. Then he resumed writing.

My darling Concha,

I fear you will soon hear your father reviled as a turncoat, a traitor and worse. Madrid is far away, but many of our friends are already leaving Costadora and not a few will make their way to you. Out of loyalty to me, you may want to turn them away. Do not. Old friends are not made in a day or a year.

I have written to Juan giving my reasons. I will not reiterate them here. Only know that I do what I do because it is in the best interests of our country. I hope the action I now take will ensure that this inevitable conflict is a short one. My

240

only wish is to spare Costadorean lives. One day you will understand all of this.

I shall tell you a secret. Your brother will soon be a military attaché in a European country. Do not let him know I have arranged this. If he speaks bitterly of me, do not turn your back on him.

Forgive me, dear Concha, if I have cast a shadow in your life.

Your loving father.

As he laid down his pen, he thought of his younger son. No point in writing to Raphael who was probably already with the rebel army. He would think what he would. He had never understood Raphael. Nor had Raphael ever understood him.

CHAPTER THIRTY-ONE

Late afternoon Minister Gilberto Gonzales was seated at his paper-strewn desk when the telephone rang. In a reflex action his hand jerked forward to lift the receiver, his expression suggesting that he anticipated trouble. Perhaps another of those frenetic calls from the Palace urging tighter control on news broadcasts. But what further steps could he take? Pre-recorded news bulletins delivered by a robot?

At the end of the line was the seductive voice of Carmen, his personal secretary, her tone imparting uncertainty. 'Someone asking to see you, sir. I can't find anything about him in the diary.'

'Who is it, Carmen?'

'He says his name is Ignacio. He didn't give a surname. Said you knew him – that you were expecting him.' The inflection of her voice implied that she thought there was something odd about the caller.

Gonzales stiffened. Some days had elapsed since Roberto Diaz confirmed that the rebels had agreed to the conditions of their horse-trading: an offer of the Commerce portfolio in a future government, in return for assisting them to overthrow Bianqui. When the time came to fulfil his part of the bargain he would be contacted by someone called Ignacio. Now that Ignacio was here, his nerve was beginning to fail.

'Tell him to come up, Carmen. Sorry I forgot to tell you about this.' The habitual smooth, easy-going tone masked his anxiety. No one had told him how Ignacio would contact him, but he had not expected him to walk boldly into the Ministry of Information.

Carmen showed the visitor in. Before withdrawing she shot her boss a concerned glance which seemed to say: are you sure this is all right? He and Carmen had their own way of silent communication. For once he avoided her eyes. Rising from behind his desk, he extended his hand in greeting. 'Pleased to meet you, Mr …. Ignacio.'

He was a youngish man. His light-brown hair contrasted oddly with the darkness of his almond-shaped eyes. With cold formality he shook the minister's proffered hand. Gonzales noted his visitor's ill-fitting dark lounge suit. Like something borrowed.

'Mr Gonzales, our time is short.'

'Quite. Quite.' Gonzales waved towards a chair indicating that the man should sit down, then retreated behind his desk. As he sank back in his chair he could feel the stranger's eyes probing him. Disturbing, hypnotic eyes. 'You were expecting me, Mr Gonzales?'

'I was told you would be in touch. How can I help you?'

The man's eyes flickered, his lips tightened; it was as though he suspected some perfidy. 'You know that already.'

A quick assessment of that hard, young face told Gonzales that it would be unwise to upset him. 'I didn't expect you so soon.'

'Soon?'

With deep unease Gonzales remembered his half-regretted promise to Diaz to hand over the broadcasting station to the rebels. With tanks on the streets, the centre of Ciu Costa was now relatively quiet. You could almost be lulled into believing the current propaganda that the government had regained control. The rebel army was steadily advancing, but Bianqui's hold on the capital was still solid. Gonzales arched his eyebrows. 'Yes. Broadcasting House. That would be difficult at present. You will have noticed that security is tight.'

The stranger's tone was dismissive. 'That's your problem.'

'Presuming it is possible, when would you want me to hand over broadcasting to you?'

243

'When our army reaches Ciu Costa.'

Gonzales flicked open his gold cigarette case and extended it to his visitor. 'You smoke?'

The stranger declined. 'You will know yourself, Mr Gonzales. I'm here to warn you to be prepared.'

Gonzales scanned the other's pale, emotionless face. 'I'm curious about one thing, Ignacio. How did you get here? There are checkpoints at both ends of the street, as well as at all entrances to the building.'

A thin smile from the stranger. 'Everything is possible, Mr Gonzales, if you have the right papers.'

* * * * *

The Metropole's Orchid Bar was filling up. Not so crowded as in the days before the exodus of the tourists, but livelier than Delaney had expected. Leaning against the bar in white linen suits were two men absorbed in conversation, the older one urbane and relaxed, the younger with a loud finicky voice. Delaney had seen them in the bar before. Paseo de Malecón types had a penchant for white linen suits.

The men sitting around tables speaking in low voices did not look like the Metropole's usual clientele. More like rustic types wearing their best suits to gain admission to places they did not usually go to. Their presence puzzled Delaney. What side will they be on when the war reaches Ciu Costa, he wondered?

'Hi, Mike. Have a drink.' Turning around he saw it was Katie Casper.

'Hullo, Katie! My turn I think. What will you have?' He ordered a couple of white polanza beers. As they perched on high stools at the bar, she leaned towards him, her voice taking on that conspiratorial whisper which he always found amusing. 'Mike, have you any idea what's going on in this damned city?'

Delaney shook his head, complaining that they might as well be on another planet. It was now four days since the fall of Sonora. She had failed to reach the rebel army, but her camera crew had been able to get dramatic pictures of the bombing of the military airport. Now nothing to do but wait for events to unfold.

Her eyes had a restless look. 'I hate just hanging around like this.'

'I don't think we'll wait long, Katie. The calm before the storm.'

Pushing her unkempt hair back from her eyes, she suddenly flashed him a broad smile. For a fleeting second it struck him that she had a raw sort of beauty. What would she look like if dressed differently? He tried to picture her in a chic dress. Hair softer – something like Helen's.

Then, in some inexplicable change of mood, her voice sharpened. 'Mike, get out of here. Fast!'

'What's wrong?'

'Don't look round.' She shoved a cigarette towards him.

'I don't smoke.'

'Yes, you do.' Her tone of voice demanded acquiescence. He took the cigarette. 'Katie, what the hell is going on?'

'I said don't look round. José Manchez has just walked in.'

Recalling his expulsion order, Delaney blanched. 'God, not him!' Manchez was an official at the Ministry of Information – the one they usually met at government press briefings.

Katie had already thought it through. 'I'll distract him,' she whispered. 'Get over to that table. The one beneath the mirror.' She pointed her thumb backwards to where three men sat smoking. 'Ask one of those guys for a light. I'll keep Manchez talking while you slip out to the terrace.'

As Delaney slid off the stool he drew sunglasses from his pocket and put them on, at the same time realising it was a futile move. Sunglasses didn't make you inconspicuous when you were more than six feet tall.

'Señor, could you oblige me with a light?' The man nearest to him smiled and flicked on his lighter. As Delaney bent down to light the cigarette, he could hear Katie waylaying the government official. Her voice rose above the background din. 'Mr Manchez, press briefings are still suspended? Nobody is giving us any information.' Delaney chilled as he heard Manchez's suave voice apologising and explaining. He was directly behind. Murmuring his thanks to the man who had given him a light, he edged his way towards the French window. There he collided with Hepworth and Renoir. 'Quick!' he hissed. 'Let me pass.'

Hepworth's eyebrows shot up. 'The loo on this floor is shut for refurbishing.'

Delaney tried to sidestep them. 'Not that sort of emergency, Tony. Manchez is here. He mustn't see me.'

Renoir, quicker to react, had already seen Manchez. Silently he seized Delaney by the sleeve and pushed him through the French window. Then he and Hepworth sauntered forth to join Katie, still berating Manchez for the lack of information.

On the terrace Delaney sank back into a sun chair. His relief gave way to irritation as he remembered he had left his drink in the bar.

* * * * *

Half an hour later his press colleagues joined him on the terrace. 'He's gone,' announced Renoir as he sprawled out in a sunchair.

'Thanks, Katie,' Delaney murmured as she handed him a white polanza. He raised his glass to her. 'Thanks for the drink. And for saving my skin.'

She accepted his gratitude lightly. 'I think you enjoy living dangerously.'

He smiled. 'Look who's talking. Got any information out of Manchez?'

'No, only misinformation. Everything back to normal according to him.'

Hepworth gave a wily grin as he leaned back in a chair. 'Manchez offered us a helicopter ride over the city to see for ourselves that all is well. Must think we're daft.'

Grabbing a newspaper from a chair, Katie deftly swatted a fly that had alighted on the table. 'A guided tour from a safe distance.'

Delaney suddenly leaned forward, pointing. 'Look at that! Over there.'

Turning towards Marine Gardens they could see a ship emerging around the cliff's head. Only just. When it stopped, most of its body was still hidden. Large, stately, even this partial view was impressive. Accustomed to seeing only fishing boats and pleasure boats at this end of the bay, ferries and cargo boats at the other, the appearance of this towering vessel was causing a stir. People were beginning to pour onto the terrace to have a closer look. Springing to his feet, Renoir shielded his eyes from the glare of the setting sun. 'Is the navy getting mixed up in all this?'

The Costadorean navy was small. There was a joke amongst Costadoreans that you couldn't dodge national service by saying you were a pacifist. They would put you in the navy. Although there was a naval base in the far west, about twenty kilometres from Arganda, the navy had not seen active service since the first abortive independence rising.

Hepworth sounded grim. 'If they start shelling, we're front line.'

CHAPTER THIRTY-TWO

At dawn next morning the rebels mortared the civilian airport south-east of Ciu Costa. Too far away to be heard in the city centre but it woke residents of the Santa Monica district including Gonzales who saw from his window the smoking skyline. Even now, with the net closing in, he had not reached a decision. There was still time to flee the country.

Before leaving for the office he put his passport and a thick wad of US dollars in his briefcase. 'I'll be back late this evening,' he told the housekeeper. 'Or if I can't get back, I'll phone you.' This was not unusual. At the Ministry of Information a small apartment was at his disposal for those occasions when he worked late and needed to stay overnight. The housekeeper asked w hat she should say if Doña Marcela phoned. His wife was spending a few weeks with relatives in the south.

'My wife can reach me at the office,' he told her. A worried expression darkened his face. Was it time to send Marcela and the children to safety?

Early morning commuters were heading towards the city but traffic appeared to be less heavy than usual. He listened to the car radio – ironically Radio Libertad; CNR would not broadcast news of the bombing without his permission. The rebel station, which had been silent for the last couple of days, was now broadcasting continuously. They confirmed that the bomb target had been the airport. 'It is no longer operational,' they announced triumphantly. 'Liberation is at hand.'

How come they have all that hardware, Gonzales mused? Outside help? The broadcast ended with advice to civilians to stay off the streets. Too late, he reflected. How many workers and students had already set out? Today colleges reopened after the summer vacation. He was glad he had taken his two sons back to boarding school the day before.

Nearing the city centre, he could see there were more tanks on the street than the previous day. Some streets were sealed off altogether. Stopped at a checkpoint, he was told to take a diversion.

'More trouble?' he asked the soldier.

'Fighting in the San Pedro district, sir.'

Turning down the diversionary route, the chauffeur slowed down as the traffic thickened. The signs were contradictory. The number of people trying to get to work suggested some sort of normality. Yet here and there you could see hapless families pushing their belongings in pushcarts, probably fleeing from the beleaguered San Pedro district. But who was fighting whom? The usual skirmishes between local residents and security forces? Or had the rebel army reached the city?

On the kerb just ahead, waiting to cross the street stood a woman, graceful in the ankle-length skirt that clung to her slender frame. Before recognising her, his attention was caught by the bag she carried. Like his wife's weekend bag. Someone else fleeing the country carrying just a few essential possessions? Then she turned towards him. Towards him, but looking beyond him without any sign of recognition. Dark hair framing her classical features. Still youthful, still enigmatic. A deep emotion stirred within him as he saw that it was Elena Diaz. Seized by a strange caprice he wanted the driver to slow down. Wanted to, but dare not ask. With a compelling nostalgia, memories flooded back of those peaceful days of his youthful passion for her; a sense of how things might have been. As she crossed the road, he stifled an impulse to call out to her.

At the approach to another checkpoint, the car slowed down. A group of youths appeared suddenly on the walls of a public garden, then leaped onto the street. The park gates had been locked since the imposition of martial law. His gaze met the eyes of one boy, the last to scale the wall. Smart in his crisp college uniform, he was laughing with glee. Elated by some boyish prank, or amused that they had found an illicit shortcut through the gardens. The boy reminded him of his own high-spirited son; his eldest. Even as their eyes met, a volley of shots rang out. The boy fell lifeless to the pavement.

As Gonzales saw the blood gushing forth from the lad's head, he reached his decision.

* * * * *

At the Metropole the mortaring of the airport dominated breakfast conversation. That and the renewed rioting on the east side. They had more questions than answers. Who had armed the rioters? Where exactly was the rebel army? Shootings at the edges of the city had intensified, while Bianqui's best units guarded the Palace and the Grande Plaza.

Delaney stirred his coffee. 'Anyone seen Katie?' In the absence of hard news Katie could always be relied upon to come up with some idiosyncratic theory. He had noticed more than once that the quirkier her hypothesis, the more likely it was to be true.

Hepworth cocked his thumb towards the door. 'I saw her out there just now with her cameraman. Looks like she's leaving. She's got her overnight bag.'

'She's leaving?' Delaney stood up. 'Must have a word with her before she goes.'

Katie was indeed about to depart. He caught her just in time. A strictly utility Katie. On her feet strong shoes, jeans so faded that the original colour was indeterminable, and that shabby old anorak. The only feminine touch was the wild hair which had a curious effect of softening her features.

'Leaving us already, Katie?'

She muttered something about a job to do on George.

Delaney's grin implied disbelief. 'Why, what's happening on George?'

'I'm looking into the refugee situation. Must hurry. Brian is waiting.'

He walked out with her onto the steps. 'Come off it, Katie. The war is here, not on George.'

'Mind your own business!' However much she liked Delaney – and some thought she liked him more than a little – he was still a professional rival.

He chuckled. 'Katie, minding one's own business is no part of this job.'

A reluctant smile from Katie. 'See you soon. Must hurry.'

He fired after her some jest about keeping out of the way of that so-called philanderer Colonel Wong. Just to let her know he wasn't taken in by her fib about refugees. He knew she was really heading for the war zone. With a toss of the head, she mouthed some obscenity, got into the car with her camera crew and drove off.

After breakfast Delaney waited for Carlos in the lobby. Waited without knowing exactly what they were going to do. The logical place to go seemed to be the San Pedro district. The street fighting there had intensified. But unconfirmed reports said that it was fighting between civilians of rival political allegiance; if true it was not necessarily where the first clashes would take place between rebel and government troops.

Renoir joined him. 'If you're looking for a taxi over to the east side, forget it. The taxi men are refusing to go. Let's go onto the roof. We might see some action from there.'

As they emerged onto the flat roof a breeze from the sea blew into Delaney's face and hair, stirring within him a sense of exhilaration and optimism. 'Look, Guy! Look over there.'

Renoir's gaze followed the direction in which he pointed. 'I know, I saw it from my window this morning.' The ship they had seen the evening before still nestled in the bay.

'But have you seen the flag they're flying?'

The Frenchman's eyes narrowed as he gazed more intently. 'It's the Costadorean flag, isn't it? The tricolour.'

Buffeted by the wind, the flag fluttered in the air, touching the morning sky with dabs of yellow, white and blue. Then as it flapped wide open, the polanza with wings outspread could clearly be seen superimposed on the tricolour. Renoir gasped in disbelief. 'The rebel flag!'

'Yes. Beautiful, isn't it? Clever too.' Superimposing this particular logo on the tricolour had a symbolic meaning. To the rebels the polanza was a symbol of liberty; to the Terani it was a sacred creature.

They strolled to the other side of the roof. From there they could see the barricades, some reinforced with vehicles, probably hijacked. No wonder taximen were refusing business. Men, clearly armed, were moving about like ants.

Delaney's gaze wandered towards the Sierra Guadaloupe. Usually hazy in the morning mist, today the mountain range looked stark and cold against a limpid sky. He remembered that it was now the beginning of autumn. Costadora had a mild climate all year round; yet even here you could feel the rhythm of the seasons. In autumn and winter the days were warm, but with a sharp drop in temperature from evening to early morning. And in a month or two the first snows would fall on the higher peaks of the Sierra.

Renoir's voice jolted Delaney out of his reverie. 'Look, Mike. Over there.' He pointed beyond the rooftops to a distant stretch of the Arganda Highway, the main road linking the capital with the west. Delaney stared, not believing what he saw: a long line of tanks approaching, flanked by columns of marching men. His heart sank. This could only mean that Bianqui had called up Varela's men from the west.

'Gentlemen, I'm afraid I must ask you to leave.'

Swinging around, Delaney saw a few paces away a bearded man he had noticed the evening before in the bar; one of those in a white linen suit. Now dressed in jeans and open shirt, he carried a rifle. He had approached so noiselessly that neither had heard him. And behind were a group of other men, all armed.

His voice had a measured courtesy as he repeated,'You must leave at once. For your own safety.'

The two journalists exchanged glances, both reading each other's thoughts. It was useless to argue

In the lobby they collided with Hepworth and Barney Mackenzie. Mackenzie and his camera crew had just arrived, having made a precarious car journey through the night from Sonora. Unkempt, bleary-eyed with fatigue, his red bushy beard looked even wilder. 'I thought we'd never get through. The rebels are beating the hell out of the government boys.'

Delaney spoke glumly. 'Not for long, Barney. Varela has sent in reinforcements.'

'You're sure?'

'We saw his army just now from the roof. Coming down the Arganda Highway. Unless the rumour about his defection ....'

Hepworth interrupted. 'Mike, there's someone over there waiting to see you.'

'Who?'

Hepworth grinned. 'The smoking haystack.'

Looking in the direction Hepworth had pointed, Delaney saw that familiar figure sprawled out in an armchair, straw hat over his eyes, cigarette smoke curling indolently into the air. 'God! Carlos. I'd forgotten him.'

Dashing over, he sat beside him. 'Carlos, sorry I was delayed.'

Carlos sat upright. 'Got you some pictures. Men on barricades and things like that.'

'Good, could be useful.' He looked thoughtfully at his photographer. 'Could you hang around for a while? If necessary I'll book you in here for a night or two.'

'Yup. No problem.'

* * * * *

In Habana Vieja, Celia loaded bandages and antiseptics from a cupboard onto a tray. At the other end of the room Alfonso was arguing with his nephew. Diaz and Alfonso had just shouldered their rifles and were prepared to leave; Raul pleaded to go with them. 'It's my revolution too.'

'Raul, you have an important job to do here,' Alfonso reasoned. 'The care of casualties is also part of the revolution.'

There was a stubborn look in the lad's eyes. 'Celia and Dolores can do that. They have plenty of helpers.'

But Alfonso was adamant. Untrained youths got in the way. If they wanted to help there were other jobs: acting as messengers, or assisting at first aid posts.

Diaz tried to mediate. 'Raul, you're not just another helper. You're in charge here. Even Alfonso and I are not going out there to fight. We're just Citizens Defence fellows, not soldiers.' The political wing of the Constitutional Alliance had formed a quasi-military organisation, the Citizens Defence Unit. A turbulent history had taught that in civil wars, bloodshed was not just the outcome of clashes between opposing armies; political divergences meant that neighbour killed neighbour and brother killed brother. The CDU was required to keep order on the streets, and act to prevent civilian atrocities, irrespective of political allegiance.

Yet Diaz's words were misleading. Both he and Alfonso knew well that once the opposing armies came face to face, every member of the CDU was prepared to use his gun.

Celia saw that Raul was not convinced. 'Raul, I hope you do stay.' She flashed him a persuasive smile. 'Who else can I rely on to fetch Dr Mendoza when things get rough?'

Raul's cheeks reddened slightly. His admiration for Celia was scarcely hidden. 'Well, if you need me ....'

Alfonso, seeing his resistance weakening, spoke briskly. 'Oh, you'll be needed all right.' While he was enumerating all the reasons why it was vital that Raul should stay, the door opened silently. Celia, nearest to the door, saw her first. Saw her and instinctively knew who she was.

'Roberto.' She uttered his name softly. Like a caress.

Diaz stared in disbelief. 'Elena!'

Her voice trembled. 'I would have come sooner but they follow me everywhere.'

He started to speak, but emotion choked his words. Dropping his rifle onto a chair, he stepped forward and impulsively gathered her into his arms. She seemed to stifle a sob.

Celia watched their reunion with a compelling wistfulness. What she had always known, but sometimes tried to forget, was now manifest: Roberto Diaz belonged to someone else.

* * * * *

254

By midday the tanks which had been seen earlier on the Arganda Highway had reached the outlying western suburbs. On the eastern side it was stalemate. The rebel army was now entrenched in an area which covered the San Pedro district and docklands, the government forces were preventing further advance. A punter would have difficulty knowing where to place his bet: so far it was anyone's war.

The beleaguered President sent for Brigadier Miranda and asked for a full and frank assessment of the situation.

Miranda looked ill at ease. 'Excellency, we are still holding out.'

It was not the heroic, sanguine evaluation that the President wished to hear. '*Holding out*, Miranda? When do you expect the enemy to be routed?'

'Difficult to say, Excellency. So far we have defended all positions of strategic importance in the city.'

The President gave the Brigadier an almost pitying look. Until now Miranda had served him well. But was he getting too old for the job? To show lack of judgement at this crucial time was worrying. 'Brigadier, are you out of touch? Didn't you know that help has arrived? Varela's tanks reached the city some hours ago.'

'I am aware of that, Excellency.' He fell silent for an instant. His next words came with difficulty. 'They are flying the rebel flag.'

Bianqui paled. Miranda went on tonelessly. 'His planes are bombing the civilian airport.' The President reached for the telephone. 'What is Paco doing about this?' Then he barked down the phone to his secretary: 'Get me the Chief of Staff at once.' Miranda raised his hand. 'Excellency, your nephew's plane took off yesterday.'

CHAPTER THIRTY-THREE

Dusk had fallen when Minister Gonzales walked up the steps of Broadcasting House. The building was surrounded by government troops. An officer of the rank of Major approached him. 'I wasn't informed that you would be coming today, sir.'

Gonzales smiled, his voice assured and firm. 'The situation is changing from hour to hour.'

The Major shot him a quizzical look. 'We are still holding out, sir.'

Gonzales went on smoothly. 'I'm taking charge here. Your unit is needed elsewhere.' From an inner pocket he drew out an envelope. It had the Presidential seal. There was a thin line where the wax had been reheated; something he thought would be undetectable in the fading light. He passed it to the Major. 'New orders. From the President personally. You need leave only two soldiers to guard each of the entrances here. I would urge you to take your troops without delay to the city's southern defences where they are urgently needed.'

The Major nodded. He gave the order to a subaltern. In less than an hour they marched off.

The Minister took the lift to the executive offices above the studios. He could scarcely believe his luck. As the lift mounted he reflected with wry amusement on his latent talent for forgery. Had he not been a politician he might have been a criminal. Some would argue there was little difference. He wished there were someone here to share the joke.

Secretaries and clerks rose as he made his way to the Director's vacant office and seated himself behind a mahogany desk. On the well-polished surface lay a single page directive signed by himself. He leaned back in the leather swivel chair. All he had to do now was await the rebels.

* * * * *

The sun rose on a troubled world. As the rebels advanced west to embrace the city, Varela's army duplicated the movement towards the east. Small boats which dotted the sea were taking frightened Costadoreans to King George Island for a price. Those carrying the poorer passengers were dangerously overloaded. Some had capsized before reaching the British island.

From his window Delaney saw the boats heading out and wondered about their safety. Although not quite a storm, the seas were turbulent. Who was leaving and why might be an indicator as to how the war was going. But he had no time to do a refugee story. This was the second day of the battle for Ciu Costa and he still had not succeeded in getting to the front.

In the lobby he met his photographer. 'Shall we try to get to the Palace, or as near as possible?'

Carlos looked dubious. 'The army is all around it.'

'How close can we get?' There had been no news yesterday evening from national television; not even the usual propaganda. Little too from Radio Libertad, save periodic broadcasts urging civilians to stay off the streets.

'Not sure. Shall we just scout around the streets and see what's going on?'

* * * * *

Grimly Delaney averted his gaze as he side-stepped to avoid the lifeless body of a young woman on the pavement. Eyes open, raised hand partially covering her face in some futile gesture of self-defence, she was probably gunned down while trying to flee to safety. Despite his experience of reporting from war zones, he had never been able to harden himself to scenes like this. Taking a deep breath, he looked resolutely ahead.

'Carlos, stay back.' Carlos, seeming not to hear, had jumped onto a now abandoned barricade and started to take photographs. In so far as they had gone along Calle de la Cathedral, rebel flags flew from buildings on each side, but bullets from God knows where still whizzed through the air, indicating that the area had not been completely routed of government supporters. It was a pattern repeated all over the city: even after areas fell to the rebels, there followed a shoot-out between civilians of opposing political allegiances.

Carlos leaped nimbly from the barricade. 'Got a good shot of the tanks around the palace. Which way now?'

'Your guess is as good as mine. Just follow our noses.'

Screams, explosions, gunfire: the sounds of war came ever nearer.

'Hi, stranger! Looking for a good time?' Delaney stared in surprise at the lanky girl with long black hair who had called to him from the doorway of a half-demolished building. Prostitutes did not usually operate in the city centre.

Go home, Carlos told her. Hadn't she noticed there was a war on? Ignoring Carlos, she called again to Delaney. Foreigners paid better.

'Señorita, you could get killed here,' Delaney shouted at her.

'Could get killed anywhere, Sweetie.' She was now tugging at Delaney's sleeve. Delaney pulled himself free and walked on.

'She's taking a bit of a risk, isn't she?' he murmured to Carlos.

Carlos looked back guardedly over his shoulder. 'If she is what she pretends to be.'

'What do you mean?'

Carlos lowered his voice. 'They say some of those girls are police agents. They lure suspects to interrogation centres.'

* * * * *

The University faced the rear of the Ministry of Commerce. While rebel forces shelled the front of the government building, students besieged its rear in Plaza de la

Universidad. Snipers fired from the roof of the government building. Delaney knew they were now in the thick of it. His voice was terse. 'This is about as close as we'll get, Carlos.'

With an unerring instinct for the dramatic, Carlos began taking pictures – the angry mob attempting to break down the ministry door; buildings falling in flames; a priest kneeling beside a dying man, raising his hand in absolution.

A volley of shots thundering through the air engulfed them on all sides; then a stampede for shelter down the side streets. As Carlos paused to photograph the fleeing students, Delaney tugged his sleeve. 'Leave it, Carlos. Just run like hell.'

They made it to a side street before the second sustained volley of shots ripped through the air. Crouching behind a burnt out car, Delaney saw that some of the students were hurt. A few were dragged along by comrades; others lay on the road. Then from some tenebrous doorway a man emerged, red armband showing his allegiance. He began lifting a casualty painfully to his feet.

Out of the darkness another man appeared, also wearing a red armband. Delaney saw that it was Robert Diaz. He knelt beside a wounded youth. Carlos, apparently recognising him, sprang to his feet. He had already positioned his camera to get a shot of the celebrated writer when someone got in the way. Standing there in the middle of the street blinking stupidly, as though unaware that danger lurked in every corner, was that balding, middle-aged tourist – the Innocent Abroad. Delaney stared in disbelief. Sightseeing? And with a war on. Or hadn't he noticed? His presence seemed to irritate Carlos who uttered softly, 'Loco! Necio!' Then stepping briskly to one side, he clicked his camera. 'Got him,' he called out triumphantly to Delaney. 'That's Roberto Diaz.'

The Innocent, appearing to hear what Carlos said, jerked sharply towards Diaz. Mouth firming into a grimace, he drew a revolver from his pocket. Then he pointed it directly at Diaz's head. Instinctively Delaney put out his hand in a wild, desperate gesture as though to stop him. As the shot rang out he shut his eyes. He opened them to see the body face downwards on the road, blood gushing forth. There was a look of quiet satisfaction in Carlos's eyes as he replaced his revolver. For a second Delaney's mind failed to make sense of what he saw. The man sprawling untidily across the roadway in a pool of his own blood was squat, and balding. Not Diaz, but the Innocent, still clutching the revolver he had no time to use. Diaz was looking towards them uncomprehending, not yet grasping that Carlos had just saved his life.

CHAPTER THIRTY-FOUR

The fourth day of the battle for Ciu Costa. Varela's Second Division, backed by local resistance fighters, had pushed government forces from all areas west of the city. Around Fisherman's Cove, and areas behind Paseo de Malecón they had begun to clean up their streets. But business premises remained closed and there were reported food shortages.

Stiff Government resistance between the San Pedro district, the business district, and all areas around the Palace still prevented Varela's forces from joining up with Moreno's. But the foreign media were speculating that the end must be in sight.

Hepworth was the only journalist in the Orchid Bar when Delaney wandered in. Leaning against the bar, he seemed to be contemplating his reflection in the whisky glass. 'Phillips checked in about an hour ago,' he said glancing up. 'Has Fielding been hit?'

'Haven't heard anything.' Delaney perched on a seat next to Hepworth. 'Still pretty rough out there. Tried to get to San Pedro district, but got stuck in the cross-fire around the Cathedral.' He glanced towards the television. For two days the screen had displayed only a typed notice to a background of the rebel anthem *Libertad*. The notice stated that transmission would resume as soon as possible. Civilians should keep off the streets. The order was signed by Colonel Wong.

Delaney turned away from the screen. 'Still only that!'

Hepworth nodded. 'Sometimes they run a tape of Costadora versus the Philippines in 1996.' He grinned. 'The only international match this island ever won.'

'Nothing on Radio Libertad either.'

261

Hepworth downed his drink and signalled to the barman for another. 'Heard something on the BBC World Service about the US asking the Security Council to support bianqui's democratically elected government.'

Delaney gave a short laugh. 'Danny will be pleased.'

'France is bound to oppose. So will China,' Hepworth continued. 'And the UN is sending humanitarian aid to the refugees on George.'

'What would a muddled UN do without refugees?' Katie Casper strode in, canvas overnight bag slung over her shoulder. She seated herself on a vacant stool beside Delaney. 'The usual, Antonio. And a packet of Dunhills.'

The barman could supply the beer, but the hotel's stock of foreign cigarettes had run out. 'Whatever you have, then. As long as it has tobacco in it.' Her usually wild hair was now pulled back severely, a sophisticated style which suited her. She wore a short-sleeved safari suit, chic and expensive-looking. Delaney eyed her appreciatively.

'Going somewhere, Katie?'

Ignoring Delaney's question, she spoke in a tone of feigned detachment. 'I smoked all the specials Varela gave me.'

'Varela!' Delaney and Hepworth repeated simultaneously.

'Didn't they show ....' Her sentence died as she glanced at the television screen. Still the same typed notice. 'I was travelling with his army. Not badly trained by Costadorean standards.'

'Interview him?' Delaney asked.

'Embargoed. You'll see it on Cosmos. I left after he linked up with Moreno.' She seemed to enjoy the impact of her words. 'Handshake for the camera and all that. I thought Moreno ....'

Whatever she thought of Moreno was drowned by a blare of television. CNT was broadcasting again.

'Colonel Wong.' Delaney identified the face on the screen.

Katie jerked round towards Delaney. 'Wong? You interviewed him?'

'Not quite.' Wry reminiscence edged Delaney's tone as he thought of Wong confiscating Carlos's film. 'Could say that Wong interviewed me.'

Dressed in army fatigues, hair well-groomed, Wong's voice had a hard-edged aplomb. 'Less than an hour ago Colonel Moreno's forces liaised with the army of General Varela ....'

His next words were drowned by a wild cheer from a couple of men sitting at a corner table. Antonio the barman, for a moment forgetting himself, joined in the cheering. The staff rarely betrayed their political allegiance. A call for quiet from a Costadorean in a linen suit, and then Wong's voice was heard again. 'There is still resistance but it is futile. Comrades in arms take no reprisals. I urge government soldiers to lay down their arms. You cannot win now. Only those who have committed atrocities, or ordered atrocities to be committed, will stand trial. A fair trial. But you, the ordinary soldier, have nothing to fear from us. For the sake of your country, your families, and to prevent further bloodshed, I appeal to you to lay down your arms now.'

'Wouldn't trust *him* as far as I'd throw him,' muttered the man in a linen suit. His voice carried to Delaney.

A rising crescendo of voices drowned Wong's next words. Was it really over? If so, what now? Wong's triumphant conclusion – Viva la Revolución – was scarcely audible.

Wong's face faded from the screen to be replaced by an image of Varela and Moreno shaking hands. A familiar background voice described the meeting. Costadora's TV presenters were adapting quickly to the new situation.

'Cosmos film.' Katie stubbed out her cigarette.

Hepworth gave a tough smile. 'Breach of copyright.'

'Favour for favour. Richard might need some cooperation from the new order when he takes over here.'

'And when might that be?'

She glanced at her rolex. 'In about three hours. Things are hotting up in the Caucasus and this little party is about over. Let me buy you a farewell drink.' She looked towards

263

the door. 'Fielding, how do you always know when someone else is buying?'

Fielding joined them, very much alive and unscathed. He wore a neat open-necked shirt, his jacket slung over his shoulder. Setting down his overnight bag on the floor, he perched on a stool.

Hepworth shifted to make more space. 'Eric! We were getting worried.'

'Everything's chaotic out there. No transport. Thought I'd never get back.' While Fielding gave a graphic account of his difficult journey, Delaney was eyeing a newspaper sticking out of the overnight bag. Folded over, the front page was only partly visible, but the photograph was clearly that of Celia Martinez. 'Mind if I see that?'

'Oh, that. The *Manila Telegraph*. Keep it, Mike. I'm off to Dagestan.'

'Can't get through via Dagestan,' Katie informed him. 'The Russians have blocked the frontiers. The only route is through the mountains ….'

Grabbed by the headline, Delaney was no longer listening. It read: "Shock Confession." Then below: "In a sensational turnabout in the Manila drugs trial, Peter Surrey changed his plea to guilty. He has also confessed to planting drugs in the hand luggage of Celia Martinez when on a Global Orient flight from London Heathrow to Ciudad Costadora. Martinez was condemned to death in Costadora, but disappeared in the recent earthquake before the execution could be carried out. Surrey's lawyer is appealing for clemency on grounds of his client's mental instability."

Did Celia know this? He wanted to dash over to Habana Vieja to tell her the good news. But it was now approaching midnight. It would have to wait until tomorrow.

Peering over Delaney's shoulder at the newspaper, Hepworth spoke in an undertone. 'Looks like she's in the clear but for the formalities.'

'You're talking about Martinez?' Fielding raised his eyebrows. 'She's dead, isn't she?'

A sudden blare from the television of the anthem *Libertad* allowed Hepworth to evade the question. 'Don't they know another tune?' Fielding muttered, then turned to Katie to probe her about what she knew of the unrest in the Caucasus.

The strong-featured man who appeared on the screen looked a little dishevelled as though he had just emerged from the turmoil of the streets; his dark eyes exuded both charm and command.

Katie turned towards Delaney. 'Who's that?'

'Roberto Diaz.'

'You're sure? Did they say he was Diaz?' Distracted by a remark from Fielding, she hadn't heard the introduction.

'Sure, I'm sure. I interviewed him.'

'So he *did* escape.' Fielding fixed his gaze on the screen.

Katie smiled coyly: 'He's quite a good looker.'

Once again the man in the linen suit called for quiet: 'Let's hear what Diaz has to say.'

'All right, Mister, keep your cool,' muttered Katie between her teeth, then flashed the man a smile that seemed to convey a charming acquiescence.

Another interruption as a group of teenagers, who didn't look like the Metropole's normal clientele, burst into the bar shouting: 'We won the war!' This time several voices called for quiet, then all eyes turned towards the screen.

Fragmented by the bar turmoil, much of Diaz's opening remarks had been lost on the listeners. Delaney could just about make out that they were directed at displaced civilians. Something about where to get food and medicines. The end was in sight, but it was not over yet. The palace was still defended.

And then as stillness descended in the bar, Diaz's voice seemed to gather power. 'You have endured much and sacrificed much, but I believe I can now promise you a better future. Soon we will begin the massive task of reconstruction – not just of burnt buildings and damaged highways – but of society as a whole. I hope to tell you more about this in the coming weeks. In the meantime I ask you to be good Costadoreans, good neighbours, and to help each other through these last few, difficult days of struggle. I urge you not to take revenge on those who opposed us politically. Enough blood has been shed already. If your enemy of yesterday can become your friend of today, that would be the best and brightest hope of a peaceful future for all our children.' His smile exuded a quiet confidence as he concluded: 'Our day has come. Viva la revolución!'

Katie murmured softly. 'So that's Diaz. I thought he'd be older.' She lit another cigarette. 'Think he'll be President?'

Fielding shook his head. 'It will be Ramos, surely.'

'Isn't he too old?'

'No older than Mandela when he became President in South Africa,' Delaney reminded them.

Diaz's image faded, to be replaced b shots of Ciu Costa's burning buildings and devastated streets. There was no commentary; just a printed notice: "Bianqui defeated".

'Wonder what Bianqui is doing now?' Fielding mused.

Hepworth's face creased into a dry smile. 'Packing his bags and hitting the road running, if he has any sense.'

* * * * *

Francisco Wong gave a backward glance as he left the television studio flanked on one side by Minister Gonzales and on the other by Roberto Diaz. 'Is it there my father denounced me?'

'He had to, Francisco,' Gonzales replied.

'I know.'

'Will you see him?'

Wong's thin smile held no humour. 'I'd rather face Bianqui's guns again.'

Diaz shot the Minister a curious look. 'You wouldn't know where our beloved ex-president is, Gilberto?'

'I doubt that Bianqui thought he would fall. My guess is that he's still in the Palace somewhere.'

Diaz gave a short laugh. 'Waiting for God or the West to rescue him.'

CHAPTER THIRTY-FIVE

It couldn't go on, everyone said. But it did. The Palace was still defended. If it held out the night, there could only be one reason – the expectation of outside help. Many citizens, unable to sleep, spent the night anxiously watching from windows. From the rebel-held west side, the sound of intensified fighting in the city centre could clearly be heard. Machine guns. Rockets. Aircraft in the sky. Thundering explosions that seemed to shake the whole world. Sometimes, too, cries of terror both animal and human.

By four a.m. Delaney abandoned any notion of sleep, dressed and went up onto the roof. It was deserted. The government supporters who had taken up positions there fled two days ago w hen the rebel hold on the area consolidated.

Glancing towards the city he saw some buildings ablaze. The dome of the Cathedral obscured a view of the Palace. He wondered if the flames rising upwards behind the Cathedral meant that the Palace had been torched.

Here, west of the city, streets were deserted. The only life to be seen was a cat stealthily crossing the road at the rear of the hotel. It paused at the foot of a tree, then with lithe grace shot up the trunk. Just in time a bird arose from a branch and escaped its claws. The creatures of the night were fighting their own war. He turned his gaze towards Habana Vieja. A rear wing which projected into the car park was just visible. A soft light glowed from one of the windows. Was Celia up and about?

A footstep caused him to turn around. It was Renoir. The Frenchman drew his anorak closer around his chest, as though feeling the morning chill. 'Where did the rebels get their ground to air rockets?'

'They liberated them in Sonora. The armoured cars, too. Can't you sleep either?'

Renoir grinned. 'Just sent off a dispatch. Rebel troops have entered the Palace. Get to work, Mike.'

* * * * *

Shortly after eight Delaney called at Habana Vieja. A clear-up job was in progress. In the flurry of activity, you could sense the keen edge of elation. People were dancing in the streets of Ciu Costa.

'Coffee, Michael?' Alfonso asked as Delaney settled into a chair. 'Dolores, go fetch Michael some coffee.'

Dolores rose from a chair. 'Something to eat, Michael? We are going to have breakfast.'

'Just coffee, please.'

Wincing slightly, Dolores placed her hand on her abdomen as though some sudden movement of the child in her womb had caused her discomfort. Alfonso looked concerned. 'All right?' She nodded and smiled. 'Our son will be born into the new Costadora. Born into freedom.'

Alfonso looked reflective. 'Pray he doesn't have to fight a war. Let's hope we got it right this time.'

Delaney leaned forward. 'What about yourself, Alfonso – any political plans?'

Alfonso threw back his head and laughed hearatily. 'Me? A politician? All I want to do now is to get on with running my restaurant.'

Dolores, who had joined in the laughter, paused at the door. 'You will want to speak to Celia, Michael?'

He held up the newspaper Fielding had given him. 'Does she know about this?'

Dolores nodded. 'She knows – we heard it yesterday.'

Delaney turned to Alfonso. 'Then there should be no trouble about her leaving.'

'None at all. As soon as the airport is operational again, she'll be on her way.' He shifted in his chair. 'Are you staying on, Michael?'

'Just long enough to cover the victory celebrations, and hopefully to interview the new president. Where is Bianqui now?'

Alfonso gave a dry laugh. 'The question we are all asking.'

'Thanks, Dolores.' Delaney absently took the proffered cup of coffee. A ripple of laughter caused him to turn around. It was Celia who had handed him the coffee. The laughter lingered in her eyes; she looked immensely happy.

'Celia!' Placing the mug on the table, he sprang to his feet and kissed her.

'You've heard the good news?'

'Yes, I know. It's wonderful.' He gave a buoyant smile. 'How does it feel to know you'll soon be home again?'

'Home?' Her eyes clouded. 'Wherever that might be!'

Delaney shot her a puzzled look.

CHAPTER THIRTY-SIX

Two das now since the fall of the Palace, and no one had seen Bianqui. Manuel, the old fiddler, thought that Ramos would find him when he came back. That's what he told Delaney who saw him once more playing his fiddle outside Marine Gardens. Manuel had seen all those fellows coming on television – Colonel this, and Doctor that – telling them not to shoot people, and to get back to work. But Ramos would sort things out.

Delaney pushed his hair back from his eyes. 'Ramos is coming back? It has been reported?'

Manuel assumed a knowing expression. Nothing on television or radio, he told Delaney. But Ramos would be here on Independence Day. Everyone knew that.

Delaney did not dismiss the old man's words lightly. Quite often the bush telegraph knew what senior civil servants did not. Sooner, or later, Ramos would return.

* * * * *

The sun shone brightly for Independence Day. Bianqui's parades had always been led by the elite fifth regiment. This time the leading regiment were attired in rebel army fatigues, many ill-matched, but they stepped as smartly as Bianqui's best. Then came the newest missiles with flybys overhead. The tanks and armoured cars were captured. Some troops rode in open vehicles, military and civilian lorries, firing their AKs in the air. The noises of war had become the clamour of celebration. Then came Varela's smart troops, well-pressed uniforms, buttons shining, stepping smartly.

Civilians marched behind trade union banners, student union banners, the banners of football clubs, youth clubs or any sort of club. If you didn't belong to anything in particular, you marched behind whichever banner took your fancy. Wearing a red armband showed that you supported the revolution.

Delaney and Celia joined the parade at the rear of the Natural History Museum. Her last day in Ciu Costa – she was taking a flight next day to London. Both wore red armbands which Delaney had bought from a pedlar selling souvenirs.

'You must look like a *proper* revolutionary, Celia,' he told her as he adjusted her armband.

She laughed. 'Buy me one of those little rebel flags as well. Or do we call them something else now?'

'Liberation flags,' suggested Delaney. He bought her one.

'It's beautiful,' she said as she contemplated the design. 'I love that polanza. Ever seen a polanza, Mike?'

'No. They're rarely seen around here. You find them mainly in the rainforests and mountains.'

And yet a story was circulating that that morning a polanza had alighted on the roof of the presidential Palace. If true, it would have made a wonderful photograph. At the time of the alleged sighting pressmen and photographers were still in bed. The citizens of Ciu Costa were already speaking of it as a good omen for the future.

The parade moved from various points in the city, converging on the palace. Spirits were high. Here and there voices were heard in various languages. Many were visitors who had gone over to King George Island for the festival, remained there as the trouble in Costadora intensified, returning only when it was all over. A group of black youths – American by the sound of them – began singing their civil rights song *We shall overcome*. This was followed by some English voices giving a stirring performance of *The Red Flag*. Everyone, it seemed, had their own freedom song. Then above all others, one voice floated through the air – clearly the voice of a professional – singing the rousing rebel song *Libertad*: a song many thought would be adopted as the new national anthem. Enthusiastically the crowd joined in.

271

A few yards ahead Delaney spotted Carlos hand in hand with a young woman. 'Carlos!' he called. Carlos turned around and seeing Delaney, waved his camera in the air to let him know that the photography would be taken care of.

'Press photographer. He works with me. Must get him to take a photograph of you tomorrow before you leave.'

'But you've got a photo of me, Mike. Remember you took one the day you interviewed me.'

'Why not another one? Just as we're leaving for the airport.'

'We …. you're coming with me?'

'I'd like to see you off. Unless you've other plans.'

'No, I've nothing planned.' She slipped her arm through his. 'I'd love you to come.'

'Celebrating your freedom, Miss Martinez?'

Celia tightened her grip on Delaney's arm as the man suddenly appeared at her side. Thin and wiry, Chinese features, neatly dressed. Delaney shot a querying look from one to the other. He could sense her fear. Then seeming to regain composure, she looked as though she were about to speak. Before she had time to do so, the stranger spoke again. 'Well, enjoy your day.' He smiled at her, gave a slight bow of the head towards Delaney, then disappeared in the crowd.

'Who is that, Celia?'

'One of the prison warders. It was a shock seeing him suddenly like that.'

'Bastard!'

Delaney's vehemence of tone, born of an instinct to protect her from harrowing memory, surprised Celia. 'Oh, no. He was a decent enough fellow. Of course, I didn't have much to do with him. Only women warders on our wing. But I saw him in places like the exercise yard and prison chapel.'

'And yet he recognised you.'

She smiled. 'Not the first time. The day we escaped Roberto and I came face to face with him in the street. I thought I was done for – like hearing the death sentence all over again. But he just looked at us coolly and walked on.'

* * * * *

272

In the crowded plaza Delaney focused his binoculars on the balcony where the revolutionary leaders had gathered to give victory speeches. Then he handed them to Celia. 'The man speaking now is Colonel Wong. The one before that was Moreno, Chief of Staff. And that fellow beside Moreno is Paez. I thought I saw Imi Timu in the background. Not too sure, though.'

Celia raised the binoculars to her eyes.

'Look, Roberto has just come onto the balcony. With some other people. And there's Elena – his wife.'

Lowering the binoculars, she looked up at Delaney. 'Do you think he will speak?'

'I'd be surprised if he didn't. Isn't he supposed to be the Conscience of the Revolution?'

Diaz was in fact the last of the speakers. As if sensing that there was a weariness of political rhetoric – the mood was for a public holiday – he kept his speech light. Amid roars of laughter, he reminded the crowd of the last time he had addressed a mass rally. It had resulted in an enforced vacation in Monteverde. When he woke up this morning he had to remind himself that he was now respectable. A few more jokes, followed by his now familiar plea for reconciliation: 'We are all just Costadoreans now.' Some people in the crowd started to shout, 'Where is Bianqui?'

'If he's still in Costadora he'll be found,' Diaz told them. 'There's no hiding place for him here. He must face trial for crimes against the people.'

A chorus rose up. 'Hang him. Hang him.'

'No, my friends. The first person to lose his job in the new Costadora will be the hangman.'

Loud cheers from somewhere behind followed that comment. He raised his hands for silence. 'People of Costadora, in time there will be elections so that you may choose your government. You will hear more about that from your provisional president, Dr Ernesto Ramos, who will arrive in Costadora tomorrow.'

The thunderous cheer drowned out whatever it was that Celia was saying.

There was a deserted feel to the Metropole. Renoir was the only pressman at the bar when Delaney entered. They exchanged a few hurried words, then Renoir dashed off to the airport to catch the Paris flight. Only two daily. Schedules were still not normal.

Jackson had already departed wearing a heroic air with his plaster-encased arm. Hepworth left for London immediately afterwards with Mackenzie, both taking their hangovers with them as they argued about Bianqui's whereabouts. Hepworth thought he was in South America. Mackenzie argued for Madrid.

Downing his beer, Delaney stepped out into the night. It was less lonely to be completely alone than in a familiar place filled with strangers. He looked towards the glassy, black sea, then with no particular purpose strolled through the hotel gardens. As the warmth of the early September night lulled his senses, his mind began to wander. From the open window of the Orchid Restaurant he could hear a piano playing, the music harmonising with garden sounds – buzzing insects and the clamour of birds. Sweet scent from trees and flowering shrubs wafted through the air, the fragrance of the cassias predominating. It had been a summer like no other. He would remember it not only for the loss of Helen, or the meeting of Celia, or even the dramatic build-up of political events. It was also imprinted on his mind in a sensuous way – the sights, smells and colours of this beautiful island. Lyrical and wonderful. He had a feeling that if he ever came back it would never be the same again.

* * * * *

Mid afternoon Delaney, Celia and Carlos alighted from a taxi at the airport. A little way back on the other side, at the entrance marked Arrivals, a large crowd had gathered.

274

'They're waiting to greet Ernesto Ramos,' Delaney told Celia. 'He's expected from Manila in a couple of hours.'

Celia looked towards the crowd. 'Yes, I heard about that on the radio. Roberto and Colonel Moreno will be there to meet him.' Her voice took on a wistful note. 'I never had a chance to say goodbye to Roberto.'

Carlos left them to join the waiting crowd. Delaney and Celia tagged onto the queue for luggage check-in. Not much luggage; only the weekend bag she had lifted from Keevers. Her original luggage had never been traced.

'You can carry that with you as hand luggage,' the man at the desk told her.

She shivered. 'No, thank you.' A note of tension edged her voice as she answered the routine security questions: Yes, she had packed the bag herself. No, no one had asked her to carry anything.

Delaney, sensing her mounting agitation, put a hand on her arm to calm her. A look of relief on both their faces as they saw the bag being sealed with security tape.

An hour until boarding time. They sat chatting in the airport cafeteria as they sipped coffee. Lighthearted chatter that seemed to mask deeper emotions.

'Don't forget you promised to see me in London,' she reminded Delaney.

'Yes, of course.' Then remembering that her accommodation at his newspaper's flat in London was a temporary arrangement, he added: 'You mustn't forget to let me know your permanent address.' It was all too easy to lose touch with friends.

'You know, Mike, in spite of all that happened to me here, I shall always love this place.'

'Me, too. God knows where they'll send me next.'

She waited for the last call. He kissed her goodbye and then for a moment her hand lingered in his.

'I'm very grateful to you, Mike.'

'Whatever for?'

'For giving me some good memories of Costadora.'

As she went through passport control, she turned around, waved and smiled. That lovely smile.

Delaney returned the wave. Why did she say she would miss this place? It had been a nightmare for her. Did she mean she would miss Roberto Diaz?

He walked towards the exit, his mind already on the job ahead. He must find Carlos. Ramos would be here shortly. He didn't see that Celia had turned around once more, watching him until he disappeared from view. Then she walked on towards Gate 10 for the London flight. On to a world that she had almost forgotten.

* * * * *

Diaz sat at a desk in the office he had taken over at the palace. It had belonged to Brigadier Miranda. Some of the elderly officer's family photographs were still there. Miranda with his wife looking somewhat younger. Their daughter and husband. His grandchildren. The long-haired, wide-eyed little girl looked to be the same age as Pilar. He hoped Miranda had been able to get his family away with him safely.

On the wall above the desk was a bright rectangle shape. It marked the place where, until a few days ago, the obligatory framed photograph of Bianqui had hung. The Palace had been searched. His country house too. But the dictator had evaded them. Mentally, in that empty space, Diaz could still see the dictator's face. See it, and feel its sardonic eyes – as though Bianqui was relishing having outwitted them. He had set great store on Bianqui's trial. A fair trial; not the farcical show trials Bianqui had given so many Costadoreans. He wanted to show that the new Costadora was a country of law and justice, where even the worst were treated impartially. But Bianqui had cheated them. He always had.

He glanced at his watch. Time to finish his speech before leaving for the airport to welcome Ramos. He was finding it difficult to concentrate. It had been a hectic morning, taken up conferring with senior civil servants; key figures whose cooperation he had mustered to keep essential services ticking over until a provisional

276

government could be set up. Remembering that he had missed a meeting of the Revolutionary Council, he grimaced. Too many meetings these days. More important for public confidence was to be seen to be running the country.

As his eyes rested again on the empty rectangular space, he reminded himself that he would have to tell Ramos that Bianqui was still unaccounted for. Worse, he must tell the people. A vision of the dictator, living luxuriously on his Swiss bank account somewhere in exile flashed across his mind and stirred him to anger.

Another glance at his watch, then he collected his thoughts and began to write.

* * * * *

The soldier was no more than twenty. It was his duty to guard the wine cellar. Bianqui's private stock would serve to entertain foreign dignitaries for many years to come.

A noise within alerted him. Looters? More likely a cunning thief. He knew the cellar was valuable, although he could not know that some of the wines were worth more a bottle than he could earn in a couple of years.
Cautiously he opened the door just a fraction and stood silently listening. That noise again. The hinges squeaked as he pushed it further ajar. A damp, musty smell filled his nostrils as he stepped inside. Thousands of bottles lying in their slots met his eyes in the dim light. Some were covered with cobwebs. He grinned. He must tell Fernando. Then he remembered and the grin faded. Often he thought of things to tell Fernando. And then remembered.

Another noise. He swung his AK towards it. In the gleam of light from the open door a mouse scuttled across the floor. That would have amused Fernando. Fernando was afraid of nothing.

Another noise. A soft noise, but nothing like a mouse. He sensed a presence like a marauding jackal in his village. Following his sense as he would the beast, he came to a

277

number of barrels standing in a corner. Nothing there. Unlike the bottles, the barrels had no labels with dates on them. He wondered what they contained. Rice wine or brandy? That would be a lot of brandy. Perhaps it was written on the other side. He walked around the outer row and found himself staring into frightened eyes. The face was familiar. He had seen it on posters. Cast in bronze. On statues. In the large photograph that hung in the assembly hall of his school.

Bianqui raised his hands. His thinning hair was unkept. His face shadowed by five days of beard. But it was the same face. Beside him were the bones of two chickens, a joint of lamb well gnawed and some fruit. A loaf of bread remained. One wine bottle was empty. The other half full.

The dictator's voice was unchanged. Deep and nasal. 'I will give you money. Whatever you ask, if you help me leave safely.'

'You killed my brother. Fernando.' The soldier's throat was tight. 'Two years ago.'

'I do not know your brother.'

'He carried a banner. Free trade unions.'

'I was not there.'

'One of your police shot him. When they gave back his body they told my father that he was shot escaping arrest.'

'It was an illegal demonstration. The police were outnumbered … it was dangerous ….'

'He did not resist. I saw it. His hands were up as yours are now.'

The staccato shots ripped into a wine barrel. Red wine mixed with the dictator's blood spreading like a great ink-blot stain on the stone floor. A shaft of light pierced the gloom.

The soldier looked at his weapon as though it acted of itself. The shaft of bright light widened. The soldier turned. Paez stood in the door taking in the scene.

* * * * *

278

Diaz put down his pen and folded his speech. The car waited to take him to the airport. He was about to rise when Paez walked in.

'We found Bianqui. He's dead.'

'Dead!' Diaz rose from the chair looking startled. 'What happened?'

'Shot while trying to escape.'

'You're sure, Emilio?'

'No mistake. We've got the body.'

Diaz glanced at his watch. No time to articulate all the questions which barraged his mind; he could not delay his departure. 'Emilio, can this be kept quiet? At least until we get Ramos here?'

A shrewd glint crept into Paez's eyes. 'Sure, amigo. Leave that to me.'

CHAPTER THIRTY-SEVEN

With brisk strides Diaz and Moreno crossed the palace forecourt and onto the western terrace. The air had an autumn feel. Diaz inhaled deeply as he looked up towards a sky heavy with cloud. Heavy, too, were the trees which fringed the well-kept lawn, their branches drooping as though the foliage were burdensome. Soon the brooding oak would shed its leaves.

'Strange weather, this,' Diaz mused aloud. 'The sun should be shining for the old man's homecoming.'

Moreno, appearing not to have heard, voiced his own anxieties: 'Did we need this? Bianqui should have gone on trial.'

'We all wanted a trial, Antonio ....' Diaz swallowed hard. 'But it was not to be.'

Diaz's calm hid deep concerns. The guns were stilled, but the propaganda war went on. Enemies of the revolution, now in exile, might well seize on Bianqui's death as evidence of arbitrary justice – proof that the new regime was corrupt and ruthless. It was too early yet to know who their friends were: the West was still hedging its bets.

'You will tell him straight away?'

'At the first opportunity, Antonio. Ramos must be informed before it becomes public knowledge.'

How long, he wondered, did a secret of this magnitude remain secret? Who else knew apart from Paez and whoever fired the fatal shot? If only there had been more time to question Paez. He spoke thoughtfully as though to himself: 'All the same, something doesn't add up. I'm not sure how we explain it to the old man.'

'You said Emilio knew.'

'I spoke to Emilio only briefly.'

They fell silent for a moment. A sudden breeze arose causing a shudder of leaves in the shrubbery. Water rippled gently in a nearby fish pond. Diaz broke the silence.

'I wonder what *really* happened.'

Moreno looked sharply towards his companion. 'You don't believe he was trying to escape ….?'

Diaz raised his finger to his lips to motion for silence. On the driveway, a few yards ahead, the chauffeue had hopped out of the sleek, black car. Giving a deferential nod of the head, he opened the rear door for them.

* * * * *

The car took a diversionary route to the airport. War and earthquake damage had left some roads still impassable. First they headed towards the docks. As the sea came into view Diaz espied a large, flat rock, lapped by turbid waves. The same rock on which Celia had sat bathing her feet on the day of their escape. In his mind's eye he could see her still. Juxtaposed against a shimmering summer seascape, the soft breeze lifting her hair. Wasn't she returning to London this week? Perhaps it was tomorrow? In the turmoil of the last few days he had forgotten.

Beond the docks they took an inland turn. Up a gently sloping hill until they reached the Tizol Fruit Canning factory. With a jerk of the thumb, Moreno indicated the work of a graffiti artist on the factory walls. Bianqui, noose around his neck, grimacing grotesquely as he swung from the gallows.

'Our revolution is producing its art.'

Diaz smiled faintly. 'Not always in the best of taste.'

A deep solitude stole over him as he leaned back in his seat. Bianqui had dominated their lives for so long. What would Costadora be without him? A better place certainly. But what sort of better place? There would be elections in a year or so. In the meantime the country would be run by a Convention of Government with Ramos as its provisional head. Few doubted that the elections would confirm Ramos as the people's choice of President.

Moreno's voice broke in on his thoughts. 'We're nearly there.'

* * * * *

At San Cristóbal International Airport they stepped out of the car. A large crowd had gathered to welcome Ramos. Diaz turned with a smile and a wave to acknowledge their cheers. Already the media had begun to notice his easy rapport with people. What would he be in the new government, they speculated? Moreno, too, was recognised as, a little more diffidently, he raised his hand in greeting. The red-headed colonel, now known as the Liberator of Ciu Costa, was the most popular of the military figures. Cameras started clicking. Diaz recognised one of the photographers.

'Look over there. I'm sure that's Carlos Garcia. The young man who saved my life.'

Moreno cast a backward glance. 'You mean when that lunatic took a pot shot at you near Plaza de la Universidad?'

'That was no lunatic, Antonio. They now have evidence that he was a government spy.'

A uniformed officer ushered them into the VIP lounge. Only thirty minutes until the arrival of Ramos. Through great windows they could see an aircraft – Global Orient flight 217 to London – skim the runway and soar into the air. Diaz watched it disappear in cloud, unaware that it carried Celia on her homeward journey.

Other members of the reception committee joined them. First Angel Delgado, manager of an agriculture cooperative and resistance coordinator in the Western Province. A fresh-faced country man, his inclusion on the committee was to represent the heroic contribution of ordinary citizens to the struggle. Then Juan del Cerro, Mayor of Ciu Costa. A moderate Bianquist, Del Cerro had opportunely switched allegiance at the eleventh hour. Old enmities were shrouded now. Del Cerro's inclusion had been opposed by some comrades – a few of the diehards. But in the mainstream political movement reconciliation and national unity had become the political buzzwords.

Moreno stiffened visibly as the sleek-haired, sharp-nosed mayor walked towards them beaming suavely. A glint of humour lit Diaz's eyes; he spoke in an undertone: 'Smile, Antonio, smile. We'll be doing business with bigger bastards than Del Cerro before the week is out.'

* * * * *

Throughout the country people watched on television as events unfolded at San Cristóbal airport. At first nothing but waiting crowds. The arrival of dignitaries to welcome the new President conveyed a sense that things were about to happen. But still they waited. The television presenter, looking twitchy, was running out of things to say. Once again, he described the colourful banners, the revolutionary songs, the mood of elation.

And then at exactly twenty two minutes past four the aircraft touched down on the runway. Just twelve minutes late.

Dr Ernesto Ramos appeared at the door of the aircraft, smiling, hands raised in greeting. Tall, white-haired, looking remarkably fit for his seventy-two years. At his side was his wife, a dignified, petite woman, demurely dressed in a neat, navy-blue two-piece. Her smile exuded warmth. 'Very much the First Lady,' opined the television presenter.

And now a running commentary as the couple descended from the aircraft. How well they looked. What must their thoughts be setting foot once more on their native soil after a long exile. What a historic moment ....

283

The telejournalist's voice trailed away. Dr Ramos disappeared from view. Images became confused. People at home began to adjust the controls on their TV sets. But still things were out of focus. Shouting. People running. Some falling face downwards. Then, in a tone of deep anguish, the commentary resumed.

'Something has happened …. There were shots …. two or three gunshots. Oh, my God, no! Has Dr Ramos been hit? Yes, they are saying that Dr Ramos has been hit. Nothing yet confirmed ….'

* * * * *

A great gloom descended on Ciu Costa in the hours that followed. Crowds gathered outside the Sagrada Familia hospital where Ernesto Ramos had been taken. A gunshot wound in the head, he was still alive but unconscious.

News was scant. Nothing yet known about the gunman, or how he managed to penetrate the airport's security. He evaded arrest by turning the gun on himself.

Tense and incredulous, Alfonso and Dolores watched on television the scenes outside the hospital. Dolores's face was tear-stained. Alfonso put a comforting arm around her, but said nothing. There was nothing to say. Both knew it was a moment of acute danger. Without a head of state anyone could seize power.

And then the images changed. Another crowd. This time outside the Presidential Palace. Unlike the silent vigil at the hospital, this was a scene of agitation. Difficult to make out what was happening. Some section of the crowd fighting with the police? Or was it a clash between rival political groups which police were trying to separate?

With deep foreboding Alfonso thought of the guns so recently stored away. Guns which he thought had no further use, save to show to children and grandchildren as revolutionary memorabilia. Would they have to take up arms yet again?

* * * * *

284

Seven p.m. a car drew up at the Palace's western terrace. Francisco Wong, dressed in his Colonel's uniform, stepped out. At the entrance to an inner courtyard he exchanged brisk salutes with palace guards. Thin-lipped men with expressionless eyes and impeccable uniforms who had until recently served Bianqui. Now working alongside former rebels, they took orders from Paez. The strategy of "neutralising the forces" was obviously working.

Once out of sight of the guards Wong's mask of cool authority dropped. Bounding up the marble staircase, he looked ashen-faced and intense.

'Something must be done,' he murmured to himself distractedly.

But what? Ramos now lay fighting for his life. At the moment the only visible authority in the country was the Revolutionary Council, made up of executives of the military and political wings of the Constitutional Alliance. Once sworn into office, Ramos had been expected to invite the Revolutionary Council to form a Convention of Government. Until he did so, anyone could challenge their authority. If Ramos did not recover, what then?

On the first floor, he came face to face with a military aide.

'This way, sir.' The soldier spoke as though Wong had been expected. 'Second door on the left.'

Wong's eyebrows lifted. Before he had time to speak the soldier answered his unspoken question.

'Colonel Anzar is waiting to see you.'

* * * * *

In an office once used by the former president, Anzar was seated at a heavy antique desk, its elaborately carved legs shaped like an animal's limbs. As he waited for Council members to arrive, he jotted down points to be raised at the hastily convened emergency meeting of the Revolutionary Council – ironically on notepaper which bore Bianqui's insignia.

285

Glancing towards the eighteenth century French clock on the mantelpiece, he saw it was already seven o'clock. A worried frown gathered on his forehead. Still no one here. Even if they hadn't received his message, surely the comrades would know that in a crisis like this, they should report immediately to the Palace. As he was about to resume writing, Wong entered.

'Francisco, I've been trying to contact you.'

A note of urgency edged Wong's voice. 'Julio, we must call a meeting. Straight away.'

The Cuban nodded. 'That has been seen to. People should now be on their way.'

Wong eased himself into the leather-upholstered chair on the opposite side of the desk. 'Any news?'

'Nothing since six o'clock.'

Their eyes met in silent angst. Desperation edged Wong's voice. 'What will we do if he doesn't last the night?'

'There is only one thing we can do.' Anzar spoke calmly. 'We elect a deputy president at once – someone who automatically takes over if the president dies.'

'Can we do that?' Wong shifted uneasily in his chair. 'Is it constitutional?'

'You tell me. I wouldn't know where to get hold of a copy of the constitution at this time of night.' He gave a shrewd, tough smile. 'We'll sort out the constitutional niceties later. There must be no power vacuum. If we falter now, there are enough opportunists out there ready to rob us of our victory.'

Wong seemed about to speak, then shook his head as though it were all too much for him. Anzar's wise, old voice rapped out the unthinkable:

'Francisco, you know what this means? We could now lose control.' He paused to let his words sink in. 'Unless we act decisively. Very decisively.'

Wong leaned back, hands clenching the arms of the chair. 'Julio, without a government there'll be bloody chaos.'

'Francisco, we *are* the government.' Anzar paused as though having a sudden doubt about this. 'Or if we're not, we must act as though we were.'

The Cuban flipped through some papers on the desk as he continued. 'You know, of course, there will be a certain jockeying for position. We need to prepare our strategy ....'

Wong wasn't listening. Rising abruptly he began pacing the room. As Anzar's voice trailed away he shot his comrade a concerned look. What was wrong with Francisco? Where was that once fearless warrior who thrived on danger? Where was the old debonair touch? Francisco now looked stressed. Burnt out.

And then came a flash of understanding. Anzar, the oldest of them, had seen it all before. He had lived through two revolutions. Years of fighting in forests, mountains and swamps sometimes took a heavy toll on even the bravest of men. For some the adjustment from war to peace did not come easily.

'Francisco, sit down. Please. We have a lot to discuss ....'

Pausing abruptly, Anzar looked towards the window. The tumult outside in the Plaza suddenly seemed shriller. Wong stiffened.

'Julio, I don't like the sound of this. We need reinforcements.'

Anzar raised his hands in a placating gesture. 'Leave the palace security to Emilio. He'll do whatever needs to be done.'

Wong eased himself back into the leather chair and lit a cigarette. He appeared to gather his composure. 'Sorry, this thing has hit me like a bombshell. You were saying?'

Anzar leaned forward on the desk. 'We have to choose a deputy president. Any ideas?'

'One of us.' There was a barbed finality in Wong's tone. 'Someone from the military.'

Anzar shook his head. 'Too narrow, Francisco. It rules out some promising peope.'

'Or joint authority. The Military High Command?'

'Francisco, I doubt if a military junta is what the people want. I was thinking ....' He paused, now reluctant to voice his own preference. The idea had begun to form in his mind that he and Wong were no longer on the same wavelength.

287

Voices outside in the corridor signalled the arrival of other Council members, giving Anzar the opportunity to change the subject.

'You are quite right, Francisco. Whatever way we sort this thing out, it must look constitutional.' He tapped the table thoughtfully while he assessed the impact of his words. 'I hope you don't mind, but I took the initiative of inviting Justice Sanchez to join us this evening. He should be here within the hour.'

'Enrique Sanchez! The judge?' Wong looked startled. 'But he's not a member of the Council.'

'I invited him in an advisory capacity. To give the proceedings some semblance of legality.'

Wong pulled hard on his cigarette. Then he suddenly smiled. 'Sanchez! The constitutional expert. Why not?'

Sanchez was a returned exile. The elderly judge's recent public pronouncement on the constitutional position was a godsend to the rebels. He had asserted that 'in these extraordinary circumstances and pending elections, Ernesto Ramos, as the most senior member of the last legally elected government, could be sworn in as provisional president.' Ramos's resignation as Prime Minister did not alter this, since that was tendered after Bianqui had illegally suspended the constitution.

Sanchez was undoubtedly a useful person to have at hand if it became necessary to choose a provisional head of state in the coming hours.

* * * * *

A tension that was palpable hung over the city. Tension that was exacerbated by a dearth of news. Each "update" simply reiterated earlier bulletins: Dr Ramos's condition unchanged; gunman's identity still unknown; viewers would be kept informed.

Fact and rumour were inextricably tangled. According to one story Señora Ramos was seen leaving the Sagrada Familia hospital by car in the company of Elena Diaz. That boded ill. The señora would surely not have left her husband's bedside if he were still alive. According to another, Colonel Moreno and Roberto Diaz left the hospital shortly afterwards and drove towards the Grande Plaza. Both looked implacably grim. Was a power struggle going on at the Palace? The night of the long knives? Rumour too had it that once more tanks had appeared on the streets.

Delaney saw no tanks as he made his way towards the Grande Plaza scouting for news. Nor were there any signs now of the agitation seen earlier on television. Evidently the police had regained control. A small crowd still milled around on the Plaza. Disconsolate and aimless, they whiled away the time trying to identify various dignitaries arriving in cars at the Palace and wondered what it all meant.

None the wiser, Delancy made his way back to the Metropole on foot. Nothing to be done but watch developments on television. Who would be in charge of the country come the morning, he wondered?

* * * * *

The same question crossed Roberto Diaz's mind as he and Moreno scaled the Palace staircase shortly after nine p.m. They had bleak news to break to the Revolutionary Council. Half an hour earlier Ernesto Ramos was pronounced dead.

As they reached the first floor, Anzar emerged from the Presidential office.

'Julio, I'm sorry to say ….' Diaz faltered.

Anzar met his gaze candidly. 'He's dead?'

'He went peacefully. I don't think he suffered.'

The Cuban nodded reflectively as though meditating the tragedy. Then he spoke briskly. 'This makes it more urgent. The meeting is about to start.'

'Everyone is here?' Moreno asked.

'Almost. As we now have a quorum let's get things moving. A new president must be chosen.'

'Tonight!' Diaz looked startled. With the spectre of counter-revolution now looming, he had assumed the object of the meeting was to deal with matters of security and defence.

Anzar nodded. 'We can't afford to wait.'

289

Things were moving too fast for Diaz. It seemed just minutes ago that he had watched the old man draw his last breath. He spoke warily. 'Julio, we need to think this through. None of us has any experience of government.'

Anzar smiled cryptically. 'Nor have we time to gain any. But there are historical precedents. When Fidel took over in Cuba he too lacked experience.'

Moreno, too, seemed unable to take it in. 'Julio, what's going on here? Do we have candidates? Already?'

The Cuban evaded the question as he thoughtfully adjusted his spectacles. 'I hope you don't mind …. but I invited Justice Sanchez along to brief us on the constitutional position. It seems that as we are now the only authority in the country, we have the right – indeed the duty – to elect a provisional president as quickly as possible.'

With the fresh and poignant image of the widow's grief in mind, this haste struck Diaz as indecent. He raised the palms of his hands as though to slow things down. 'Surely out of respect for the old man we should wait. The Revolutionary Council can run things for a few more days. Let's have some period of mourning.'

'And while we're mourning some crackpot out there will declare himself head of state.'

Anzar's sober realism momentarily silenced Diaz. And then a shadowy suspicion. Did Anzar himself want to be president? As a hero of the revolution, he was entitled to Costadorean citizenship.

Moreno spoke tentatively. 'We do of course need to get the question of a successor sorted out.'

Diaz was now convinced that he had guessed correctly. And was Anzar such a bad choice? Although surprised that the manoeuvring for position had begun already, he reflected that they could do worse. He had come to admire the veteran revolutionary's calm, empirical mind; his dedication and courage.

'You are right, Julio.' Diaz spoke tranquilly. 'Ramos would expect us to do whatever needs to be done to keep the peace.'

'Well, then.' Anzar smiled enigmatically as he motioned towards a nearby door. 'Just step in here a moment, Roberto. Justice Sanchez needs you to sign something.'

While Diaz and Moreno exchanged bemused glances, the Cuban continued in a dry, pragmatic voice as though a matter of some import had already been decided.

'You will appreciate that we cannot proceed to election without the written consent of candidates.'

Diaz had the impression that he swayed a little. Hunger? He hadn't eaten since morning. The Cuban was looking at him intently.

'You are asking me to stand? As a presidential candidate?'

Anzar smiled encouragingly. 'You seem to be the odds-on favourite.'

Diaz's voice rose in protest. 'Surely there are others more suited ....'

Anzar cleared his throat. 'Two comrades did express an interest.' He seemed reluctant to elaborate.

'Francisco?' Diaz did not know why the name came to him. A revelation from the depth of his subconscious. He knew his old friend to be ambitious.

Anzar's voice droned on. 'I persuaded Francisco to stand down. So as not to split the vote. That leaves Rojas still in the running.' He gave a wily smile. 'You'll beat Rojas easily. There is really no contest.'

Diaz saw Moreno nodding his head as though to endorse what Anzar was saying.

And then a rough, west province voice boomed from behind. 'Amigo, please. We need you now. Don't let us down.'

Stunned, he found Paez at his elbow. A hard-liner; a dedicated military man who always seemed contemptuous of the politicos, someone who might be expected to favour Wong's candidature. Paez, of all people, was appealing for him to accept nomination.

In what could only have been a few seconds, Diaz experienced a thousand conflicting emotions. Human enough to feel a stab of regret at any hurt to Wong, his boyhood friend;

yet politician enough to see that if he had the support of the likes of Paez, the prize was his.

But did he really want this? Surely he should be given time to consult Elena. It was a matter that also affected his family. Yet he knew what Elena would say: he must do his duty.

And then a surfacing of an image deeply etched in his memory of that other world of long ago – the look on his father's face on learning that his boy had won a scholarship to the country's most prestigious school. 'You'll go far, my son,' said the poor fisherman, his voice trembling with pride and love.

My dear father, Diaz thought, you could never have guessed it would be this far.

Anzar's voice intruded. 'Well, Roberto ….?'

Anzar, Moreno and Paez were looking towards him with an intensity of expression which seemed to convey that refusal was not an option. An immense sense of responsibility welled up within him; he spoke with a penetrating calm:

'Thank you for placing this trust in me.'

* * * * *

They waited until morning to break the news of Ramos's death. It sidelined the announcement of Bianqui's demise, briefly reported as "accidentally shot when he startled a young guardsman". Grim and composed, Colonel Moreno appeared on CNT to assure early morning viewers that the Revolutionary Council was still in control. A matter of constitutional importance would shortly be announced.

By midday Costadora, and the world, knew that Roberto Diaz had been sworn in as head of state. A provisional government would be in place the following day. While in the streets of Ciu Costa the sense of relief was palpable, in Fisherman's Cove the overwhelming feeling was one of pride. He was, after all, one of them. The mantle had fallen on the shoulders of the fisherman's son.

At San Miguel University lecture attendance dropped to an all-time low as students watched developments on television. Those who had taken part in that now legendary demonstration which led to Diaz's arrest held a heroic status in the eyes of younger students. Like the veneration given in China by a younger generation to veterans of the Long March.

At 6 p.m. Roberto Diaz gave his first televised Presidential address to the nation. A strong, confident speech which lost nothing by being hastily prepared; rather it held a compelling spontaneity. First the formal, gracious words of thanks for the trust that had been placed in him, followed by a tribute to the late Ernesto Ramos who in exile had kept the torch of freedom shining for them. Then a statement of objectives and priorities; this broadly reiterated the reforms and social principles outlined in the Constitutionalists' manifesto.

Characteristically, he ended with a plea for reconciliation: 'In particular I extend a hand of friendship to those whom we defeated. We need you too – your talents and your commitment are vital to building a better future for all. Let us now bury the past. The most precious legacy we can leave to our children is peace.'

Good speech, mused Delaney as Diaz's face faded from the screen. He sounds presidential already. It was difficult to gauge the reaction of the handful of people who had gathered in the hotel bar. Inevitably responses were muted. Those who supported Diaz must still be reeling from the shock of Ramos's death. Those who did not would be careful to hide their feelings.

Leaning against the bar, looking grave and tentative, were two middle-aged men in navy blazers, their badges showing membership of the exclusive Malecón yachting club. Unlikely adherents of the Constitutionalists. Yet the fact that they had not fled the country suggested that neither were they die-hard Bianquists. If Diaz could win over types like these, his vision of One Nation was certainly attainable.

Delaney had been watching them during the speech, hoping that, by look or word, they would betray some reaction. One of them, the well-rounded man smoking a Benito cigar, did not shed his gravity. The other, tall and silver-haired, nodded his head thoughtfully now and then as though becoming convinced of something that Diaz was saying.

Whatever their politics, they no doubt grasped that there was a price to pay for peace. And was it such a heavy price? The revolution might well have swept to power a more extreme politician than Roberto Diaz.

And then Delaney saw Egghead hovering behind the two men, his face as expressionless as ever as he adjusted his hearing aid. With something of a shock, Delaney noted that he looked inconsequential, even frail. The assumption that this old fellow had been one of Bianqui's secret agents suddenly seemed ridiculous. Such was the paranoia that repressive regimes could generate, notional dangers often appearing more menacing than real ones. He remembered that he had never entertained the slightest suspicion of the Not-So-Innocent-Abroad.

He glanced at his watch. Still time for a stroll on the beach before meeting Carlos for dinner in Fisherman's Cove. A farewell dinner. The day after tomorrow he was heading home.

* * * * *

Delaney sat on a rock near the pathway that led down to the beach. A deserted beach. There was rhythm in the sound of waves breaking on the shore; a rhythm which evoked tranquillity and nostalgia. The light of a pale moon gave the waters a glassy brilliance.

He glanced at his watch. 7.15 in Costadora – that would be 3.15 a.m. in London. By now Celia must have heard about Diaz.

'So, your friend is now the top man, Celia,' he murmured. 'What do you think about that?' He tried to picture her reaction. Tried, but no coherent picture came to him. That thing which had for so long teased his mind would remain an enigma.

And then he saw in silhouette a couple, still some distance away, walking along the water's edge. Like the day of the earthquake. He watched until they came closer. But not too close. He did not wait to see that it was not Celia and Diaz. He wanted to guard the illusion. As he walked back up the path towards the hotel, he reflected that that had been a day they would always remember.

All three of them.

Printed in the United Kingdom by
Lightning Source UK Ltd., Milton Keynes
137369UK00001BA/17/P

9 781849 233477